THE FIFTH WARD

GOOD COMPANY

DALE LUCAS

www.orbitbooks.net

ORBIT

First published in Great Britain in 2019 by Orbit

1 3 5 7 9 10 8 6 4 2

A CIP catalogue record for this book
is available from the British Library.

ISBN 978-0-356-50940-2

Printed and bound in Great Britain by
Clays Ltd, Elcograf S.p.A.

Papers used by Orbit are from well-managed forests
and other responsible sources.

MIX
Paper from
responsible sources
FSC® C104740

Orbit
An imprint of
Little, Brown Book Group
Carmelite House
50 Victoria Embankment
London EC4Y 0DZ

An Hachette UK Company
www.hachette.co.uk

www.orbitbooks.net

For Bryan, Donald, and Mike, who stoked the fires

CHAPTER ONE

There were a great many things that Rem loved about his job as a watchwarden in the city of Yenara. First and foremost, he was rarely bored. Even if he did find himself so, he knew, down deep, that that boredom wouldn't last long. Sooner or later, something somewhere in their ward would go tits up and he and his dwarven partner, Torval, would be called in (or would stumble in) to set it right.

Likewise, there was the sense of secret fellowship—of clandestine knowledge—that came from stalking the streets from sundown to sunrise, existing within and bearing witness to a side of Yenara that most workaday folk would never see, or did not want to: the nocturnal half of the citizenry who plied their trades and sold their wares only after dark, and the certain streets that were, in daylight hours, wholly unremarkable and half forgotten, that came to life only after dusk, supporting activities that would make a brothel-keep blush.

There was the action—sudden, violent, bloody, and sometimes (though Rem hated to admit it), damned bracing. Rem gained no pleasure from hurting people, but there was a certain sense of accomplishment—of primitive pride—in knowing that you could hold your own in a row if you had to.

And then, of course, above and beyond all other considerations, there was the fact that, once in a while, he felt that he was doing some genuine good: returning much-needed coin to innocent victims of a robbery or a short con; apprehending a murderer; freeing a stolen or lost child from the clutches of a thieves' ring or unsavory trafficking band; rescuing terrorized spouses and children from drunken, abusive mates and parents. All of those things and more gave him a feeling of real purpose, pride, and satisfaction.

But then there were incidents like the present one: answering—for the fourth time in five weeks—a call from the neighbors of Geezer Fassler and his wife, Rikka, because the two were trying to kill one another. *Again.*

Gods, the neighbors cried, *they're killing each other! Come quick, watchwardens, I smell smoke! They're liable to burn the whole building down! Bless me, it's grown quiet in there—I fear one's finally done in the other…*

Variations on a familiar theme. Rem was certain that Torval, like him, was tempted not to respond at all. To shrug off the cries for aid and carry on with their patrol. To make some idle jest and assume that this bout between Geezer and his belligerent bride would be just as bloody, just as vexing, as the dozens of others they'd responded to in the past.

"It's pointless," Rem said to his partner.

The dwarf, Torval, nodded solemnly. "Most likely."

Rem shook his head. "It'll be just like always. She won't charge him, he won't charge her—"

"I know," Torval said.

"—we arrest them on trivial charges, they pay their fines, and next week, it's the same bloody business."

Torval gave a final, curt nod. "Aye, that. And yet…"

Rem instantly knew what Torval was suggesting. The one time they failed to answer the call—the one time they dismissed it all as routine business or reduced it to a jest—that would be the one time it would take a fatal turn. Torval had a little aphorism he offered in those moments when they were faced with hue and cry they'd rather not respond to.

Ours isn't to judge the call, he would usually say. *Ours is just to answer it.*

Thankfully, he didn't say the words now. He didn't need to.

Rem sighed, nodded, gestured expansively. "Shall we?"

Torval led the way and Rem followed.

Rem knew they'd find a familiar scene upon arrival: Geezer and Rikka, mutually bloodied, one or the other or both armed with whatever hasty implement was at hand—a broken bottle, a frying pan, a bread knife, logs from the fireplace. They'd be shouting at one another, provoking each other with horrible names and curses. And when Rem and Torval tried to intervene, the truculent pair would, inevitably, come to one another's aid, as though their violent conflicts were some private tryst that watchwarden interference violated the sanctity of.

Oi, now, that's not right, Geezer might say. *We's just having a rassle, watchwardens! I'll not have you hauling my ladylove into your drafty dungeons over this, no sirs!*

No, no, no, Rikka might say, suddenly donning a mask of sweetness and light when, just moments before, she'd been threatening to make a coin purse of Geezer's bollock-bag. *You misunderstand, lads. Geezer was just a bit pissed—too much brew, you see—and he came home on a bit of a tear. It's all worked out now, sure as can be. We're terribly sorry for the upset. Can I offer some victuals for the road? Cooked meself, just an hour or two ago . . .*

Rem and Torval had each tried, more than once, to get one or the other to admit to being scared of their partner—fearful for their life and safety—thus obligating an arrest and severe charges that might finally break the vicious cycle. Half the watchwardens of the Fifth could attest to the injuries they'd seen the two wreak upon one another, the mess they'd made of their various rented rooms, the casual passersby who'd been thumped headwise by flying objects intended for the snarling Rikka or her quarrelsome husband. Oh sure, they'd been hauled in for disturbing the peace, property damage, and unintentional battery on strangers, but they always simply got a dressing-down, laid out their coin, then were sent on their way.

Again, again, and again. It made Rem want to vomit.

They heard the commotion when they turned the corner: curses, taunts, iron clanging, wood creaking, the crack of splinters, and the occasional strident crash of broken glass. A large crowd clogged the street before Geezer and Rikka's residence, a three-story riser capable of housing six different families. Geezer and Rikka's window, on the second floor, was brightly lit, and the sounds of their conflict spilled into the balmy night, offering a counterpoint to the distant thunder of a coming storm and the idle chatter of the gawkers.

"Move!" Torval barked. "Wardwatch coming through!"

"He's killing her!" someone said. At that instant, from above, Rem clearly heard Rikka call her beloved Geezer "a gods-damned damp squib if ever there was one, all mouth and no trousers."

Aemon, the barbed tongue on that woman...

"She's a menace, that one!" an old man in the crowd said as Rem and Torval shouldered through. "Mark my words, if you lot don't lock her away, we'll find her baking Geezer in a pie one of these mornings! Just you wait."

Rem leaned toward Torval. "If only."

Torval shook his head. "I swear, lad, if either one so much as frowns at me, I'll put them both on their backs and clap them in irons. We need an end to this."

"We're not carrying irons," Rem pointed out.

Torval shot him a vexed glare. "Don't be smart. Now, no mollygagging about this time, eh? We haul them in, period. Follow my lead."

Rem nodded, and they moved through the dark, close little doorway of the block of flats. They passed through a short, stale-smelling vestibule, then mounted the dark stairs toward the second floor. Above, the sounds of the brawl were loud but indistinct, dampened by several layers of wood beams and plaster.

"A fool's errand," Rem said as they climbed. "They'll pay their fines and once more be on their way, as always."

"Then we need them to threaten someone *other* than each other," Torval countered. "Officers of the law, perhaps?"

Rem stopped. Torval was a few stairs above him, looking back over his shoulder. Though the stairwell was dark, Rem thought he could see something like a sly smile on the dwarf's broad face. That didn't give him any confidence in the dwarf's scheme.

"You're not serious?" Rem asked.

Torval turned and kept climbing. "Just wait and see how serious I am."

When they made the landing, the racket from inside Geezer and Rikka's apartment assailed them, louder and clearer now.

Clang. Crash. Thump.

"Missed me, you loopy cunt! Why don't you try again?"

Thump. Crash. Rumble. Groan.

"Ha ha, didn't miss you that time, did I, you numpty skiver?"

"You daft cow," Geezer growled slowly. "I'll make you pay for that. Bleedin' like a stuck pig..." Even through the closed door, they could hear Geezer's slurring words. He sounded to Rem as if his head had been bashed in, or his mouth was full of gravel. That didn't bode well. Maybe Rikka had made a killing blow?

Torval stepped forward and kicked in the door. Before he'd passed over the threshold, he had his maul in hand and full command of the situation. Rem slid in behind him, hand on his sword hilt, ready to draw. For the barest instant—before Torval spoke, before Geezer or Rikka could react—Rem took in the chaotic scene before him.

Every bit of furniture in the room, save the little table where they ate their daily meals, was shattered. Several iron and copper frying pans and cookpots lay about. A few shelves, once mounted on the walls, had fallen. Broken crocks of flour, butter, lard, and spices made a colorful, queasy desert out of one far corner. If there was a glass implement—phial, goblet, jar, or wine bottle—still in a single piece, Rem could not see it. There was a terrible smell—piss and shit—emanating from a far corner where a tin chamber pot lay overturned.

And there they stood, like familiar and most unwanted friends: Geezer, blood sheeting down his pockmarked face from a nasty wound on his forehead, clothes disheveled and torn, and Rikka, breasts threatening to fall out of a half-unlaced corset, smeared blood and snot besmirching her lips and chin, one eye blackened and already swelling. The pair of them were not past forty, but they looked as if they'd lived a hundred lifetimes instead of barely one each.

Rikka held a bent iron poker. Geezer brandished a knife.

Why do they do it? Rem wondered, his belly tight with disgust. *Why won't she just turn him over to us? Why won't he just leave her?*

Then the opportunity to assess the scene before them ended. Geezer and Rikka turned toward the kicked-in door and blinked simultaneously, as though awakening from a shared dream.

"Hey, now!" Rikka said. "Don't go knocking that door about—the landlord'll make us pay for that!"

"What's all this?" Geezer snarled, studying Rem and Torval with a bitter, predatory gaze that gave Rem no comfort. He shot a venomous look toward Rikka. "More of your coinjacks, you filthy slag?"

Rem felt a deep, instinctual offense at that. As if he'd give a wild-eyed mongoose like Rikka the bells of the hour...

"Shut it," Torval suddenly snapped. "Both of you, drop what's in your hands and don't say another word. You're in big trouble this time. Don't make it worse."

Geezer, who'd been crouched in a strange defensive stance, now stood to his full height. He was a big man—taller than Rem. With unbelievable bravado, he wiped his hand over his face, clearing away a great deal of the blood covering it and smearing the remainder like war paint. He then flipped back his long, blood-caked forelocks and brandished the bread knife in his hands.

"Trouble," the big man said. "Why don't you caper over here, master dwarf, and see what kind of trouble I can give you."

A strange hissing invaded the world, accompanied by a dull, distant roar. Rem glanced toward the open window of the apartment, directly opposite where he stood. Rain began to fall in sheets, beating hard on the wooden shingles of the apartment building's roof. Rem wished he were out in it, right now, instead of in here, smelling piss and shit, seconds away from having to defend himself and his partner against this foolish man and his equally foolish wife.

Torval took another step into the room. Rem slid sideward, trying to position himself directly in front of Geezer, who was ahead and on their right. He let his hand close on his sword grip now, to make it clear that he'd draw the blade if need be.

"You two," Torval said, and Rem thought he heard real sadness in the dwarf's craggy voice. "How many times are we going to come down here? How many times do we have to haul you before the magistrates?"

"Maybe until you get the message," Rikka said. "This man and I, we ain't your problem, watchwarden. It's just a little domestic spat, that's all."

"Aye, that," Geezer said, offering a genuinely agreeable nod that put Rem in fear for the shared sanity of the two. Moments ago, they'd been trying to kill each other. Now that the authorities were on hand, they were a united front against the interlopers. What sort of fool logic was that?

"Well," Torval said. "I'm afraid your little domestic spats are too loud, too costly, and too bloody to be left unaddressed. Drop the poker, drop the knife, come with us. That's your last warning."

"Last warning," Geezer said. "You threatening my lady, master dwarf?"

Torval turned his narrowed gaze toward Geezer. "I'm sorry, was that solely your job?"

Geezer took a step forward, raising the knife. "You'd best watch your tongue—"

"Geezer," Rikka hissed suddenly. Rem studied her. Her blood was settling now. She knew what was happening, what was at stake. She might not like having to interrupt their little dustup, but she didn't want to end the night in the watchkeep dungeons, either.

Geezer, however, hadn't come to understand that just yet. He took another step forward, all but ignoring Rem, his hostility directed entirely at Torval.

"Threaten her again," Geezer said to the dwarf. "Utter a single unkind word and see what happens."

"Put that knife down," Torval said flatly, "or the only person in the room to feel its sting will be you."

Rem half drew his sword, the blade almost sighing as it peeked from its scabbard. Part of him wanted to loose it entirely, but he was afraid that if he did so, he'd set off Geezer. If they could just get him to stop advancing, to drop that knife . . .

Be ready, Rem thought. *You might only have an instant. If he moves for Torval, it's on you to put him down—*

"You should go," Rikka said from across the room. "We're done now, watchwardens, truly. We're so very sorry—"

"Shut your cock-sleeve, woman," Geezer snarled at her. "These two copper-gobbling maggots need a lesson in manners."

"Are you threatening us?" Torval asked.

"Geezer, stop!" Rikka shouted.

"Bleeding right I'm threatening you!" Geezer growled, then lunged for Torval.

Things happened fast then. Geezer charged Torval, but the dwarf had his maul up quick, swinging it in a broad sideward arc that knocked the bread knife from Geezer's hand. There was a sickening, wet crack as the blunt metal head of the maul connected with Geezer's outstretched fist. Rem guessed that every bone in Geezer's hand shattered with the blow.

Geezer screamed and retreated, yanking his broken hand close. "You half-pint tonker son of a whore!" he roared. He raised his eyes to Torval, wide and white in his sweaty, blood-streaked face, teeth gnashing. "I'll break you in two for that!"

Rikka was on him then, arms around Geezer's hunched shoulders. "Stop it!" she hissed. "Stop now, Geezer, love, or this'll—"

"Off," the furious man grunted, and tried to shrug his wife from his shoulders.

"Geezer, love, come on now—"

"Off, I said!" Geezer shouted, and used all the force of his body to throw Rikka clear. Her feet left the floor and she fell backward, screaming as she went. In the next instant, her head connected with the sharp stone edge of their hearth and she was instantly silent. When Rikka's body hit the floor, it did so without a speck of life in it: rag-doll limp, empty.

Rem instinctively took a step toward the fallen woman, but Geezer was in his path and snarled like a rabid hound.

"Don't do it, lad!" Torval said. "He's mad, that one!"

Rem froze, seeing the hate and fury in Geezer's eyes. He tried to speak to him. "Geezer," he said, "just look. I think Rikka's hurt."

Geezer's eyes swung back and forth—from Rem to Torval, then back to Rem—before he finally stole a quick glance behind him and saw Rikka lying there. She wasn't moving. She wasn't breathing.

"Get up," Geezer said.

Rikka didn't respond.

"I said get up, woman!" Geezer shouted, and kicked her nearby foot. Her body shook, but she made no move. Rem guessed she never would again.

Geezer turned now, almost forgetting about Rem and Torval. He still clutched his broken right hand close to his body. Little by little, Rem could see the anger and violence seeping out of his face, like wine draining from a broken skin. Only a blunt, pale shock remained. He stared at Rikka.

"Rikka, lass? What's going on?"

Rem and Torval exchanged sorrowful glances.

Geezer fell at Rikka's side. He shook her with his good hand. "Come on, now. Just a bump on the noggin. You'll be fine..."

He tried to pull her up by her corset. Her body sagged limply in her clothes, nothing but flesh and bone now—wholly lifeless, a bundle for the lichyards. Since he had only a single hand and no good grip, Rikka fell to the floor again with a thump. Geezer was left kneeling beside her, staring, mouth working and no words coming out.

Torval took a tentative step forward. "Come on, Geezer. We'll see to her. Just come over here and calm down—"

Geezer bent over Rikka, held her face in his good hand, and tried to pat her cheek. The gesture was gentle, loving even, and it made Rem feel a terrible pang of sorrow and loss, a barbed arrow that pierced right through the center of him.

"Rikka," Geezer rasped.

"Geezer," Torval insisted, "come on now."

"Rikka!" Geezer shouted, shaking the dead woman who lay before him. Rem could see that a widening puddle of blood was staining the floorboards under Rikka's mound of disheveled curls. Whether it was a cracked skull or a broken neck or both that had killed her, he couldn't say...but clearly the result had been the same.

Geezer turned on them now. His sorrow was apparent, but something else rose beneath it. That rabid fury that he'd displayed when squaring off with the two of them returned with a vengeance. Rem could see it in his eyes: Geezer finally understood that Rikka was dead, and clearly he held Rem and Torval responsible.

Rem felt his hand tighten on his sword hilt, unbidden.

"You two," the grieving man spat, tears cutting tracks through the drying blood on his face.

Torval raised his maul. "Stay where you are, Geezer," the dwarf said quietly.

"You murderers!" Geezer said, shakily regaining his feet. He looked around him, found a shattered bottle, and took it up by its narrow end.

"Torval," Rem said, knowing what came next. Geezer's eyes were fixed on the dwarf. The jagged edges of that broken bottle were clearly meant for Torval.

"I'll have your flayed skin, you bloody stump!" Geezer shouted, and lunged toward Torval.

Rem's sword cleared its scabbard and flashed in a broad, flat arc. Rem felt steel bite flesh, saw Geezer shrink from the blow and bend double. While Rem's eyes drank in the sight, his body followed through, almost independent of his conscious mind. He used the momentum of his sideward swing to bring his sword up, point leveled, then drove it forward in an angled downward thrust. The blade bit deep into Geezer's rib cage on the left side. The drunken man shouted and cursed, then stumbled to the floor, the deep thrust bringing forth a great gush of blood.

The bottle fell from his hands. Rem kicked it clear, resheathed his sword, then rushed to Geezer's side. He had binding ropes in hand, ready to tie the man and make sure he could do no more damage. Gods, there was so much blood, more pouring out every second!

"You killed me," Geezer said, blinking as though his vision was failing him. He tried to slap Rem's hands away, but Rem rebuffed his resistance easily. Geezer's strength fled fast. It was staining the floor all around them.

"We warned you," Rem said, trying to keep from vomiting. He wanted to comfort the man, to reassure him, but he heard only anger and reproach in his own voice. "It's not our fault you wouldn't listen!"

He gave up trying to tie Geezer's hands—what was he thinking?—then struggled instead to yank up the man's blood-soaked shirt and get at the wound. It wasn't large, but it was deep: his thrust had passed between the fourth and fifth ribs, just below Geezer's left nipple. As Rem watched, dark-red blood pumped forth rhythmically, spilling over Geezer's prone frame, turning his once-white shirt into a dark-red funeral shroud.

"Rikka," Geezer moaned, sense leaving him as his blood pressure dropped. "Rikka, love, talk to me."

Torval stood over the two of them, staring down, face a mask of pity and regret. "You'll see her soon, Geezer. Don't you worry..." Torval then hurried across the room to the window. He let out three long, shrill bleats of his watchwarden's whistle, then began shouting. "Somebody get a surgeon! Move! We've got a dying man up here!"

Rem looked around for anything he could find. He seized upon a kitchen rag encrusted with old stew stains and stinking of sour beer. He snatched up the rag, made a wad of it, and pressed it hard against Geezer's flowing wound.

"Aemon," someone breathed.

Rem looked to the doorway. Emacca and Tembryna—two of their female comrades from the wardwatch—had arrived. They stood just outside the door, as though they were loath to enter the room and let the bad fortune swirling there settle on them. Tembryna's soft young face and great green eyes betrayed horror and sadness at the ugly scene before her. Emacca, born to a hard life on the Tregga Steppe and rarely inclined to displays of emotion, simply stared, stoic and silent.

"Oh, this is just a fine way to end it," Geezer said sadly. As his life ebbed out of him, his sanity was returning. "Bleeding out like this, done in by you lot..."

"Calm down," Rem said, trying to get the fidgeting Geezer to hold still. "We've called for someone. We'll not let you die tonight."

"Says the man who killed me," Geezer retorted.

"Well, we warned you!" Rem shouted back, suddenly losing his patience. "How many times, Geezer? *How many?* Beating her? Threatening us? Making a mess of…of…of everything! You're a fool, and if this is the way you end, you've only yourself to blame!" Immediately Rem regretted his words. They seemed cruel, somehow, no matter how true they might be.

"Rikka, lass," the dying man said. "I can't see her. Where is she?"

Torval was at Rem's side now, lifting the rag Rem held just long enough to study Geezer's wound. The dwarf looked to Rem and gave a slight, almost imperceptible shake of his head. He wasn't going to make it.

"Curse you," Geezer wheezed. "Curse you both. I call down Hyryn's wrath…beg for Serath's snare…"

"Go on," Torval said dismissively. "Blame us, you sod. This is all on you."

Geezer's face was so white now, his eyelids drooping. "May you be broken on Ghagar's table," he whispered. "Swallowed by Meimis…snatched by Kraet…"

Rem stared, forcing himself to bear witness as the man died. His eyes were half shut now, face white as ash, expression immobile. He stared upward, into the night sky, as if he could see through the ceiling, through the roof, beyond the rain and clouds to the hidden, distant stars…

"We warned him," Rem said. "Bloody fools—we warned them both."

Torval's hand fell on Rem's shoulder. "No regrets, lad. You did your duty."

Geezer's last breath escaped him like a shuddering cough.

Rem stood and backed away. He moved to the window and stared out into the night, wishing he could be out in that rain right now, its inexorable fall washing all the blood and the guilt and the pointless waste right off him...

CHAPTER TWO

A local barber-surgeon who'd heard the commotion arrived soon after Geezer's heart stopped. When it was apparent his clinical skills were no longer required, Rem and Torval asked the man to give a sworn statement to either Emacca or Tembryna, then told him he could be on his way. Down in the street, more watchwardens arrived. They immediately busied themselves with taking statements from those in the crowd willing to give them, and dispersing those who had nothing of use to offer. Upstairs, Rem and Torval gave their versions of the event to Emacca and Tembryna before allowing their two female comrades to study the crime scene, a standard practice among the watchwardens when fatalities or serious injuries were involved. Once the two women had completed their hasty recording of Rem's and Torval's separate recollections on scraps of parchment and appended their own observations, they promised to see the statements delivered to the watchkeep before the end of their shift. By the time the lich cart arrived to haul the remains of Geezer and Rikka away, the crowd had thinned, but a steady rain yet fell, turning all the world into a muddy screen differentiated only by smudges and shadows, and churning the uncobbled streets to thick, sucking mud. It felt as if they'd passed a whole night's shift in that cramped little apartment. In fact, less than two hours had elapsed since their arrival.

In no hurry to get themselves soaked to the bone, Rem and Torval lingered in the cramped, dark vestibule of the apartment house, each lost in thoughtful silence.

Rem knew he'd done the right thing—Geezer had killed Rikka with his anger and carelessness, then clearly threatened Torval with that broken bottle. What else could Rem have done? There had been no other choice.

But *doing* the right thing and *feeling* that it was the right thing were two distinct states of being, weren't they? Truth be told, Rem didn't care how right his defense of his partner had been—he hated the feeling of taking life, especially in the course of what should have been such a simple, routine encounter.

"Are you done yet?" Torval asked.

Rem glanced at his partner. "Done with what?"

"With all of your brooding," Torval said. "Because if you are, I'd like to head back to the watchkeep."

Rem shrugged. "Let's go, then."

"Hold on," Torval said, stepping into his path. "Look at me—right into my eyes. Right at my ugly mug."

Rem forced himself to do so. In truth, consciously looking Torval in the eye felt strange and unnerving. No doubt the two of them spoke eye to eye all the time, but making the decision consciously felt like opening himself up—inviting something he wasn't sure he could withstand…

"I know it's cold comfort," Torval said slowly, "but you did what you had to."

"I know," Rem said hastily.

"Do you?" Torval asked. "Because I'm fairly certain it's still weighing on you. I know killing anyone never becomes easy, or normal, but you've been doing this nearly a year now. If you strike anyone down because they were threatening you, or threatening me, then it was a good call, plain and simple. Say a prayer for them, but don't carry the weight of it. We gave Geezer a choice. He made the bad one."

Rem nodded. "I understand that...It's just...it seems like such a waste."

"It is," Torval said. "But there's nothing for it. Those two were headed for some sort of reckoning—some bloody, unwelcome end—since they first fell into the same bed. Somewhere in their haunted hearts, I have no doubt they harbored love for one another, but that love was volatile. If it didn't get one of them killed, it would've taken someone else. We did our jobs by making sure *they*, and no one else, paid the price of that reckoning."

"I just don't understand it," Rem said, "no matter how many times I've seen it. Isn't love supposed to make you care for things? Guard them? Protect them?"

"Some love, yes," Torval said, his voice soft and unusually tender. "But there's another sort...a dangerous sort. It's a love that doesn't just warm—it burns. It blazes. And ultimately, it devours things. That kind of love doesn't protect—it kills."

Rem sighed and lowered his eyes. "Gods save me from a love like that."

"Well, now," Torval said, and gave Rem a friendly clap on the shoulder, "what say we make a dash through that downpour? The sooner we're back at the watchkeep, the sooner we can scratch out our bloody reports and be done with this ugly business."

Torval led the way through the rainy streets, keeping a steady pace in an effort to get them through the rain and out of it as quickly as possible. Their progress was a zigzagging game as they darted from one overhang or portico to another, trying to keep from spending too much time in the rain, and hoping at each brief stop for an abatement that never came.

They were just blocks away from Sygar's Square and the watchkeep, the thought of the crowded common chamber and the quiet, thoughtful scratch of a quill-tip on parchment already making Rem feel warmer and drier, when Rem heard a strange series of sounds behind him: first, a light, tinny rattle— the sound of chain mail on a moving body—followed by an impact, a curse, and a loose clickety-clacking, like something solid skating over a bumpy surface, followed by a dry rattle as pieces of something hit the mud. Rem stopped and turned to scan the street behind them. Just a few feet away, he saw a trio of slate roof shingles lying in the mud beneath the over-hanging eaves of a peak-roofed warehouse. He tilted his gaze upward, to see where they might have come from, and scanned the steeply slanting roof for signs of damage.

"What are you gawping at?" Torval shouted from up ahead. "I turned back and you were gone!"

Rem's eyes made the peak of the roof. There, visible in dark relief against the black sky, was a strange, solid figure strad-dling the roof's center. For a moment Rem wasn't sure what he was seeing. Maybe it was just a misshapen chimney? A large alley cat? A stray dog that had somehow climbed to a height it couldn't find its way down from?

Then a short, sharp flash of lightning illuminated the hud-dled shape and Rem saw clearly that it was none of those things; it was, in fact, a man. He wore what looked like royal livery of some sort—a soaked, colorful surcoat over gleaming chain mail—and his hair was lank and plastered to his head in the rain. In that brief lightning flash, Rem not only saw his quarry; his quarry saw him. Realizing that he'd been discovered, the man on the rooftop spat a curse, then rose, still straddling the peak, desperately searching for an escape.

"Torval?" Rem called, and pointed toward the roof above them. "Did you see that?"

"Bollocks," the dwarf cursed under his breath. "I did."

"You there!" Rem called. "Get down here! This is the wardwatch!"

The man, now an inky blot, suddenly disappeared. He'd flown his perch, probably gone sliding down the far side of the pitched roof.

"Around the other side!" Rem shouted, and broke into a run, right past Torval, rounding the front corner of the big warehouse. Even as he approached, Rem could vaguely hear the commotion of the climber's rough descent and landing: the sound of his body sliding over the uneven roof, the rattle of falling shingles as his passage tore them loose and sent them tumbling earthward, then a wet splat as the man fell and hit the mud. Rem was just rushing into the mouth of the alley on the warehouse's far side when he heard his quarry curse again.

Lightning flashed once more. Rem gained a momentary glimpse of the dark alley. The rooftop bandit, pulling himself out of the mud, was trying to orient himself and locate an egress. When darkness returned, Rem could still pick the man's form out of the slate-gray shadows and used that blot of black on black to guide him.

"Stand fast," Rem said, bolting forward. "You'll only make it worse on yourself if you run."

Of course the fellow ran, turning his back on Rem and pounding down the long alley toward the far end, splashing through the standing puddles and sheets of rain. Rem broke into a sprint after him. Some small part of him supposed he should let this one go—that no good would come of this sudden, intense desire to run a single roof-hopping burglar to ground when they'd already dealt with such foul business at Geezer and Rikka's—but Rem simply couldn't resist the urge. So what if it was a shit night? If he couldn't lay hands on this single clumsy sneak thief, what sort of watchwarden was he?

He was closing, but not fast enough. The man was twenty paces ahead. In seconds the bastard would hit the side alleys that fed into the one they now traversed, and if he made it around either of those corners, Rem was fairly sure he might lose him entirely.

Maybe that's for the best, Rem thought as he ran. *This is foolish. You're already soaked to the bone. Depressed. Angry. Just stop. Let him go. There's no point in—*

Just as his quarry made the corner and started to turn, something thick and muscular leapt from the shadows and collided hard with the fleeing thief. He gave a shout, then hit the mud with stunning force. Rem wondered what had just thrown itself at the man. He found out when another flash of lightning gave him an instant of slanting light in the alley.

It was Torval. The dwarf sprawled atop the fallen thief, having tackled him full force. He must have circled around the opposite side of the warehouse. The old stump now struggled to set himself upright while keeping his considerable weight on the fallen burglar's back. Rem slowed, struggling to catch his breath. He wished he had Torval's night vision. At present, all he could see was an airy, murky darkness, a pair of forms squirming just a few feet away from him, their visibility more dependent upon their movement than upon anything Rem could clearly make out.

"Good watchwardens," the thief said from the ground, "how fortunate! I was just in pursuit of some offending footpad who'd absconded from my rooms."

"Nice try," Torval said. Rem heard struggles and grunting.

He assumed Torval was tying the thief's hands behind his back before yanking him upright again.

A flash of lightning. Rem had an instant to study the man's face: unshaven, vaguely handsome, long dark hair, anywhere between thirty and fifty. Torval was, indeed, binding his hands.

"Let me guess," Rem said. "You don't normally traverse rooftops, but you were so concerned about this burglar's spoils you were willing to risk it all to get them back."

"Exactly," the man said. "Personally, I'm terrified of heights."

Rem heard grunting and knew that Torval was now pulling the man to his feet. He saw the blotted forms of their prisoner and Torval coming toward him. He fell in step beside them as they headed back for the mouth of the alley.

In moments they were back on the street, and Rem and Torval were better able to see their new prisoner by the dim light of a few nearby post lamps and from the secondhand glow of lit windows on the street around them. The man was strangely calm, even his attempts at an explanation sounding like rote banter instead of true, well-intended excuses. *Clearly he's done this before*, Rem thought.

"It's been my experience," Torval said to the thief, "that no one goes for a midnight stroll on a rooftop without considerable practice and a definite aim. Whether that aim is murder or just plain thievery remains to be seen."

"Look, gents," the man said, sounding eminently reasonable, "I'll only say this once: let me go, forget you ever saw me. You'll be happier if you do so, trust me."

"Listen to this prat," Torval said, shaking the bound prisoner a bit. "Only our well-being at heart, eh?"

"Forgive us," Rem said to the prisoner, "we've heard better excuses offered with greater sincerity. I'm afraid it's the watch-keep for you, my friend."

"Honestly," the man said, and he almost sounded sad about it, "you'll be sorry."

"We're already sorry," Torval said at his elbow, then shoved him along the street. "It's been a shit night and we're both soaking wet. Nabbing you might be the only bright spot in our evening, truth be told."

"Just remember," the man said as he began his walk through the rain back to the watchkeep. "I warned you. You could've saved yourselves."

Rem wanted to laugh off the man's bravado as pure clap-trap, but there was something in the man's voice—an earnest regret—that put him on edge. Rem didn't voice his concerns, but he failed, no matter how he tried, to wholly banish them.

CHAPTER THREE

They found a livery stable wherein the owner was hard at work forking hay into the stalls and getting his beasts bedded down for the night. There they sheltered until the rain subsided and they could carry on to the watchkeep. For the hour or so that they passed there, hunkered around a fire in a brazier, trying to warm themselves despite being waterlogged, they shared few words with their prisoner. More than once, in the flame-burnished near darkness, Rem stole glances at the mysterious thief, tied to a post just a few strides away. Who was this man, espied on a rooftop and captured as he fled the scene?

"You're staring," Torval said.

"Does he look familiar to you?" Rem asked, voice barely above a whisper.

Torval studied their quiet prisoner and shrugged. "Something in his face rings a bell," Torval said, "but damned if I can work out what it might be."

Rem regarded the bound man. He'd stood there, without a word of complaint, for the whole time they'd been sheltering in the barn, as patient as a man on a street corner hoping to cross after a tide of heavy traffic.

"Would you like to come closer to the fire?" Rem asked.

"Thank you, no," the thief said. "I'm just peachy where I stand."

Torval shot Rem a doubtful glance. What was this sneaky bastard up to? His demeanor, his calmness—they were all wrong.

"Care to tell us what you were doing on that rooftop?" Torval asked.

The man shrugged. "I already told you. You didn't believe me."

"We still don't," Rem said. "That surcoat—aren't those noble colors?"

For the merest instant, the prisoner looked profoundly annoyed, as though Rem's eye for heraldry presented an unexpected obstacle. Then his resigned smile returned and he gave an offhand shrug.

"I was caught unawares in a boardinghouse. These were the only clothes at hand."

"Right," Torval said. "Good boots, well-sewn breeks, a nearly full suit of chain mail, and a surcoat denoting service in the house of some duke or another—just lying around, easiest thing to slip into when chasing a burglar over rooftops."

The man nodded, as if resigning himself to something. "Very well, then. This is what is called an impasse. If you do not believe what I tell you and I cannot convince you otherwise, there's no point in talking. I'll just stand here and keep myself to myself, thank you."

The stabler joined them now, tossing aside his pitchfork and studying the bound prisoner for himself. He was a leather-skinned, stooped old man, face so lined it appeared to be carved from tree bark, a wild tangle of white curls on his head. Despite his advanced age and bent back, there was yet an air of confidence and command about him—as if he had once been a man of importance and was now struggling mightily to ignore the march of time as it gnarled his body and carved ravines into his countenance.

"Funny sort," he said, making an appraisal of his own. "Looks all rough spun, like a woodsman or road agent, but talks all fancy, like someone highborn."

Again Rem caught that fleeting, barely perceptible annoyance on the prisoner's face. Just as before, it was erased by a forced smile and another resigned shrug. "Now the stabler's an expert in linguistics," he snorted. "Rich."

"He's right, though," Rem pressed from his place beside the fire. "You talk like someone raised in a lord's house. I should know—I was myself."

"Groom's son," Torval said, and Rem caught the unmistakable note of incredulity in his voice. He turned to his partner, and the dwarf gave him a challenging look. Rem had told Indilen the truth months ago, but he'd left Torval in the dark. Clearly he wasn't fooling anyone...

"My, my," the prisoner suddenly said, glancing toward the half-open door of the stable. "Looks like the rain's subsided. What say we carry on to the watchkeep, gents? Leave this poor sod and his horses alone for the night?"

Rem and Torval looked toward the stable door. He was right. The rain was barely a trickle now, its roar on the roof having abated and made the world quieter. In one of the nearby stalls, a horse whickered. An ox bellowed sleepily in answer.

"Well, then," Torval said, "I guess it's time to press on."

Rem moved for the prisoner and began the quick work of untying him from the post that he'd been bound to. As he did so, he looked into the man's eyes. The prisoner stared back, unafraid, unaffected, unmoved. His cordiality and self-control, far from making Rem feel at ease, put him on edge. Clearly the man knew something—planned something—that Rem and Torval had no reckoning of.

"Thank you for the use of your barn," Rem said as he led their prisoner by his rope lead toward the stable door.

"Anytime, watchwardens," the old stabler said, raising a hand. "Appreciated the company."

The prisoner turned and spoke to their host as he was led toward the door. "Check that dappled mare in the last stall, old man," he said. "She favors her hind right when she's shuffling about. Might be stone bruised. The shoe might even be loose."

Rem froze in his tracks and studied the man. The prisoner's face was implacable, as though he'd said nothing unusual, offered nothing out of character for a roof-dancing sneak thief.

"Know something about horses, do you?" Rem asked.

The man shrugged again, a practiced gesture. "A little something," he said, then smirked, ever so slightly. "Though a groom's son from the north probably knows far more than a simple woodland boy like myself."

Rem looked to Torval, wondering if he'd caught the veiled insinuation. *You're no groom's son*, the man seemed to say, *just as I'm no simple woodland boy.*

The dwarf had stopped. He scowled at the prisoner, then turned his scowl on Rem, as if awaiting an answer.

"I didn't tell you I was from the north," Rem said.

"The Marches are in your every word," the prisoner said, "groom's son." He snorted a little at those last words, as if they were a fine joke.

"Come on," Torval said from the doorway. "The sooner this one's in the lockup, the sooner we can call it a night."

Four bells rang from the Tower of Aemon in the city center when they finally reached the watchkeep off Sygar's Square. True to form, their headquarters was pleasantly disordered, even at such an oppressive hour. As they led their prisoner in through the vestibule and down the length of a side aisle in the administrative chamber, Rem took in the familiar sights and sounds that greeted them almost every evening and early morning.

There were Firimol and Pettina, trying to corral an unruly mob of underage pickpockets and footpads, all tied together in a long line to discourage flight. At a nearby desk, the barbarian Hildebran loomed large in the vision of a big, wide-shouldered bruiser—a Kosterman, just like Hildebran himself—while Hildebran's partner, Blein, scribbled a hasty report nearby. A female dwarven watchwarden, Gnupa, played referee between a cursing, infuriated prostitute and her belligerent, wheedling pimp, while partners Sliviwit and Demijon argued in front of their tired-faced prisoners regarding who should do the questioning and who should have to write the report for the prefect.

Nothing out of order, except everything; it was the friendly, familiar chaos that Rem had come to know and love during his year on the force.

Their favorite desk—at the end of the row, nearest the back corridor that led to the dungeons—was occupied, currently hosting old Blotstaff and Pello as they put the screws to a swarthy Magrabari merchant whose florid insistence upon his own innocence was matched only by the colorful motley of silks and jewelry he wore. Rem marked most of the man's glitter as fake—pure costumery—and guessed that his arrest probably had something to do with just such pretense. With an impatient sigh, Rem searched the chamber, found them another desk—on the opposite side of the aisle, back the way they'd come—and led Torval and their prisoner along to it.

Rem offered the prisoner a stool, which the man took with a muttered thank-you. He sat there, straight backed, tied hands in his lap. Rem fished about for some parchment, a quill, and an ink pot. Torval mounted the nearest desk and sat upon it.

"Sundry hells, old stump!" Cumenia, the female watchwarden at the desk, protested. "I'm working here!"

"Not on this very corner you're not," Torval snapped. "Carry on." With an irritated shake of her head, Cumenia did just that, doing her best to ignore the dwarf sitting just a foot away from where she scratched out her narrative.

Rem dipped his quill and set it to the page. He looked to their prisoner. "Have you a name?"

"I do, yes," the man said.

Rem waited. The prisoner offered nothing.

"Is this how it's to go?" Rem asked.

Torval smacked the man's skull. "He asked you a question," Torval said.

The prisoner looked as if he was fighting down the urge to answer that strike. Instead he simply straightened up again and drew a deep breath. "Indeed he did. And I answered it. Yes, I have a name."

"What is it?" Rem asked.

"I'd rather not say," the man answered curtly.

Torval scooted off the desk and lunged into the man's smug, serene face. "I'm warning you—"

"What difference does it make?" the man asked, and for the first time, Rem thought he heard something like annoyance in his voice. "Just lock me up, will you?"

Rem put his quill back in the ink pot. He studied the prisoner again, now in the far steadier light of the administrative chamber, provided by a wealth of hanging and standing lamps. Again Rem was overtaken by the sense he'd seen the man before, that his face was somehow familiar. But from where? That small fact eluded him, and the constant sense that this man was known to him, coupled with his inability to wriggle out just how, was driving him mad.

Try deduction, then, Rem thought. *You're a watchwarden. This is your job.*

And so he studied the man. Studied him very carefully and took all that he observed and piled it together with all that he'd already deduced from the man's speech and manners.

He was highborn—or, at the very least, raised in a lord's house. His polite demeanor and self-control suggested that. If he was not, then he was the most effective autodidactic street urchin Rem had ever encountered.

His accent was urban and courtly, but not precisely Yenaran. There was a slight lilt to his words, to the rhythm of his speech, that suggested he had been raised in some other clime. Perhaps farther inland, nearer the foothills or the mountains? And definitely a little farther north than Yenara—though not so far as Rem's own homeland in the Marches.

"What are we waiting for?" Torval asked.

"Indeed," the man said, "I'd really like to see a cell now."

Rem held up a hand. "Just give me a moment." He continued his study.

So he had a man who spoke in a courtly manner, seemed to be of other than Yenaran birth, and yet…he looked like a road agent or a turnpikeman just out of the wilds. His hair was long, almost to his shoulders, and, although he did not wear a full beard, his face was clearly unshaven, showing off a growth of several days at least.

Then there was the mystery of his dress: ducal livery, chain mail, and good boots, a combination that suggested he was a house guard for someone of importance—or, at the very least, masquerading as one.

"Rem," Torval began again, clearly impatient.

Rem held up his hand. "Just...wait, will you?"

The prisoner looked to Torval. "Does he do this all the time? Gawp at strangers sitting right in front of him, not saying a word?"

Torval leaned into their prisoner's face. "Maybe he does, you prat. Just keep your gob shut. We'll tell you when to speak."

Courtly in character, yet rough in appearance. Dressed in house livery, but not possessed of the natural discipline or manners befitting a well-trained, well-clothed professional guardsman. And yet they'd found him traversing a rooftop. That took some sort of courage, didn't it? Some sort of confidence and daring?

Then understanding dawned in Rem's whirling brain like a sudden sunrise.

"Gold and white on blue," Rem said. "That's the livery of the Duke of Erald, isn't it?"

The man made a show of studying his own garments, then looked to Rem as if quite puzzled. "I'm not sure, is it? As I said, it was the nearest thing at hand—"

Torval drew back a fist in threat.

"Answer his questions," the dwarf said slowly.

The prisoner's gaze met Torval's and never wavered. "If you strike me," he said quietly, "I shall give as good as I get. Do you understand?"

Torval shot a fell glance at Rem—*Did you hear that? He threatened me!*—then returned his attentions to their prisoner. "You're in no position to make threats, you whoreson. Now answer this young man's questions, or I'll see you hung on a rack for days to come before ever you stand before the tribunal."

The prisoner straightened up. He leveled a hard gaze of his own at Torval, then said, quietly and without enmity, "Just remember what I said."

Rem thought Torval would surely cuff the man then, so he interrupted, eager to get back on their questioning. "You're no house guard," Rem said. "Your lank hair and unshaven face tell me that. But you're highborn. I can hear it in your speech."

"As I can hear it in yours," the man said, finally losing his patience again. "What's the point of all this? Just lock me up, will you? I'm tired and I could use a good piss—"

Torval struck—or tried to, anyway—a loose-fisted, back-handed strike.

But it missed.

CHAPTER FOUR

It happened in seconds, before Rem could even spring up out of his chair. Their prisoner leaned backward, avoiding Torval's whizzing fist, then launched from his sitting position. In a single breath, Torval was flat on his back, the prisoner kicking him hard to keep him stunned, then laying one boot on Torval's throat. By the time Rem had risen and lunged to Torval's aid, by the time he saw other watchwardens closing from all sides to drag the prisoner off the fallen dwarf, the man had already removed his boot from Torval's throat and withdrawn of his own accord.

"I warned you," the prisoner said quietly, before a half dozen watchwardens fell upon him and yanked him away. "Hit me and I'd give as good as I got."

Still smiling, proud of his display of speed and strength, the prisoner let himself be drawn away. The commotion sent the whole administrative chamber of the watchkeep into a flurry of activity, curious prisoners and watchwardens pressing forward for a better look. Rem, relieved that Torval was safe, offered a hand to the prone dwarf. As their enigmatic prisoner with his unshaven woodsman's face and inexplicably expensive boots and knightly surcoat was dragged away, Torval's eyes never left him. Something about the way Torval stared set Rem on edge.

It wasn't fear, precisely—Torval rarely, if ever, betrayed fear. His gape-mouthed expression instead suggested both awe and respect. The man's sudden movement and attack had left Torval *impressed* by him, creating of an enemy a grudging admirer. Torval took Rem's hand and regained his feet. A stone's throw from them, the prisoner stood still and unresisting, surrounded by wary watchwardens, all ready to arrest another attack if need be.

"You all right?" Rem asked quietly.

"Fast, that one," Torval said. "Did you see him?"

"I saw a blur, then you were on your back," Rem said. "What say we lock him up and question him later?"

"What say we offer him a job?" Torval asked.

Rem felt a strange twinge in the center of him—bitter, unfamiliar. "That's enough of that," he said to his diminutive partner. "I'm still standing here, you know."

Torval turned his blue eyes on Rem. He smiled a little, then patted the young man's cheek with patronizing softness. "The Bonny Prince is jealous," he said, with no small amount of satisfaction.

Rem threw off Torval's hand. Without any retort to offer, he turned to the watchwardens still surrounding their prisoner. "Take him below, please?" he asked. "If there's an empty cage, lock him up in it."

Their prisoner—already mysterious enough—responded strangely, pressing his hands together, prayer-like, and nodding. He offered a very genuine smile. "My sincere thanks, watchwarden. You've done good work this night, both of you."

Then he was gone, whisked away to the dungeons. Rem turned back to Torval. The dwarf looked just as puzzled as he. Their night had taken a very strange turn.

"I've a feeling I never want to see that man again," Rem said. "No good will come of it."

Torval nodded. "Aye, that. Thank you, though—for getting him off me."

Rem shrugged, still amazed at the man's speed. "Better late than never."

As they turned to resume their report writing—they still had to offer their own summary of that nasty business with Geezer and Rikka, after all—Rem realized they were being watched. Ondego, the prefect of the Fifth Ward watch, stood on the far side of the desk they'd been using, assessing the scene with his customary scowl. His second-in-command, Hirk, loomed at his elbow. Rem and Torval both froze under Ondego's weighty gaze, not sure if they were about to be commended or censured.

"What's the story on that one?" the prefect asked.

Rem looked to Torval in a last-ditch effort to defer to the seasoned dwarf and let him explain. Torval, to his great chagrin, said nothing. He only shook his head and swept out his hand, as if he and Rem were both trying to pass through the same narrow doorway and only one could go at a time. *After you, Bonny Prince.* Annoyed, Rem set about answering the prefect's question.

"We found him on a rooftop," Rem said. "Probably wouldn't have caught him if he hadn't slipped and fallen into our laps."

"That was house livery of some sort, wasn't it?" Ondego said, raising one eyebrow. "Strike you as odd, finding a rooftop burglar in a knight's surcoat?"

"Most certainly," Rem said. "That's part of the reason we went after him. Skulking on rooftops is one thing—even if we didn't catch him red-handed in the commission of a crime—but dressed like that? It's a puzzle, indeed."

"Get anything out of him?" Hirk asked.

Torval finally joined the conversation. "Not a whit. Though the Bonny Prince here made some fine deductions."

Rem summarized. "You saw him—unshaven and long-haired, like an itinerant lute player, but wearing that surcoat and fine kid boots. I recognize that livery, too—gold over blue, parted by a white chevron and sporting a falcon: that's a uniform for the Duke of Erald's house guard. So we've got a scruffy scoundrel in what I'm guessing is a stolen uniform who addresses us in courtly speech, in an accent foreign to Yenara."

"Has a familiar look about him," Ondego said thoughtfully. "Wouldn't you say so, Hirk?"

The second shrugged. "Just another goon in dress-up, you ask me."

"I had the same thought," Rem said to Ondego. "I told Torval as much! I could swear I've seen him before, I said, but can't say where. It's been eating at me all night."

Ondego nodded slowly, mentally chewing on Rem's proposition. After a long consideration, he asked another question.

"You're sure it was Eraldic livery?" Ondego asked.

Rem shrugged. "Fairly. If I could get a look at a book of patents, I'd be sure—"

"How about some men in the same getup?" Ondego asked, nodding toward the far door of the chamber.

Rem and Torval turned to see what their prefect now stared at. Crowding the main entryway to the administrative chamber were five men, gathered in a tight knot. They wore freshly washed surcoats atop well-oiled chain mail: gold over blue, parted by a white chevron and sporting the likeness of a falcon. The leader of the party was a stiff-backed, patrician sort—level, hawkish gaze, proud profile, square shoulders—and his gray-flecked black beard was trimmed close to his jutting chin, a near-perfect bit of face grooming. His four companions were clearly his subordinates. As they haunted the doorway, their leader scanned the room with his raptor's gaze, eyes swinging slowly but surely toward the spot where Rem and Torval stood beside Ondego and Hirk.

"I guess that settles it," Rem said. He elbowed Torval and indicated the new arrivals. "See? What did I say? Look at that man's neat hair and trimmed whiskers. I told you our prisoner couldn't actually be a ducal guard, looking the way he did."

The newcomer's gaze finally found Ondego. He appraised the prefect—command recognizing command—then led the quintet of men across the room in an orderly march, passing right through knots of curious watchwardens and lingering prisoners without so much as an excuse-me or beg-your-pardon. As he approached, Rem had another chance to assess him—his regal bearing, his apparent age and wisdom, all borne about in a well-exercised, well-cared-for, still-strong body. *Formidable* was the word that came to mind. The man projected strength, grace, and cunning—a most impressive combination.

Then he stopped just a few feet from Rem and Torval, his men silent behind him, eyes locked on Ondego. There was a long, tense pause as the man once more studied and weighed all those before his gaze—Torval, Rem, Ondego, Hirk—before finally deigning to speak.

"Who commands here?" the stranger asked.

"That'd be me," Ondego said, stepping forward.

The guard commander carried on. "I am Harcta Kroenen, lord marshal to Verin Lyr, the Duke of Erald. I offer my badge of office and a written mandate from my sovereign."

With great efficiency the lord marshal drew a leather wallet and a small matching leather scroll case from his belt. He flipped back the lip of the wallet, revealing a golden signet, well tooled and polished, bearing the ducal seal of Erald.

Ondego whistled. "Shiny." He turned to Hirk. "Can we get some of those?"

Hirk shook his head. "Won't do. Remember the old gold badges? Always getting stolen?"

"Not for everyone," Ondego said, suggesting the watchwardens at their business around them. "Just you and me. Prefect and deputy prefect. We, at least, should have a fine, shiny badge of office like that..."

Rem studied the lord marshal. His face was largely immobile, but the twin ghosts of annoyance and impatience floated just below the surface of his apparent calm. Clearly he didn't care for Ondego's joshing about.

"Excuse me," the lord marshal finally said, and tucked away his walleted badge again. He offered the small leather scroll case this time. "My master's mandate, for your perusal."

"Keep it," Ondego said. "Clearly you are who you say you are. Missing a man, are you?"

The newcomer raised an eyebrow. "Missing...?"

"One of your pretty little bluebirds? We just locked up a fellow wearing your uniform not moments before you arrived."

The lord marshal's back stiffened at that. It was a subtle gesture, but Rem caught it. The man's eyes widened. "Is that so?"

"'Tis," Ondego said. "So what say you state your business?"

The lord marshal tucked away his little scroll case and held out a hand to one of his subordinates. "The circular," he said.

The soldier addressed went rooting in a satchel slung at his side and produced a sheet of stiff, folded parchment. Gingerly he unfolded the parchment and handed the well-creased leaf to his master. The lord marshal took the parchment, then handed it to Ondego.

"We've gone watchkeep to watchkeep, inquiring after our quarry. Is this the man in your custody?"

Ondego took the parchment and studied it. His eyebrows rose and he whistled low, clearly impressed by something he saw on that folded leaflet. He shared a conspiratorial glance with Hirk, who'd been studying the sheet over his shoulder, then handed it to Torval. The dwarf took the leaflet and held it out before him, making sure that Rem could see it.

"Now we know why he looked familiar," Ondego said to them. "Go rooting around on our wall of shame over there, crammed with Wanted posters, and you'll find a leaflet just like this."

Rem and Torval studied the creased parchment together. There, staring back at them from a subtle and strikingly accurate woodblock portrait, was their prisoner. His hair was even longer in the image, and his beard fuller, but the resemblance was undeniable. As Ondego had said, that explained the man's familiarity; Rem was almost certain that he'd seen that Wanted leaflet more than once, probably when it was first circulated, then later, hanging in the rogue's gallery on the far wall, gradually obscured by newer leaflets that got nailed atop it.

"Wanted," it said, "dead or alive. The notorious outlaw road agent known as the Red Raven. Charged by His Lordship Verin Lyr, the Duke of Erald, with theft, murder, kidnapping, conspiracy, and extortion. To whoever presents the living person of said outlaw, or undeniable proof of his death, let it be known that the duke shall remit to said presenter a fabulous reward of one hundred pieces of gold."

Rem threw a glance at Torval. His partner was already staring back at him.

Rem had heard stories of the Red Raven, the first of them during his journey toward Yenara, still more in taverns and taprooms since his arrival. It was well known that the Raven and his band of robbers—called the Devils of the Weald—haunted the Ethkeraldi Forest, a vast, untamed woodland through which the northeasterly road from Yenara to Erald wound. Though Rem's own approach to the city had not taken him through the Ethkeraldi—the merchants and pilgrims he'd traveled with had given the wood's eastern borders a wide berth—he'd heard more than a few harrowing tales of the Red Raven's daring and villainy around many camp cookfires and hearths of roadside inns between Lycos and Yenara.

Not a man but a ghost, some said.

Not a man or a ghost but a beast, countered others. *A trickster. A shapeshifter. Inhuman.*

Balderdash, the incredulous scoffed. *He's a man, all right, but quick and cunning, unlike any you could meet. Fearless, rich as a king on the tons of gold he's stolen from those passing through the forest, and likewise a slaver and raper of women.*

You're giving him too much credit, still others insisted. *He's not so posh. Just a common robber and woodland scum, as like to skin you and eat you as rob you.*

Rem knew well that legends often obscured reality—that a person's reputation usually far outstripped the actuality of who they were and how they comported themselves—but the very fact that the Red Raven had so many people talking about him, and that the stories were so vast and varied and colorful, told Rem that, whatever the reality behind the legend, it was likely to be almost as exciting, almost as intriguing, as the stories themselves.

How much crime did an outlaw have to indulge in, after all, to warrant such a princely sum for his capture or death?

Watchwardens were paid twenty-five silver andies each month. With twenty-four andies to the gold piece, a year's wages for one of them added up to just over twelve and a half pieces of gold. How much could Rem and Torval accomplish for themselves and their loved ones if they were granted even a portion of that one-hundred-gold-piece reward? Even if they handed over a fifth to the watchkeep coffers and another fifth to Ondego himself—as was proper—that would still leave them with sixty pieces of gold—five years of wages—to split between the two of them!

"How did this man come to be in your custody?" the lord marshal asked, interrupting Rem's daydreams about what to do with the reward. "Was there violence? Damage to person or property?"

"He fell into our laps," Torval said.

"Literally," Rem added.

"Shush," Ondego hissed. Rem knew the look on the prefect's face well, the look of an annoyed father whose chatty child had just said too much. The prefect then looked to their visitor. "Step into my office, lord marshal. What say we hash out all attendant issues of jurisdiction and extradition...as well as remuneration?"

Lord Marshal Kroenen nodded. "That will do, Prefect. Lead the way."

In short order they were all crammed into Ondego's little, airless office, with only its single tiny window placed high on the wall to allow in some fresh air. Hirk offered the lord marshal a chair, but Kroenen cordially declined and simply stood—back straight as an iron rail. Rem and Torval pressed themselves into a far corner of the room, while Kroenen's chosen assistant—a youngish soldier who bore, if Rem was not mistaken, a quite striking resemblance to Kroenen himself—stood in the doorway.

"I know not how often you venture beyond your city walls," the lord marshal said to the prefect, "but the Red Raven and his brigands have been terrorizing the Ethkeraldi for some time now."

"Going on ten or fifteen years, isn't it?" Ondego asked, almost wistfully. "I used to hear tell of him when I made my home in Kaarth. Devils of the Weald—isn't that the preferred moniker for the Raven's men?"

Rem thought of the man they'd just locked up. *Ten or fifteen years?* Had he embarked on his life of crime when he was a teenager and gained fame so young? Not so unusual, Rem supposed... but something in that reckoning—the years of activity considered against the relative youth of the man they'd arrested—just would not sit easy with him.

"Just so," Kroenen said. "And devilish they are. Kaarth, Iskera, Erald, Yenara... All the free cities round the Ethkeraldi have felt the sting of the man's villainy. He's orphaned a hundred children, crippled twice as many brave soldiers or travelers who dared to challenge him, and his greed knows no bounds. That he steals such fabulous sums and still lives like a savage in the woods should be proof enough that he's mad as well as villainous."

"Don't the forest folk speak well of him?" Hirk offered. "I've heard some even call him a hero."

"Wood-folk," Kroenen said dismissively. "These are people who live in caves or primitive hovels and subsist on tree bark and underfed rodents. Should it come as any surprise they would lift up such a dishonorable man?"

"One man's outlaw is another man's equalizer," Ondego offered, and Rem could see clearly that he was teasing the lord marshal. It was not beyond the prefect; though he took his duties seriously, he also had an almost reflexive disdain for well-groomed men in bright, shiny uniforms.

"Prefect," Kroenen said, cocking his head doubtfully. "You cannot, with any seriousness, countenance or approve of this man's criminality?"

"Oh, no," Ondego said. "Surely not. Just saying that is, at times, the prevailing wisdom. If the Red Raven gives the wood-folk something while the free cities give them nothing, why *wouldn't* they lift him up and defend him?"

"In any case," Kroenen broke in and carried on, clearly trying to put the conversation back on track, "you say you now have the man. Let me get to the point: if we see your prisoner and verify that he is, indeed, the notorious Red Raven, I should expect his swift remand to our custody for transfer back to our home city. There the duke's justice shall be meted out to him."

"Hold on, now," Rem said, suddenly stepping forward. "We're all for cooperation among jurisdictions, Prefect, but we've yet to even work out what the man's done that's against the law."

Kroenen regarded Rem with a dismissive glance over his shoulder. The look became a strange, puzzled double take. For a moment it was as though the lord marshal thought he recognized Rem. A beat later, he once more regarded Rem with nothing but annoyance.

"Prefect," he said, "if you could please control your men."

"Tried and failed, *so* many times," Ondego said with mock resignation. "In this case, however, the lad raises a fair question: What's this Red Raven done—here, in Yenara—that we should hand him over to you?"

"What's he done?" Kroenen asked, disbelieving. "Prefect, you said yourself you've heard the stories."

"Aye, and they're most engaging," Ondego countered. "But the fact remains, we arrest and charge people based on the commission of crimes on the sovereign soil of *this city*, not based on hearsay and campfire spook tales."

"But your men," Kroenen said, suggesting Rem and Torval

lurking in their corner, "they themselves arrested the man, did they not?"

"We found him on a rooftop," Torval said. "We deemed that suspicious. But we haven't even searched the man for stolen goods or wormed out any proof of wrongdoing yet. By rights, if we find nothing, we have to let him go."

"Prefect," Kroenen said, for the first time appearing somewhat flustered, "you cannot set this man free."

"What's he done, then?" Ondego pressed. "You show me proof of a crime, on Yenaran soil, and I'll remand him to you."

"Breaking and entering," Lord Marshal Kroenen said, overcome with sudden inspiration. "This very night, the Red Raven gained access to a person of some significance to the Eraldic court."

"Someone significant to the Eraldic court," Ondego said slowly, "in this city? In my ward? I'd hate to think a foreign duke was here, under my very nose, without me or my compatriots in law enforcement being made aware of the fact. There are protocols, after all."

"I am not at liberty," Kroenen began.

"Then neither are we," Ondego broke in. "To remand our prisoner, that is."

CHAPTER FIVE

"Prefect," Kroenen countered, "this is most ungracious—"

"Almost as ungracious as a perfect stranger marching into my watchkeep and asking for one of my prisoners without so much as a summary explanation or probable cause," Ondego snapped. He was letting his impatience show now, and Rem could see from the lord marshal's gaping mouth and wide eyes that he was totally unprepared for it.

"I can take this matter to the high magistrate," Lord Marshal Kroenen said. "Even the Tribunal or the Council of Patriarchs."

Ondego nodded. "There's the door. Do as you must. If need be, I'll fight them just as I'm fighting you now. There aren't many rules in this game of ours, but we try to honor the few laid down."

"Why do you resist me?" Kroenen asked.

Ondego leaned back in his chair and folded his hands on his belly. "Could be your pretty blue surcoat. I'm off the color. Gives me the queasies."

Rem saw the lord marshal's eyes narrow. "Treat fairly with me, Prefect. I am not a man to be trifled with."

"Neither am I," Ondego said, and Rem could hear the lowering of his voice, a darkening. "Though I think you thought I might be? Old roughneck, ordering watchwardens around in a dingy old watchkeep. Drunk, probably. Ready to roll over.

Sure to be dazzled by your surcoats and your jangly mail and your shiny gold badges. Well, sir, let me tell you: not bloody likely. If you want a fair shake from me, you need to speak to me like I'm your peer and not your subordinate, savvy? Otherwise you can take your well-heeled arse out that door and back into the street."

The lord marshal studied Ondego for a long time. Rem could almost imagine the wheels turning in the man's mind as he appraised the prefect and his belligerence. He was probably trying to work out what Ondego's angle was...what the prefect hoped to accomplish. For a man like the lord marshal—proud, polished, long associated with pomp and power and courtly intrigue—a man like Ondego probably gave the impression of being dirty in some way, morally compromised or suspect. What a man like Lord Marshal Kroenen might have a hard time accepting was that Ondego had just told him precisely what he wanted and why: he felt disrespected, and until he got the respect he was due, he would be intractable. It really was that simple.

"Shall we try again?" Ondego asked, breaking the silence and offering a mirthless smile. "You mentioned that the Raven broke into a home, here in Yenara. Am I to assume that the Duke of Erald is here, in our fair city, breaking dozens of long-standing diplomatic protocols by not announcing himself to the authorities?"

"Not the duke," Kroenen said. Rem could see that he was loath to share more information but could find no way around it. "The duke's bride-to-be. This very night, the Red Raven forced his way into the lady's chambers."

Ondego looked to Hirk, then to Rem and Torval. *Interesting*, his raised eyebrows and frowning mouth seemed to say. *Very interesting*.

"Who is she?" Ondego asked. "One of Yenara's favored daughters?"

"No," Kroenen said. "Her name is Tzimena Baya, daughter of the Countess of Toriel, in Estavar. An honor guard from her mother's court brought her this far. We were to meet her here and see her back to Erald safely. Unfortunately, the Raven ambushed us in the Ethkeraldi. He and his Devils killed a handful of our men, stole our supplies, and scattered our horses—we that you see are all that remain. Before we could reach the city, the Raven and a small contingent of his men did. They gained access to the Lady Tzimena by presenting themselves as us. Only good fortune and borrowed horses brought us here close on his heels."

Borrowed horses. Hearing those words brought to Rem's mind the image of an itinerant family in a laden wagon now sitting alone in the Ethkeraldi, their mounts having been stolen from them outright by the lord marshal and his men.

"See now?" Ondego asked. "That's all you had to say. That makes sense. I'd like to hear testimony from someone in this lady's retinue—just to confirm the facts—but here and now, we're square. Care to see your little caged bird?"

Kroenen nodded. "At once, Prefect, if you please."

Ondego looked to Rem. "Lock-up keys, please, lad? Let's all take a little walk on the dark side..."

The familiar litany began the instant the door to the dungeons clanked open and Ondego marched in. The cells were not overly full tonight—a dozen miscreants, twenty at most—but those present made themselves known. Hands were thrust from between the bars as eager faces pressed between them, wide-eyed, beseeching.

"Prefect, sir, I swear, as Turawa's my witness, I've no recollection of where my breeches got off to..."

"Prefect, sir, listen to me! The coin-mongers of the Yenaran bank are holding my assets presently. If someone could but set me free and see me to their offices..."

"Prefect, sir, this is most embarrassing, but the truth is, I'm a very important man where I come from. The word doesn't translate directly into Yenaran, but some might say it's equal to *prince* or *potentate*..."

Rem almost smiled. Ah, the smell of desperation in the wee hours of morning. It wasn't pleasing, precisely, but it did have a certain welcoming familiarity to it.

Ondego led the way along the three banks of chambered cells. He found their quarry locked up alone in one of the smaller cages, sitting with his back against the outer wall, staring off into the gloom as though daydreaming. As he stared, his lithe, rough fingers picked at a reed of straw, alternately bending and straightening it. Rem recognized the aspect—the staring, the busy hands, the deliberate silence. The man was thinking, plotting.

Ondego stepped up to the bars and presented the prisoner to Lord Marshal Kroenen. When the lord marshal narrowed his eyes, straining to see the man's face in the inky shadows, Ondego snatched a torch from a nearby wall sconce and thrust it through the bars of the cell. The Red Raven squinted against the heat and glare of the burning torch, but kept his gray eyes fixed on the lord marshal. During a long, tense silence, the two men studied each other across the space between them, hunter and quarry, predator and prey, each sizing the other up.

Rem looked to Torval. "He doesn't seem terribly worried," he whispered.

Torval shrugged. "Perhaps he isn't," the dwarf said. "Slippery eel like that? He's sure he'll worm his way free again if he just bides his time..."

"Did you see the size of that reward?" Rem asked, voice still low.

Torval's broad face betrayed a sly smile now, blue eyes flashing greedily. "Aye, that, Bonny Prince. What would the likes of us even do with all that gold, if we had it?"

Rem returned the sly smile. "I'm fairly certain we could think of something."

"Lord Marshal Kroenen," the Red Raven said.

"At last," the lord marshal answered. "Right where you've always belonged...in a cage."

"Won't you greet me by my proper name?" the Red Raven asked.

Kroenen's eyes narrowed and his mouth bent into a frown. Rem saw it. Torval saw it. Rem was sure Ondego saw it, too.

"Would that I could choose just one," Kroenen said finally.

The Raven smiled from the corner of his cell. "Just one will do."

"So," Ondego broke in, "I take it that's your man?"

"It most assuredly is," the lord marshal said.

"Therefore," Ondego added, "you'll be taking him back to your duke, to face justice?"

The lord marshal stepped away from the bars and faced Ondego. "If you would be so kind as to release him to me, yes."

"Then let's talk now of remuneration," Ondego said. "Seeing as we've delivered this notorious road agent into your hands, I'd say me and my men are entitled to that promised reward. One hundred pieces of gold, was it?" Ondego threw a glance at Rem and Torval: *Go on, lads—back me up.*

"That's what I read," Rem said.

"As did I," Torval confirmed. "For I can read now, thank you very much. And that's what it said."

Kroenen nodded deferentially. "As you say, gentlemen. I

give you my word, that gold shall be yours... contingent upon my safe return to Erald with my prisoner. We could summon a notary and I could write you a promissory note, sealed with my duke's signet—"

"Don't trust him," the Raven said, now standing and sauntering forward. "He's all square shoulders and proud declarations now, but let him out of your sight with his prize and you'll never see that money. Not a single coin." He had removed the blue surcoat and chain mail and tossed both into a corner. He now wore only those good boots, leather breeks, and a simple wool under-tunic.

"I don't recall asking you," Ondego said, almost wearily. "What say you go back to braiding the hay, right? Let the grown-ups talk."

The Raven was on the bars now, gripping them, gaze spearing right through them and meeting Ondego's own. "You don't know this man like I do, Prefect. I'm just looking out for you."

"How dare you impugn my honor!" Kroenen snarled, a real fury starting to stir in him. "Prefect, I beg you, dismiss any words that come from this verminous pickpocket—"

"Tell you what, Prefect," the Raven now said, smiling and whispering through the bars, friendly and conspiratorial. "You know who I am now. You know I've stolen boatloads of booty from this fool and his duke. What say I double the reward? Two hundred gold pieces."

"Three hundred," Ondego said casually. "There's me and my two men here. Three'll split more easily."

The Raven shrugged. "Fair enough. I can cover that."

Ondego looked to Kroenen. "Counteroffer?"

Kroenen looked as though Ondego had just suggested the

lord marshal's daughter be passed around for fertility rites. "Prefect! You wouldn't—"

Ondego rolled his eyes impatiently. "Of course I wouldn't! Belenna's bunting, you're a tight one, aren't you?" The prefect looked to the Raven as though they'd been sharing a wonderful jest. "Can't take a joke, can he?"

The Raven shook his head, smiling. "You have no idea."

And then Ondego's fury came, thundering out of him like an explosion in a mine shaft: sudden, terrifying, deafening. Rem actually jumped at the sound of it.

"Wipe that bloody smile off your face, you radge cunt!" the prefect roared.

The Raven leapt back from the bars, clearly frightened of Ondego's sudden change of aspect. Rem looked to Torval. It never failed. The man let his inner beast loose with uncanny suddenness and precision, like a boxer whose left hook you never saw coming.

"You're a highwayman on a Wanted leaflet," Ondego sneered. "Why, in the name of all that is holy and consecrated, would I believe a single word you say, you piece of cack?"

The Raven tried to hold on to his composure, though Ondego had clearly shocked him. "No insult intended," he said. "I just thought we were negotiating."

Ondego suggested the lord marshal. "*We* are negotiating. *You* are cooling your heels in a cell because you're a gods-damned villainous, pig-fucking bushwhacker. So do me the honor of not mistaking my intentions. I intend to sell your hide like a drake-skin and make fine flash while I do so."

Lord Marshal Kroenen turned toward the Red Raven, smiling, exultant.

"And don't you start patting yourself on the back," Ondego

snarled at the lord marshal. "I'm not finished with you and your gods-damned bluebirds yet, either. Not by a long shot."

"Are you saying we are not in agreement?" the lord marshal asked.

Ondego looked to Rem and Torval. "Catches on quick, doesn't he? Come on."

With that, the disgusted prefect pushed past the lord marshal and headed for the door to the dungeon. Torval marched after him, leaving Rem standing there holding the keys and staring at the dumbfounded lord marshal. Finally Rem just swept his hand toward the door.

"After you, sir," he said.

The lord marshal turned and threw a last glance at the caged Red Raven, then strode through the dungeon door. As Rem followed him, he heard the Raven from his cell.

"Your prefect won't listen, lad, so maybe you should," the outlaw said, pressed against the bars. "I meant what I said: *do not trust that man.*"

Rem turned back, still able to see the Raven, though at a far more oblique angle than before. "We don't trust anyone around here," he said. "That's why you're in a cage."

Then Rem took his leave, locking the door behind him.

CHAPTER SIX

Rem made it home shortly after dawn to find Indilen just washing up for the morning and preparing to put on some real clothes instead of the nightdress she slept in. Seeing his lover, drinking in the sight of her, he felt turbulent pangs of unparalleled joy and deep foreboding. How lucky he was to have found her, to have saved her when she fell into the clutches of vile slavers, to have started a new life with her here, in this city, so far from the place of his birth. Even now, with the sun's first light barely peeking over the rooftops, the small sounds of singing birds and a waking city invading their quiet little rented suite, and she probably just moments out of bed—even now, Indilen was the most beautiful thing he'd ever seen.

But soon, too soon, he'd have to leave her. He didn't fancy breaking that news.

Indilen smiled as he closed the door behind him. "There's my big, tough watchwarden. I'd almost given up on seeing you before I left."

Though her eyes were still tired and puffy from sleep, her auburn hair still a wild tangle, Indilen's natural beauty nonetheless shone through. Her freckles, her big, bright, brown eyes, her wide, sun-bright smile.

Again, the pangs. Rem moved to her and swept her into his arms. He kissed her lips, her cheeks, her forehead, then held her close and breathed in the musty morning scent of her hair:

faint traces of jasmine and vanilla from her favorite hair oils, along with the comforting funk of sweat and that deep, undeniable scent that was her...the very essence of her, stripped of all perfumes and accouterments. He wanted to throw her back into bed and ravish her, but that wouldn't do. He knew that she had two clients already lined up for the morning, and failing to meet with either would be disaster for her reputation as a scribe and notary.

He felt her arms tighten around his middle and relished it. She giggled a little, face pressed against his chest.

"There, there," she said teasingly, "I missed you, too."

He lowered his face into the soft storm of her hair, breathed deep, then kissed her forehead again. "It's been such a night," he said. "Such a long, long night."

Indilen pulled away from him, just enough to look into his eyes. "Now, what's that I hear in your voice?" she said, as much to herself as to him.

Rem shrugged. "A great deal. But you've got to be going."

Indilen shook her head. "I've still got to finish dressing. Tell me while I prepare."

Rem obliged. He plopped onto the bed, yanked off his boots, and tossed them aside as Indilen finished her morning freshening and began to dress herself for a proper day's work. She owned only four dresses—all flattering colors, but of simple design and sturdy make. She chose a dark-blue one trimmed in delicate ivory stitching. Rem assisted by lacing it up in the back and making sure all the knots were secure. As she dressed, he recounted the night to her.

He started with the call to Geezer and Rikka's, and Indilen immediately turned and swept him into her arms again when he told her about having to put Geezer down. She knew he hated to kill anyone in the line of duty—even the worst, the most deserving—and she had long ago stopped trying to assuage his guilt and grief whenever his watchwarden's duties forced him to take a life. She knew, based on their shared experience, that Rem's lethal encounters weighed on him less if he could fully feel them—bitter, dolorous, painful, even. Much like fresh wounds, Rem wanted to clean and tend to those things he did in the line of duty that aggrieved him—not pretend they weren't there so that they could fester and trouble him later.

"You poor thing," Indilen said, stroking his hair, kissing his forehead as she stood and he sat on the edge of the bed. "I can't imagine how that feels..."

"You don't want to," Rem said quietly.

He let her hold him, comfort him. Then, after a time, he pulled away and carried on with his tale as Indilen pulled up a chair, sat, and held out her bare feet so that he could help her put on some shoes. When Rem saw that she planned to wear her good sandals—beautifully tooled and possessing a complex lattice of leather laces that climbed all the way up her calves and shins—he shook his head.

"It rained in the night," he said. "I'd recommend close-toed."

"Bollocks," Indilen muttered, then tossed aside her sandals and gathered her everyday shoes. They were neither expensive nor overly fashionable, but they enclosed her feet and kept the mud and shit in Yenara's churned-up streets off those precious toes of hers. Rem knew that Indilen looked forward to spring and summer, warm months meaning she could wear those favored sandals a little more often—but a wet day wasn't the time to enjoy them. Resigned, Indilen propped up her right foot and let Rem go about the business of shoeing her and lacing her up. It was a familiar ritual, one that they both silently relished.

"Anyway," Rem said as he bent over his work, "after that business with Geezer and Rikka, we thought we'd had our fill of excitement, but then some sneak thief crossing the rooftops literally fell into our laps. And could we then relax and tell ourselves this was just good fortune? That finally we could do some simple police work and throw the man in the dungeons? No such luck."

Indilen stared. He'd moved on to her left foot now. "I don't understand," she said.

Rem sighed. This was the part he'd been dreading: the lead-in to the terrible news he now had to share with her before she went out into the world for her workday.

He told her about their immediate sense that the rooftop thief was more than he appeared. The courtly speech and manners, the ducal livery, the complete absence of any stolen merchandise on his person, and his apparent resignation to being locked up. He then told her about the man's attack on Torval, the arrival of the lord marshal, and, finally, the revelation about the man's true identity.

Indilen's eyes grew wide. "*The* Red Raven? The Scourge of the Ethkeraldi? The Demon Prince of the Devils of the Weald?"

"The same," Rem said.

"Well, that's nothing to be troubled by," Indilen said, clearly trying to cheer him up. "You caught a notorious outlaw! There's got to be a huge reward! Certainly you should be entitled to some portion of that!"

Rem nodded. "Oh, we shall be—Torval and I. There's just one catch."

Indilen cocked her head, inquisitive. "A catch."

Rem nodded. Drew a deep breath. Spat it out. "We've got to go to Erald to claim it."

★   ★   ★

Indilen stared. Her eyes narrowed. Her mouth opened as though she might speak, then closed again. She put both feet—now firmly in their shoes—on the floor and folded her hands in her lap. Rem worked hard to keep his mouth shut. Indilen would be quiet now, to chew on the news before asking questions, then offer portents of doom.

It was a familiar ritual. He'd learned it was best to let her follow through with it. Trying to interrupt or explain it away would only further trouble her.

"You and Torval will go to Erald," she finally said. "To claim the reward?"

Rem nodded. "The lord marshal offered a promissory note, but Ondego refused. Privately, he told Torval and me that he didn't trust the man to honor whatever note he had written—notarized or not. And so that was the compromise reached: Torval and I will accompany the lord marshal's train back to Erald, present the Red Raven in person to the duke, then collect our reward and hurry home."

"Home," Indilen said. "From Erald."

"That's right," Rem said. He hoped she could see his own reluctance in his gaze. He wanted that coin—could already dream of so many wonderful things it could do for them. They could acquire a house for themselves and let out the extra rooms! He could buy her a trunk-load of dresses! He could get himself an even better sword than the one Torval had bought for him when he first joined the watch—maybe even have one custom made!

But he knew that she knew the cost of claiming that treasure might prove too high.

Yet it was just a mission, wasn't it? A job—no more, no less. He'd be a few weeks on the road to his destination, then a few weeks coming back. Before either of them knew it, he'd be right here in her arms again.

It sounded so simple...and yet something still gnawed at him and filled him with fear.

The world outside those walls was far more unpredictable and chaotic than the city in which they made their home. Strange to say that—to even contemplate that anywhere in the world could be *more* chaotic and unpredictable than Yenara itself—but it was the truth. The wilderness was wild, untamed, dangerous.

Sometimes deadly.

Bollocks, Rem thought. *I don't relish this. Not one bit.*

"Erald is a hundred miles from here," Indilen said.

"More like ninety," Rem said. "As the crow flies, anyway."

"You'll go by the Pilgrim's Road?" she asked.

Rem shook his head. "Afraid not," he answered, loath to lie to her—though that option had occurred to him. "That adds fifty or sixty miles to the trip, since it goes due west and only turns north-ward past the hills and the forest. No, the lord marshal swears that he and his soldiers can take us by the Ethkeraldi road safely, and that we'll reach our destination far sooner. That route gets us close to those ninety miles. We should be there in eight or nine days. Ten at most." He considered. "Two weeks at the outside."

"So," Indilen said, "I'm to go about my business as though nothing's untoward, while you go off on a monthlong round trip to the nearest sovereign city through a forest rife with bandits and roving orcs and who knows what sort of hungry wildlife?"

Rem nodded. "I'm not pleased about it myself—but that reward, Indilen—"

"Oh, I know," she said, shooting to her feet and stepping away as he tried to pull her close and hold her. "You don't think I've already come up with a hundred ways to spend that coin?"

Rem tried to feign offense, if only to get her laughing. "Here, now, lass—that's *my* coin. You neither apprehended this notorious outlaw, nor will you join me on the road—"

"Take me with you," Indilen said.

She was serious. Rem shook his head. "Absolutely not."

"You don't think I can handle it?" Indilen asked.

Rem shook his head again. "I'm not sure *I* can handle it," he said. "And I don't just mean surviving a journey through the Ethkeraldi. I'm talking about worrying about you when I'll already be worried enough for myself. Besides, I can't just bring my lover along…"

Indilen nodded. "I know, I know…It was a foolish thing to say. But honestly, Rem, something in this makes me uneasy…"

"You're not the only one," he answered. "I feel like I've just gotten to know this city, its rules—spoken and unspoken—its people. A week or more on horseback in the wilderness? A rugged wilderness hiding who knows what sort of dangers? That's uncharted territory—literally and figuratively."

"Can't someone else go?" Indilen asked.

Rem shook his head. "Believe me, Torval and I already had that conversation. Ondego isn't keen to send us, but he wants his share of that reward, as well—not just for his own pockets, but for the watchkeep coffers. That money could do real good for the ward—for all the watchwardens. This isn't just about Torval and me collecting something for ourselves—we're collecting for *everyone*."

"And what about the return journey?" Indilen pressed. "You'll be part of the lord marshal's train when you go, but when you come back—"

"We'll come back by the Pilgrim's Road," Rem said. "It'll take longer, but it'll be infinitely safer. Who knows—if we hire ourselves out as bodyguards to a pilgrim train or something, we might even make a little more coin on our way back to supplement the reward money."

Outside, morning bells pealed from the Tower of Aemon. Indilen lowered her head, counting the gongs in silence. Rem fought the urge to press her, to try to explain away her worries and fears. Just as he hated to suppress his feelings of grief and guilt after a kill, Indilen hated to have her own feelings invalidated by his clumsy attempts at appeasing her or assuaging whatever it was she was feeling. It was an old argument, and each of them had finally, after months of effort, managed to learn just what the other needed at a given time.

Thus he knew it might make him feel better to try to convince her that there was nothing to worry about, but she would feel better only if she could wrestle with her worry alone, and not have it taken from her.

The bells finished their tolling, eight peals in all.

"I have to go," she said finally. She raised her eyes to Rem. He saw the worry in them, the sickness. She was ready to blow off her morning clients.

"Go," Rem said. "Just hurry back when you're done. Knowing that we'll need sleep and strength, Ondego gave us tonight off."

"Tonight," Indilen said. "How soon do you leave?"

Rem drew another deep breath. "The day after tomorrow."

CHAPTER SEVEN

Rem made the most of his limited time with Indilen, spending the late afternoon and evening of that first day wandering the streets with her, shopping for a few home supplies, and feeding their fancies by occasionally inquiring after townhomes, houses, or pubs they saw for sale. They slept well beside one another that night, a deep melancholy lingering between them that kept them staring at one another, stroking one another, holding one another tightly, but never daring to break the solemnity of their shared solitude with anything so coarse or prosaic as lovemaking. The following day, Rem went shopping for some travel clothes that he knew he'd need: new wool undershirts, a padded studded doublet to provide a little extra protection on the road, and a woodsman's mantle with an attached cowl. Then he got his sword and his two daggers—a long dirk for his belt and a small dagger for his boot—sharpened at a local bladesmith's. When evening came, Rem and Indilen joined Torval and family at the King's Ass for an impromptu going-away party, so that the two of them could venture off into the world smothered in best wishes and good fortune.

That night, he and Indilen made love, and it was spectacular...though laced with a terrible sadness. Rem did his best, both before and after, to lighten the mood with sweet whispers and a little jesting, but try as he might, the pall never totally left either of them. By the time he felt himself drifting off to sleep in Indilen's arms, he knew that the dewy wetness he felt on his chest was her silent tears. He hoped she would not notice that he had shed a few of his own.

This is foolish, he told himself. *It's just a journey. There and back again. Three weeks gone. Maybe a month. Why should that trouble us so?*

The answer was readily apparent, staring at him from the dark recesses of his imagination like a precocious, overly wise child. *Because you're venturing out there*, that smug inward voice said. *Beyond the walls. Into the wild. Away. Apart.*

All sorts of terrible things can happen out there. That's why you were so relieved when you finally reached Yenara after your month or more of wandering away from home. Why this place welcomed you when no other had. Yenara, for all its insanity and chaos, is still bounded, protected, orderly after its own fashion.

But out there? Anything can happen out there . . .

He well remembered the reports from travelers on the road of bloody business both in the Ethkeraldi and on the Pilgrim's Trail. Robberies, rapes, murders, kidnappings . . .

Rem finally slid into dreamless sleep and woke with the cock's crow, long before their landlord had agreed to wake them. He slid out of bed as softly as he could, washed up, dressed in his traveling clothes—not fancy, but fiercely practical, most newly acquired just for the journey—and waited for Indilen to stir. After a while she, too, pulled herself from the murk of sleep. Without much coaxing she rose, washed, and dressed. By the time their landlord knocked on their door, calling that it was the appointed wake-up time, they were both ready.

The agreed-upon meeting place was Roylan's Square, adjacent to the famous Dragon's Roost Inn near the city's East Gate, since that would give the train direct access to the road that would

ultimately take them through the near hills and into the Ethkeraldi. However, before Rem and Torval could join the train for
their departure, they were required to deliver the Red Raven to
the lord marshal. Thus Rem and Indilen walked together, holding hands, from their rented rooms in the Third Ward to the
watchkeep in the Fifth, there to meet Torval and collect their
prisoner before doubling back toward the Third Ward and the
East Gate. Rem carried his supplies in a small pack on his back,
and in the secondhand saddlebags Ondego had issued to him and
Torval from the watchkeep stores.

This was not Indilen's first visit to the watchkeep, though
Rem did his best to keep her away from the place. For one
thing, Rem felt he got more than enough of that den of iniq-
uity nightly; what need had he to be there—or to drag Indilen
along—if he wasn't on duty? Added to that were the boisterous atmosphere and coarse company. Oh, Indilen didn't seem
to mind, surely; very little shocked or surprised her. Nonetheless, Rem always found himself worried and on edge when she
was around. Perhaps it was the way the prisoners leered at her,
or the way his comrades sniggered and teased him—or worse,
the times those roles were reversed and the prisoners did the
teasing while his fellow watchwardens did the leering. Worse
than the teasing or the leering, though, was the flirting. Be it
dusky-skinned Djubal or Rem's frequent sword-sparring partner, Emacca, or someone else entirely, there was no shortage of
Rem's cohorts doing their level best to banter with Indilen and
embarrass Rem whenever she was around. Indilen thought it
all charming and hilarious. Rem, not so much.

Torval waited for them on the watchkeep steps. He greeted
Indilen warmly when he saw her, drawing her into a tight,
wholehearted bear hug. Indilen, after giggling at Torval's
aggressive embrace, gave the old stump a kiss on his bald

tattooed head and begged him to put her down. After obliging, Torval offered Rem his hand and let his brotherly love fly.

"She's too good for you," he said. "You know that, don't you?"

"You never fail to remind me," Rem said.

"Fine, clever girl like her," Torval continued. "She should get herself a proper lord or a scholar or a man of the law, not some poxy, pretty-faced whelp like you."

"I like poxy, pretty-faced whelps," Indilen said with a smile. "I always preferred puppies to alley cats."

The smile she gave Rem made his heart leap.

Torval started laughing, a deep, raucous sound that rocked his whole diminutive, muscular body. "Ha!" he shouted. "She called you a puppy!"

"Are you finished?" Rem asked. "The both of you?"

Indilen offered a sad but warm smile. "Got to get my licks in now," she said, then drew up on her tiptoes and kissed him on the cheek. "I shall have no one to tease for nigh on a month."

Rem had no answer to that. He only offered a smile of his own, then led them up the steps and into the watchkeep.

Indilen waited in the common room while Rem and Torval descended to the dungeons with Ondego and a few more hands to fetch the Raven. To Rem's great relief, they found the outlaw in his cell, snoring on a bed of straw, bare chested, his filthy shirt rolled up beneath his head as a pillow.

Ondego batted the bars of the cell with a watchman's stave, making a terrible racket. "Rise and shine, you filthy mug! Time for a long, slow stroll to your standing appointment with an Eraldic gallows."

The Red Raven stirred on the cell floor, rose, and studied the men and women of the watch who'd come to collect him. Rem half expected some quip or a caustic jest, but the man only nodded, unlaced his breeks, and pissed into his cell's slop bucket as they all watched. When finished, he relaced his trousers and slipped back into the shirt that had been serving him as a pillow. He indicated his bare feet.

"Do I get my boots back?" he asked.

Ondego unlocked the cell, opened it, and threw something at the prisoner's feet: the very same finely tooled guardsman's boots he'd been wearing when arrested.

"The better to bear you homeward," the prefect said with mock solemnity.

The Raven slipped into the boots, then offered his hands for binding. He got a surprise when he learned that he was to have not only his wrists manacled but also his ankles. He was also to have a chain locked around his middle and a catchpole with a leather noose at its end—the sort used to subdue rabid hounds—wrapped around his throat. Fully encumbered and surrounded by his watchwarden escorts, Rem thought the Red Raven looked like the most dangerous man in the world. Torval bore the trailing end of the chain locked around his middle. Rem handled the long pole whose noose encircled the man's throat. Four more watchwardens, including Ondego himself, spread in a loose circle around the prisoner—a most dishonorable honor guard.

All this security for one man. Could he honestly, truly, be *that* slippery? That dangerous?

Ondego gave a nod. "Follow me, lads. Next stop, Roylan's Square."

Off they went, back up to the surface, through the common room, and out into the ubiquitous mists of the Yenaran morning. Indilen fell in behind them and followed at a safe distance.

The ward revealed its familiar morning rituals in the thinning fog around them as they marched. Blacksmiths pumped bellows and fired forges. Fresh-baked bread and morning rolls were drawn from hot ovens, exuding their warm, buttery scents through open doors and windows. Wives, daughters, and younger sons fetched water from city wells or emptied slop jars, while shopkeepers and mongers of all sorts opened their windows, wedged their doors, and adorned their little sellers' stalls with the goods they hoped to divest themselves of as the day wore on. Amid it all, an almost perpetual array of day laborers—longshoremen, stonemasons, carpenters, diggers, roofers, tillers—came forth from their rented rooms, their cramped homes, and their warm beds into the streets, most half-asleep and drifting like wraiths in a somber dream.

Through the midst of these the party marched, keeping gawkers at a distance and urging any and all curious parties to mind their business and carry on. To be sure, several watchwardens leading a single well-chained, dog-collared convict toward some unknown fate through the streets was a strange sight. There were often parades of prisoners from the watchkeep to their meetings with the Tribunal on Founder's Hill, but in those cases the train usually consisted of several prisoners all strung together. Rem, from his vantage behind the Raven, still holding that pole attached to the collar that held him, noted that their prisoner was quite courteous to those they passed. He nodded with brotherly solemnity at the men, smiled and gave curt head-only bows to the women, even spoke to the occasional gaggles of children who fell in beside them to follow the train, calling eager questions as they went.

"Is he a murderer?" one dark-skinned little ragamuffin asked.

"Is he a brigand?" asked a stout, towheaded boy.

"He's too pretty for the gallows," a girl on the cusp of her maidenhood said.

"Why so many of you?" one snaggletoothed waif asked. "He's no bear—more like a possum!"

Rem and his fellows did their best to shoo the children away. More than once, the Raven responded, working his peculiar, charisma-based magic upon the little street urchins.

"Do you know who I am?" he asked one cohort of filthy, lice-ridden boys.

"The God of Death incarnate!" one guessed.

"Some prince off to the debtors' house?" said another.

"I'm the Red Raven," the prisoner said, and winked at them.

"Go on!" a third boy shouted. "You lie!"

"It's the solemn truth," the Raven said.

"The Scourge of the Ethkeraldi?" one boy asked.

"First bow 'mongst the Devils of the Weald?" asked another.

"The same," the Raven answered proudly.

"He lies," the smallest boy among them said. "The Red Raven's too smart to be caught by the likes of these cunts." He offered an expansive gesture that took in Rem and all of his badge-wearing companions.

"Scat, now!" Torval barked suddenly. "All of you! Before we throw you in the same cage!"

The boys obeyed and scattered, laughing derisively as they went.

"Coarse language from such little mouths," the Raven said to no one in particular. "And so disrespectful—"

Torval shoved him. "Keep your sauce box shut," he said.

"It's this city," the Raven carried on, almost wistfully. "It hardens them. Roughens them."

"I'll roughen you if you don't be quiet," Torval growled. "Now keep pace, and no more conversations with the passersby."

The Raven gave a diffident shrug and marched on. Torval threw a glance at Rem: *Can you believe this sod?*

Rem could only offer a shrug of his own. In truth, he wasn't paying much attention. There was only one thought in his mind, turning round and round like a waterwheel spinning in a steadily rolling stream.

Soon I'll have to leave her, he thought. *Soon I'll be riding out those gates, to meet the gods know what, and she'll be left here. Yerys, Belenna, and Elimena, bring me back to her. Don't let us lose one another now, after finding each other under such unlikely circumstances . . .*

In short order their little party came to Roylan's Square, which marked the last city blocks before the city's East Gate and the world beyond. The square was huge and bustling, even at such an early hour, lorded over on its north side by a mid-size Aemonic church and on its western verge by an enormous six-story, block-wide inn, the Dragon's Roost. That great edifice—red stucco crisscrossed by dark cedar beams, a honeycomb of curtained windows and several layers of overhanging eaves—was one of the largest inns in the west, capable of housing almost a thousand guests at any one time, lauded far and wide for its many luxuries and amenities: a fancy bathhouse in its basement, a grand courtyard tavern at its center, and two special chambers on each floor that allowed guests to actually flush their piss and night soil down a complicated piping system into the sewers beneath the city. Waste disposal! *Indoors!* Truly, wonders never ceased . . .

In the great flagstone- and cobble-paved square before the vast inn stood the Fountain of the Forebears, larger than any of its water-bearing cousins in the whole of the Fifth Ward. Two stories at its apex, the fountain was adorned with a magnificent, multifaceted marble sculpture depicting the whole history of Yenara in a single complex tableau, woodland settlers from its founding age intermingling with the pioneer women of its boom years, who in turn were lorded over by fully armored Horunic officers from imperial antiquity. Rising above the rest, clear in heroic relief against the sky, were the figures of Velerens, one of the city's chief benefactors and most beloved founders, as well as Duke Roylan, the Most August, him for whom the whole square was named, one hand on his armored breastplate, the other raised elegantly in the air, gesturing expansively toward the heavens. Beneath and around the ennobled Roylan, an ever-cascading rush of dancing waters flowed from the pressurized plumbing within, the roar of the falling, splashing waters echoing through the whole square.

Rem gaped as they approached. He'd been here only a handful of times before, but he had yet to tire of the fountain and its artful engineering. Even now he was most impressed by its strange visual sinuousness, the way all its contours, corners, and planes were harmonized so that each dynamically poised marble or bronze figure interlocked with its neighbors, one body blending seamlessly into the next, their forms mutated and transformed by perspective as one circled the great assembly. The chalk-white streaks of bird shit dripping down the contours of Roylan's bronze face only marginally subtracted from the overall grandeur of the display.

In the shadow of the fountain, arrayed with almost military precision, stood the train of Lord Marshal Kroenen and his soldiers from the city of Erald. There were five of them in all—the lord marshal and four subordinates—along with a troop of saddled horses and a single four-wheeled, ox-drawn supply wagon laden with provisions and camp gear. Attached to the aft end of the supply wagon was a separate, smaller, two-wheeled cart supporting an iron cage. Rem guessed that was where the Red Raven would be riding.

Even at their distance, Rem saw clearly that the yellow-blue-and-white-clad Eraldic honor guard were not alone, for mingling among them were soldiers with black-and-scarlet tabards, clearly of separate origin. Rem had never been gifted when it came to memorizing the many arms and colors of all the great houses of the west, but he knew that scarlet was a color frequently employed by the peerage in Estavar, far to the south. And hadn't Kroenen said that the Duke of Erald's bride-to-be was the daughter of an Estavari noble? The Countess of Toriel, if Rem remembered aright.

The Estavari soldiers were five in number, their chain mail of a rosy, coppery tint, as opposed to the polished steel gray of that worn by Kroenen and his men. Their scarlet tabards sported a gyronny-of-eight device of black and yellow beneath a fierce rearing stallion, also rendered in black and traced in silver thread. Rem and Torval approached with the prisoner, the lord marshal and his Estavari counterpart deep in negotiation, each standing square shouldered, their helms beneath their crooked arms. As the commanders treated, the rank and file stood by in stalwart silence or busied themselves with simple preparations: checking their mounts, strapping down their saddlebags, securing their weapons, and the like.

It was only when they were almost upon the group that Rem realized every member of the Estavari guard was a woman.

Most impressive, that. Rem had met any number of warrior women on the wardwatch or espied them in taverns with their male or female companions, but he'd never seen a whole platoon of them, all arrayed in armor and house livery.

Their little band led the Red Raven across the crowded square toward the waiting train, drawing curious onlookers and gawpers as they went. When they hove up to the close gathering of horses, women, and men, Ondego broke from the cordon and stepped forward to effect the transfer.

"Your prisoner," he said flatly.

Lord Marshal Kroenen studied the Raven as if inspecting him, then swung his gaze back to Ondego. "No, Prefect, *your* prisoner. If your men are to accompany us, the Raven will remain their charge until we reach Erald. I and my men will be more concerned with assuring the safety of this train, and Captain Tuvera here"—he indicated the female officer from Estavar, whose light-brown skin and black hair suggested she had some equatorial blood in her—"has the sole task of protecting the Lady Tzimena during our long journey." The lord marshal now looked to Rem and Torval, his narrow-eyed appraisal suggesting that he thought very little of them indeed. "Everyone on this expedition will do their duty and pull their weight. Are the two of you equal to that task?"

Rem and Torval exchanged incredulous glances. It was on the tip of Rem's tongue to say something snide, but Torval beat him to it.

"We caught him, didn't we?" Torval said.

"Very well, then," the lord marshal said. "You have your assignment. See to it."

He and Captain Tuvera returned to their discussion of riding order and watch schedules. Ondego, realizing he was now being ignored, cleared his throat. The lord marshal looked at him as if surprised to still find him there.

Ondego indicated the cage. "I presume that's for him?" Up close, the cage looked to Rem just big enough for a single person to sit in comfortably, though standing up or lying down at full length would probably prove impossible. It was the sort of thing one might find in a traveling circus, small enough to be hitched to a cart or even just a strong horse, but stout enough to hold something fierce and compact within. Its only comforts were a bed of straw, a ratty old cowhide blanket, and a stoppered gourd of drinking water dangling by frayed twine from one of the overhead bars.

"It is," the lord marshal said.

"Is there a key?" Ondego pressed. "We can't very well lock him in without it."

The lord marshal frowned, severely annoyed at Ondego's belligerence. Finally he called for one of his companions.

"Wallenbrand!"

A broad-shouldered old soldier appeared from amid the Eraldic company—probably the same age as Ondego or older, but still hale and strong. He had a bushy gray beard, a raptor's piercing gaze, and more than a few scars on his tanned old face.

That struck Rem as rather strange—a veteran of a duke's house guard all tanned and scarred like a common sellsword? Was he a new hire?

"Milord?" the old man asked.

"The key to the cage," the lord marshal said, waving dismissively at Ondego. "From now until the time we reach Erald, that key shall remain in the charge of these two watchwardens."

The old warrior nodded curtly and fished the key from a pouch at his belt. It was iron, only slightly rusted, and hung from a long leather loop. Old Wallenbrand handed the key to Ondego, and Ondego passed it to Torval. The dwarf threw the long loop over his head and the key hung on his chest like a talisman. The circle of watchwardens round the Raven pivoted en masse, angling their prisoner toward his home for the road.

"Only the finest accommodations," the Raven muttered mordantly. "Clearly my reputation precedes me."

Ondego stepped toward the bound man and cuffed him—hard and swift—right across the mouth. Rem, Torval, and their fellow watchwardens were all shocked by the move. It was fairly rare to see Ondego stoop to physical violence when not directly threatened or engaged in an interrogation. The Raven spat out a wad of saliva and blood, then resumed his straight-backed stance, unbowed by the prefect's attack.

"You two listen, and listen well," Ondego said, addressing Rem and Torval but glaring at the Raven as he did so. "Your task is to deliver this piece of woodland trash to the Duke of Erald, collect the reward promised, and speed your arses homeward. But if, at any point in the journey, this smug son of a whore troubles you or threatens you, you have my permission to kill him where he stands and come home empty-handed. I want that gold, but I want the two of you back in my ward more. Savvy?"

Rem and Torval each gave an affirmative, along with a curt nod. When Ondego saw their acknowledgements, he turned back to the Raven.

"There is it, then," he said quietly. "You might be worth a hundred pieces, but if you trouble these good men, I don't care if they gut you and leave you for the crows, gold or no gold. Understood?"

"Understood," the Raven said—rather earnestly, to Rem's ears. "Thank you, Prefect, for your honesty."

"Fuck off," Ondego answered, then turned to his watchwardens once again. "Lock him up."

The Raven was locked in his cage, the catchpole collar loosed from his throat and the chain around his waist withdrawn. His ankle and wrist manacles remained. Once the cage was locked, Torval dropped the key, still hanging from its leather loop, under his shirt, so that it was in no danger of being torn off or falling.

"Nice and tidy," Ondego said, studying the caged-up prisoner with some small satisfaction. "Enjoy your ride back to Erald, good sir. You've been a most gracious guest."

"For the last time," the Red Raven said, addressing Ondego directly, "don't leave your men in this man's care, Prefect. You'll never see them again." Rem didn't care for the man's tone. It seemed far too honest, too genuinely concerned, to simply dismiss.

"What part of *fuck off* did you not understand?" Ondego muttered, then wandered away from the cage. As he trudged off, he waved impatiently for Rem and Torval to follow him. When he had the two of them and the rest of the watchwardens gathered a little apart from the train, he presented the young man and the dwarf with some provisions for the road, carried in sacks by their fellows who'd helped in the transfer.

"As promised: barley meal from the watchkeep stores for porridge, hardtack from the seaman's refectory on the waterfront, dried and salted meat—not sure what sort, but it isn't moldy, so it'll do—and a pair of skins filled with small beer. They're survival rations, but they'll also keep you on your toes. You're always a little more wary if you're underfed. Save these for the hard times on the road and buy fresh stuff from the inns and peddlers you pass."

Rem took the bags full of supplies and thanked the prefect. He actually felt gratitude. Supplying them wasn't Ondego's responsibility, but he'd said from the beginning he intended to contribute, and he had.

The other watchwardens present all offered wishes for a good journey, accompanied by handshakes or hearty claps on Rem's and Torval's shoulders, then began to disperse. At last only Ondego remained. Rem studied the strange look on the prefect's hangdog face and realized there was something like real worry there; it was the look of a father sending his youngest sons off on a dangerous journey.

The prefect stepped closer to the two of them, then placed one of his hands on a shoulder of each of them.

"Don't trust these cunts farther than you can throw them," he said quietly. "Not the Raven, not the lord marshal, not the shield-maids—*not a one.*"

Torval huffed. "As if you have to tell us."

"We won't let you down, Ondego," Rem said, and was quite surprised when he realized how deeply he meant those words. This man—this gruff, profane, blustering prefect of theirs—had become a sort of surrogate father to him in their year together. Rem hadn't realized until this very moment how much Ondego's respect and concern meant to him.

"You'll only let me down if you get yourselves killed," the prefect said with a wry smile. "Eyes open, fists clenched, back to the wall. Or a tree, if there are no walls about."

He smiled wider at his own joke, clapped their shoulders, then turned and marched away. No goodbye. No "Good fortune." No word at all. Rem supposed that was as it should be.

Rem spun quickly to look for Indilen. Gods, he hoped she hadn't heard the Raven's warning, or Ondego's. If she honestly thought there was something to fear in this, she'd work mightily to get him to beg off. And he had to be honest with himself: reward or no, if she looked into his eyes and said she had a terrible feeling and beseeched him not to go, could he really refuse her?

But Indilen, when he found her, was otherwise engaged. For one, she'd been joined by Aarna—the mistress of his and Torval's favorite tavern, the King's Ass—and Torval's entire family: his sister, Osma; his daughter, Ammi; and his sons, Tavarix and Lokki. There they all stood, far apart from the Eraldic and Estavari soldiers and their arrayed mounts, Aarna and Torval's brood all bearing sacks and baskets.

"What's this?" Torval said, sounding more than a little annoyed. "I told them not to..."

"Which is why they did," Rem said. "Come on, old stump—let's get the goodbyes over with."

They approached their launching party, the children rushing to their father and surrounding him before he'd even taken four strides. As Torval hugged and wrestled with his sons and held his daughter close and urged her—in his most fatherly tones—to watch after the boys and help Aunt Osma however she could, Aarna edged nearer and gently laid a heavily laden bag on the flagstones at her feet.

"What's all that?" Rem asked.

Aarna pulled Rem forward, gave him a quick kiss on the cheek and a summary, one-armed hug, then withdrew and regarded the bag. "Supplies," she said. "I know it looks like a lot, but you should be able to divide it between your saddlebags."

"Supplies?" Torval parroted.

"Aye, supplies," Osma said. "We came together to make or gather them."

Rem shot a glance at Indilen. He knew she was eager for some time alone with him, as he was for time alone with her, but they both knew instinctively that those quiet, stolen moments before their parting would be easier to embrace when the rest of their ad hoc family had attended to its business and was out of the way.

"There's a slab of smoked bacon," Aarna said, opening the mouth of the bag and staring in, "as well as a half wheel of well-aged cheese that should be good for the road. If it molds, just trim it. You can still eat it."

"There's also two jams," Osma said, "elderberry and apricot. We put them in gourds instead of jars or crocks, so they wouldn't be so heavy."

"Oh!" Aarna said, as if finding sudden inspiration, "there's also dried apples! And a small hogshead of Joedoc's red. The Old Thumper is too strong and doesn't hold up well outside a nice, cool cellar. Water the red down as you tap it, it'll last longer."

"Oh, and pickles!" Osma said. "Pickled herring, pickled cucumbers, and those pickled eggs you like, Torval. Those are all in jars—though they're well wrapped—so you'll have to be careful with them."

Aarna indicated the bags. "So who gets these?"

"I do," Torval said. Rem saw a big, broad smile on the dwarf's face. He strode forward, gave his sister a big, hearty hug, then turned to Aarna and opened his arms. Before he even knew what she intended, the taverner leaned forward, drew him close to her comfortable, middle-aged body, and squeezed him ferociously. Torval, being two-thirds Aarna's height, had his face pressed comfortably against the lady's ample bosom. The dwarf's eyes were closed—a sign of contentment, Rem thought—peace, even. Finally Aarna dipped her head, gave Torval a soft kiss on his bald pate, then let go of him. When they separated, Torval was left with the look of a love-struck puppy and the big bag of food.

"Safe travels," Aarna said, giving each of them a wave and one of her always-warm, always-wide smiles. "I shall count the days 'til the two of you are back at my bar, making nuisances of yourselves."

Rem nodded. "You and us both," he said. Having already

gotten a hug and a kiss from Aarna, Rem now moved to Osma and swept her into an embrace. "Thank you, Auntie," he said, using his most frequently employed pet name for her. "Torval can have the eggs, but I plan on eating all the rest."

As they pulled away from one another, Osma's eyes met Rem's. There was the glint of tears in them, despite the fact that the dwarf woman was still wearing a well-intentioned smile. "Bring him home safe," she said quietly, so that only Rem could hear. "Those children need him far more than I do."

Rem nodded. "On my life," he said solemnly.

Osma nodded, blinked away those promised tears, then looked to the children. "Everyone's said their farewells?"

They all agreed they had. With a few last well-wishes and blown kisses, Osma and the children turned and marched away, leaving only Indilen alone with Rem and Torval. At their backs the soldiers had all fanned out to their individual horses and were deep in final preparations to mount up and depart.

Rem looked to Indilen, eager to have his last quiet moments alone with her. Unfortunately, his lover was distracted by something. She was staring toward the great fountain.

Rem followed the line of her gaze. Indilen was watching a woman perched upon the broad, water-beaded lip of the fountain. She wore a sturdy but finely sewn traveling dress with a matching embroidered cloak, and as she sat, a stout servant woman—probably her full-time nurse and chaperone—was bent at her feet. The servant woman was adjusting the laces of the lady's riding boots, making sure they were tight. Rem was reminded of how he'd just been lacing up Indilen's shoes like that, the day before yesterday.

But he was reasonably sure Indilen wasn't remembering the sweetness of what had passed between them—so common, so prosaic. No, she was clearly staring at the lady herself: young, poised, raven haired, slender, and impossibly beautiful. Rem took in the lady's face and figure with a glance, knowing that a longer perusal could get him brained with a heavy object, but that glance was enough. He noted the long, rolling ebony tresses, how they framed her beautifully sculpted face and accentuated her dark-olive skin and pale, flashing green eyes. A picky man might suggest that her nose was too long, or that her eyebrows were too heavy, but Rem wagered that would have to be a very picky man indeed. By his hasty reckoning, everything about her was perfection...

Clearly Indilen had come to the same conclusion.

"Who in the sundry hells is that?" she asked pointedly.

Rem's mouth worked soundlessly before any words tumbled out. "That must be the Lady Tzimena Baya. Did I not mention she's one of our traveling companions?"

Indilen's silence answered his question. Clearly he had forgotten to mention that.

CHAPTER EIGHT

Rem knew what was required. He stepped toward Indilen and swept her into his arms.

"She's the daughter of the Countess of Toriel, from Estavar," he said quietly, as though the young lady might be embarrassed should anyone be overheard speaking of her.

Indilen stared back at him, mouth set, one eyebrow cocked curiously.

"I believe the lord marshal said she was betrothed to the Duke of Erald."

Indilen blinked but still said nothing.

"The Red Raven tricked his way into her chambers the night that we caught him," he said.

"I'm sure she was terrified," Indilen said drolly. "I don't remember you including a countess's daughter on the list of travelers in this little caravan."

"Well," Rem said, "I guess...I suppose...It probably just didn't—"

Torval was beside them. "You know," the dwarf began, "tall-folk women don't generally do much for me—"

Rem thought of Aarna. He wanted to blurt, *That's a lie!*

"—but that one," Torval continued, indicating Tzimena Baya, "could be the prettiest longshanked lassie I've ever seen."

"Torval!" Rem hissed. He stole a glance at Indilen. She still stared, that single eyebrow raised, as if waiting for words that Rem had yet to summon.

"Worry not, love," Torval said to Indilen in a hoarse mock whisper, "if this fool betrothed of yours so much as offers that broodmare a refill from the hogshead, I'll box his ears 'til they swell like cauliflowers."

"You do that," Indilen said with the first hint of a smile. "I knew I could count on you, Torval."

Torval nodded, thoroughly proud of himself, and continued to linger beside them. Rem stared at his partner, silently willing him off. The dwarf remained—stubborn, oblivious—studying the swirling activity about them, the dutiful soldiers, the shuffling animals, the Lady Tzimena...

"Torval," Rem finally said, "why don't you go get those foodstuffs stored in our saddlebags?"

"What, on the horses?" Torval asked.

"Yes," Rem said. "On the horses. Make sure they're balanced. Put what you can on your mount and I'll take the rest on mine when I get there."

"I can wait for you," Torval said. He was certainly capable of lingering just to vex Rem intentionally, but he seemed honestly clueless at this moment regarding Rem's deep, desperate need for some privacy.

"Go away," Rem said flatly. "*Please*. Just let us..." He didn't finish his thought, but hoped that his beseeching tone and needy expression made his requirements clear.

Torval rolled his eyes and sighed. "Fine, fine...Let me go make myself scarce so you can whisper a flock of sweet nothings into this poor deluded girl's ear..."

He threw a knowing wink at Indilen as if the two of them were sharing the most hysterical of jokes, ribbing Rem as they were. Indilen managed a smile for Torval, but the moment he'd left them, Rem saw a sadness in her eyes that the smile had clearly been meant to mask.

Rem swept her into his arms and tried to kiss her. Indilen turned her face away.

"Are you serious?" he asked, becoming impatient. "You're jealous of a complete stranger?"

Indilen shook her head impatiently. "It's not her, honestly... I just know the time's almost here. And, of course, I don't really relish you being on the road with"—she jerked her head toward the Lady Tzimena—"*that*."

"She's a pretty girl," Rem said. "So what? The world's full of them. And I've got the prettiest, right here in my arms."

Indilen sighed. "Pretty girls don't frighten me. The road through the Ethkeraldi Wood does."

Rem lifted her face in his hands and kissed her, long and slow. He had things to do, true. Presently, though, his only duty was to assure his lover with his kisses, with his eyes, and with his enfolding arms that he was unafraid of this inconvenient little journey and eager for only one thing: to return to her.

The kiss broke. Indilen withdrew a little. She was smiling now—a sad smile, but a smile nonetheless.

"Don't mind me," she said, her brown eyes meeting Rem's and melting the center of him. "I'm sad you're leaving. Sad and frightened. Angry, even."

"I'll be back before you know it, with gold in my purse," Rem said with all seriousness and a reassuring smile. "I'm not wasting all this time away from you and putting my hide on the line just so I can see the countryside."

"Just remember," Indilen said slowly, "your only job is to come home to me. That prisoner doesn't matter. The gold doesn't matter. That irritatingly beautiful young lady by the fountain doesn't matter"—she smiled when she said that. "Only one thing matters. And that is...?"

Without even thinking about it, Rem fell to one knee on the flagstones, drew Indilen's hand up to his mouth, and kissed it long and slow. "I swear, as all the gods of the Panoply and ruined ages past are my witnesses, I shall come home to you, my beautiful girl, with all speed." When he raised his eyes to Indilen's, he saw the glint of tears in them. He stared at her— steady, even, true—holding her hand in both of his.

Indilen wiped the first bloom of a tear from one eye, then gently yanked on his hands. "Stand up," she said. "If you make me cry here, I shan't forgive you."

Rem shot to his feet again and drew her into his arms for what he promised himself would be the last time. She held him tightly. He drew in the scent of her hair, the feeling of her warmth and softness against him.

"I love you," she said.

"And I you," Rem answered, fighting the urge to say something more, something that would ruin the bittersweet simplicity of the moment they were sharing.

Indilen then stood on her tiptoes and kissed him, holding his face in her hands this time. When the kiss was done, she stepped away. It was a definitive gesture—sudden, jarring, but clear in the message it carried: *Time to get this over with*. She still held his hand, and she held it tightly.

Then Indilen looked past Rem and scanned the onlookers. "Torval?" she called.

Torval appeared from behind a horse nearby. "Oi?"

"Bring him back in one piece," Indilen called, dead serious, "or it's your hide, do you understand me?"

Torval made a fist and held it over his heart. Rem had seen

him make that gesture only a few times, usually with his children; it was a dwarven sign indicating that a solemn promise had been made. "Upon my children," the dwarf said.

Rem remembered his quiet promise to Osma and smiled.

Indilen looked to Rem. She was smiling now, though there was still sadness in it. "There," she said. "I feel better."

"I need to get at it," Rem said.

"Go on," Indilen said. "You're on duty now, and not off again until you're back in my arms. I'll go."

"There's no need," he began.

"There is," she said, then kissed him one last time, turned, and marched away. Rem watched her go, wondering if she might turn back before joining the traffic on Eastgate Street and disappearing into the crowd. She did not.

Rem turned toward the line of horses. As he did, he caught sight of the Lady Tzimena, now inspecting what Rem assumed to be her own mount. It was a fine chestnut mare with a long flaxen mane, a brilliant, buttery ivory against its rusty brown coat. The lady was looking right at him, smiling brightly. Clearly she'd seen what had passed between him and Indilen, and it seemed to have given her pleasure. Rem, not sure what to do, simply gave a curt nod and trudged on toward his waiting horse.

When he arrived, Torval eyed him suspiciously. "I'm watching you," the dwarf said.

"Shut up," Rem spat back. "Let's get to work."

Torval said that Wallenbrand, the lord marshal's second, had identified the mounts intended for the two of them: a shaggy pony for Torval, twelve or thirteen hands high, with a stocky frame and good strong limbs, and for Rem a dappled gray gelding, sixteen hands high, compact but elegant, with a long, thick mane and tail. He knew he'd have to give the animal a closer inspection, but something in him loved the beast instantly.

First, though, he'd have to get Torval situated on that pony. The dwarf had packed his saddlebags but hadn't yet attempted to mount.

"Now, listen," Rem lectured as he double-checked the pony's harness and tack, "I'm going to warn you that it may take some time for this little fellow to become accustomed to you. Try not to take his reluctance personally—he's just trying to figure out who you are and what he can expect from you."

"Sounds reasonable," Torval said, patting the buckskin-colored flanks of the pony. "I myself tend to warm up slowly."

"If ever," Rem muttered.

"What was that?" Torval asked.

"Nothing," Rem said. "Come on, into the saddle."

That took some doing, since Torval had, he admitted, not ridden more than two or three times in his whole life. Rem tried his best to give Torval some proper grounding in technique—mounting from the left, using the pommel as lever-age and swinging his right leg up and over. After two or three false starts, Torval finally managed to mount and settle himself, but the shortened stirrups were still too long for his stocky little legs. Rem immediately set to adjusting them, knowing that the long ride they were about to embark on would be miserable indeed for both pony and rider if Torval couldn't comfortably rest his big feet in those stirrups. Rem also noted—and was most impressed by—the fact that even though the pony was small and its stirrup straps equally so, whoever had chartered the animal had made sure to have a set of large stirrups attached to the short straps, knowing that a dwarf, though short of leg, would be large of shoe.

So, Rem thought as he struggled with the straps, *the lord marshal and his men are cunning indeed. No detail escapes them, no contingency is unforeseen.*

He wasn't sure if that made him feel better or worse.

"There," Rem said at last, straightening. "You're all set."

"Good," Torval said, "now get me down from here."

"Oh no," Rem said. "You're all set, and it was hard enough getting you up there. Take him for a few circles around the square. Get to know him. Let's not have your very first ride be out of that city gate."

Torval looked troubled by that thought, but Rem knew he'd be fine if left to his own devices. He anticipated a great deal of swearing and grumbling on the dwarf's part, but he reckoned that soon enough pony and rider would reach an accord. Satisfied, Rem turned to his own mount and began his inspection. The shoes on the gelding looked fairly new, and his hooves were smooth and unblemished, showing only the most superficial cracks. Rem led the animal forward and back, then in circles, to check his gait for irregularities, and finally counted himself satisfied. The gray wasn't eager to bite him, nor did he shy away when Rem stroked his muzzle. All in all, he was a fine, solid animal, and Rem thought he'd prove a splendid companion for their journey.

"I picked that one myself," someone said.

Rem turned. It was one of the younger soldiers in Lord Marshal Kroenen's squad—the one who Rem had noted bore some resemblance to the lord marshal. The young man had the same patrician features—a long proud nose, pronounced cheekbones, a square jaw, and a direct gaze—but both his hair and eyes were lighter than Kroenen's own. He also exuded a different energy: enthusiasm and friendliness in place of the lord marshal's unbending authoritarianism.

Rem offered a hand. "He's lovely," he said. "Truly."

The young guard was attending to his own mount, a handsome bay. The horse's tack and saddle were far finer than those on the horses tagged for Rem and Torval, which struck Rem as odd. If they'd hired the horses from a local vendor, shouldn't all their saddles and harness be roughly equal in terms of functionality and ornament?

The young guard took Rem's hand and shook it. "Brekkon," he said. "Good to meet you . . . ?"

Rem broke the handshake. "Rem," he said, then indicated the gray gelding. "I'll take good care of him. You have my word."

"I should hope so," Brekkon said. "I bought him. Once we're back in Erald, he'll be all mine. I must say, I'm impressed. I saw you inspecting your friend's mount and your own, and you seemed to know what you were looking for. Not a skill I'd attribute to a lad from this city."

Rem felt a twinge of inward fear. Was this young man truly intimating something? Suggesting something? Or was he simply curious? His friendly eyes and easy expression suggested no ill intent, but most people could lie well enough if they were deeply interested in doing so.

And he's a royal guard, Rem thought. *Spent his whole life in service to a nobleman, probably seen plenty more come and go through the Eraldic court . . .*

"I was a horse groom," Rem said, "when younger. Changed my line of work, but I still love them, you know? Get far too few opportunities to mount up and go for a ride in this job."

"But you're not *from* here?" Brekkon pressed, still looking perfectly friendly and casual, not eager or doubtful in the least. "You sound like you're from up north—"

"Lycos," Rem said shortly, "near Great Lake. That's where I

did my, er, grooming. In the house of a lord. Eventually tired of it and wandered down here."

Brekkon nodded agreeably, then took in their surroundings: the milling crowd, the big marble fountain, the enormous, looming Dragon's Roost Inn on the far side of the street. "Long way from Lycos," he said amiably.

Rem decided agreement was all that would snuff the boy's infernal curiosity. "Aye, that, sir. Aye, that." He forced a laugh, then turned back to his horse and busied himself with rearranging the provisions and spare clothes in his saddlebags. He prayed Brekkon wouldn't keep speaking or press the issue. To his great relief, he didn't.

Rem raised his eyes, looking over the rump of his horse toward the rest of the lord marshal's train as they secured the supplies on their four-wheeled ox wain in preparation for departure. Wallenbrand and a smaller, more wiry man were lifting a shallow, heavy wooden chest with a stout iron lock into the hands of the biggest man of the company—a tall, broad fellow with thinning hair on his head but a thick growth of black whiskers on his face. As the big man took the heavy chest from the two men below and moved to stow it in the cart bed, Rem suddenly realized there was something rather strange about the big wain. Though it was of average dimensions—about six feet wide by ten or eleven long—the forward and side walls of the wagon bed were extremely high. A man standing in that cart bed would be able to peer over them if he stood on his tiptoes. Torval would have no hope of seeing over the wagon walls at all. Moreover, though there were a great many supplies arranged in the bed, they came nowhere near filling the cart entirely. It seemed a rather strange vehicle to have chosen, considering very little of its bed space was actually used. Rem half wondered why the Red Raven hadn't simply been chained therein, instead of the lord marshal's spending the extra money required to rent or purchase that separate cage cart for him.

Then Rem realized what use such a high-sided wain might afford in the wilds: protection. If they were attacked on the road, a number of the company could fall back into that cart bed and use it as a fortification of sorts, the high sides affording great cover against attack.

Knowing that the lord marshal had prepared for such an eventuality—even just to be cautious—gave Rem no pleasure.

Suddenly Rem became aware that there was someone standing between him and the cart. It was the lord marshal, having wandered into Rem's field of vision at some point during Rem's contemplation of the cart and its defensive uses. The lord marshal was staring directly at Rem.

Rem tried to decide what he should do. Smile and wave? Ignore him? Quickly lower his eyes and pretend he wasn't being stared at, like a nervous fugitive? Finding no better options, he simply gave the lord marshal a curt, professional nod, then returned his attentions once more to his saddlebags. Seconds later, he furtively raised his eyes to see if he was still being watched.

The lord marshal had gone about his business.

Gods...what had he gotten himself into? He was about to embark on a long journey with a group of men who—by nature of their origins and duties—were the most likely to recognize him of anyone he'd met in his year since leaving home. Lycos and Erald hadn't had many direct dealings, aside from a little trade—they'd been too far apart for anything else—but Eraldic embassies had visited the court of Rem's father more than once in his life. If just one of these soldiers had been part of a security detail for one of those embassies...

It's time, Rem thought grimly. *Indilen's kept my secret for months now. Torval needs to know it, as well.*

After all, he might have to help me lie to these men if they get too curious...

"Company, mount!" old Wallenbrand suddenly boomed. "When everyone's ready, we ride."

Rem lifted himself into the saddle. The animal met his weight with practiced calmness, swiveled his head a little, then shuffled his hooves, as if impatient to be underway. Farther up the line, the Lady Tzimena mounted her chestnut mare with practiced ease. Apparently her skirts were divided for riding. No sidesaddle for that one, as for many other noble young ladies from Estavar to Kosterland. Instead the Lady Tzimena sat her horse regally, straight backed, and gripped her reins like an experienced equestrian.

Hells and bells, Rem thought, *she looks ever so regal atop that animal...*

Torval's pony shuffled up beside Rem, Torval still looking quite stiff and uncomfortable in his saddle. "Seems an agreeable beast," he said. "Tends to walk in circles if I don't direct it, though."

"Better than charging off after butterflies," Rem said.

Everyone was ready now. All the soldiers—Eraldic and Estavari—sat their horses, save one man in Eraldic livery who perched on the driver's bench of the supply cart. At the fore of the line, the lord marshal turned his horse round so that he could face everyone in the company. Satisfied, he gave the order.

"Move out," he shouted, then with a flourish, spun his horse round again and led the group toward the city's East Gate at a brisk canter. Each rider fell in line behind him, their order clearly having been decided upon already. The Lady Tzimena and her chaperone moved in the midst of their own retinue.

As Brekkon prepared to join the moving line, he turned to Rem and Torval.

"You two ride behind the cart," he said. "Keep an eye on the prisoner. Elvaris and Sandiva, from the countess's house guard, will bring up the rear." Without waiting for an affirmative from Rem, the young guardsman urged his horse forward. Rem and Torval waited for the cart to rumble into its place in line, then, good soldiers that they were, fell in behind the jouncing, creaking little cage on its two-wheeled cart that held their prisoner.

The Red Raven was delighted to see his arresters and waved.

"Bollocks," Torval snarled. "Are we to be stuck staring at that smug bastard all the way to Erald?"

"Just ignore him," Rem said. "And don't let your temper get the best of you. We want him to reach our destination in one piece, don't we?"

CHAPTER NINE

They left by the East Gate because they were a large party, bearing both a prisoner and a great many supplies. Such official contingents, carrying bonded cargo, had to leave via the East Gate to satisfy Yenara's many customs and immigration regulations. Once beyond the gate and the city walls, their column took a side road that bent southward and joined the snaking line of the Embrys River, meandering through the bustling suburbs that had sprouted up like toadstools in the lee of the city's defensive walls and through the haphazard growth of shantytowns and cheap grogshops beyond. That road—narrow, muddy, really no more than a well-beaten path—ran roughly parallel to the north bank of the river, bending southeasterly. The city receded at their backs, a line of hills rose far off to their left, northward, and the bristling treetops of low-country forests effaced the horizon directly before them. At one point in their progress, as the last of the outer shanties fell away and the untamed countryside asserted itself, Rem turned his horse from the path to try to get one last, long look at the city that he'd called home for almost a year now. There, nearly a mile behind them, Yenara brooded, ageless and silent, sprawling across the line of the flowing Embrys, largely obscuring the misty blue vastness of Hatarau Bay on its far side. Her three high hills peeked over the walls like the humped backs of slumbering dragons, scaled with villas and close-packed town houses, horned and spined by sleek towers and glowering tenements. The old keep and the civic council halls crowned the sharp knob of Founder's Hill in the foreground, lording over it all, eternal and implacable.

It was a lovely view and filled Rem with a strange, dual-pronged pang of both dread and sadness.

You'll be home soon enough, Rem thought. *Two weeks. Maybe three. Four at the outside. You'll be back in Indilen's arms, walking the streets with Torval at your side. You'll be back to the drudgery of being a watchwarden and the pleasant sameness of mornings or evenings drinking at the King's Ass.*

Soon enough. The time will fly by. You'll see . . .

He nosed his horse round and spurred it, rushing to rejoin the train.

On they went.

By midday, when the sun was highest, they were well into the countryside, the only signs of civilization being a few scattered freeholders' houses widely spaced among tilled fields and unmowed meadows, all bounded by ill-tended hedgerows marking the old land plots. It being late spring on the cusp of summer, many of the fields were rife with low green shoots and sprouts, indicating that soon enough, the crops would start to rise and the planted fields would start to look like proper farmland.

"Why are we going south?" Torval grumbled, rocking uncomfortably atop his shaggy little pony. "I thought the Ethkeraldi was to the northeast, around the Kaarten?"

"It is," Rem said. "But the road that runs through it peels off of the road we're on right now. If we want to meet it, we've got to go south before turning northeast and eventually entering the forest. But, of course, before we get to the forest, we've got to climb into those hills"—Rem indicated the rolling green slopes, patches of woodland, and bald, rocky outcroppings that snaked along the northern horizon—"traverse the valley on the far side, and cross the Kaarten River. We won't enter the Eth-keraldi proper for another four or five days."

"No wonder my people prefer to stay home," Torval said, punctuating his statement with an impatient huff. "Every-thing's so blasted far away from everything else. I remember our journey down here, from the mountains. The scale of it all—the vastness—never really sank in because we'd only travel for a day or two at a time, then stay where we could for as long as we could. A little crossroads trade post, towns, villages… Osma and the children and I might stay for months or years, earning wages and saving until we felt it was time to move on to the next place."

"I'm guessing," Rem said, "you came by the Pilgrim's Road. That's farther east. Stretches from the icy wastes of Kosterland all the way to the red hills of Estavar. There are more settle-ments along the Pilgrim's Road, not to mention greater safety and less rugged terrain. I took it myself, when I came south."

"South," Torval said, staring off into the distance over his pony's crown. "From Hasturland." The animal's ears were wiggling to drive away a cloud of gnats.

Rem looked to his partner. There was something in the dwarf's voice that he didn't care for. An incredulity. An unspo-ken intimation.

Torval stared back, half smiling, as if challenging Rem. "From where you grew up as a groom in a lord's house," the dwarf recited. The timbre of his voice made it clear: he knew the story well, but he didn't precisely believe it.

Rem drew a deep breath, then slowly blew it out. About ten yards ahead of them, the Red Raven lounged in his cage on its little two-wheeled cart, his gaze facing forward but his ear clearly cocked toward the two watchwardens riding in his wake. For all Rem knew, the man could be lost in thought, not hearing a single word that passed between them...or it was just possible that he could overhear their conversation. One couldn't exactly whisper to one's riding partner while in transit, after all.

Rem took a quick glance behind them. Two Estavari guards, Elvaris and Sandiva, rode ten or twenty yards behind them. There was a third, Rem knew, currently nowhere to be seen. That one brought up the rear—a scout of some sort, sweeping their wake and watching for any unwanted followers. Again, probably too far to hear anything clearly, but there was always the chance...

Rem turned back to Torval. "I'll make a deal with you," he said. "I'll tell you the truth of it—the absolute truth—before we reach our destination. Provided there's a good time for it."

"A good time?" Torval said, as if insulted.

"I trust you," Rem said. "Implicitly. *With my life*. You know that. But I can't trust anyone else in this party. And while there is no shame in what I'll tell you, there is still hazard in it. I can never forget that, especially not in such...mixed company."

Torval nodded, understanding Rem's reasoning. "Fair enough," he said. "And lad, please don't misunderstand...I never meant to force you—"

"You're forcing nothing," Rem said, trying to smile but knowing that it probably looked a little wan, a little sad. "You're family now, Torval—one of the two people I love and trust most in this world. Indilen's known the truth for some time now. In light of that, I shouldn't keep it from you any longer."

"Sing for us," someone said.

Rem sought the source of the voice. It was the Raven, still reclining in his cage as casually as a lord on a divan. He was looking out through the bars, wearing that smug, satisfied half smile of his, chewing on a piece of straw.

"What was that?" Rem asked.

"I said, sing for us," the Raven answered. "I love the riding songs of the Hasturfolk. 'O Merrily, We'll Canter On'...'Over the Hills and through the Dales'...'Hail and Farewell to the Ladies of Rhaim.' Surely a bonny lad like you, working all his life with horses, should know a few? Have pity...it'll be a long trip."

"Not much of a singer," Rem answered, his voice sounding too loud in the wild stillness where only the tumbling waters of the river and the hitching winds made any sound.

"I've got it," the Raven said, now shifting his body and sitting up on his knees. "'The Last Light of Eve.' That's a fine one!"

Rem knew exactly what the man was intimating. He didn't care for it, nor for the bent smile on the prisoner's face. "That's a court song," Rem said curtly. "I heard plenty but I never bothered to learn them."

"Never bothered," the Red Raven said. "Maybe you've just forgotten?"

They were in sparsely populated farmland when the sun declined at their backs and the lord marshal gave orders to make camp for the night. The lord marshal's forward scout—a big, dark, broad-shouldered bruiser named Croften—was sent to the nearest farmhouse to make sure the holders knew they meant to camp in peace and posed no threat, and the rest of them bent to their work.

The site chosen was a fine one—a little clearing surrounded by a few lonely alders and sycamores, within sight of the willow-choked Embrys banks, tilled fields stretching beyond a low line of hedgerows to the north. The two troops of soldiers—Eraldic and Estavari—went to work with surprising efficiency, as though a plan for preparing camp had been arrived at before they'd ever departed Yenara. While two soldiers—one of each party—set about digging a firepit and encircling it with stones, another mismatched pair disappeared into the brush in search of firewood. Those not bent to the fire saw to their mounts. Rem and Torval unhitched the Red Raven's cage cart from the supply wagon, rolled it to the farthest edge of what would be their encampment, beside a pair of stunted laurels, and left it there. Concurrently the supply wagon was unloaded and a small, modest pavilion raised for the Lady Tzimena between two cottonwoods.

With the Raven secured, Rem decided he would educate Torval on the care of horses, starting with immediate water and forage. After he showed Torval how to remove his pony's saddle, the two led their mounts down to the river and let them stand for a good long while, munching on the high grasses and drinking their fill. As they watched and waited, Rem and Torval treated themselves to an afternoon snack of salt pork and barley bread, then slaked their own considerable thirsts and wet their faces to wash off the dust of the road. It was in the midst of this quiet and welcome respite that they were joined by a pair of their traveling companions.

"And here I thought we'd found a quiet corner," someone said, yanking Rem and his partner out of a lovely silent reverie.

Torval and Rem turned toward the voice to find two of the Lady Tzimena's female soldiers. They were the two who'd ridden at the tail of the party through the day, young Sandiva and her partner, Elvaris. As Rem and Torval watched, the women led their horses to the water's edge just a few feet away. Rem sized them up at a glance: tall, trim Elvaris, clearly at home in her armor and scarlet tabard; short, stocky, baby-faced Sandiva, seemingly playacting—a brash girl dressed up for a masque in her big brother's uniform.

"We thought the same," Torval said to the young woman. "Apparently we were wrong."

Sandiva smiled crookedly as she stepped away from her now-drinking horse. "He's a grumpy dwarf, isn't he?"

"You have no idea," Rem said, almost to himself.

"I have a name," Torval said to her.

"Well, I don't know your name," Sandiva countered, clearly trying to sound friendly but just coming off as childish.

"So ask him," Rem said.

The young lady rolled her eyes. "Fine. What's your name, good dwarf?"

"Torval," the dwarf said.

"And I'm Sandiva," she said. "And this is Elvaris."

"We know," Rem said. He didn't dislike her...he just missed the silence that he and Torval had been enjoying before she arrived. He studied the two of them. Elvaris was taller, darker, with a long face and sharp features, her black hair woven in a tight braid that trailed down her back. She might look severe, even gaunt, but for the glint in her dark eyes and a curl at the corner of her lips that suggested both prowess and playfulness—the quiet confidence of a first-rate warrior. Her companion, Sandiva, wore her hair down, untied, but had it cut to shoulder length. She was clearly quick to laugh and jest, but Rem sensed that all her laughter was only a mask for fear and uncertainty. She was clearly the youngest member of the Estavari company, and probably the least sure of herself.

I know you, Rem thought, smiling a little. *Masking all your fear and insecurity with jests and mock bravado. Gods, I've been you.*

"Fine," Sandiva said. "Now we all know one another. I have a question."

"And that is?" Torval asked.

She indicated his pony. "What's it like, riding on that oversized mouse of yours?" She laughed at her own jest. Rem caught Elvaris shooting a doubtful glance at her partner, suggesting that she didn't find it so funny.

"I'll be happy to tell you," Torval responded, "if you'll first tell me what it's like being an oversized mouse way up there in a horse's saddle."

Elvaris snorted, as did Rem, in spite of himself. Sandiva stared, not getting the joke. Then, suddenly, a bright smile split her face.

"Oh, he's funny!" she cried, clearly delighted by Torval's insult. "Did you hear that, Elvi? The dwarf is funny!"

"Funnier than some," Elvaris said quietly, then knelt by her drinking horse. Before bending to get herself a handful of water, she winked conspiratorially at Rem.

As Elvaris knelt and drank, Rem found himself suddenly staring at the sword sheathed at her hip. Sandiva was chattering at Torval about one thing or another, and a quick sideward glance told Rem that the dwarf was being patient and indulgent, but did not care for her boisterous company or brand of humor. That all mattered little, though, because Rem's attentions were focused on Elvaris's blade—specifically its beautifully tooled hilt, grip, and pommel. The handle was wrapped in a leathery material with a strange, pebbled texture to it, while the crosspiece and pommel bore elegant, distinctive lines and engraving that suggested an uncommon level of care and meticulousness in its creation.

Elvaris caught him staring. When Rem realized that she might think he was admiring the line of her bent, slender legs—even though they were clad in leather and chain mail— he raised his hands, an instant, silent petition for understanding.

"That sword," Rem said. "Is that a Taverando?"

Elvaris looked to the blade as if just noticing it. She gripped the hilt and drew it forth, just an inch or two. Rem instantly saw the telltale engraving along the fuller, just above the hilt.

"It is indeed," she said proudly.

Rem leapt to his feet and moved nearer. He was sure his mouth hung agape and his eyes were as wide as a child's at a mummer's show, but he didn't care. He'd heard for years of the glory and elegance of Estavar's Taverando blades. He'd seen one or two in his younger years, usually ceremonial sorts, with little real use in combat. But he guessed this woman's sword was no ceremonial blade for state feasts or holy days— she didn't look like the sort to carry anything that was merely ornamental.

"May I see it?" Rem asked.

"Oh, that blade of hers," Sandiva muttered. "Everywhere we go, she's being asked to bare the thing and show it off. Too pretty for my taste. I like something a little more simple, a little more utilitarian—"

"Shut up," Torval said, suddenly at Rem's elbow. "What's this all about?"

Elvaris drew the sword with blinding speed and handed it over. Rem reached out and closed his hand around the grip, then slowly took it from its owner and marveled at it. It was not ornate, precisely—there was nothing showy or ostentatious in its design—but its undeniable grace and delicacy, along with its alluring heft and perfect balance, made it a work of art. Within the fuller groove was the maker's mark: a long, elegant, stylized rendering of the swordmaker's oft-whispered name.

"This, Torval," Rem said with reverence, "is a blade forged by the master swordmaker Talis Taverando. From Kosterland to the Magrabari blight, these weapons are spoken of with reverence and dreamed of as the apex of the bladesmith's art."

The dwarf stared, studying the blade. "It's certainly pretty," he said. "But the blade looks awfully flimsy. It's barely two fingers-widths and thin as a razor."

"That's what makes them so special," Rem said. "Talis Taverando is renowned for folding his steel hundreds of times and driving the metal to the very edge of its capabilities. It looks light and elegant—flimsy, as you say—but feel it." He started to hand the blade to the dwarf, then looked to its owner. "With your kind permission?"

Elvaris nodded. "I suppose if the dwarf runs off with it, I can catch him at a sprint."

Torval shot the warrior woman a dismissive frown, then accepted the blade from Rem. The instant it was in the dwarf's hands, his eyes widened.

"Well, I'll be," he breathed.

"Heavy, isn't it?" Rem asked. "Heavier than it looks, anyway, but perfectly balanced."

Torval stepped away from the group, gripped the sword in both hands, and took a few practice swipes. Rem knew that the sword wasn't Torval's preferred weapon, but he still had good enough form with it, even when the weapon was so oversize and ill suited to his frame. The awe on the dwarf's face as he felt the heft of the blade in his hand was, to Rem, infinitely satisfying.

At last Torval handed the blade back to Elvaris. Rem was a little hurt that the dwarf hadn't handed it back to him, but before taking it, Elvaris nodded his way. "Go on," she said, "I know you're not done with it."

Rem smiled and took the blade from Torval. He studied it from every possible angle, and when his close study was done, he stepped apart from the others and moved through a few fencing iterations, letting the blade whistle and buzz and slice the air. It was magnificent.

"Pay attention," Elvaris said to Sandiva. "*That's* proper form."

Rem felt a swell of pride and fought the urge to smile.

"What's that on the grip?" Torval said as Rem went through his paces. "Didn't feel like leather."

"Sharkskin," Elvaris said. "Repels moisture and maintains its friction, even if your hands are sweaty."

Rem finally forced himself to hand the weapon back to its owner. "That's a beautiful blade. You must be proud."

Elvaris nodded as she resheathed the Taverando. "Most proud, indeed. It was given to me by my father. My elder brother renounced his inheritance when he joined the Aemonic church as an acolyte—he's a high priest now. When I came of age, my father knew the family lands and title would pass to me, so he gave me this and told me to go out in the world and hew myself a path with it. Someday I'll pass it on to my own son or daughter."

"With a blade like that," Torval said drily, "I doubt any man eager to breed would come near you."

Sandiva burst out laughing. Rem turned to Torval, a look of shocked incredulity on his face. "Torval!" he hissed, thoroughly mortified.

"It's all right," Elvaris said, smiling easily. Very little ruffled her, apparently. "I get that all the time. What I decided, master dwarf, was that the only man who gets to call me wife is the one who can best me in a duel against this blade. If he can draw blood or disarm me, he can have my hand. Providing he wants it, that is."

Torval, despite his rude pronouncement, looked thoroughly impressed. "You may be dressed as a soldier, milady," the dwarf said slowly, "but you strike me as a queen."

Elvaris smiled broadly and bowed. "Nothing so grand. Only your most humble servant, master dwarf." With that she took the reins of her horse and looked to Sandiva. "Come on. We should be getting back."

Still laughing, Sandiva agreed. The two women led their horses away, leaving Rem and Torval alone with the mud and willows at the riverbank.

"Tall and wispy like an elf, that one," Torval said, "but, by Thendril's braids, she's got a dwarven spirit. All fire and stone inside."

Rem nodded, still thinking of how good that blade had felt in his hand. "These Estavari women," he said, "I've never met their like."

Once the animals had drunk their fill, Rem and Torval led them back up the bank to the camp. There Rem showed Torval how to tie his pony in a good spot for further foraging. Rem then moved on to a crash course in brushing their animals down—currycomb first, followed by the brush. By the time they were done, Torval seemed to have taken a genuine liking to his pony, whispering to it warmly all through its combing and brushing, admonishing it like one of his own children if it whickered or snorted at him in a manner he found less than respectful.

By the time Rem got to work on their own supper—bacon and hardtack, with some cheese on the side—the other parties were already well into their meals. The lord marshal's men were bent over what looked like camp rations—simple porridge with some speck and carrots thrown in, accompanied by some foul-smelling smoked kippers—while the meal prepared by the Lady Tzimena and her lady-in-waiting for their own soldiers looked and smelled like something from a well-regarded tavern: spiced sausages, relishes of pickled vegetables, and wine-braised mushrooms along with fire-warmed flatbread and a cask of good wine.

Rem wasn't sure what impressed him more: that the Estavari company was eating so well, or that it was their charge—the noble lady whom they protected—who did all the cooking for them. Clearly, highborn or not, the Lady Tzimena was not one to sit by and let others do everything for her.

Torval plopped down beside Rem at the fire and lifted the jar of pickled eggs that Osma had given him.

"These," Torval said, brandishing the container of eggs in their green-tinged vinegar, adrift with various herbs and spices, "these are a kingly gift indeed. I shall have to bring Osma something back from Erald in answer to this."

"You keep those eggs," Rem said. "I just want a pull of that beer from Aarna."

Torval nodded, looking a little insulted on behalf of his eggs, and scurried back to their supplies to dig out the hogshead.

Rem was no great camp cook, but he could handle himself with a frying pan. He let some of the sailor's hardtack procured by Ondego soak in water for a bit while he fried up some rashers of bacon over the fire. Once the pork was nice and crisped, he threw the softened hardtack into the grease and let it break down further over the heat. This greasy, lumpy, salty mess filled their bellies and warmed them, tempered on their palates by some nuts and dried fruit as dessert. Torval provided tin cups of Joedoc's red ale, cut with water from the river. It was thin and weak, but it still reminded Rem of home, back in Yenara. As they ate, Rem recalled how he'd first learned to make bacon and hardtack, from his father's master-at-arms, Evengor, on his very first long hunting expedition when he was eight years old. It was, in truth, a rather unpleasant meal—but for some reason, it still reminded him of happier times and simpler joys.

Remembering the home I left, Rem thought wistfully, *longing for the home I've adopted*.

There was little talk, except among the closest companions present, and those words were usually short and exchanged in breathy whispers. Every now and then, Rem caught members of the two parties—Eraldic and Estavari—glancing at one another across the fire, as if trying to build up the courage to start a conversation but never finding it. He thought it quite strange that the traveling companions could not bring themselves to simply talk and get to know one another, but the awkward silence persisted. To make up for it, though, there was the bright beauty of a million stars strewn across the moonless, cloudless sky, and the comforting whisper of May winds rattling the leafy alders and sawing through the bankside willows, not to mention the low, watery susurration of the slow-moving river. It occurred to Rem that he didn't mind the silence, really. It had been so long since he'd been out in the country at night, under the stars and blessed with none of the sounds he had come to find familiar in a city of Yenara's size: squalling cats, barking dogs, drunks singing as they reeled home, lovers fighting, babies bawling, stairs creaking under the weight of climbers.

"Excuse me?" a voice called out of the darkness. It was the Red Raven. "I know I'm a prisoner, but I should hate to think I'd starve before being brought to justice."

Rem and Torval looked to one another. Rem felt his own face, hot and flushed with embarrassment.

"Sundry hells," he muttered. "I totally forgot about him."

"There's some hardtack and bacon left here," Torval said, suggesting the frying pan between them.

"We've got some leftovers," the Lady Tzimena offered.

"Some dregs of porridge here," Croften said, peering into the Eraldic cookpot.

"He'll have not a crumb from our stores," the lord marshal snapped.

"But, Father," Brekkon said. "We've all eaten."

"It's just a mouthful or two," Wallenbrand said.

"I said no," the lord marshal countered. "It's a waste, and I will not countenance it."

"What was that?" Rem asked.

"I said," the lord marshal answered, with patronizing slowness, "feeding that man from your own stores is a waste. The rest of you do as you like. But no one from my company will give that man even a crumb of stale bread, is that understood?"

"Well, now," Torval broke in, "it's a good thing he's our prisoner and not yours. Otherwise the poor sod might starve before he hangs."

The lord marshal's eyes narrowed. "I only thought to advise—"

"You made each of our tasks abundantly clear before we set out," Torval snapped. "You'd get us to Erald safely, these good ladies of Estavar would guard the Lady Tzimena, and my partner and I would watch the Red Raven. What say you do your job, lord marshal, and let us do ours?"

Rem was proud of Torval. He knew the dwarf had no love for their prisoner, but he also knew Torval hated bullies even more than he hated bandits and outlaws.

The lord marshal stared in stunned silence for a long time. Finally he lowered his eyes. "Do as you will, then. As you say, the man is *your* problem on the road, not ours."

Rem nodded. "See, lord marshal? Each to his own duty. That's the way we do it in Yenara." Then off he went into the shadows, to see their prisoner fed.

When Rem reached the Raven's cage, he handed the frying pan through awkwardly, having to tilt it almost onto its side to pass it into the man's waiting hands.

"Sorry," Rem said without real contrition, "no implements."

"My hands will do nicely," the Raven said, and sniffed at the pan, since it was too dark to see what he'd been handed. "Pork and biscuit?"

Rem nodded, unsure whether the Raven could even see him clearly. "I'll be back for the pan in a bit. Feel free to eat what's left."

Rem set off then, trudging onward through the high grass toward the deeper darkness near the hedgerows and the fields. He was eager to find himself a nice, dark tree to piss under. In no time the night engulfed him, and he relished it, reveling in the brilliant starlight, the rasping grass and creaking trees spread so widely around him. He thought he could just see a low, dark mass off in the distance with a small, warm light burning in a tiny window: a farmhouse, perhaps. The air was cool but not cold, the breeze sweet.

He did his business, then started his walk back to the camp, taking a slow, meandering path because he so enjoyed the darkness and the solitude. As he neared camp, he realized he'd managed to approach the Red Raven's cage cart once again, even though he'd intended to return by a different path. The cage and its occupant were silhouetted against the red-gold light of the great campfire, and it was clear, even from this vantage point, that the Raven was scraping every last bit of mushy biscuit and bacon grease from the frying pan. Beyond the cage Rem saw the small, half-lit figures of the lord marshal, his men, the Estavari soldiers, and the Lady Tzimena's maidservant, all gathered round the roaring campfire, the hitching winds tugging greedily at the flames and driving cyclones of sparks and embers before them.

It was only when Rem saw a willowy female figure detach from the surrounding darkness and approach the outlaw's cage that he realized the Lady Tzimena was not by the fire with the rest of them. How could she be? She was right there, a stone's throw from him, a moving shadow on a barely lit world, as obscured and phantom-like as the caged Red Raven himself.

Rem froze where he stood, afraid another step might give him away.

As he watched, the Lady Tzimena approached the Red Raven's cage. She handed him something through the bars: bread, perhaps, maybe a small cup. The Raven took the offered gifts. Though it was very dark and they were nothing more than flat shadows on his night-dulled vision, Rem thought he saw the Raven's hand and the lady's own linger together on the same bar of the cage.

A moment later, she withdrew and bustled back into the dark at the edge of camp.

Rem waited, not sure what to do. The Raven remained up on his knees, watching the lady go, then finally reclined again and dug into his clandestine supper. Rem decided the best course of action was to slowly, quietly withdraw and return to the camp by the way he'd come. With luck, no one would know that he'd seen what he'd seen.

What had he witnessed, in fact? A young maiden's mercy? Kindness from one stranger to another?

It could be. But Rem thought of that lingering gesture, when both of their hands were clenched together around the same bar.

Kindness, yes. Mercy, certainly. But that small, simple gesture suggested to Rem that it was very unlikely the Lady Tzimena and the Red Raven were complete strangers.

CHAPTER TEN

Rem and Torval chose a line of whispering willows as shelter against the increasingly persistent winds that scoured the campsite through the night. Torval took first watch, so Rem got at least a few hours of good, uninterrupted sleep in before being awakened to watch their prisoner through the early-morning hours and past dawn. The whisper of the willows and the gurgling of the river often threatened to send Rem off to sleep again, but when that feeling overcame him, he'd simply rise and move briskly about, doing his best to keep himself awake without disturbing anyone else. If the fire threatened to subside to ash, he'd stoke it and throw a few more branches on. Time and again, Rem was overcome by the feeling of being watched. He could've sworn the source of that feeling was the Red Raven himself, curled up in his cage, feigning sleep but watching—always watching. And yet every time Rem's paranoia got the best of him, he would approach the cage and stare intently, only to find the outlaw fast asleep, snoring placidly. Or pretending to with great skill.

Then, suddenly, it was morning. Gray light crept into the world from its far-eastern edges. Birds began their songs from the alders and cottonwoods, and a gentle silver mist slithered up from the riverbank and the nearby hollows, making of the world a dewy, half-obscured landscape out of a child's fairy story.

Fasts were broken with uncooked victuals: dried fruit, nuts, bread, and cheese. Torval wolfed down one of his pickled eggs and seemed more than a little vexed by the gathering light. Rem asked him what troubled him as they prepared their mounts for another day's ride.

"It's so bloody bright," the dwarf said, looking around through squinted eyes. "And so bloody...*open*. Wide open."

"Suffering a bit of the dwarf's distemper?" Rem asked, trying to sound casual and joking so as not to offend his partner.

"Don't forget," Torval said, "I didn't just start my life underground—I also work nights. Daylight hours are not, and never have been, terribly agreeable to me."

Rem nodded. He could definitely see where that might be true. They harnessed their horses, secured their saddlebags, and made sure the animals were fed and watered. Concurrently, the rest of the campers made their own preparations to once more take to the road. It was on the tip of Rem's tongue to tell Torval about what he'd seen the night before—the Lady Tzimena secretly visiting their prisoner when she thought no one would notice—but in the end he decided to keep it to himself. For the present, at any rate.

They were underway again in no time, the rising sun climbing over the jagged horizon far to the east and nearly blinding them as they rode on, more or less right into its brilliant golden light. Soon the morning mist dissipated and the world was a riot of empty blue skies bearing only long, ruined streamers of white cloud, green grass, and the roiling, rumbling rush of the Embrys River on their right. Off to their left, to the north and northeast, the high hills that lay between them and the Kaarten River valley rose, ridgelines swathed in mist or obscured by swaying ranks of sentinel pines. On the gently rolling land between the river and the hills, they saw farmland and pocket forests, the tiny figures of tenants and yeomen tending their just-rising crops or clearing fallow fields for late-spring planting visible as the party passed. The company was quiet that day—unusually so—but Rem was glad of it. For some vague and inexpressible reason, he suddenly longed to know just whom he could trust among their traveling companions—who could be truly relied on if the need arose. Elvaris and Sandiva had seemed a good pair—friendly enough, and clearly dedicated to their duties as protectors of the Lady Tzimena. If the rest of their group was of the same mettle, it seemed they might prove the ones to look to—the ones to stand beside—in a moment of crisis. The lot of them seemed to have an almost familial bond, the soldiers serving the Lady Tzimena and Tzimena serving them in turn, after a fashion. The lord marshal's men were more tight-lipped, even among themselves. Rem had barely heard words shared between them, except in the form of furtive whispers and simple orders. Though they all wore the same livery and served the same hard taskmaster, it was as if they were strangers.

All through the day, whether they were riding or taking a short respite by the roadside, their safety rituals remained. Galen, the outrider for the Estavari company, watched the company's rear rank, disappearing for intervals on the road behind them or into the woods they passed through. At the vanguard the lord marshal's own scout—the big, broad-shouldered one called Croften—repeatedly rode ahead, crossbow strapped to his back, disappearing over the horizon or into passing copses for unmeasured intervals before eventually reappearing to give the lord marshal a report.

Rem also noted that the lord marshal's son, young Brekkon, tried on numerous occasions to urge his horse up alongside one or another of the Lady Tzimena's female bodyguards. The boy would try to strike up a conversation—too far away for Rem to hear, but easy enough to embellish given the lad's forced smiles and visible attempts at affability. Always he was met with cool detachment—short answers or none at all—and sooner or later, he'd get the picture and fall back into line again.

Rem almost felt sorry for the boy and wondered what it was in him and Torval that had moved Elvaris and Sandiva to speak with them, when the rest of their company seemed determined not to offer any similarly friendly gestures to the lord marshal's own soldiers.

When the persistent silence vexed him, Rem and Torval talked at intervals, usually of the familiar things they were already starting to miss. Torval spoke warmly of his children—how Tavarix had graduated from the first form of his dwarven stonemason's apprenticeship to the second; how Ammi had started earning coin watching the children of working parents in their bankside neighborhood; how little Lokki was passing through a rather troublesome phase of mischief making and open defiance, constantly causing trouble and all but laughing when challenged over it. It was true, Rem and Indilen spent a great deal of time in the company of Torval and his family, but these finer points of everyday life—the children's growth and triumphs and setbacks, and Torval's feelings about them—were seldom witnessed or discussed between them. It was only here, now, on the road and bored with the monotony of their journey, that Torval managed to talk of more domestic matters, and how they moved him.

"Oh, now get this!" Torval suddenly spat, interrupting his own train of thought as some new revelation burst upon him. "My sister has a suitor!"

Rem turned to stare at his partner. "Osma?"

"Well, not a suitor, precisely," Torval said, "but a most

persistent burr that won't see fit to remove itself from her skirt-tails."

"Do tell," Rem said.

Torval obliged. "You know she often sells secondhand wares and baked goods in the market, yes? Well, apparently, more afternoons than not, there's a dwarf comes sniffing around, showering her with compliments and always buying one of her mutton pies—if there are any left. They often sell out by midday."

"So who is he?" Rem asked.

"She says his name's Whurin," Torval continued, now starting to look a little sour about it all. "Blond, braided, and short bearded. Younger than her, too! Imagine…"

"Well," Rem pointed out, "your sister's been a widow for some time now, yes? Going on twenty years or something?"

Torval grunted and nodded.

"And she's a lovely woman with a lot to offer any man—or dwarf, as the case may be. Why shouldn't she remarry if a worthy suitor presents himself? Is there anything in dwarven culture preventing it?"

Torval shook his head. "Far from it. In fact, among my people, remaining indefinitely unmarried after being widowed is seen as rather selfish…or self-indulgent, at the very least. We are made, we are told, to marry and procreate. If we can do any of those things and we *choose* not to, we are not fulfilling our purpose."

"Do you think she'd want to marry again?" Rem asked.

Torval shrugged and grunted again.

"And how would you feel about it if she did?"

Torval's head whipped toward Rem, as if the question itself shocked him. The dwarf's broad face screwed up, an unmistakable indication that he had been posed a question he had no ready answer to. Now, under duress, he was rooting around in the corners of his mind and heart for an answer. Finally the dwarf shrugged again and blew out a heavy sigh.

"She's a grown woman. I could not stop her if that's what she wanted."

"I didn't ask that," Rem said. "I asked how you'd *feel* about it."

Torval wriggled in his saddle. "I would wonder what it might mean. For the children. For myself."

"It'd mean you'd have to hire a maid," Rem countered. "Osma keeps your home in order. If she skipped off to start her own—"

"And why shouldn't he live among us?" Torval said suddenly. "Are we not worthy of this ragamuffin? He's a blacksmith, apparently. That's not so grand, is it? Is a blacksmith any better than a humble watchwarden and his children?"

"It might have nothing to do with that," Rem said patiently. "If Osma likes this fellow and if—*if*—something grew between them, don't you think they'd want their own home, like any husband and wife?"

"That's how it works among your folk," Torval said. "Not ours. Dwarves see safety in numbers, and comfort in closeness. If this man married Osma, he could move in with us—"

"Or you all would move in with him," Rem offered. "If he's a blacksmith and well-to-do, he might have a very large house, indeed. Could have three, even four rooms!"

Torval looked as if he was growing impatient with this line of questioning. Rem thought he might shrug off his questions or tell him to shut his gob, but instead the dwarf suddenly changed the subject.

"Well, what of you, then?" Torval demanded. "You and Indilen took rooms together months ago. Will you marry her, or won't you?"

"A fine tactic," Rem said, putting his eyes back on the river road. "Changing the subject."

"Well?" the dwarf pressed.

"I suggested it, when we moved in together," Rem said. "She was the one who wanted to wait."

"Bah," Torval said. "She's testing your resolve. Have you asked her again?"

Rem shook his head.

"You fool!" Torval shouted, his voice scaring a flock of sparrows from a nearby tree. "Don't take her silence for indifference, lad, I warn you! Even if she keeps rebuffing you, you must keep digging it up."

"And why is that?" Rem asked. "I should think I know my ladylove better than you, old stump."

"You may," Torval said, "in most ways. But I see the way she looks at you when we're all together. The way she stares at you when you're prattling on about one thing or another that no one else gives two shits about. Hells—the way she looked at you yesterday, when we rode out. She loves you, lad—truly, deeply. If you love her, and you're under the same roof in any case, there's no reason not to make her an honest woman."

Rem supposed that was true. She knew the truth of things now, anyway, and that was a relief. But still, Rem felt a deep, abiding fear of something—he could not articulate or even give a face to it. And that subtle, creeping, unnamable fear within him often stood between him and Indilen and a High Council–sealed marriage license.

What was it, then? What could it be?

Late in the day, as the sun was at their backs and threw their shadows, garish and elongated, upon the uneven ground before them, it started to rain. Though it was early summer, the clouds had blown down from the mountains. The rain from those clouds was cold, sharp, and unfriendly, driven by hard, insistent winds. Riding along in the sudden downpour, the falling water turned honey gold by the sun's declining light, shining out upon the world from beneath the lowering clouds, was most surreal. Rem drew up his forester's hood to keep the rain off and yanked out his traveling cloak to try to stay dry, but he knew that if they remained out in this weather for too long, they'd be waterlogged before they reached their destination.

Luckily it appeared on a rise before them within an hour of the rain's advent: the little coach-stop village of Kribb. By the time they reached the hamlet and all hurried into the common room of the inn—named, in rather aspirational fashion, the Crossroads Palace—the whole party was soaked, good riding cloaks or no. The Red Raven was left in the rain, his cage parked near a window, where they could easily see him, hunkering in his moveable prison beneath the single rough cowhide blanket afforded him. The innkeeper, a short, round fellow of rosy cheeks and agreeable aspect, instantly set about directing everyone to bath chambers where they could strip their wet clothes, wash themselves, and slip into something comfortable while their raiment and armor dried through the night.

There were two bath chambers. The Lady Tzimena, her nurse, and her soldiers had one of those chambers all to themselves, while Rem and Torval crowded into the men's chamber with their Eraldic traveling companions. It was a large room, built for multiple users at once and sporting at least four copper and two wooden tubs for bathing, but it struck Rem as considerably less spacious with six men and one dwarf crammed inside. As the lord marshal's men began to strip off their gear, Rem realized they had unfinished business outside.

"That cage is wide open," he suggested to Torval. "Perhaps we should wheel it into the barn?"

"He's bound for the gallows, good watchwarden," the lord marshal broke in—rather testily, Rem thought. "What difference does it make if he catches cold while in transit?"

"It's not right, sir, with respect," someone else said. It was old, whiskered Wallenbrand. "Prisoner or no, he's still a man. He deserves some courtesy until such time as the duke's justice is carried out."

Sitting there, now half-stripped and barefoot, the lord marshal regarded Wallenbrand with more than a little irritation. Wallenbrand's level stare made it clear that, despite any differences in rank, he expected to be treated as a peer, not a subordinate. Just as evidently, the lord marshal didn't care to be publicly contradicted—certainly not by one of his own soldiers. Rem could read the ongoing argument in the silent looks the two men gave one another. He could not decide, though, if this was a disagreement between two old comrades or two complete strangers.

"So honorable," Kroenen said with a sneer. "So gallant."

"Perhaps," Wallenbrand said, unmoved by the lord marshal's apparent dismissal. "Or maybe I'm just practical. What happens if our prisoner catches his death and expires before we make it back to Erald, eh?"

"Then he will save us the use of the gallows," the lord marshal answered. "And he's not our prisoner"—he looked to Rem and Torval—"he's *their* prisoner."

"What of our reward, then?" Torval broke in. He was already naked save for his undergarments, which consisted solely of a breech-clout wound about his broad middle.

"I pledged on my honor that you'd be paid," the lord marshal said. "You've already impugned that honor once, by insisting on riding along with us instead of accepting a sealed prom- issory note. Do you now dare to impugn my honor further, master dwarf?"

"No one's impugning anyone's honor," Rem said. "We just want to remind you we're not on this trek for thrills and wonders. We've come along to collect a reward *you* promised us, so anything that undermines our whole purpose for being here—"

"Why are you even asking me?" the lord marshal said abruptly. "He's *your* prisoner. If you want to go back out there and move him into the barn, do so. I would also expect you to spend the night in that barn, watching him...since he remains *your* charge until we arrive in Erald. Make yourselves useful, in some fashion?"

"Useful?" Torval snarled and stepped forward. "Have you forgotten that we did what you and your men couldn't? How we caught him while you and your pretty little companions here were still marching into the city because the Raven's men had stolen your horses? If anyone's making good on the work of others and reaping rewards they haven't earned, it's you, you bristling, ramrodded son of a—"

"Torval," Rem broke in. "I'll take care of it." He made for the door.

"What are you doing?" Torval asked.

"I'm going out into that blasted rain and I'm going to roll the Red Raven's cage into the bloody barn. Then I'm coming back here for a bath and some supper. And when it's time to retire, we—that is, you and I—will go keep watch over the prisoner through the night and let the good lord marshal and his men enjoy the beds and braziers of the Crossroads Palace." He stared at the lord marshal as he unpacked that plan, eager to make sure the bastard knew he was serious.

"There now," the lord marshal said, standing and starting to unlace his breeks. Though the hair on his chest was largely gray and there was clearly some of the fat of age on him, his shape and muscular frame remained impressive. "There's a good lad. I'm sure your horse-groom father would be proud."

"He was always proud," Rem muttered, heading for the door, "just not of me."

Torval still stood by, with only his loins still covered. "Lad, do you need help?"

"No worries, Torval," Rem said as he left the bath chamber. He had redonned his tunic, but it hung on him loosely, unlaced and with nothing beneath, like a stolen garment. Its sogginess was unpleasant. "I'll use my horse."

Rem worried over his careless words all through supper.

He was always proud . . . just not of me.

Why had he said that? What had made him so eager to prod and provoke the lord marshal, even if it was just with muttered asides and snide retorts?

Because he reminds you of him, he thought. *He may look nothing like your father, he may sound nothing like your father, he may not be of noble birth like your father . . . but in every meaningful way, he is your father. The smug self-satisfaction, constantly looking down his nose at everyone and everything, the impossibility of argument or disobedience. They are two swords forged of the same stubborn pig iron, and dealing with a man like that when you've so long been out from under his thumb . . .*

It unbalances you.

You must control yourself, Remeck. Provoking that man will profit you nothing.

It was easier to accept that idea having bathed and swaddled himself in dry clothes. They all looked remarkably refreshed postbath, gathered in small groups at their various tables, dominating the common room for their nightly meal as the handful of guests not of their company were pressed to the far corners. The innkeeper and his wife served them generously, though they explained, time and again, that they would have offered more if they'd known such a big party was coming. They had no roasted meat, but several loaves of bread had been thrown into the ovens when they'd all stomped into the common room earlier. Now that fresh, hot bread was served with a good, nutty cheese, rashers of bacon, savory country sausages, and eggs fried in grease. Porridge and soup were offered, as well, but most of them were satisfied with the heartier fare that came from the oven and the frying pan. Unknown to Rem, Torval quietly paid the innkeeper for an entire barrel of locally pressed cider and bade the brew be served liberally until it was gone. Concurrently, Captain Tuvera sprang for a dozen bottles of wine from the innkeeper's cellars, and that made the rounds, as well. Even the strangers in the common room benefited from the largesse of the Estavari captain and the humble dwarf. When Rem caught Torval and Tuvera toasting one another across the common room—he with cider, she with wine—he knew they had at least one ally among their traveling company.

Rem and Torval occupied a small table in a cozy corner of the common room, hunched over their meals and wolfing them down with great haste and relish. Rem barely even raised his eyes as he ate, and when he finally did, he saw that Torval was a mirror image of himself, sopping up the last golden remnants of the runny egg yolks and droplets of fry grease with a still-soft hunk of warm bread. To wash it all down, they gulped the tart cider that Torval had sprung for, then immediately refilled their cups and gulped again.

"That," Rem said, "was most satisfying."

"Aye, that," Torval said, reclining a bit in his seat. "Didn't even realize how hungry I was."

They sat for a time, letting their bellies do their work as they looked about the room and studied their traveling companions. The Eraldic guards all shared a single four-seat table, while the lord marshal sat apart, alone, eyes on his plate. Rem had been more than a little infuriated by the man when his son, young Brekkon, had tried to sit with him and the lord marshal had given only a curt, "Soldiers mess together. Officers eat alone," to chase him off. The boy, predictably, looked both angry and crushed.

The Lady Tzimena, meanwhile, sat at a long trestle table with her chaperone and all the women who accompanied her. They laughed and spoke with ease and seemed to genuinely enjoy one another's company. Though it was easy enough to hear every word said by her and her companions, it was impossible to actually understand them. Rem spoke three languages and could passably read a couple more—but none of them were Estavari. It bore some resemblance, in syntax and word forms, to Old Horunic, but the speed and lilt of their speech made identifying the similarities and picking out useful root words beyond his ability. Whatever they discussed, though, it was clearly entertaining. They smiled easily, laughed effortlessly, joked and cajoled without embarrassment. In short, though Tzimena was clearly their charge and the warrior women were clearly her servants, there was something undeniably loving about how they interacted with one another, especially here, in this out-of-the-way place, so far from their shared home.

More than once their whole table burst into laughter in answer to someone's joke or friendly insult. Whenever that happened, Rem noted that the lord marshal, alone at his table, would raise his head the slightest bit and turn—ever so subtly—toward them, as if it was always on the tip of his tongue to scold them like rowdy children.

The lord marshal's men, meanwhile, talked among themselves and did a little bantering, but generally kept their voices, and their heads, down. Wallenbrand, Croften, and the wain driver, Wirren, seemed familiar with one another. Most of the words exchanged were among the three of them. Poor Brekkon sat at their table, eating in silence, occasionally offering a word, but being frozen out of their conversation by curt answers or awkward silence.

Rem was lost in a reverie, considering the many differences between the two bands, when the innkeeper returned, bearing a full jug of cider.

"More, good sirs?" he asked. He struck Rem as a truly kind man, the sort well suited to his chosen profession because taking care of people—feeding and sheltering people—came naturally to him.

"Most assuredly," Rem said, trading the empty jug on their table for the full one offered. As the innkeeper gathered up their empty plates, he ventured a question.

"Forgive my asking, if it's an intrusion," he began, voice low but still easy, "but just where is it you're all off to? And how did you two end up with all of them?"

"They're from Erald," Rem said, indicating the lord marshal and his men. "They're from Toriel, in Estavar. And we're from Yenara. We're all on our way to Erald. The lady over there is to marry the duke, and my partner and I are guarding a prisoner."

"A prisoner?" the innkeeper said, eyes wide. "That fellow in the cage?"

"The same," Torval said. "Ever heard of the Red Raven?"

The innkeeper's blue eyes grew as big as saucers. "No!"

Rem nodded. "Yes indeed. We caught him in Yenara. Didn't even know who he was."

"Well, now, that is something!" the innkeeper said, still standing there with two empty plates teetering on one arm and an empty jug of cider in his other hand. "You're not going by the forest road?"

Rem and Torval both nodded.

The innkeeper's expression dropped. "Oh, good sirs . . . honestly, I'd recommend another route—"

"What's going on here?" the lord marshal snapped. Rem hadn't even noticed, but he'd suddenly appeared at the innkeeper's elbow. Though not in uniform or armor, he still gave the impression of being taller than anyone, the straightness of his back and the squareness of his shoulders sufficient to bully and intimidate.

"Just having a conversation," Rem said. "Officers may eat apart from their men, but watchwardens can fraternize as they wish, last time I checked."

Torval snorted and lowered his face, stifling a laugh.

"Have you considered," the lord marshal said, "that sharing too much about our prisoner and our destination might prove risky? No matter how friendly the hearer?" He gave the innkeeper a dreadful side-eye, silently suggesting that the man could not be trusted.

"Oh, good sir," the innkeeper began.

"Lord Marshal," Kroenen corrected.

"Lord Marshal, Your Highness, good sir," the innkeeper sputtered, "I meant no disrespect. I was just making conversation. Why, I was just telling these two fine fellows that you should all shun the forest road. The Ethkeraldi's crawling with brigands."

"Crawling with brigands?" the lord marshal asked, suggesting that he needed details.

"Why certainly, sir," the innkeeper said. "There's the Devils of the Weald, of course, but there's still more besides. The Wastrels—they's just a lot of feral children, but quite cunning. Slaymaker and Sons—they're new, but they've hit a caravan or two. And the Bloody Boskers—heavens and hells, that lot won't just rob you, they'll cook you and eat you! And still more! Why, there's even been talk of late that there are orcs roving the woods, in search of no one knows what! And that's not even accounting for blighted ruins like Hobb's Folly, where unquiet spirits still linger, or the wood nymphs eager to draw young men off the road, or the bears..."

"Bears," Rem repeated, looking right at Torval.

"I could kill a bear," Torval said. "Easy."

The innkeeper turned his worried gaze on Torval. "Oh, good master dwarf, they're very *big* bears."

"Ghost stories and foolish folklore," the lord marshal said. "The forest holds dangers, surely, but most of what you're telling me is twaddle. For every truly dangerous brigand band like the Raven's Devils, there are a dozen others that are starving, inbred, backcountry rubbish on legs. The only people who fall to their blades are those too foolish to outwit them or too weak to outfight them."

Rem snorted in spite of himself.

"Did I say something amusing, boy?" the lord marshal asked.

"Some bits were more amusing than others, surely," Torval said, not smiling at all. "Suffice to say, in our line of work, we've seen more men undone by overconfidence than almost anything else."

The lord marshal had no response. He simply gave the two of them one last, lingering look of disdain and condescension, then turned and crossed the common room back to his table. The innkeeper looked to Rem and Torval. He looked genuinely worried.

"Too proud, that one," the man said under his breath.

"To the point of folly," Rem said, shaking his head. "But don't worry, sir—we'll take your words to heart, even if he won't. Maybe with a little luck and wide-open eyes, we'll make it to Erald unscathed."

"Well, best of luck to you," the innkeeper said, and offered a most genuine smile. "I shall light candles for you both on the family shrine and say prayers."

Away he went, leaving Rem and Torval alone once more. For a time they sat in silence. Finally the dwarf spoke.

"I grow tired of this company, lad," he said. "What say we go take up our appointed duty in the barn?"

CHAPTER ELEVEN

As barns went, Rem thought their accommodations for the night warm and welcoming. The clapboards were all well fitted, the roof free of leaks, the hay well baled, and the stalls all neatly arranged and well kept. Most of their horses had been brought in, but there was not room for them all, so a few had been crowded under a lean-to outside usually reserved for cordwood in the winter. The Raven's cage stood in the very center of the earth- and hay-strewn floor, listing forward because it had only two wheels and its hitch rested on the ground. When Rem and Torval entered, they found the Raven quite at ease in his mobile cell, staring off into the middle distance and chewing on a sprig of straw.

Rain still fell on the barn's shingled roof, but it had let up somewhat since their arrival and now offered more of a light patter than the stinging roar of the earlier downpour. In the stalls lining either side of the barn, their company's horses whickered and snorted. One of them raised his tail and farted proudly. Thankfully, he was at the far end of the line. Rem prayed they were upwind.

"Look here," their prisoner said when they trotted in out of the rain. "My captors, come to keep me company through the night."

"Come to keep you from slipping off, more like," Torval said. To reinforce the fact that they were on duty, and not simply opting to sleep in the barn, Rem and Torval had brought both their saddlebags and their weapons with them. "I'll say it now, and not give you another warning: we're here to keep an eye on you and the only conversation we'll want is with one another. Talk more than either of us likes and we'll gag you, if need be."

The Raven nodded agreeably. "As you wish, master dwarf."

"Now, then," Torval spat back, suddenly agitated. "What is all this 'master dwarf' cack? Do I look like the master of anything to you?"

"Just being polite," the Raven said.

"Well, stop it," Torval said, so irritated that Rem was almost tempted to snicker at him. "Your brand of politeness does little to ease my spirit, you scheming snake."

The Raven seemed honestly hurt by that, as though he'd said something intended as a kindness that had been taken as an insult. "Very well, then. I apologize."

"You'll have to forgive Torval," Rem said as he hung his saddlebags over a stall divider and leaned his sheathed sword against a nearby support beam. "He's not a big one for obsequies or chitchat. He puts up with me, but that's just because I've been chained to him for so long now."

"Save it," Torval said, taking a seat on an empty hogshead. "The more you talk to this one, the more he'll talk back."

"I'm a brigand and an outlaw, it's true," the Raven said, shifting in his cage so he faced the two of them. He sat cross-legged, like a street-corner tale swapper ready to launch into a tenpenny epic. "But you gents have my word, so long as you treat fairly with me, I mean you no harm. If I make conversation, it's just because I'm infernally bored."

Torval made a low, rumbling sound in his throat but didn't reply. If Rem was not mistaken, the dwarf looked almost contrite...but contrite for Torval was really just "not actively hostile," so it could be hard to tell. Rem, for his part, leaned on a sawhorse and crossed his arms. Having been mounted in the saddle all day and settled upon the hard chairs of the inn's common room all through dinner, his rear end was ready for a little standing before he turned in for the night.

"You want to talk, fine," Rem said. "What were you doing in the Lady Tzimena's chambers?"

"Are you daft?" Torval asked.

"Not in the least," Rem answered, confident. "We've heard the lord marshal's story. Let's give the prisoner a chance to speak. I'm not saying I'll readily believe him."

The Raven stared at Rem. His neutral expression slowly widened into a friendly grin. "You're a bright one, aren't you?"

Rem jerked his head toward Torval. "Not if you listen to the old stump, I'm not."

"He has his moments," Torval said, hands on his knees, sitting straight backed on the hogshead as if it were some rustic throne. Rem was impressed; his dwarven friend actually cut quite a kingly figure, despite his simple attire and humble surroundings.

The Raven's eyes moved back and forth between them—slowly, deliberately. Rem was sure the man was trying to read them—to measure their openness, their potential for understanding. Finally he lowered his eyes and shrugged. "I thought the lady could speak on my behalf, given her, uh, closeness to the duke. I only wanted to make an appeal, nothing more."

Rem thought his voice had the sound of honesty in it, but he couldn't be sure. Even if he was telling the truth, after a fashion, it was clear that he was leaving something out, as well.

"And it had nothing to do with her position?" Torval asked. "Her value?"

The Raven raised his eyes, suddenly troubled. "What does that mean?"

Torval stood and moved toward the cage, fully in interrogation mode, as though they were back at the watchkeep. "It means a noble lady betrothed to a duke is a valuable bargaining chip," Torval said. "If you went to all that trouble to gain access to her, it's because you were trying to kidnap her for ransom. But you were surprised and had to make a hasty escape—which is why we found you in your guard costume, running like a madman over the rooftops."

"Maybe there's some truth in that," the Raven said. "But I swear to you both, she was safe with me. I would never hurt her."

Rem appraised the man. He spoke calmly and freely, without the long pauses and careful syntax of a man inventing a story on the fly. He did not trust the Red Raven overall—it was incontestable that he was an outlaw and a killer, after all—but he still got the impression that there was more to him than simple wickedness. As if he were the sort of man who did terrible things, but for some loftier purpose, if only in his own mind.

"All right, then," Rem countered, "answer me this: Is what the lord marshal said about his company true? Did you, in fact, ambush and murder a number of his soldiers, then steal their horses and ride for Yenara in their livery?"

The Raven's eyes sank again, then rose to meet Rem's when he finally answered. "There was an ambush, and there was a plan. Kroenen's men fought hard, and many of them died because they would've killed us otherwise. But my plan—my *intention*—was to take them all alive and hold them while we went about our business in the city. Those not killed were captured. None escaped."

"Now I know you're lying," Rem said. "Clearly some escaped, or the lord marshal and those men wouldn't even be here."

"Wouldn't they?" the Raven asked. Rem didn't care for the wry, narrow-eyed smile the man now wore.

"Where are those captured men now?" Torval asked.

The Raven smiled a little—only a little. "If my Devils have held to my orders, they're still prisoners in the wood. If you want to see how badly the lord marshal wants me dead, broach the subject with him. Tell him I've told you both that I'll see those men released to him, alive and well, if he'll but release me. I'll wager good coin he won't do it. He'd rather let his own men die than let me go now that he has me."

"And just why is that?" Rem asked. "What makes you so bloody special?"

The Raven's smile changed. Rem thought he saw some sadness in it. "You wouldn't believe me if I told you, so I won't bother. Let's just say we have a history, the lord marshal and I."

"Tosh," Torval spat. "It's clear enough: you've been a burr in the collective boots of the duke and his soldiers for so long, they want to hang your corpse from the city walls and let everyone see the crows picking at your soft bits. That doesn't make you special, just annoying. A nuisance, like a fox that keeps raiding a farmer's henhouse."

Rem knew Torval could be right...but he wasn't entirely convinced. There was something about their prisoner—a quiet assurance, an earnestness—that impressed him as somehow honest and forthright, criminal career notwithstanding.

"See?" the Raven said. "You don't believe me even when what I tell you isn't hard to swallow. I won't force-feed you the rest of it."

"What is it?" Rem asked. "What's the rest of it? Maybe we can help."

Once again the Raven's expression took on a great and terrible sadness. He shook his head slowly. "You seem a good pair. Kind. Honest. Maybe just a little hardheaded. I haven't lied to you when I've warned you not to trust the lord marshal. But I'll tell you right now, if I told you my story, and he knew it, you wouldn't just be in danger—I'd be signing your death warrants. I honestly don't want that. I'll figure my own way out of this, and I'll do my best to leave you two out of it."

"The sundry hells you will," Torval broke in. "You're worth a lot of money to us, you ponce, and we'll not waste all this time and risk our hides on the road just to see you skip away into the hills."

"Aye, that," Rem added, trying as hard as he could to make his point without overmaking it. He looked the Raven in the eye when he spoke next. "Mark me, here and now: I don't care what's between you and the lord marshal. I don't care what you are or are not guilty of, and I don't care whether you're ultimately punished or not. We're here to collect a reward that we earned by catching you. We *need* that money. Our families *need* that money. If your escape looks like it might cost us that money, I swear by Aemon, Lattis, and the *Scrolls of the Thrall* that I'll see you dead before I see you prancing off into those woods."

The Raven's expression hardened, but the smile remained. "That sounds like a challenge, boy. Are you sure you want to challenge me, knowing as little as you do?"

Rem offered a smile of his own. "Maybe you should ask yourself the same question."

A silence fell between them, tense and uneasy, broken only

by the rain on the roof and the soft breathing of the stalled horses. That is, until the barn door creaked and a sweet voice surprised them all and drew their eyes toward it.

"Oh, goodness," the Lady Tzimena said as she drew back her cloak's rain-soaked cowl, "I didn't know anyone was out here."

Rem stood at attention, as though Ondego or Hirk had just come into his presence. Torval turned himself toward the lady as well and squared his shoulders. Strange how conditioned they were to look disciplined and presentable when a well-heeled female came into their presence.

Rem stole a sidelong glance at the Raven. The outlaw stared at the Lady Tzimena, then lowered his eyes. It was a strange gesture, indicative to Rem not of indifference, but of an attempt to *appear* indifferent. It was as if the Raven was struggling not to stare at the lady, not to drink in the sight of her and let her beauty bring a smile to his face.

She stepped into the barn. A small bundle wrapped in a scrap of linen was clutched in her hand. "Am I interrupting something, good sirs?"

"Nothing," Rem said. "Just having a conversation with our prisoner, milady."

"Understood," she said, moving closer. She made right for the cage, not toward Rem or Torval off to one side.

"I wouldn't," Torval said, stepping in front of her. Rem had to remind himself that Torval hadn't seen what Rem had seen the night before—the lady stealing away in the dark to deliver some food to the caged Raven. So far as the dwarf knew, this was the first time the two would interact. "He's dangerous, milady."

The Lady Tzimena paused before speaking, as though weighing her words carefully. When she spoke, she smiled girlishly, but Rem instantly recognized a feint when he saw one. She was trying to make them think that, whatever she intended to do, she was doing it as an afterthought—a whim—not a deliberate action.

And she was lying.

"You would know better than I," she said to Torval. She then held out her bundle. "I brought him a heel of bread, a bit of cheese, and an apple." She stepped forward and spoke to Torval in a whisper; trusting, conspiratorial. "I know the lord marshal said to starve him, but that's unnecessarily cruel, don't you think? And these scraps, they're not so much, really..."

Torval took the bundle, nodded, then turned to Rem. When Rem saw the dwarf's face, he could see the puzzlement on it. Torval sensed the lady's subterfuge, as well. He was no fool, and often a better reader of silent markers and tells than Rem himself. Torval's expression seemed to silently impart a judgment and ask a question all at once.

Do we trust her? Should we feed him?

Rem shrugged. *What could it hurt, really?*

Torval gave the little piece of bread a couple hard squeezes, just to make sure there was nothing useful hiding in it, like a lockpick or a blade, then handed it through the bars to the Raven, followed by the palm-size morsel of cheese that had been brought with it. The Raven took the food, threw a thankful glance at the lady, nodded, and set to eating, tearing off one bit of bread at a time and chewing it completely before swallowing and tearing off another.

The lady stood, watching the man, gaining some silent satisfaction. Rem was uncomfortable with the lady's presence here—there was no telling what the lord marshal would think if he found her out here, near the prisoner and the two of them. He could tell by Torval's frowning mouth that he was equally uneasy about it.

"Was there something else, milady?" Rem asked.

Tzimena raised her eyes, as though his words had just reminded her of his presence. "What's that?"

"Something else?" Rem asked. "I'm guessing you're out here secretly—"

She smiled and nodded. "Indeed. Slipped away to make water, or so I told them. My nurse won't worry about me too soon."

"But there's the lord marshal," Torval said.

Tzimena frowned and all but shuddered. "Ugh. That man."

Rem smiled in spite of himself. "Between us, milady, we have no love for him, either. But he *is* the leader of this little expedition, and if he finds us here, with you—"

"Or you near him," Torval said, suggesting the Raven in his cage.

"Just so," Rem continued. "Be it the prisoner or the two of us, he might find us all less than suitable company for a lady of good birth."

"And what business is the company I keep to him?" Tzimena asked, raising her chin a little. "Besides, if I'm to be married to his master, he should probably get used to taking orders from me, don't you think?"

Rem instantly admired the spirit in the small gesture and the timbre of her voice. She didn't strike him as naïve or a petulant child. Instead she struck him as more like Indilen: intelligent, willful, more than familiar with her own mind and desires. No doubt that if the lord marshal found her here and tried to make something of it, she'd readily fight about it.

And though Rem thought her equal to butting heads with the lord marshal, he seriously doubted their stiff-backed expedition leader would back down for anyone or anything, even a noble lady betrothed to his master.

"That's a fair question," Rem said, "but despite what we may think of the man, I gather we can all agree he's not to be trifled with?"

"Aye, that," Torval added. He spoke softly, as though to his own daughter, Ammi. "And consider, lady, he may not be capable of punishing or challenging you—but the two of us? We're just humble tagalongs. He would have no qualms taking his ire out on us, if it came to that."

Tzimena looked from Torval to Rem, then back to Torval. Gods help him, Rem instantly admired her. She'd barely spoken twenty words with him, but her good heart and keen wits were clear as a day without fog. She impressed Rem, wealth and entitlement notwithstanding, as a good soul.

"Very well, then," she finally said. "I won't have anyone suffering for my indiscretions. I'll be off. I trust my visit will remain in confidence between us all?"

"Of course," Rem said.

"Pledged," Torval added.

"As always," the Raven answered.

Rem looked to the prisoner. The Raven was smiling at her. It wasn't his normal smug grin, nor even the sly half smile that he so often defaulted to. Instead his smile was warm and loving, indicative of great and sincere affection.

To Rem's great dismay, the Lady Tzimena wore a similar smile and held the prisoner's gaze. Gods, what had they stumbled into?

"Quiet, you," the lady said, then turned and hurried out into the rainy night again, drawing up her cowl as she went. Long after she'd gone, Torval finally turned and stared at Rem again. He wore a worried expression that told Rem he'd sensed what had just passed between the lady and their prisoner, and he didn't like it one bit.

The Raven kept eating. After his bread was gone, he reached for the stoppered gourd that hung from the bars of his cage. He displayed it for Rem.

"Could you fill this, please?" he asked. "I'm guessing there's a rain barrel outside?"

"I'll do it," Torval said, taking up his own canteen and stalking away toward the barn door. "If we get in hot water for this," he called back over his shoulder, "I'll crack that skull of yours myself! Reward or no reward!"

"Thank you, master dwarf!" the Raven sang as Torval slunk out into the rain.

"He only suspects," Rem said to the man in the cage, "but I know. I saw you with the Lady Tzimena last night."

"I know," the Raven said. "You didn't think I heard you, tromping through the high grass and trying to hold your breath when you came upon us?"

Rem stepped closer to the cage. "What are you playing at? Are you using that girl?"

The Raven shook his head. He looked genuinely hurt by that accusation. "You know nothing of what we share. Of who she is to me or I to her."

"You're right," Rem said. "And I don't want to know."

"Then don't ask," the Raven said, and Rem thought he saw a genuine plea in the man's eyes—a deep and abiding dread of revealing any more of himself. "I am a cunning man, but I prefer truth to lies. If I'm asked an honest question one too many times, I'll tell the truth. And when you know the truth—"

"I know," Rem said. "Or so you've said. Just...please. Let's keep our mouths mutually shut and not take this association any further than we must."

"As you wish," the Raven said, his eyes still down but his mouth starting to turn up into that half smile again. "You strike me as a man who can keep a secret well—even from his own brave partner."

Rem felt something coil in him. It was on the tip of his tongue to ask what the outlaw meant—but Torval then returned, carrying his full canteen.

The dwarf grabbed the Raven's drinking gourd, filled it from the canteen, and thrust it back between the bars. "Take it," he said.

The Red Raven accepted the offered gourd and drank in short, shallow sips, savoring the water.

Rem withdrew from the cage. Torval followed him.

"I don't like this," the dwarf said.

"Nor should you," Rem said quietly.

"You know something you're not telling me," Torval said, staring at his partner.

Rem nodded. "When next we're alone, I'll tell you everything."

Everything, Rem assured himself. *Every single thing that I've been holding inside for so long. Secrets are dangerous, after all . . .*

CHAPTER TWELVE

It was in the waning light of their fifth day on the road that the company finally arrived at a wall of shadowy pines marking the entrance to the Ethkeraldi Forest. They had crossed the Kaarten River via an ancient stone bridge early on that same day and were now on its north bank. From their vantage point, two by two along the road, stalled before the forbidding barrier of trees and darkness ahead, Rem noted that even the river's curling line was obscured. After a single bend in the river, about five hundred yards on, the forest alone held sway. Even the mighty Kaarten was just one more piece of the landscape that the vast woodland dominated.

The party halted while both scouts, Croften and Galen, rode ahead in search of dangerous road conditions or possible ambush sites. As everyone waited, all atop their horses save Wirren the wain driver on his bench and the Red Raven in his cage trailing the main wagon, the dark wilderness ahead all but beckoned them to enter. To Rem, it looked placid enough: close ranks of spruce and redwood, alder and hemlock, every space among the great trees crammed with bright-green ferns, big-leafed rhododendrons, and leather-leafed salal bushes heavy with dark-blue berries, the silence and stillness broken only by the insistent tap of woodpeckers and the trill of wrens. Behind it all lay the sluicing rush of the river—now tumbling over rockier, more uneven ground than it had back west—underscored by the winds whispering in the gently swaying trees.

It was peaceful. Unspoiled.

And yet Rem could not deny that something about it filled him with a deep and primal fear. The closest thing he could compare it to was the feeling of being a child, alone in his bedchamber at night after the one candle left burning at his bedside had gone out, sure that something—something hungry and unnatural—waited in the dark beneath his bed, or just over the sill of the open window...

Torval leaned in his saddle. "What are we waiting on?" he whispered.

"They're trying to understand it," the Raven said from his cage, a stone's throw ahead of them. "It's a common reaction. Submit to it."

"Hardly," Rem said, attempting to dispel the Raven's mind games as quickly as possible. "They're scouting the road. They'll be back any minute."

"What's to understand?" Torval barked back at the Raven. "It's a forest, isn't it? Trees, rushing water, a bunch of sly beasts and insects—"

"Oh, but the Ethkeraldi's so much more than that," the Raven said, moving forward and grasping the bars of his cage. He was truly relishing this. "The Ethkeraldi's the oldest forest near the coast, and it's hosted fugitives and rebels and bandits since time immemorial. When all of its sister woods to the north, south, and east were being hacked down to build the free cities or the great castles of the kings and queens of Keramia, or to feed winter fires or shore up mine shafts, this great lady's remote location in her long, meandering valley kept her safe—kept her mysterious. The Horunic Empire, which quelled this part of the world more than a thousand years ago, refused to venture in there after a whole legion was lost and never heard from again. That bridge we crossed earlier is the only thing the Horunii left behind. In later days, when this area was part of the Kingdom of Keramia, those who managed to escape Mad King Merrick's persecution and imprisonment usually made their homes here, alone or in small bands, knowing the likelihood of anyone following them was low. After the kingdom's collapse, the worst of her soldiers haunted these roads as brigands and thieves, ranging not just through the valley but over the mountains, as well. And then, of course, there's Hobb's Folly..."

Rem felt a shudder in spite of himself. Hobb's Folly: their sundown destination, where they would make camp and wait, through the long, dark woodland night, for the sunrise. He'd heard the stories and he thought himself a reasonable chap—not prone to excess superstition or unreasonable fear—and yet there was something about the thought of passing a night in that fell place that did not sit well with him.

The sound of hooves preceded the sight of Croften and Galen emerging from the wood on their mounts. The big male scout hove up beside the lord marshal and gave his report while his female counterpart rode back along the line to give her own impressions to Captain Tuvera and the Lady Tzimena.

"Looks like we might be moving," Rem said.

Up ahead, the lord marshal gave a curt order. Their train trundled on, slowly but surely, ever closer to the looming redwoods and glowering pines. The Red Raven's cage creaked and jostled along before them over the stone-strewn, unkempt forest road. At the fore of the company, Galen spurred her horse and went riding back into the woods, apparently now playing forward scout. In a similar change of duties, Croften galloped from the train's head to its rear, carrying on into their wake until he disappeared along the river's muddy bank. Clearly the two scouts had decided to exchange places for a bit.

"What's Hobb's Folly?" Torval asked after a moment's silence.

Rem answered before the Raven could. "An abandoned trade post just a league or so ahead of us, well inside the wood. Legend has it that about five hundred years ago, an impious merchant named Remus Hobb decided what the Ethkeraldi needed to escape its long-darkened reputation was a permanent settlement—a way station of sorts. He laid claim to a large clearing by the river and funded a building project at fantastic expense, bleeding coin for years in order to get workers and materials up here and make his little trade post a reality."

"You know the stories," the Red Raven said with an admiring smile. "You're not even bad at telling them, I'll bet."

"Would you prefer to take over?" Rem asked.

"Wouldn't dream of it," the Raven answered.

"Will someone tell the rest of it?" Torval snapped. "I'm waiting!"

"As the story goes," Rem said, "Hobb got his wish. He built the beginnings of a small town: a lovely inn, a big barn and stables, a few small satellite taverns, a trade post, and some storehouses. For a year or two, everything went just as he'd hoped: travelers did not simply pass through, but were actually drawn there, to see what he'd built out of pure grit and determination. He made back most of his investment, built himself a reputation, and the town grew to a permanent population of about three hundred. There were even children and a school administered by an Aemonic priestess. And the town got a name: Sanctuary."

Rem stopped and drew a deep breath. The smell of the cedar and pine and rank, moist forest loam was intoxicating.

They were passing under the canopy now, the world darkening around them.

"And then?" Torval asked, clearly anticipating a coming disaster.

"And then," Rem continued, "a fierce winter came—the worst in a hundred years by all accounts. The snows in these mountains are, according to most, mild by comparison with those farther inland, in the Ironwalls, or farther north, in my homeland—but that winter, snowdrifts choked the passes in this area more than a month before the winter solstice, cutting off the valley for months. It wasn't until well after the spring thaw that anyone made it to Sanctuary to check in on those trapped through the winter."

Torval stared. Clearly he was engrossed. Rem let his dramatic pause hang in the quiet air. The world around them was close and dark now, a strange, muffled deadness enveloping all they heard, including the dim clop-clop of their horses' hooves. As they passed, he heard small, furry bodies rattling stands of globe sedge and saw clearly the wink of tiny dark eyes peering from the shadows under knots of sorrel and sword ferns. Rem told himself that the world around them was simply wild—alive with rodents and songbirds and scuttling insects and ground fowl—but telling himself that, again and again, did nothing to assuage the feeling that they were being watched.

He carried on, eager to crush his growing paranoia. "Some fur traders stopped in the town and thought it deserted. Eventually they located a great many of the settlement's grown residents—or what was left of them. All that remained were bones, stripped and bearing the marks of gnawing teeth, all piled into a mass grave just fifty paces from Remus Hobb's own house. While the bones were all in a jumble and specific numbers couldn't be identified, they estimated a couple hundred, at least."

He stole a glance at Torval. The dwarf was staring, nose crinkling the slightest bit in disgust, mouth agape in childlike wonder. Rem fought the urge to smile and continued.

"What they found in Hobb's cabin was far worse. Clearly the winter had been terrible, and the people of the town had been forced to start eating one another to survive. Not so unusual, no matter how grim, but it was the scale of the carnage that impressed the trappers. Every man, woman, and child in the village had been murdered and devoured, most of their bones deposited in that grave, but many more built up as grim trophies in the darker corners of Hobb's cabin.

"Hobb himself hadn't made it. They found his desiccated head, still bearing flesh and wisps of hair, laid upon a grim altar as a sort of totem or object of worship. The only survivor of that winter, it appeared, was a single girl child. When they found her, she was sucking the marrow out of the tiny bones of an infant. Some say she even offered the marrow to the newcomers, as though she was completely unaware of what an abominable act she was engaged in.

"It took several months to coax the whole story out of her, but apparently, it went something like this: When food became scarce and the snows hadn't abated, Hobb had taken it upon himself to gather all the children of the village—two dozen or so—into his home. He said it was to protect them, but most felt it was to hold them hostage. Then, with the help of a few accomplices, he gradually worked his way through the town—quietly at first, more deliberately when his plans were no longer deniable. He murdered every one of the adults and ate them, feeding them to the children to keep them fattened and ready for consumption if need be. Any who tried to escape were hunted down and slain by his abettors. When he ran out of victims and only his loyal companions remained, he started getting them to turn on one another. Finally they were all eaten, as well, and only he and the children remained.

"But by that time, the children themselves were accomplices. They had not only grown adept at butchering the victims that Hobb brought them, but had also acquired a taste for the flesh they supped upon. Little by little, Hobb started to note that his supply of children was dwindling, yet the children's hunger remained sated. About the time he tried to tell the children that he, and he alone, would decide who lived and who became meat, the children decided that he—so fat and well fed—could feed them all.

"But they kept his head, as a sign of respect. Those who found that lone girl still dwelling in his cabin said she spoke to the thing, as though Hobb could yet converse with her."

"Gods and devils of the deep...," Torval breathed.

Rem nodded. Even now he tried to imagine what he might feel—what he might try to tell himself to make sense of it all— if he found a child alone in a charnel house eating the remains of a baby. He honestly could not imagine. Even in light of all the wickedness he'd witnessed in Yenara, he was fairly sure that such a horrible sight would simply defy understanding.

"At any rate," he continued, suddenly overwhelmed by the silence, "that's how the place earned its name. Sanctuary became Hobb's Folly, and it's been a locus for legend and superstition ever since. It's obviously just a ruin now, since it has no permanent residents, but most who pass through here still say the place is home to unquiet spirits, and most sensible travelers refuse to camp within sight of the place."

"And that's where we're bedding down tonight?" Torval asked. "Whose bright idea was that?"

"Thank the lord marshal," the Raven said with a smile. "He's bound and determined to show everyone in these woods that he's not afraid of anything—old superstitions and ghosts least of all."

Rem was about to assure Torval that there was nothing to fear—the stories were just stories, after all, and Rem himself did not believe unquiet spirits still haunted the ruins of Hobb's Folly. But at that moment Galen returned to the company at speed, riding right past the lord marshal and hurrying to her captain and her mistress. Rem could not hear her hasty report, but he saw the looks on the women's faces when they received it.

"What is it?" the lord marshal cried from the front of the column. He turned his horse round and rode back along the line toward where Galen sat her own mount, in conference with Tuvera and the Lady Tzimena. "I'm still the leader of this expedition," he barked as he approached, "and I demand to hear your report."

It was Captain Tuvera who answered him, calling so that he could hear, even at a distance. It was her raised voice that allowed Rem and Torval to receive the news, as well.

"Bodies, Lord Marshal. Fresh. Just up ahead."

There were three of them, discarded haphazardly some distance off the road, about halfway between the beaten track and the river, farther south. The whole party hobbled their horses on the road and trudged into the woods behind Galen as she explained to her captain and the lord marshal what had led her to leave the road and investigate. Wirren, the wain driver, and young Brekkon stayed with the cart, the horses, and the prisoner while the others hiked a short distance through the wood to the kill site.

"My horse smelled them," Rem heard Galen say. "When the beast started balking and stamping, I thought she'd gone mad. Then the wind changed and I smelled it..."

They broke through dense underbrush and emerged in a semicleared grove, ringed by madrone and white alder. Almost immediately Rem saw the bodies: one sprawled facedown, the earth beneath him stained darker by all the blood that had run out of him; another speared to a tree on the far side of the copse; a third who seemed to have expired after trying to crawl away, the half-bent positions of his arms and legs and the long, ropy trail of intestines unfurled in his wake suggesting that escape—even survival—had been a foolish dream. Several broken fern fronds, scraped portions of the thick forest loam, and obvious footprints made it clear there had been a great deal of hasty activity there. A few travelers' packs lay strewn about, turned inside out to spill their contents chaotically over the open ground.

"Hit and run, I'd say," Galen continued, as she moved to the dead man sprawled facedown across the clearing. "This lot was here, resting from a hike or something of the sort, and someone hostile found them and beset them. But that's not even the worst part."

She knelt beside the dead man, took a handful of cloth from his thick wool tunic, and yanked. The man's head was drawn up with his body, and they all saw what she meant.

The dead man's face had been torn away. A sharp line of black, coagulated blood suggested that it hadn't been ripped, either, but methodically cut. All that remained was a sticky red ruin, exposing muscle fiber and white bone, all now littered with specks of woodland soil and already crawling with flies.

Rem shot a glance at the Lady Tzimena. To her credit she didn't look away. The young woman stared, grave and somber, just like everyone else, drinking in the horrid sight of that man without a face.

Galen laid him back down again and suggested the others. "The one speared to the tree is missing several fingers and looks like he had teeth yanked right out of his gums. And you can see the crawler's entrails. Someone gutted him and left him to die slow. Probably took every ounce of strength left in him just to make it to the far side of the clearing..."

"Why are we here?" the lord marshal asked. "What is it we're meant to see in this?"

Galen stared at the lord marshal for a moment before turning to her own commander. Captain Tuvera swept her eyes over the grim scene before them. "This slaughter would appear to be its own lesson," she said. "There are dangerous folk about."

"Not just men, either," Croften said, staring at something in a muddy patch of ground on the edge of the scene. Everyone closed on the big scout, and he knelt to show what he'd found: a large broad footprint, clear as an etching, in the moist loam.

Rem recognized the shape of that footprint immediately. Only Torval spoke.

"Orc," the dwarf said.

"He's right," Galen agreed, and crossed the clearing, pointing to yet another small clue lost among the chaos of the scene. "Look here."

Rem saw that she was pointing to an arrow, protruding from a large spruce like a small, sickly limb. The arrow was unusually short, the shaft painted black, fletched with crow feathers.

"Orcish?" Elvaris asked.

"Close," Galen said. She swept her dark, tight braids away from her wrinkled brow. "Goblin."

"Aemon's bones," Wallenbrand said, searching the ground around them. "So that's what this is? Orc-sign? And they've got at least one goblin archer among them?"

Galen shrugged. "So it would seem."

Everyone in the company exchanged worried, wary glances, then began a slow, individual scan of the trees and landscape surrounding them. All at once, the Ethkeraldi Forest—already so dark and ancient and unwelcoming—seemed actively hostile. Carnivorous. *Hungry.*

Rem looked to Torval. His partner was already scanning the trees and the forest shadows around them, all but willing the brutes to show themselves. Rem cursed inwardly. This was the last thing they needed. If there were orcs abroad in this wood and they threatened the caravan, Torval wouldn't beg off until every orc—or he himself—was dead.

It seemed the unquiet spirits haunting their yet-to-be-reached campsite would be the least of their worries...

A little over an hour later, as the day's light faded toward a bruised and dusky purple and the shadows of the forest deepened around them, their party arrived at its ill-starred campsite.

Rem felt a strange sense of disappointment when they rounded a bend in the forest road, saw the tree line before them thinning, and realized that the low, dark huddle of structures up ahead was the infamous ghost town. As they rode into the overgrown clearing that had once been a thriving trade post, Rem thought the place almost welcoming, and certainly more prosaic than he'd imagined. Most of the buildings had collapsed after centuries of neglect, but several of the larger structures still stood under sagging, shattered roofs or behind log walls sprouting hoary moss and colonies of toadstools. The largest of them, squatting in pieces on the south side of the forest road, looked like it might have once been an inn—two stories, broad and tall, with what looked like a long, covered porch along two sides and numerous well-spaced windows in its facade. Sometime before their arrival—decades, probably—a massive spruce had fallen, crushing the sagging roof and shattering the old inn's eastern wall. That fallen tree was now little more than a worm- and insect-riddled shell filled with piles of wood pulp and sprouting fungi, but the mess it had made upon collapsing was unmistakable.

Though the empty foundations of small, long-abandoned houses yet lined the forest road, the greater measure of the little burg's buildings were clustered on the north side. The divided stalls of a onetime stable were unmistakable, even in ruin, as were the squat, round stone base of a granary and the tumbledown bones of an Aemonic church. But lording over them all, raised upon a small knoll and still possessed of both solid walls and the vague sweep of a peaked roof, was the building Rem marked as the manse of Remus Hobb. Surely the man who'd built this place would have chosen that site for himself—elevated, tucked away in the northwest corner of the village, close to the open space that had probably once been a town square and close beside a rocky stream. A tree had fallen on that structure, as well, opening its back end to the elements long, long ago. But if any building on the site had been the home of the arrogant fool who'd tried to make this place thrive, that had to be it.

Rem had never seen anything like it; it was, very literally, a town where no one lived. Not entirely ruined, yet certainly far past its prime and long abandoned. There was just enough form and function remaining in the village's bones to suggest order, a kind of homey neatness, yet sufficient blight and decay to make the camp's long and storied history clear at a glance. It did not frighten him so much as sober him: *Look how easily the natural world crept in to reclaim what mankind had tried to wreak upon it.* At the end of everything, time, nature, and the elements always won.

They chose as their campsite the little clearing that might have once been a town square, on the north side of the road, with old Hobb's ruined manse on one side and the skeletal Aemonic church on the other. The stream was close by, and there was plenty of grass for forage, so the horses were unsaddled and set loose to graze while the company set to its nightly duties. With Wirren's help, Rem and Torval unhitched the Raven's cage from the ox wain and rolled it over uneven ground to a spot just beyond their campsite, nearer the ruins that Rem had marked as onetime stables. The prisoner would be in their line of sight all the time, but at the edge of any light the fire might provide, and too far away to speak or converse with anyone regularly. Concurrently the lord marshal's men and Captain Tuvera's swordmaids split into mixed pairs and began a survey of the area, to work out where the watch posts would be and what approaches provided the most cover for possible attack. As everyone else bent to their labors and prepared to pass the night, the Lady Tzimena and her nurse, Kolia, built a fire and started cooking everyone's supper. This seemed to be the one task the soldiers from Tzimena's retinue and the lord marshal's men would allow her to do in peace, with only minimal objections or intimations that such labor was beneath her.

Rem and Torval were just completing their own hasty camp setup when the Raven deigned to speak with them.

"Could I get out of here?" the Raven asked from behind his bars. "My legs are cramped and my back is killing me. I can't stand up in this thing—"

"I'm fairly certain that's the idea," Torval said as he shoved stones under the cart's wheels to brace them. "You *are* a prisoner, after all."

"Keep me tied," the Raven said. "Keep me chained. I just want to stand upright for a few minutes and have a piss in the bushes instead of through the bloody cage bars."

"Not happening," Rem said. "Even if we trusted you and wanted to allow it, the lord marshal never would."

"So you work for him now?" the Raven asked, putting himself upright on his knees and starting to undo his trousers. Even in such a strange position—crouching, not standing—the Raven still had to turn his head sideward a bit to keep from thumping his skull on the cage bars above him.

"You know gods-damned well we don't work for him," Torval said, truly offended. "We're not going through this again."

"Of course not," the Raven said, loosing a stream of urine through the bars onto the ground below. "I've heard you say it a hundred times now: I'm nothing but a pay purse for the pair of you."

"See?" Torval said to Rem. "He's learning."

"The good news is," Rem said, "there doesn't appear to be rain in store tonight. So there's no need to put the tarp on you. You get to sleep under the stars, with nothing but the sounds of the forest and the wind in the trees around you."

As if in answer to Rem's description, a horrible scream tore through the stillness of the woodland evening. Rem heard the beat of bird wings in answer to the scream, fleeing that sound for a safer perch elsewhere. A quick glance at the campsite told him the others had heard it, as well.

Torval looked genuinely frightened. "What in the sundry hells was that?"

Rem clapped the dwarf on the shoulder to reassure him. "Just a hillcat. They can be dangerous one-on-one, but it won't come around here—not with so many of us tromping about."

The Raven settled back into a sitting position again, his trousers laced. "Let's just hope the lot of you make it through the night," he said smugly. "This place . . . There's a blight upon it. Maybe it's haunted, or maybe it's just poisoned ground, but most who dare to camp here flee before the night is done. I've never known a single person to spend a whole night here without something terrible befalling them."

"Something terrible," Torval huffed. "Like what?"

The Raven shrugged. "Hard to say. The place knows you. It can look right into the center of you. It'll know what it needs to show you to expose your fears, your darkness."

"Poppycock," Torval muttered, trying to forcibly shove his fear of just moments ago aside. He trudged away toward the ever-growing campsite, twenty yards from where they'd secured the cage.

Rem was about to follow his partner when the Raven's steady gaze caught his own. For what seemed an eternity, the two men stared at one another. It was an appraisal, Rem knew. A sizing up. He did his best not to look intimidated.

"I'm not exaggerating," the Raven said quietly, calmly. "This is dangerous country. Surely the bodies you found earlier prove that."

Rem shuddered, recalling the dead man with no face.

The Raven made a strange face: a mask of both worry and sadness. "I can't help you if you don't give me a reason to."

"Help me?" Rem asked, incredulous.

"The both of you," the Raven said, "you and your little partner. I told you, I bear you no grudge. But when things get bad—"

"Stop right there," Rem said, moving close to the cage. "You think we're a pair of babes in these woods? That we've never faced death? Never killed? That's our stock-in-trade, sir. Every gods-damned night we wander about looking for your kind: criminals, miscreants, whoremongers, and thieves. For the record, I don't trust you *or* the lord marshal, but even distrusting you both, I'm not afraid of you, either. And neither is Torval. So stop trying to intimidate us."

"I'm trying to make sure you make it home alive," the Raven said slowly, earnestly. "You don't understand what you've stumbled into the middle of here, or that you play no important role in it whatsoever. When things get bad—and they *will* get bad, now that we've entered the forest—you and your companion become the two most expendable members of this expedition."

"What should we do, then?" Rem asked. "Run home, empty-handed?"

"Better," the Raven said, still speaking under his breath. "Get me out of here and I'll pay you myself. You know who I am. You know I've got treasure troves all through these woods."

"And earn the ire of a duke and his lord marshal?" Rem answered. "No thank you."

"I'll treat fairly with you," the Raven said. "They won't."

"The lord marshal's a hard man," Rem countered. "Unbending, a bit of a prig, but he's bonded by a ducal seat and subject to his own sense of honor. He'll treat fairly with us, if only to prove to himself what a fine, upright fellow he is. You, on the other hand, do nothing but try to ingratiate yourself to us—to earn our trust, or our pity. Which of those two people should I trust, I wonder? The one who honestly doesn't give two shits about me but who values his own honor and reputation, or the one who keeps trying mightily to be my friend because I have the keys to his cage?"

The Raven shrugged. "Fine. I've said my piece. Done my best. When it all goes sour, I'll still try to do right by you and keep you out of danger—but I make no promises."

"As it should be," Rem said, and turned to leave. "I wouldn't trust any promises you made to me in any case." He walked away then, knowing that if he allowed it, he would stand there verbally sparring with the outlaw all night.

CHAPTER THIRTEEN

"So let me get this straight," Elvaris said from her side of the crackling fire. "There are close to fifty thousand souls in your ward, but there's only a hundred-odd guardsmen to keep them all in line?"

"We prefer the term *watchwarden*," Torval said, "because they're not all *men*."

"Aye, that," Rem added. "And there's more like two-hundred-odd—one company on the day shift, one on the night."

"But only a hundred on the streets at any given time?" Redriga, the executive officer of the Lady Tzimena's company, broke in. She was a handsome woman, between forty and fifty, wearing her armor with ease but with a soft, placid face like a schoolmarm or a baker's wife.

"That's right," Rem said. "As for fifty thousand, that's probably a fair estimate, because that'd be about one-fifth of the city's population, but truth be told, it's probably more. By all accounts, there are more people crammed into the Fifth than any other part of the city."

Elvaris raised her cup and toasted the two of them. "Huzzah to you and the dwarf, then. From where I sit, that's madness." She drank, not waiting for anyone else to join her toast. She was a good soldier—a good mate—based upon Rem's little interaction with her—honest and forthright, if a little blunt and graceless. But wouldn't he like to see her put that Taverando blade of hers to use?

"Sounds mad," young Sandiva added, shaking her head in disbelief. "They don't even put you in armor?"

"The city guard gets armor," Torval said, taking a bite of one of his pickled eggs. "Pretty toffs, that lot. And useless."

"The city guard," Captain Tuvera said. "Those were the men in chain mail and surcoats who guarded the gate?"

Rem and Torval both nodded.

"And here I thought they were the ones who patrolled the streets," the captain said, almost to himself.

"That would require them to get up off their well-heeled arses and move," Rem responded, hearing the bitterness in his own voice. "Not something they take to without the right motivation."

"Well," began the scout, Galen. She reminded Rem of Emacca, the Tregga horse nomad, back home: a hard, striking face under ropes of tight black braids, her eyebrows permanently knitted into a contracted scowl. "From where I sit," she continued, a sly smile now spreading across her stony countenance, "these lads are like some Kosterling heroes from the sagas of old—two brave souls against a pitiless world, damn the consequences, never backing down—"

"You'll have to forgive Galen," Redriga said. "She's a bit of a romantic."

"We have a saying," Torval said, meeting Galen's gaze over the fire. "*Eyes open, fists clenched, back to the wall.*"

Galen's sly smile widened to a grin. She nodded approvingly. "I like that! I like that very much!"

"It's hard work," Wallenbrand said. "Keeping the peace."

"Never took to it, myself," big Croften said, then belched and smiled crookedly. "Disturbing it is more my speed."

Rem laughed at the scout's pronouncement, but stole a glance at the lord marshal as he did so. As he'd suspected, Harcta Kroenen was glaring at the two men as if the very act of joining in a group conversation or making a jest was tantamount to dereliction of duty.

An epiphany struck him, wholly unbidden. *They're not his men*, Rem thought. *There's no camaraderie, no discipline, no shared history. Wallenbrand, Croften, Wirren... He barely knows them. And yet here they are, in his employ... Why?*

"Well, you're certainly a brave pair," Captain Tuvera broke in. Rem guessed she was about ten years his senior. Old enough to be experienced, but still young for a command role. She was either some important person's cousin, or she was actually as good as her position suggested. "I, for one, wouldn't relish wandering the streets of that city of yours. I'm sure she has her charms, but what I saw of it just left me impatient and claustrophobic. So many people crammed behind those walls..."

Rem's pondering was thrust aside. Now Captain Tuvera's words reminded him of home, and he felt wistful. He still remembered his own first impressions of Yenara: the bustle, the crowds, the interminable fog and the clouds of stinking smoke and the way the bent and meandering streets betrayed no pattern, suggested no inherent sense in their arrangement...

"'A city of smoke and shadow,'" he quoted from memory, "'the place from which all the roads of the world unravel and to which all the pilgrims of the world strive. She is Yenara. She is her own mistress, and she will have no master.'"

"Tyr Lyrios," the Lady Tzimena offered. "*A Traveler in the West.*" They all raised their eyes. She'd retreated to her pavilion a short while earlier, but had now returned. Almost as one, all those around the fire—Rem, Torval, the Eraldic company, the Estavaris—shot to their feet and stood at attention.

"Heavens," Tzimena said. "That's hardly necessary. Sit down, the lot of you."

They did as she bade. Even after they'd resumed their seats, the lady kept standing. Tuvera quickly stood from her place on the log that she and her companions shared and offered her mistress a seat.

"Milady," she said, by way of invitation.

"Sit down, Captain," the Lady Tzimena responded. "I've spent all day in the saddle. I'm perfectly content to stand for a bit."

Haltingly, Tuvera obeyed.

Tzimena's eyes were back on Rem now, betraying something like amazement and admiration. "You're well-read, sir. And such a memory…"

"I think that bit's been swirling through my head since I arrived in Yenara, milady. I never understood it, really, until I saw her for myself."

"Nor I," Tzimena said. "I'm most impressed you had that quotation so ready at hand."

"With respect, milady," Torval said, "you shouldn't be too impressed. The Bonny Prince here's always got some pretty bit of dusty old poetry tumbling out of his yapping gob. Not the sense the gods gave a goat, though…"

The soldiers all laughed, instantly recognizing good-natured brotherly ball-breaking when they heard it. Rem smiled, but in truth, he knew he had probably turned beet red. *Was that really necessary, Torval? In front of the lady … ? In front of them all … ?*

"Bonny Prince," the Lady Tzimena said, as though trying to make sense of the words.

"A most unfortunate nickname," Rem quickly interjected. "One this obstreperous little bastard won't let go of. I assure you, I'm as lowborn as they come—"

"Well, look at him," Torval said, suddenly reaching out and pinching Rem's flushed cheek. "He's so very pretty!"

The soldiers, male and female, all burst into laughter again at that. Rem yanked his face out of Torval's grip. "That's enough," he hissed to his partner.

"Not nearly," Torval whispered back.

Rem thought the laughter was warm and welcome, however irritating it might be to be its subject. He wondered why it had taken them all so long to come to an evening like this—easy talk, sharing their own stories, a real sense of oneness and common purpose binding them. Then he realized what was different.

They were camped in Hobb's Folly. Benighted. Haunted. Accursed.

Perhaps that was where all this warmth and fraternity was coming from? For the first time, they felt out of their depth, off the proverbial map...endangered.

It wasn't that they had grown to love and respect one another. It was that they were reaching out, seeking solace, sharing strength.

Rem certainly knew it was true of himself. He would simply assume it was true of the others.

"Well," the lady said, "I, for one, know just how you felt. I was only in Yenara for a few days, but I thought it a most wondrous place. Frightening at first—overwhelming, really—but so alive. So deeply, dangerously, beautifully alive."

"All due respect, milady," Redriga broke in, "but I'll take our homeland any day. There's no place finer or more beautiful."

"And what's in Toriel?" Torval asked. "Grass and goats? A few pretty storybook castles?"

Redriga looked like she might be mildly insulted. She sat

up straight and set her palms on her knees. "No doubt, master dwarf, you've a different notion of what beauty might be, but I can assure you, there's more in Toriel than grass and goats."

"It's a good-sized city, as I recall," Rem said. "Twenty thousand or so?"

"Aye," Captain Tuvera said, nodding. "You're not just a reader, you're a geographer."

"She stands on a high hill above a rolling plain," Redriga carried on. "Golden sandstone walls enclosing close, quiet streets and shady plazas. From her battlements you can see the Red Mountains off to the southwest, and on clear days you'd almost swear you could see the Ironwalls on the northern horizon..."

"That sounds lovely, indeed," Brekkon broke in. The young soldier wore his enthusiasm and earnestness on his sleeve, the complete opposite of his tight-lipped, implacable father. Rem often felt sorry for the boy. "But surely none of you have seen Erald. She sits on a promontory, where highlands slope down to the fields of the surrounding valley. The Kaarten River flows right through the center of the city, including Reiken Falls. You can sit in a paved plaza, enjoying mead and honey buns, staring at the roaring waters as they tumble down the hillside and carry on, foaming west toward the bay and the sea."

"A waterfall in the middle of the city?" Elvaris countered. She shook her head. "If I had to listen to that roar all the time, I'd never stop needing a piss." She suddenly remembered the Lady Tzimena was still present. "Apologies, milady—"

The Lady Tzimena, to her credit, only smiled like a rueful babysitter and shook her head. "You're incorrigible, Elvaris. As you were, everyone." And with that she turned and drifted away again, once more swallowed by the darkness beyond the firelight.

"You're from the north," Brekkon said to Rem. "Don't you

ever miss it? Your homeland? Certainly, whatever Yenara has to offer, it's not the place that bore you and bred you? The place you're from?"

"We're not always from the place where we belong," Rem said, without even thinking. A moment later, the words having left his lips, he thought of Indilen. In that instant—so far from her, around a fire with a bunch of strangers, thinking of how he'd found her, like a treasure just waiting for his discovery— he missed her more than he had in all the days previously combined. He positively ached for her presence.

Beside Rem, Torval raised his mug, the beer inside sloshing. "True, that," the dwarf said, and let his blue-eyed gaze fall over all around the fire. "Here's to home—wherever we may find it."

They all raised their cups. "To home!" they said, and drank.

Only the lord marshal was silent, sitting straight backed on his folding camp stool as if all this warmth and nostalgia were the lowest of indulgences.

When Rem had emptied his own cup, he realized that he was long overdue for a piss himself. He rose, his legs—cramped from daytime saddle soreness and now from using that same saddle as a too-low stool to sit upon beside the fire—screaming in protest.

"If you'll excuse me, everyone," he said, then stepped over his saddle, making a beeline into the darkness toward the stream, in search of a nice, lonely thicket in which to relieve himself. It wasn't until he'd put some distance between himself and the campfire, and meandered through a few far-strewn, twisted trees, that he remembered where he was once more.

Hobb's Folly, at night, in the dark.

If there was a moon or stars above, the trees obscured them. With the chatter of the men and Torval now behind him, the only sounds were the scrabble of tiny claws in the underbrush and the sighing of the wind snaking plaintively through the tall pines and glowering redwoods surrounding them. Somewhere a screech owl let out a foul, barking hoot.

Rem stopped. Looked around. Blinked. He wanted his eyes to adjust. Traipsing off into all that darkness, all that emptiness, left him more than a little uneasy. He found a nearby tree and put his back to it.

Enjoy this, he thought. *The silence. The darkness. Think of Indilen. Think of home. We'll be through these woods in a few days, home in a few weeks. Soon she'll be back in your arms.*

The wind subsided and the trees stopped whispering. In the darkness Rem suddenly heard voices.

"...Don't understand," someone said. It was a woman, trying to speak low, but still audible. "Why won't you tell them?" It was the Lady Tzimena.

"Those watchwardens won't believe me and your soldiers won't care. The lord marshal holds all the cards here. He's the one I've got to neutralize and overcome." That was the Red Raven.

"I could vouch for you," the lady said.

"Then you'd be as good as dead," the Raven answered. "No. Keep your mouth shut, as you promised. I'll get us out of this, but you have to trust me."

Rem felt a strange shudder run through him.

I'll get us out of this, but you have to trust me.

Gods, what was he planning?

"They're coming for you," Tzimena said, "aren't they?"

A long silence.

"Just be ready," the Raven said. His voice was low, earnest, grave. "They'll free me, and we can be away. I gave them strict orders to hurt no one, so long as they pose no direct threat to our escape."

The words echoed in Rem's mind. *Just be ready. They'll free me, and we can be away.*

Rem felt a chill run through him, starting at the base of his spine and radiating to the tips of his fingers. *They.* The Devils of the Weald. They were going to free their master.

"There's got to be another way," Tzimena argued.

"I'm still waiting for a viable suggestion," the Raven answered. Rem could hear the smile in his voice—the irony. Even here, now, whispering with the young lady in the dark, he was still using his considerable charms to set her at ease. "Hurry back now. They'll miss you if you're gone too long."

"I trust you, Korin," the lady said. "Don't make me sorry that I did."

Away she went, her light, fast footsteps barely audible, even in the near silence of the big, black forest.

What had she called him? *Korin?* An old Keramian name, that. Probably not too common outside of noble families. And didn't Rem once hear of a nobleman hereabouts with that name? Where was it? When was it?

Then it hit him.

The shudder ran all through him this time.

No . . . no, that couldn't be, could it?

It wasn't easy drawing Torval away from the others without raising any curiosity among them. Luckily, the night was winding down and everyone was preparing to settle in for a good sleep, so all Rem really had to do was gently steer Torval aside, far from their camp, all the way across the forest road to a small, tumbledown ruin on its southern verge. In the light Rem had marked it for a onetime smithy. In the dark it was just a deeper darkness in which to enfold themselves.

"We need to talk," Rem said quietly.

"Look, I was just having a laugh, was all," Torval said, sounding contrite. "Don't take it to heart, lad—"

"It's not about that," Rem said.

Torval straightened, face turning grim. Clearly he heard the need in Rem's voice.

Rem took another look around. Listened for the sound of footsteps or breathing. They appeared to be alone.

"I overheard the Lady Tzimena and the Red Raven talking. She snuck off to see him and didn't realize I was off in the brush."

Torval shook his head. "Thendril's tits..."

"Wait," Rem said, "it's worse than just that. He told her that his friends here in the wood—or *someone*—will try to spring him. He kept telling her to be ready."

"We've got to tell the lord marshal, then," Torval said.

"No," Rem countered. "I'm still not finished. Torval, Tzimena called the Raven by a name—*his* name, I suppose. Korin—an old name, Keramian, basically only used sparingly in a few noble families in this region."

Torval was staring, his eyes narrowing suspiciously. "Go on."

"It nudged something in my memory—just like his face did, when we first brought him back to the watchkeep. I kept trying to figure out where I'd heard that old name attached to a living person before, because I was sure I had. Then it hit me: five years ago, the newly crowned Duke of Erald died in these woods, murdered by bandits on a hunting expedition. It was terrible news and it made the rounds of all the noble families from the Marches to the Red Mountains. That young man's brother became the new Duke of Erald—the one we're about to deliver the Red Raven to. The present Duke of Erald's name is Verin Lyr, and his brother's name—"

"His brother's name was Korin," Torval finished.

"Exactly. Korin Lyr, the Duke of Erald, lost in *these* woods."

Torval nodded thoughtfully. "Aye," he said. He was staring at Rem now, doubtful.

"Do you see what I'm suggesting? I don't know why he disappeared—maybe he was actually threatened, or kidnapped, or held for ransom. But one way or another, he was taken for dead by his family and country, while he lived on here, in these woods, as an outlaw."

"Mmm," Torval grunted. "But didn't Ondego also say stories of the Raven had been making the rounds for ten or fifteen years? I couldn't swear on it, but I'm fairly sure I heard tales of him back when I left the Ironwalls."

"Puzzling," Rem said, "but not impossible to reconcile. Maybe there was already a Red Raven, but the heir took his place? Maybe the Devils of the Weald actually did take Korin Lyr hostage, but he eventually earned a place among them? Those would be my guesses."

"Mmm," Torval said again. He was staring now.

"Why are you looking at me like that?" Rem asked, knowing damned well why.

Time's come, he thought. *Give it to him.*

"How do *you* know all this?" Torval asked. "The prevalence of an old name among Keramian noble houses? The disappearance of the heir? The way that disappearance shook the nobility far and wide?"

Rem took a deep breath. "Well, I suppose that's the rest of it, Torval," Rem said, doing his best to keep his gaze steady. "You've let me escape this for a good long while now. I suppose it's time you knew. I trust you, after all—trust you with my life."

"Knew what?"

"I'm not just a groom's son raised in a lord's house," Rem said. "I'm not even a younger son of some rich family out looking for adventure. I'm Remeck Stromm, son and heir to Kürek Stromm, the Grand Duke of Lycos...and I died to get away from home."

CHAPTER FOURTEEN

Torval was silent for a long time. Waiting through that long, interminable silence that would decide whether the two of them would remain friends henceforth, or whether Rem's subterfuge had destroyed what they'd built, was a mighty struggle. In the interim Rem scanned the woods and the campsite around them. The others were busy with their presleep rituals near the campfire. The horses, tethered in a small copse on the other side of the road, cropped placidly at the grasses about their hooves, silent and resigned. Again an owl screeched in the distance, and Rem wished the damned, accursed old raptor would just shut up already.

"What do you mean, *you died*?" Torval asked.

"I mean I faked my death. I went for rides in the woods alone quite often—more often than my father wished. Slipping my bodyguards and setting out on my own was a favorite game of mine, even as a grown man. After planning to make my exit, I abandoned my horse in the woods, left blood around the scene, then used a stolen skiff to speed downriver and put some distance between myself and my home. Traveling in yeoman's clothes, no one gave me a second look. The news of my apparent death didn't even start to move up and down the Pilgrim Road until I'd made it almost all the way to Yenara, a month later."

"Why?" Torval asked. The word was spoken quietly, but the

command in it was implicit. They weren't having a conversation now. This was an interrogation.

Rem kept his gaze steady. "Everything I've told you about my father—how hard of heart he was, how unwelcome I felt in his presence—that's all true. The only part I withheld was the truth of what he wanted from me, and what I denied him. He'd been angling for years to align with one of the other grand duchies of the Marches, to try and consolidate holdings and maybe create a new monarchy in Hasturland. I was his pawn in those plans. My whole life had been pushed and prodded toward that unwavering destiny, to bring a crown and a true throne back to the people of the north. But it also meant I never had choices. I couldn't choose my friends...my lovers...my confidantes or counselors."

"So," Torval said, his voice carrying a note of bitterness, "you ran away."

"Children run away," Rem said, as he'd once said to Ondego. "I left."

"Men *without* responsibilities leave," Torval said. "You ran away, leaving your family and your whole country in the lurch, no doubt. What do you think happened after you disappeared, eh? Was there another heir? Or would your father's duchy—all that he'd inherited and built and hoped to build—now forfeit because his snot-nosed brat couldn't handle the responsibilities bequeathed to him?"

Rem felt sick to his stomach. He'd expected one of two things: either Torval would laugh off the news and tell him he'd suspected as much all along, or he'd storm off in fury, hurt and angry that he'd been lied to. But for some reason, Rem had not expected *this*—a pointed, purposeful challenge to his motivations and desires, a questioning of his very worth. And yet he should have expected it, shouldn't he? Torval was the best of men—or dwarves. He'd only broken with his own folk when they refused to accept his petition for change. But he'd never abandoned his family or his personal responsibilities. Instead he'd marched off into the world to meet them, head-on, and woe betide anyone who dared stand in his way.

"You know what the responsibilities of feeding your family—and your children—feel like, Torval," Rem finally said, working hard to keep his voice low. "But you have no idea what the weight of a kingdom and a crown feels like. Especially when the person who should be teaching you to do it all for yourself—to better *become* yourself—is making all of your choices for you and using you as little more than a puppet for their own ambition."

"Answer my question, gods damn you," Torval said. "Was there anyone to take your place?"

"If I had to choose, I'd have handed it all to my sister, Anjevine," Rem said. "She was regal from the womb, and smarter and more responsible than I would ever have been. But, knowing my father and the ways of the Hasturfolk, who aren't fond of female rule, it probably fell to my little brother, Leriok. I had faith he'd do just fine. He was irresolute, perhaps, but a good lad with a good heart. I had to trust he'd learn to stand up for himself, even if he hadn't already."

That part was a bit of a lie, but Rem hoped Torval could forgive him for it. In truth, Rem had never been sure Leriok could handle the strain of ruling in his stead. If there was any part of his flight from home that still haunted Rem when he was sleepless or nostalgic, it was that: What had become of Leriok? Had he, ultimately, been able to embrace his fate as the newly dubbed heir apparent and flourish? Or had the weight of it all crushed him? Would all those competing voices and influences, from their own iron-willed father to the various self-interested courtiers of the privy counsel, help him better become the man he was always meant to be, or forcibly mold him to sit a throne that never should have been his?

Rem's guilty reverie was shattered by a sudden hard, loud sound. It was the sound of Torval's calloused hand striking Rem's face. It was a heavy, muscular hand, and it hurt. Rem felt his face flush. A fury shot through him, like fire in his veins.

But the fury wasn't outward. It was inward. *You should have known it would come to this*, he thought. *You were wrong all along, foolish all along. He's not wrong to be hurt by this, or to think less of you—you were wrong to think you could ever shirk your duties . . . your responsibilities.*

And Torval—the best of men, or dwarves—knows that.

You've let him down, and it kills you, doesn't it?

"Does Indilen know?" Torval asked. The fact that he kept his voice barely above a whisper was truly impressing Rem. Clearly he was angry, but he hadn't lost his self-control.

Rem nodded, trusting that Torval, with his dwarvish night vision, could see him well even in the dark. "Months ago, after that mess with the stonemasons. She understood. She's still by my side, isn't she?"

"Well, so am I," the dwarf said, sounding both angry and earnestly committed all at once. "But this . . . All this . . . What you did . . ."

"You left your people behind—your whole world—because they denied you a choice. I did the same. I know I fled my duties and my responsibilities, but I also never asked for them— just like you were never asked whether you'd rather be a miner or a warrior."

Torval grunted, turned, and began to pace. Rem felt a little better at that. The pacing meant he was thinking, and when Torval stopped to think about things, he almost always made the right decision—the compassionate one. The silence that fell as Torval paced and Rem waited was some of the bitterest, most lonely silence that Rem had ever known in his life. This dwarf—this excellent, honorable, courageous, ardent dwarf—was the best friend Rem had ever known, and a companion whose respect—whose understanding—meant everything to him. If finally revealing all of this cost him even a small speck of all the respect he'd earned, he would never forgive himself...

"So you think," Torval began, "that our Red Raven pulled the same sort of stunt—faked his death to duck the crown, then found he liked a life of banditry and murder?"

Rem was puzzled. "Torval, you do understand—"

"This isn't about *you* anymore," Torval hissed. "We've got bigger fish to fry. Do you think that's his angle? Royal heir gone bad? Essentially just a troublemaker and runaway?"

Rem thought about that, then shook his head. "No. And I'll tell you why: Tzimena. We've barely interacted with her, true, but she doesn't strike me as a shallow or wicked young lady. If she's still worried about him—still invested in him, somehow—then we have to assume there's some honorable angle in what he's doing. Something she can use to convince herself that he's trustworthy."

"But *is* he?" Torval asked.

Rem shrugged. "Probably not. It could be he genuinely has some affection for her, and doesn't want to see her hurt, but my impression of him is one of cunning and craft. If he wants something, he'll find a way to get it. If he has to wait for it, or take great pains to achieve it, he's got the patience to see it through."

"Why would he run away from his crown, then?" Torval asked. "Why the subterfuge?"

"That brings me to another part of their conversation," Rem

said, silently glad that they were no longer discussing him. "He told Tzimena that she shouldn't make his identity known or speak on his behalf—that if she did so, she'd be in danger, namely from the lord marshal."

"So he doesn't trust the lord marshal," Torval said. "We already knew that."

Rem nodded. "But there was surety in his voice. He also told her that when his people attack, no one would be harmed if they did not pose a direct threat."

Torval straightened. "Do you believe that?"

Rem shook his head. "Why do you think we're talking?"

"So he didn't just run away," Torval began.

"He fled," Rem finished. "He's not in Erald, on his throne, because he *can't* be. Maybe his supposed death, on that hunting trip, wasn't planned by him, but by his brother? The one who now holds the title? Or the lord marshal himself, trying to eject an independent young duke for a more tractable one?"

Torval nodded slowly. "That makes a little more sense."

"But you see why I'm worried by all this?"

Torval nodded again. "Oh, aye. That snake's waiting for his highwaymen to attack, those Estavari swordmaidens will fight to the death to defend the lady, and the lord marshal clearly wants the Red Raven dead—and he'll probably be willing to murder anyone—you, me, and the Lady Tzimena included—to keep him from either escaping or proving to the world who he really is."

Rem sighed. "And here we are, caught in the middle."

Torval hung his head. "Bollocks."

"We can't let on, can we?"

Torval considered carefully. "No. Sick as it makes me, we can't. I don't care to sit around waiting for the Devils of the Weald to ambush us, but if we try to confront the lord marshal with this—"

"—We're dead for sure," Rem finished.

Torval shook his head, ran his hands over his bald scalp, then stamped his feet in frustration. "Gods, what've we stepped into?"

"No point asking that right now," Rem said. "The next question is, what do we do?"

Torval resumed his pacing, and Rem waited patiently for a reply. After a minute or so, the dwarf offered his only solution.

"We wait. We keep our eyes peeled. When and if the Devils attack, we keep our skins intact. I want that gold as badly as you do, boy, but from here on, I'll settle for just making it home."

"And what if the Raven was lying to Tzimena?" Rem asked. "What if the Devils don't give a damn who they kill when they try to spring him?"

Torval shrugged the slightest bit. "Then we kill the Red Raven, to deny them their prize—and we kill any of the bastards who threaten us. *Home*, lad—that's all that matters now."

Rem thought of Indilen. He was sick with missing her, with needing her. He'd say a prayer to every god he'd ever petitioned as he fell asleep tonight, hoping to make it home to her in one piece.

"Home," he said to Torval, the single word carrying greater import than he ever could have imagined it was capable of bearing.

CHAPTER FIFTEEN

Rem slept fitfully that night, his mind trying to iterate all the ways in which the Red Raven's freedom from that cage could materialize, and all the ways in which that freedom could kill Rem and Torval. He wrestled with the guilt of self-interest; with a certain amount of shame in trying to prepare himself not to do his duty, to let a notorious outlaw flee without a fight; with the sincere hope that, whenever the attack came, it would come quickly, and he and Torval could withdraw from the violence without injury and then be on their way home. He was even reasonably sure he would spend another night camping in the terrible ruins of Hobb's Folly if it meant he was heading back toward Yenara and not farther away.

He fell asleep for a time, but woke in short order, hounded by a horrible dream. In it he'd been sleeping in Hobb's Folly, the fire crackling, wind tickling the trees above him, a hillcat screaming in the distance. Everyone around him lay still, a few snoring.

Rem had risen, filled with a terrible sense of urgency—a gut-deep dread that urged him to go to the Raven's cage, to check on their clever prisoner.

But it wasn't the Raven in the cage. It was Geezer. He lay on his side, face ashen in the moonlight, eyes staring sleepily into the maw of death as blood seeped out of him and stained the straw lining the cage.

"I curse you," he whispered, as though reciting a prayer before sleep. "I curse you both. I call down Hyryn's wrath, beg for Serath's snare..."

I'm sorry, Rem tried to say, but he had no voice.

Cold hands settled on Rem's shoulders. He smelled lavender and grave mold. A woman's voice—Rikka's voice—whispered in his ear.

"You shall be broken on Ghagar's table," she rasped. "Swallowed by Meimis, snatched by Kraet—"

He opened his eyes, heart hammering in his chest. He lay awake for a long time after that, trying to banish the dream from his mind and failing miserably.

By morning, it felt like he hadn't slept at all, but he knew that wasn't entirely true. There had been dreams—some terrible, some prosaic, some just plain bizarre—and the ghosts of them ran circles round the empty spaces in his head as he clawed his way up out of the murk of exhaustion and welcomed the gray dawn light of a new day. Sullen and tired eyed, Rem trudged down to the riverbank, stripped naked, and gave himself a bracing bath in the frigid waters of the Kaarten, hoping to both steel and awaken himself for whatever the day might hold. By the time he had made it back to camp, fasts were already being broken and the soldiers were preparing their mounts to begin the day's ride.

Torval had taken the initiative that morning and made breakfast for the two of them: cheese; dried fruit; a bag of roasted, salted nuts; and some beer from the little keg Aarna had sent along with them. The dwarf even offered one of his prized pickled eggs, but Rem politely refused.

"Fried, yes, pickled, no," he said. "But I do appreciate the offer."

Torval shrugged, fished one of the eggs from the jar, and

went about wolfing it down. When he had nearly made it disappear, he leaned closer to Rem and spoke quietly, blowing sulfuric breath with the astringent tinge of vinegar toward his partner.

"I want to apologize," Torval said. "For last night."

Rem stared at him, honestly puzzled.

"I shouldn't have said those things," the dwarf said. "Sometimes I forget that the boundaries of honor are not so clearly drawn as we would have them. If your father truly used you as you said, and if you were truly trapped, as you said, then you were right to go. You owed them nothing. Your life is your own."

Rem studied the dwarf. He saw the sincerity in his eyes, the earnest desire for understanding and reconciliation. For a moment he thought of Leriok again: a fresh-faced boy, five years his junior, always eager to please and slow to complain, capable, but hardly gifted. He imagined that boy mourning his big brother, lost to bandits in the woods...and then imagined that same boy, his youth instantly snuffed out when the expectations and requirements of a future throne were thrust upon him.

Your life is your own, Torval had said. But was it?

Rem thrust the thought of his brother—his guilt—from his mind, shrugged, and made sure no one was nearby to hear them. So assured, he offered his own apology.

"I'm sorry I kept it from you for so long," he said.

"Your life is your own," Torval said again, this time with a portentous emphasis. "You owe no one an explanation—not even me."

"That's where you're wrong," Rem said. "I was born into my family—pure accident, no choice in the matter. But you, old stump, you're the family I've chosen. You are the brother and friend that I want—that I need. Let me swear, from this moment forth, to never keep secrets from you again. I trust you with my life. I hope you know you can trust me with yours."

Torval held up his beer mug. "Aye, that, my brother. I know it all too well."

They touched mugs lightly, then drank. After a moment Torval sighed.

"I shan't call you Bonny Prince anymore," he said.

Rem raised an eyebrow. "Oh?"

Torval shrugged. "It's just not funny if it's actually true."

The dwarf looked at Rem askance then and gave him a crooked, mischievous grin.

Rem could only laugh and shake his head.

They were underway as the first rays of the rising sun cut down through the treetops, made solid by the lingering mists. Deep in the recesses of the wood, thrushes and warblers made merry, and the sound of the tumbling Kaarten echoed through the empty cathedral of the pillared sylvan landscape like the murmuring of slowly waking gods in chambers beneath the earth. The air was alternately warm and cold, welcoming and biting, as strange breezes whipped among the redwoods, set the willows murmuring, and slithered through copses of fern and sorrel. Rem and Torval tried to occupy themselves with occasional idle conversations about home and the humdrum—funny anecdotes about their coworkers, tales of family life, remembrances of some of their favorite collars in their shared year together. But try as they might to keep things casual and freewheeling, Rem could still sense that there was a pall over everything. Up ahead of them, the Red Raven sat placidly in his cage, for once not engaging them in conversation. He amused himself with grabbing close-passing boughs, then slowly, methodically pulling leaves from them, as though counting inwardly or taking some silent inventory.

Rem studied the man, finally eager to see if he could manage a true, unbiased appraisal of him. He was a little older than Rem—probably thirty, maybe even thirty-five—but though hard living had lined his face, he still had a young man's vigor and spirit. His ability to chat up a stranger, to laugh, to seem thoroughly earnest and open when, in fact, he was probably just sounding for a weakness to be exploited, all suggested that he hadn't lost any of the diplomatic or political acumen that he'd gained during his years in the Eraldic court. He might look like an itinerant lute player, but he was still a political creature.

But what had happened to him? That was what occupied the greater measure of Rem's curiosity. If it was true that his brother had sought to murder him and seize the duchy for himself, how, then, had Korin Lyr escaped the assassin's blade and managed to become an already-famous woodland outlaw? Rem supposed there could be any number of explanations. He could have ingratiated himself with the real Red Raven and then been deemed a worthy successor when the man died or retired. He could just as easily have challenged or murdered the previous Red Raven and claimed his mantle. If the Devils of the Weald were outlaws, they would respond to a show of force and superior prowess, wouldn't they? Or perhaps they were the ones who'd legitimized him? Perhaps he'd joined their company after a period of captivity as a rank-and-file robber, only to prove his worth and eventual superiority to their previous leader? If the robbers backed a new leader, there was little their old one could do about it.

Look at yourself, Rem thought. *You left home without a destination, without a plan. You ended up in Yenara. You were arrested after a drunken brawl, saved the watchward prefect from a would-be murderer, and then talked your way into a job. Must it have been so different for this man? Hells, couldn't you have been him? What if you'd decided to go to Kaarth instead of Yenara? You could've been passing through these very woods as a traveler, been taken captive by the Devils, then managed to talk your way into their ranks just as you did into the wardwatch.*

Is it so hard to imagine? So impossible to consider?

No. No, the strange part, after the most surprising and adventurous year of his life, was that absolutely nothing sounded too strange for Rem to believe anymore.

But what did it matter how Korin Lyr had become the Raven, or why? The real question was what happened now. If his gang attacked their caravan today, or tomorrow, or the next day or the next, would Rem and Torval make it out of the encounter alive? Or would they end up dead by the road, like the lord marshal and his men?

That was the worst part of their predicament, Rem realized: there was no one to trust. The Raven was an outlaw, suspicious from the start. The lord marshal was a foreign military man and clearly had an unspoken agenda; hopeless. And the Lady Tzimena? She struck Rem as a good woman, trapped between opposing forces in an untenable situation. She might be sympathetic, but she probably had as little control over this situation as Rem and Torval did.

They had no one to trust, no one to rely on. It was Rem and Torval, alone, in a world of murderous thieves and political machinations that was very far above their humble pay grade.

Late in the morning, at about the time when they might have stopped for rest and a midday repast, they came to the place where the road led on a gentle incline down the riverbank, right into the swift waters of the Kaarten, before emerging again on the far side. There was neither bridge nor ferry crossing.

"A ford?" Torval asked, staring at the Kaarten with dread.

"No bridge that I can see," Rem said. "What's the matter, old stump? This isn't the first stream we've forded on this journey."

"But it's the widest," Torval said, trepidation turning his face to pale stone. "And the deepest. And, by the look, the swiftest."

Rem didn't like the look of fear on his partner's face. "It's perfectly safe," he said.

"Safe for all you tall folk," Torval said with a huff. "May I remind you that I'm half your size and I can't swim?"

"Don't sell yourself short," the Raven said from his cage, now sitting idle about ten feet in front of them. "You're three-quarters his size, not half."

"Did I ask you?" Torval snapped. He was clearly nervous. Rem supposed that if he himself were unusually short, thick with muscle, and unable to swim, it'd probably scare him, as well.

"It'll be all right," Rem said. "That pony's probably a fine swimmer. Just stay in the saddle and—"

"What do I do if I fall?" Torval asked. He was staring at Rem now. "If this beast lurches and I lose my purchase . . . If the waters take me . . ."

Rem had never seen anything like the look that he now saw in the dwarf's eyes. The old stump was honestly frightened. He might even be on the verge of panic. He reached out and laid a hand on his friend's muscular forearm.

"Torval," Rem said, "you'll be fine."

"Could I ride with you?" Torval asked, his look that of a beseeching child eager to sleep with his parents after a nightmare.

"With *me*?" Rem asked.

"You heard me," Torval said. "There's room for me, isn't there?"

"Torval, stop it," Rem said, leaning close. Up ahead, the lord marshal had sent Croften into the churning Kaarten. A line of hemp rope trailed behind the big scout and his mount, held on the bank by Wallenbrand and young Brekkon. Rem suggested the sight to Torval. "See there? Croften's fording ahead, and leading a line across. We'll be able to hold on to that when we cross."

"A line," Torval said, rising in his saddle and struggling to get a better look at what was unfolding. When the high walls of the oxcart made a clear view impossible, the dwarf gave his pony a little kick in the ribs, and the animal shuffled forward toward the end of the road.

"It'll be fine," Rem said. "Just stay in the saddle, keep your feet couched tight in those stirrups, and you'll reach the far side safe and sound. Wet, but safe. They'll be rolling the wagon and the cage across, after all. If they can make it, certainly you can—"

"Small chance of a supply wagon or a crow's cage being washed downriver," the Raven said. "But a single dwarf on a pony—"

"Shut your mouth," Rem snapped. "This isn't the time."

The Raven grinned from his cage. "Just teasing the old stump. No harm meant."

Torval's head swiveled slowly toward the Raven, eyes narrowing. "What did you call me?"

" 'Old stump,' " the Raven said. "Isn't that what your friend just called you?"

Torval pointed at Rem, but kept glaring at the Raven. "He calls me 'old stump.' My mates and my prefect on the ward call me 'old stump.' You, you sneaky twat, don't get to call me 'old stump.' "

The Raven raised his hands in surrender. "Apologies, master dwarf. Just trying to put you at ease."

"When I need my ease from the likes of you," Torval said, turning back toward the unfolding fording of the river, "I'll work it out with my maul and my fists."

Rem shot the Raven a silent warning: *He means it. Keep your mouth shut.*

The Raven, to Rem's great surprise, looked honestly hurt and embarrassed. He nodded the slightest bit, then settled down in his cage again, silent and patient.

Across the river, Croften was just emerging. Rem hadn't been watching during the crossing—the exchange between Torval and the Red Raven had drawn his attention—but clearly the big guardsman had never gotten more than hip deep in the river, his horse's withers and head always above the flow. That was good. Torval's pony might be hard-pressed to cross without some paddling, but that meant the water was still shallow enough to not be so treacherous as Torval imagined. There was, of course, the current to worry about: swift, but not violent or turbulent. But certainly Torval could keep his mount upright and keep himself in the saddle for such a brief crossing? His panic was entirely misplaced. How much force was required to knock one dwarf off a small mount and wash him away?

On the far bank, Croften swung out of his saddle and started tying the other end of the lifeline he'd carried to an alder just a stone's throw from the river's edge. On the near bank, Wallenbrand and Brekkon found a pine and tied their own end of the line. Just like that, the way was clear: they now had a wet, sagging lifeline leading from one side to the other. If they each crossed upriver of it, then, in case of disaster, they could snag the line as the current swept them along.

At least Rem hoped that was how it would work.

The lord marshal turned his horse. "Bring up the wagon and the cage first!"

Brekkon was tapped for wagon duty, to lead the way across the ford and make sure the cart followed the shallowest and least treacherous path. The young man hurried from the riverbank, swung into his saddle, and took up a position on the edge of the forest road. The other riders at the head of the column— the lord marshal, Wallenbrand, Tuvera, Redriga, Kolia, and the Lady Tzimena—all moved their mounts off the road so that Wirren could bring the big oxcart forward to the river's edge.

Rem could not see Wirren, perched on the driver's bench of the cart and hidden by its high sides, but he heard the snap of the reins. The whole assembly creaked and jostled forward toward the ford, the ox trudging lazily along, pulling the cart behind as though it were a child's toy.

The Red Raven knew what he was about to be subjected to and prepared, stripping his coat and the main ox pelt he'd been using as a blanket inside the cage and squeezing them both through the bars of the cage roof. He laced them through well enough to keep a grip on them, then stood as upright as he could manage in the cramped little cage.

The wagon slowed as it began the downward slope into the ford. On the far side of the river, Croften stood sentinel at the water's edge, ready to dive in if need be to aid his comrades. Rem wondered if, perhaps, more hands should have been engaged to get the wagon and the cage across, but almost as soon as the thought occurred to him, he realized why they hadn't been.

This was the most dangerous part of their fording of the river. Though each was heavy, the wagon and the cage also represented major obstacles for the rushing waters. An ill-timed surge in the current or a poorly placed depression in the riverbed itself could throw the cart and the cage sideward and spill them into the river.

If the cage toppled, the Red Raven was likely to drown in it before any number of them could right it again.

Rem guessed this was part of the lord marshal's plan: Keep everyone safe on the banks. Hazard his least important soldier and his prisoner, with only his boy—mounted, and thus safer— to try to keep everything from being lost. Better to risk their supplies and their prisoner than anyone else in the company.

And wasn't that convenient? If the Raven drowned here because of a freak mishap, that would make the rest of their journey far simpler, wouldn't it?

They were halfway across now, the wagon rocking against the pressure of the current, the waters tumbling unimpeded through the half-submerged cage. The Raven looked miserable, the waters rising and churning around him. Since they'd first arrested the man, Rem had never seen him once look nervous or out of his depth. Now, though, even at the widening distance between them, he could see it clearly. He could read it in the movements of his body and the wideness of his eyes. Caught in that cage, the cold waters of the Kaarten battering and foaming about him, the Red Raven was, for the first time, frightened.

The whole forest seemed to hold its breath as the wain and the cage wobbled across the rocky ford, battered by the foaming current. Finally, after a veritable eternity, they reached the far side and began to climb the bank. Croften scurried down into the water to meet them, to snag the ox's bridle and urge it forward as Wirren shouted and whipped it from behind. Brekkon pushed his mount onward, pounding up the bank to the road on the far side, then dismounted and hurried back to aid in physically urging the big ox as it trudged up the bank. After a few minutes, both the cart and the cage were out of the river. Rem could see, even here, that the Raven was shivering and miserable in his rolling cell. As the cart mounted the flat land beyond the bank, the Raven settled back down into the bed of his cage, slipped into his still-dry coat, and wrapped himself in the still-dry ox hide blanket.

The lord marshal looked to Tuvera. "After you, Captain."

Tuvera gave her orders, and they were carried out. Single-file, the lady of Toriel and her servants crossed the river. Rem was quite impressed with the Lady Tzimena's confidence atop her mount. She drove the animal right into the water and across in one long, smooth, unbroken action, never once hesitating or allowing the animal to balk. She even managed to slip past the two guards ahead of her and make the far bank before any of her soldiers had. At last there she was, sitting her horse, clothing soaked and clinging, waiting on the summit of the bank as the rest of her retinue scurried up after her.

The lord marshal rode nearer to Rem and Torval. "On, good watchwardens. We'll bring up the rear."

Rem looked to Torval. "We're ready," he said with finality.

Torval nodded. His eyes were still wide, anxious, the same color as the cold blue waters that were about to batter the two of them. He made no attempts to beg off or delay, however. No, to Rem's great astonishment, the frightened dwarf just drew in a deep breath, nodded, and spurred his mount.

"Let's get this over with," he muttered under his breath.

Rem nodded and followed. He let Torval move ahead of him, reasoning that if anything went wrong, it would be easier to help from behind. Torval's pony was entirely unmoved by the spectacle of the flowing Kaarten, and only shied the slightest bit when its hooves first splashed into the cold, roiling waters. Torval started to curse, but Rem rode up behind them and smacked the shaggy pony lightly on its rump. The animal shook its head, whickered, and plunged into the water with a great splash. Torval launched an onslaught of curses and invective so loud that they echoed into the forest like the crack of lightning-struck trees. The soldiers on the far bank, hearing his curses, laughed loudly in answer.

"It's gods-damned cold!" Torval shouted. His mount was moving into the deeper water now, struggling to swim and keep its head above water as the current pressed against it. Rem imagined the animal doing a series of leaps and landings beneath the river waves, its hooves hitting the rocky bottom of the riverbed, its head momentarily below the water's surface, then springing up again and swimming forward for a few feet before sinking again. Each time his head was dunked and surfaced again, Torval came up sputtering.

"Hold on!" Rem shouted by way of encouragement. "You're doing fine, old stump! We're almost across!"

Rem's own mount showed no distress at all, moving smoothly along without so much as a stumble in its gait. Torval was right, the pressing waters were cold—horribly so—but the going was steady, if a little slow. In no time they'd be on that far bank...

Once more, Torval's pony plunged under, taking him with it, then leapt up and swam forward again. Amid the splashing and noise, Rem heard Torval shouting.

"On, you blasted pack beast!" he roared. "Move those short, stumpy legs of yours! *Hyah!*"

Rem smiled in spite of himself. He really hated to laugh at the dwarf's discomfort, but there was something mildly endearing about the normally unflappable Torval being well and thoroughly flapped by anything—even if it was the prospect of being swept away in a river current and drowning.

Rem turned in the saddle. He wanted to see what was happening behind him. The lord marshal and Wallenbrand had driven their own mounts into the water. In no time they'd be across, as well, and this whole nasty episode would be behind the lot of them. Rem sincerely hoped they would stop for a time to build fires and dry out. While the day itself was warm and pleasant enough, the water was bone-numbing, and riding onward in soaking-wet raiment would do no one any good.

He was thinking about how good a fire would feel, how nice it might be to sit before it—even in the middle of the day—when his horse suddenly lost his footing. Rem wasn't sure what had happened—whether the gelding had stepped on a loose stone that shifted out from under him or suddenly stumbled into a depression. In either case, the animal tumbled sideward, thrashing as he went. Rem got one look at Torval, atop his splashing pony, just mounting from the river onto the bank, turned to his right and saw the foaming, swirling waters rising to meet him, then hit the water with terrific force and was dragged under.

His horse was struggling to get upright again. In his flailing about, he had yanked Rem under the water. Try as he might, he could not free his right foot from its stirrup.

Rem yanked and jerked, his horse's struggles trapping him beneath the waves, the roaring, freezing, churning waters of the Kaarten closing over his head like a mountain avalanche.

CHAPTER SIXTEEN

Rem knew how to swim. Water, even swift water with a deadly current, didn't frighten him in and of itself. What frightened him now—panicked him, really—was his inability to loose himself from his stirrup or from the protests of his fallen horse. He clawed at the water, tried to climb out of it in fact, but only managed to break the surface once or twice, each time desperately yanking in a lungful of breath and foam before being dragged down into the roaring depths again. During one of his short breachings, he heard shouts from the shore, splashing, as someone waded in after him. Vaguely he recalled the line that Croften had strung across the waterway and let his hands strike in every direction in search of it. If he could find that line and gain some stability, some leverage, he might be able to finally free his foot.

Then, as quickly as the thought had come to him, he was suddenly loose. He kicked upward and managed to break the surface, but what he saw after drawing a deep, coughing draft of air gave him no comfort.

His horse was upright now, swimming for the shore, desperate to be on dry land. Elvaris, Sandiva, and Croften had all waded in toward him, shouting, trying to reach out—but Rem was already being swept away, the ford and his companions shrinking as the current yanked him swiftly downstream. Once more, he struggled to find that line to cling to, but he must have missed it entirely. Rem was borne on, tumbling and tossed on the churning river waters. At a bend he hit a series of rocks, rolled, and spun end over end as the currents rushed past. As he fought to break the surface and draw breath again, a whirlpool formed where the current bent in on itself. That whirlpool yanked him under, spun him around. Just as he thought he might have to open his mouth to drink air that wasn't there for the drinking, he was ejected on the far side of the whirlpool and kept flying with the current.

He broke the surface. Breathed. Searched. His companions were nowhere to be seen.

Gods, he could be carried miles from them! He had to arrest his drift and make shore, fast. Rem started swimming, employing long, strong strokes that would use the current to his advantage while pushing him ever nearer to the bank.

Up ahead he saw a fallen cottonwood, branches half-submerged in the current, roots still stuck in the eroded soil of the riverbank that it had once called home. That was his target. If he could let the current carry him into that toppled tree, his motion would be arrested and he could climb out. Providing he didn't miss. Or get swept under the fallen tree by the current and pinned there. Or impaled on one of the broken branches protruding from the horizontal trunk.

He paddled one way...saw the fearsome points of a shattered limb protruding just above the water...paddled back the other way...realized there were too many branches, that if he didn't hit exactly the right span of naked bark, he'd end up sucked under or skewered...

He corrected. The tree rushed up on him, as though the current were eager to smash him upon it—

—and suddenly he'd made it. The waters slammed him hard into the moist gray skin of the dead cottonwood, the current battering him flat against the trunk while his scrabbling hands and wheeling feet sought purchase. Then, finally, he managed to snag a slender limb above him, to rest one foot on a random stone below, and he forced himself upward. Little by little, hand over hand, he drew himself out of the river, onto the fallen tree, then climbed, squirrel-like, along its length toward the muddy, eroded bluff where its roots were still half-embedded. When Rem finally made the shore, he clambered over the storm of upturned roots, fell end over end, then landed, facedown, on the moist loam of the riverbank. He lay there for a time, drawing deep, desperate gulps of air, enjoying the feeling of being still, unmoving. Dimly he imagined the bank that he lay on deciding to give in to its long-pending erosion and collapse back into the river, so he forced himself to wriggle forward a few feet, to put some distance between him and the precarious edge. There, amid brush and trees and lichen and stone and damp, cool river mud, Rem sprawled again, facedown, happy to be out of danger.

In the distance he heard voices calling for him. Chief among them was Torval's. The dwarf sounded like he was calling for one of his children.

"Over here," Rem said, but realized immediately that he hadn't been loud enough for anyone to hear him.

Footfalls. Rattling scrub and bracken. The voices drew near. Torval called his name, again and again.

"Over here!" Rem shouted, though his shout sounded more like a child's plea for succor in the night. *Help, Papa, the thing under the bed! Mama, please, there's something in my cedar chest!*

Rem raised his eyes and searched around him. He could hear his companions nearing with each second. But it wasn't any of them that his eyes fixed on. It was something else, directly ahead, deep in the woods and the brush.

There was a face staring back at him. It was a mildly frightened face—a shocked face, amazed to see Rem, apparently discovered in the midst of some private action. And that face wasn't human.

Gray-green skin. A sloping forehead. Pale, deep-set eyes. A ferocious underbite and the bright wink of small tusks peeping out from thick, chapped lips. Rem blinked. The face blinked back.

Across a span of twenty or thirty feet, Rem was staring at an orc.

Rem's exhaustion fled. Wholly on instinct, he scrambled to his knees, staring straight back at the watching orc.

The creature didn't look angry or ill intentioned or ready to attack. Instead it looked rather confused...embarrassed even, as though caught in some act.

Rem waited, not sure what to expect. Would it speak? Attack? Run away? Should he speak to it? Explain that he and his companions meant no harm?

No. It was too far away. To speak with it, he'd have to raise his voice. And if he raised his voice, his nearing companions would hear. Torval would hear. And if Torval arrived and saw an orc—any orc, no matter that it meant them no harm—there was likely to be a fight. A bloody one at that.

Rem raised a finger to his lips. *Shush*, that gesture said. Then he raised his empty hands and showed them: *I'm unarmed. There's no reason for trouble.*

The orc suddenly rose. It had been crouching. It seemed to be hiking up its breeches and hastily tying their laces.

Hyryn's cock...had he caught that orc while it was having a quiet shit?

Before Rem could make another gesture or say another word, the orc turned and lumbered away, still trying to get its breeches in order as it went. A second later, its enormous frame was swallowed by the close-packed greenery of the forest and it was gone, only a memory.

Torval rocketed out of the brush off to his left. The dwarf very nearly tripped over Rem's barely upright form. The two partners stared at one another, then the dwarf stomped forward and threw his big, muscular arms around Rem.

"There he is!" he cried in his craggy old voice. "By the Maker, I thought I'd lost you, boy!"

"Just fine," Rem said, both happy to see his partner again and strangely uncomfortable at being hugged by him. They were still like that, dwarf embracing man, when a number of their party appeared out of the woods to join them. There were four of them—Brekkon, Croften, Redriga, and Elvaris—and they all stopped when they saw the dwarf rocking his wet, muddy partner in his arms. Elvaris, still soaking wet from wading into the water to rescue him, gave a deep sigh of relief.

"Midday swim?" she asked with a cock of her brow.

"Pitiful," Brekkon added good-naturedly. "Can't you cross a bloody stream without hazarding yourself?"

"That wasn't my fault," Rem said. "The horse slipped—"

Croften clapped Torval on the back. "You need to watch this pup more closely, master dwarf. He's like to find trouble wherever he goes."

Torval pulled away from Rem and nodded. Rem couldn't tell if Torval's face was just wet from his fording of the river, or if those were tears on his cheeks. "You have no idea," he said to the soldiers. "He's like my fourth child, this one! But not half so obedient..."

Rem stumbled to his feet. "I'm fine," he said, trying to dust some of the sticking weeds and detritus from himself. "Honestly, I'll be fine. Is the horse all right?"

Croften nodded. "Fine as can be, lad. He made it out while you were tumbling downstream."

Rem nodded. "Good news, then. The horse is fine. I'm fine. We're all fine. Let's head back."

He took a few steps, then realized Torval was standing there, staring off into the woods at something. He studied his partner, saw the slight flare of the dwarf's wide nostrils, then realized what must have happened.

The breeze had shifted. Torval smelled something.

"Torval," Rem said.

"Wait," the dwarf answered, then went tromping off into the brush, right toward where Rem had seen the crouching orc.

Rem looked to the others. He wasn't sure whether to offer an explanation or send them on their collective way while he went after Torval. When they all moved to follow the dwarf, he knew that he'd lost control of the situation.

They all gathered where Torval had come to a halt, in a tiny little glade of fir and madrone beside a big redwood. There was a smell in the clearing that assailed Rem's nostrils instantly: excrement, but of no sort he was familiar with.

Torval stared at a pile of scat in a shallow, hand-dug hole. He looked to his partner.

"Do you know what that is?" the dwarf asked.

Rem nodded. "I do. I saw the one who left it."

Croften took a look. His mouth twisted. "Orcs!"

Rem nodded again. "When I looked up, I saw one sitting right here. Doing his business, I suppose."

"You're lucky he didn't kill you," Elvaris said. She had one hand tight on the hilt of her Taverando blade now.

Rem shook his head. "Honestly, he looked a little embarrassed, like I'd caught him in the act of something."

"As you did," Redriga quipped.

"Where there's one there's more," Torval said, scanning the woods around them for some other sign of impending trouble. His concern for Rem and happiness at recovering him were all fled. Now he was in defensive mode: a sentinel on guard; a killer ready to wet his blade.

"He saw me, clearly," Rem said, "then hiked up his trousers and ran. I'm willing to guess he doesn't want trouble if we don't chase or challenge him. What say we just head back to the others?"

"He might've let you go," Croften said darkly. "But the dwarf's right. Orcs don't travel alone much—certainly not this far from the mountains. If you saw one, there are more."

"Then let's give them a wide berth and get back to the others," Rem said, perhaps too forcefully.

"I'm all for that," Redriga agreed. "The question is, will they do us the same courtesy?"

"This changes everything," Captain Tuvera said.

"This changes nothing," the lord marshal countered. "This fool nearly drowns crossing a river and reports a single orc in the woods and the lot of you are moved to hysteria?"

"There's no such thing as a single orc," Torval said, clearly without respect for the lord marshal's title or lineage. "They move in bands—everyone knows that!"

"Aye," the lord marshal said wearily, "everyone knows that...just as everyone knows dwarves remain among their own kind and keep to their own traditions. Isn't that right, master dwarf?"

"Fine," Redriga argued, "there's just a single orc. Or two. Or three. Need we remind you about the dead men we found yesterday? That poor sod with his face peeled off? The fact is, we know they're out there now, so we know they pose a threat."

"*Do* we know that?" Rem asked. He was crouching by a hastily made fire. He'd changed into the only other clothes he'd brought with him while his original garments hung on rough drying racks made of secondhand twigs and tree limbs. It was barely past midday, but his little jaunt in the river had made him feel as if sundown should be upon them at any moment.

Tuvera turned to glare at Rem. "Of course we know that," she said. "They're orcs."

"Forgive me," Rem said, doing his best to sound conversational and not insistent, "but my partner and I have had a lot of experience with orcs in Yenara. Contrary to popular belief, conflict with them is not a foregone conclusion."

"So *you* say," Torval sneered. "If we're able to sometimes treat with them without violence in the city, it's only for that reason: we are *in the city*. They are not in their element, they have very little advantage, and they're only in the city because they want something. We have leverage against them there. But out here..."

"Help me out, will you?" Rem shot back. He returned to Tuvera and the lord marshal and their soldiers. "It is possible to avoid confrontation, if we just leave them be. But if we adopt a defensive stance and draw swords at the first sign of them—"

"I see orcs," Elvaris broke in, "I draw my sword. That's not even a question."

Rem threw up his hands. "Then they'll draw, and words will be exchanged, and then come blows, and finally blood."

"At last the boy talks sense," the lord marshal said.

"I'm not saying we shouldn't be cautious," Rem said. "I'm just saying we've no reason to look for a fight. We carry on, eyes peeled, and if these orcs show themselves, we try to talk to them before fighting them."

"Forgive me," Torval grumbled, "but I shall have to disagree with my partner on this point. They're beasts, every one of them, and you can't be too careful if you encounter them. If they show themselves, we have to be ready to hit first and hit hard."

"A sound plan," Tuvera agreed.

Rem shook his head. "Fine. Go off with your crossbow half cranked and ready to fire. You'll get us all killed."

"Far be it from me to interrupt," the Lady Tzimena suddenly broke in, "but if there are, in fact, orcs about, shouldn't we be moving on, with haste?"

"I'll second that," Croften said. "With respect, milady."

The Lady Tzimena gave the big scout a nod.

Croften carried on. "Orcs or no, threat or no, we need to push on before dark. We've only got a few hours left, and the road ahead is winding."

"Then police yourselves," the lord marshal said with finality. "We move out again in a quarter hour." He made a point of glaring at Rem. "Those not ready will be left behind."

"Does anyone want to know my thoughts?" the Red Raven asked from his cage.

"No," the lord marshal, Tuvera, and Torval all said in unison.

The Raven shook his head, sighed, and carried on anyway. "Orcs are the least of your worries now. Crossing that river put you well into the wood—into the very heart of it. This is bandit country now."

"You would know about that, wouldn't you?" the lord marshal asked as he prepared his horse.

"Better than some," the Red Raven said. Rem caught the inherent provocation in the statement, but noted that the lord marshal refused to acknowledge the Raven's taunt.

Tuvera approached the cage. She eyed the Raven levelly, then finally spoke. "Just know, sir, that if your Devils of the

Weald try anything untoward, you'll be the first to meet the sword."

Rem threw a glance at Torval. If only Tuvera knew...

The Raven stared back at Tuvera through the bars of his cage. "My Devils are the least of your worries, Captain. This forest is crawling with brigand bands. The Wastrels. Slaymaker and Sons. And let's not forget those Bloody Boskers—"

"Bah," Croften said from beside his own mount. He was checking his horse's girth straps and inspecting each hoof, one after the other. "The Bloody Boskers are a gods-damned bedtime story. You'll have to try harder than that."

"They're no story," the Raven said with assurance. "My own Devils have had run-ins with them. I've lost men and women to their inhuman hunger. If you ask me, they're to blame for that bloody scene you found yesterday, not these roving orcs. Orcs don't peel people's faces from their skulls—but the Boskers do. I promise you, if we meet them on this road, not a one of us is likely to come out of the encounter intact."

"And why is that?" Elvaris asked, incredulous.

"Because you're not unified," the Raven said simply. "The Boskers are inbred cannibals. Cunning, savage, nigh inhuman. We'd be better off meeting those orcs. At least the huffers will only kill us and take whatever we might have of value. The Bloody Boskers, though—they'll drag every one of us back to their camp, then flay us, butcher us, and make meals of us for weeks to come. Since the lady and her nurse are pretty women, they might take their faces and keep them as heirlooms. The clan daughters will certainly scalp them and keep their hair, for braiding and twine-making."

"Be quiet," the lord marshal said, not even looking at the outlaw.

"You know it's the truth, Lord Marshal," the Raven said.

Rem sensed a sudden change in the man—a desperation, a sudden increase in the nervous energies he exuded. Was he trying to unbalance the lord marshal? To force a confrontation? It struck Rem as a rather inopportune time to do so...

"I said, be quiet," the lord marshal repeated. He threw a fell glance at the Raven in his cage. "Don't make me command you again."

"How would your darling duke feel then, eh?" the Raven asked. "You, tasked with one simple job: bring the caged bird home for plucking. But what happens? We all end up under the Boskers' knives, salted for jerky or bobbing about in a stew pot—"

The lord marshal finally broke from beside his mount and stalked toward the Red Raven's cage. "I won't tell you again," he said.

"Please," the Raven taunted. "Tell me again. Tell me again how affrighted I should be of a gods-damned liar and usurper! A kin murderer and—"

The strike came so quickly, as such a blur, that Rem barely understood what had happened until after it was already enacted. The lord marshal was holding his riding crop. With blinding speed he shot the blunt end of the crop—the hard, wooden handle—through the bars of the cage and slammed the Red Raven right in the teeth. The outlaw reeled and sprawled, grunting, and the lord marshal stood, staring, awaiting another clever retort. None came.

The Lady Tzimena broke from where she'd been preparing her saddlebags. "Lord Marshal!" she shouted. "Stop it, this instant!"

He turned on her, his glare stopping her in her tracks. "I will stop nothing," he said. Rem saw the Lady Tzimena's face turn white. Eye to eye with the lord marshal, the Lady Tzimena had just, for the first time, realized how fierce—how serious—the man was. Rem could feel it, even from where he stood: the cold and pure force of will that emanated from the old soldier's dread gaze. In that instant Rem was reminded of his own father. Despite himself, he shuddered.

"This man," the lord marshal said slowly, "is nothing to you. This man, Lady Tzimena, is a criminal. I would strongly urge you to keep to yourself in his presence, milady—to say nothing to him, to acknowledge him in no meaningful fashion, and to concern yourself, instead, with your own safety and your impending wifely duties."

"How dare you," Tzimena said. She was trying to be defiant, but Rem saw that she was failing in the face of the lord marshal's quiet fury. He didn't blame her. Rem himself would've had a hard time standing fast against that man.

"How dare *you*," the lord marshal countered. "You are a guest among us. You are a prize—"

Tuvera shot forward then, hand on the hilt of her sheathed sword. Rem saw that her face was red, her brow furrowed. "A prize?" she shouted. "You son of a whore!"

Her sword rasped as it started to leave its scabbard.

Wallenbrand lunged between the captain and the lord marshal then, arms out. "Only through me, Captain," the old lieutenant said.

"Easy enough," Elvaris hissed, and drew her own blade. The Taverando caught a spear of sunlight and flashed coldly.

Rem found himself on his feet only a breath later, his own sword snatched up from where it lay nearby. His response was wholly instinctual, but what else could he do? In the two or three breaths following Elvaris's drawing of her blade, everyone armed in the clearing hastily prepared themselves for a melee. Only the Lady Tzimena, her nurse, Kolia, the caged Red Raven, and old Wallenbrand had no weapons in hand.

This is wrong, Rem thought, *all wrong*.

He studied the frozen scene, trying to decide who was serious and who was merely making a display. The lord marshal's hand was on his own sword, but he hadn't drawn. Tuvera's blade was half-exposed, never having left its scabbard. Elvaris had her Taverando level and ready. Brekkon held his own sword, but his hands clearly shook. Croften had gone for his crossbow and kept sweeping the tip of the loaded bolt back and forth over the company. Redriga had a hand ax, Galen a compound bow, arrow already nocked and drawn, and Sandiva stood ready with both her sword and a matching dagger, ready to enter the fray two-handed. Near the oxcart, Wirren held the hatchet that the company often used to hack up firewood.

Rem looked around for Torval. The dwarf was a few paces behind him and to his right. His maul hung at his side, at ease, but ready for action.

"Don't be foolish, Captain," the lord marshal said. "This young lady's honor isn't worth dying for."

"You tell me," Tuvera said. "You're the one who'll pay for questioning it."

"Say the word," Elvaris urged.

"Be quiet," Tuvera hissed back.

The lord marshal swung his gaze back to the Lady Tzimena. "Forgive my bluntness, lady, but my only task is to deliver you, safely, to my master in Erald. After that you become his problem, and no longer mine."

Kolia, the lady's nurse, was at her elbow now, trying to draw her away. "Leave him be," she said.

"I'll see you censured for this," the Lady Tzimena said.

"You're welcome to try," the lord marshal answered. "Once we are back in the city, back among the court. But here, in the wild? *This* is my court, milady. Here, I am the law. I am all that stands between you and the likes of that man in the cage, and the knives of the other outlaws that haunt these woods. Vex me further and I shall throw you to them as a ready prize when the time comes. Remember that."

He went back about his business. The Lady Tzimena stood, staring into the air, shocked and humiliated by the lord marshal's dressing-down.

Rem, satisfied that no one would try to kill anyone, at least for the next few minutes, threw down his sword, moved away from the fire, and snatched up his still-damp gambeson. As he slipped into the protective coat, he looked to the Red Raven in his cage.

The Raven was upright again, but his mouth was bloody and swollen. He peered through the bars at Tzimena, the intensity of his gaze holding in it an unspoken command of some sort. Rem stole a glance at the lady and saw that she seemed to be offering a silent retort.

There's history there, Rem realized. *Only two people with such a history—two people deeply in love—can speak without words like that.*

He's telling her to keep her mouth shut, to bide her time.

She's telling him she wants the lord marshal's head on a plate.

Gods . . . what have we stumbled into?

CHAPTER SEVENTEEN

Within an hour they were back on the road. Their mounted train snaked along, the supply wagon trundling behind the silent, sullen ox dragging it. The river, on their right since their descent into the Ethkeraldi, was now off to their left, sometimes within sight, sometimes trailing far away into the wood, lost among the redwoods and hemlocks and ground-choking ferns. It was a sunny day, but the canopy was so thick that very little light penetrated. The sylvan world around them was a patchwork of light and shadow, deep wells of darkness hugging the roots of great trees and shaggy fern beds and gnarled deadfalls as lonely spears of sunlight hosted whirling clouds of insects and dancing dust motes. As they rode, Rem heard the rush of small furry bodies among the ferns or heard the clockwork knock of woodpeckers. Every sound that reached his ears caused him to stiffen and search the brush for signs of danger.

When a covey of grouse burst from beneath a fallen cedar, winging upward toward the pine boughs, Rem reflexively wheeled his horse round toward the disturbance and sat for a time, staring, sure that there was something in the brush he needed to see.

Torval rode nearer. "There's nothing there, lad."

"Do we know that?" Rem asked quietly. "Do we know that for a fact?"

Sandiva and Elvaris, who'd been bringing up the rear of the

party, joined Rem and Torval where they sat their mounts, staring into the woods, almost willing some unseen enemy to show itself.

"Orcs again?" Sandiva asked teasingly, her youthful glibness suddenly irritating.

"What is it?" Elvaris asked. Rem could hear a combination of honest concern and impatient condescension in her voice. She was a hardened soldier. She knew when a companion was too nervous—too paranoid—to be trusted. The fact that she gently tried to bring Rem out of his edgy reverie made him more than a little ashamed of himself.

"It's nothing," Rem said finally. He couldn't bring himself to meet the swordswoman's level gaze. He spurred his mount, and the horse cantered on.

Up ahead the cage leaned a little as it rounded a bend in the road, blocked from sight by the enormous trunk of a fir tree, fringed all round its base with shaggy brush.

Elvaris hove up beside Rem on her horse. "Something's troubling you," she said. "Tell me what it is."

Rem shook his head. "Sorry," he said. "Clearly, I'm being a fool." Torval fell in beside him and kept pace. Only half-satisfied, Elvaris finally withdrew and fell in beside Sandiva again, bringing up the rear as they had all morning.

"You need to let it go, lad," Torval said, barely above a whisper.

Rem's response was quiet. "It could come at any time."

"Aye," the dwarf said. "And if it does, you need to be ready to fight. As you are, you're prone to panic or freeze. We can't have that."

Rem nodded again. The dwarf was right. He needed to get his head straight. In his current state, he'd be of no use in a fight. He threw Torval a grim look.

"Forgive me," he said.

* ★ * ★ * ★

They rode on. Hours passed. The waning day, thankfully, would not mimic the excitement of its first half. Rem's clothes were nearly dry now. That hour before a fire had done them wonders.

On all sides the forest hemmed them in, a textured fairyland of emerald greens, deep rusty browns, mottled grays, and rich umbers. It was a lovely view, Rem thought—their quiet little train making its slow progress along the road, thousands of sentinel trees and fern stands surrounding them, teasing glimpses of the bright-blue sky peering intermittently through chinks in the forest canopy.

Then, from behind, there came a loud crack. It wasn't a breaking twig or a snapping limb; it was the sound of a calving iceberg or a hilltop oak riven by lightning. The sound was sudden and loud and echoed through the wood with portentous fury. Rem's horse reared under him in protest, as did Torval's pony. As he struggled to calm his mount, Rem's eyes darted all around him, wondering just what could have made that terrible sound. It had come from right behind.

His horse turned. Rem saw a giant redwood toppling, almost gracefully, before it crashed down with enormous force across the road. Sandiva's mount was so affrighted, it threw her from the saddle. Elvaris dismounted quickly, holding her own horse's reins as she moved to get the cursing Sandiva back on her feet.

Rem looked to Torval. The dwarf, struggling with his balking pony, caught Rem's gaze.

"Hold," Torval said. "Don't panic." He sounded as though he was trying to convince himself as much as Rem.

There came another crack, this time from up ahead. Rem wheeled his horse round just in time to see another huge redwood smashing across the road before the train. The horses at the fore reared and screamed and threatened to bolt. Croften was thrown from his mount and hit the ground cursing. The Lady Tzimena was nearly tossed from hers, but leaned against her animal's withers and held fast.

Blocked ahead. Blocked behind.

Boxed in.

Rem looked to Torval again. The dwarf swung out of his saddle.

"All right," he said, yanking out his maul and taking a defensive position behind his pony. "Get ready."

Rem dismounted and drew his sword, then followed Torval's lead and swung around his horse, taking refuge behind it. He and Torval were now back to back, sandwiched between their two skittish mounts, the animals' flanks providing some measure of protection against outside attack, if it came.

Elvaris had Sandiva up now. They stood, taking in the scene around them, Elvaris holding her horse's reins in one hand. The other hand had fallen to the hilt of her sheathed sword.

"You bloody nag!" Sandiva shouted into the foliage where her bolting horse had disappeared. "I'll cook you and eat you for that!"

"Bottled in," Torval said behind Rem. "They'll come fast now, from the flanks."

"Get away from here," the Raven said from his cage, ten feet ahead of them. "If you stand between me and them—"

Rem heard a percussive thump, just ahead, past the Raven's cage, on the outer wall of the ox wain. Squinting, he realized that a still-vibrating arrow fletched with goose feathers was now embedded finger-deep in the outer wall of the supply wagon, just above the rear wheel. On the opposite side of the wagon, two more thumps followed, along with two more quivering arrows.

"Cack," Torval said.

Arrows came whizzing out of the forest on all sides. Not one hit a live target, but all came dangerously close. They fletched the earth around the horses' skittish hooves; they stuck fast in tree trunks just over the shoulders of the exposed members of the company; more than half a dozen were visible on the side of the ox wain that Rem could see. He supposed there were probably just as many on the other side.

"Form ranks!" the lord marshal cried. "To arms!"

"Protect the lady!" Tuvera shouted, her horse stamping in a circle.

Atop the wagon, Wirren bent over the cart wall behind the driver's bench, reaching for a crossbow propped just a few feet below him in the cart bed.

"Those were warning shots!" someone shouted out of the forest. The voice was female, powerful and clear, but impossible to pinpoint. "Draw your weapons and we'll skewer the lot of you!"

The lord marshal drew his sword.

An instant later, an arrow whizzed out of the brush and bit deep into his horse's chest. The lord marshal's mount screamed and fell, and the lord marshal—sword and all—was thrown onto the muddy road.

Rem studied the scene: the lord marshal prone; his horse on its side, screaming in pain at the arrow that had pierced it; Croften trying to use his horse as a barricade, his big crossbow hanging precariously under one arm; the forward Estavari swordswomen all closing in around the Lady Tzimena while Elvaris and Sandiva still sought their attackers at the rear; young Brekkon swinging out of his saddle and helping his father to his feet; Wallenbrand still mounted, whirling his horse around and around as if in search of their hidden assailants.

"We only want the Raven and the girl!" the woman in the woods shouted now. "Throw down your arms and stand fast while we take them, and none of you will be harmed. You can walk out of these woods alive!"

The moment the lord marshal was on his feet again, he shoved his boy off and surveyed the company before and behind him. "What are you waiting for?" he cried. "Defensive positions! We're under attack!"

Another arrow shot out of the brush. Rem saw it an instant before it hit its target and thought for sure it was meant for the lord marshal.

Instead it drove itself deep into young Brekkon's surcoated chest. The boy fell with a small, breathless sound. The young man lay still, lifeless. The lord marshal stood over him, eyes wide, mouth agape.

From somewhere off to their left, Rem heard voices in the woods.

"Kallend, you dumb shit!" someone hissed.

"I was aiming at the lord marshal!" another hissed back.

"Torval," Rem said.

"Down," the dwarf finished.

The partners hit the dirt in unison as a flight of arrows cut the air above them. Rem could see very little, because when he fell, he landed flat and kept his head down, but he heard both his horse and Torval's pony scream and go staggering away, leaving him and his dwarven partner suddenly unprotected. Behind him Elvaris called Sandiva's name. Up ahead the Lady Tzimena shouted, as well, while someone else in her company—Tuvera, maybe, or Redriga—started barking orders. The cart thumped and rocked as more arrows bit deep into its wooden flanks. Rem dared a glance and saw that even the Red Raven was hunkered flat in his cage, desperate not to be hit by a stray shot.

"Move," Rem shouted at Torval. "Under the cart!"

"Right behind you!" Torval snapped back.

Rem started crawling forward, as quickly and flatly as he could, all knees and elbows. In seconds he was right underneath the Raven's cage, and he stopped there. Torval wriggled in behind him. There was not so much space under here as there would be under the main cart. Rem listened as the arrows whizzed and thumped in the world above him. There was a break in the volley and the faint sound of rattling ash in quivers.

"Move," Rem hissed to Torval. "They're preparing another round!"

Rem scrambled out from under the cage cart, sprang to his feet, and threw himself clumsily into the bed of the wain. An arrow split the air that he'd occupied just a moment earlier. As Rem scurried farther into the cart bed, over the piles of provisions and tarps that covered it, Torval vaulted up behind, scurrying in as fast as he could. The walls of the cart were thumped in chorus. Arrow tips bit through here and there, glinting meanly in the forested half light.

Torval then leaned out over the rear lip of the cart. Rem wasn't sure what he was after—had he dropped his maul? Was he helping someone else? As the dwarf hung over the rear gate, reaching for something, Rem saw an archer rise up on the great tree felled to block their escape—directly behind them. The outlaw aimed his arrow at Torval as he drew.

"Torval!" Rem shouted.

The dwarf yanked hard on something and came rolling up into the cart bed again. Apparently, he'd been trying to reach the rear gate and draw it up so it could give them a little more protection. The gate rose and clanked into place vertically just as the loosed arrow from the archer on the fallen tree bit through it. As Rem watched, Torval darted to each side of the rear gate, unlocked the inward-swung doors hinged above that gate, and slammed them shut.

The cart was now secure—somewhat. To a height of five feet on all sides, Rem and Torval were protected.

Rem turned to see if Wirren had taken cover. The cart driver lay slumped over the fore wall of the cart, an arrow protruding from his bleeding throat, dead.

Rem poised one foot on a chest filled with tools and materials for repairing leather and keeping armor rust-free. His plan was to launch himself upward, if only for an instant, to peer over the fore wall of the cart and see what was happening out on the road. He didn't relish exposing himself, but there was no other way to get a good look at what was unfolding.

"Are you daft?" Torval growled from where he hunkered. More arrows thumped against the outer walls of the cart.

"I promise," Rem said, "I'll only be a moment."

With that he leapt, got a tenuous grip on the lip of the cart's fore wall, and called on all his strength to pull him up so he could see.

It was a terrible sight. At least three of the horses lay dead. The rest were nowhere to be seen, having bolted into the woods. Croften was propped with his back to the fallen tree that blocked their path, an arrow in his shoulder, awkwardly trying to reload his crossbow from his compromised position. Brekkon lay where he'd fallen. Kolia, the Lady Tzimena's nurse, was down, as well. Tuvera and Redriga were hunkered low, faces in the mud behind their fallen horses. At intervals arrows still flew from the brush surrounding the road, some falling to the earth without a target, some finding purchase in the dead.

But where was the lord marshal? Or the Lady Tzimena?

A thunderous knocking suddenly sounded from the cart bed, as though arrows were thumping against the underside of the carriage. Rem released his hold on the fore wall and fell back into the cart, arms shaking from the strain of holding himself up. Torval stared at the cart bed, clearly puzzled by what he was hearing.

It came again, fast, urgent. *Thump-thump-thump-thump-thump*.

"What in the sundry hells is that?" Rem asked.

"Help us!" someone said from underneath the cart. It was a woman's voice. "There's a hatch down here!"

Was that Tzimena?

Rem and Torval stared at one another. A hatch? At the moment all they could see was the tools, weapons, and supplies piled in the cart bed, clearly covering any hatch that might exist beneath. Torval started yanking items aside first. Rem followed suit an instant later.

In seconds they'd cleared a span of the cart bed and revealed that there was, indeed, a small, square hatch in the floor. Rem pushed aside the wooden bolt that held the hatch in place and lifted it. Below he saw the mud of the road and two dirty, flushed faces: the Lady Tzimena and the swordswoman Elvaris.

Torval offered a hand. "Hurry up, lass. Come on!"

Tzimena took the dwarf's proffered hand and clambered up through the hatch into the cart bed. Elvaris followed. The two women scooted away from the hatch, and Rem slammed it shut. The four of them sat there, trying to catch their ragged breath, hunkered down in the cart, listening as arrows continued to thump into the outer walls of the cart or whiz overhead.

Rem studied them both. Elvaris, though a hardened soldier, was clearly shaken by something. Rem guessed what it might be.

"Sandiva?" he asked.

Elvaris shook her head. "Tried to charge an archer behind a tree. Took two in the chest." Rem could see the need to lament her lost companion vibrating through her—the lost look in her eyes, the way her lip trembled and her hands shook. But he also saw that Elvaris was fighting the urge to indulge that feeling at present. She was distracted, lost in thought, probably trying to work out some plan to protect the lot of them.

"Kolia, too," the Lady Tzimena said miserably. "She grabbed me, shielded me. Aemon's tears—if we don't find a way out of this, they'll kill us all."

Torval was making a racket, hastily searching the weapons arrayed in the cart by the lord marshal's men. "We've got axes, spare swords, a few pikes, even some shields...but not much that can help us against those bastards surrounding us."

"Wirren had a crossbow," Rem suggested. "That's something."

"Aye," Elvaris said, "but just one. Accurate, yes. But fast? No. You won't get far against experienced bowmen with that thing."

Outside, someone screamed. It was a sound of shock and surprise—a man suddenly overtaken by an unseen adversary. A breath later, the scream was choked off.

"On your right!" Rem heard. It was the bandit woman, the one who'd first addressed them on the road. "There's one among the trees! He got Wicklow!"

Rem sighed.

"Music to my ears," Torval said.

"What's happening?" the Lady Tzimena asked.

"One of our party made it off the road and into the woods. Clearly they just took out one of the bandits."

"But they know there's an enemy among them now," Elvaris said. "Advantage spent."

"But not ours," Torval said. "If only a few of them start

watching their own backs and seeking the killer, they won't have the time to rain arrows down on us. If we could just find something in here to give us an edge—"

"What's in there?" Tzimena asked, suggesting a heavy, locked chest crammed into a far corner of the cart. The chest bore an iron padlock—the sort only employed if something very valuable lay within.

Torval snatched up an ax from the weapons pile. "Let me try to break into it."

"Wait," Rem said, then scurried to the fore of the cart bed and yanked Wirren's corpse down to join them. The driver hit the bed with a heavy thud, in a most disrespectful position. Rem hastily rolled him over, laid him flat, and started searching his clothing.

"What are you after?" Torval asked.

"Keys," Rem said. "Infinitely faster if we can find them— and we just did."

His hand plunged into a pouch on Wirren's belt and emerged with a set of keys on a brass ring. Rem hurried to the locked chest and tried every key in the heavy lock. The first three didn't even fit its keyhole. The fourth slid in. He unlocked the chest with shaking hands. When he threw back the heavy, reinforced lid, he froze.

He wasn't sure what he'd thought he'd find, but this wasn't it: the interior of the chest was divided into nine square cubbyholes, each packed with knots of dried meadow grass, hosting several round, smooth objects about the size of large apples. The apples even had stems of a sort: a thick, stiff piece of tightly wound cord protruding from a small hole in the crown of each. Though there were nine holes, there appeared to be only six of the curious little objects.

Rem drew one from the chest and examined it. It was heavy—probably made of iron—and smooth all over except for a line of engraved script around the middle.

The script was runic—dwarven, to be precise.

Rem looked to Torval. He saw his partner's eyes grow wide and his mouth fall open in wonder.

"Impossible...," Torval muttered, eyes never leaving the object in Rem's hand.

"What is it?" Rem asked. He saw by the expressions on Tzimena's and Elvaris's faces that they were just as ignorant of what the iron spheres in the locked chest might be. But clearly Torval was not.

Torval snatched the heavy object from Rem's hand. "Do you have your flint and steel?" he asked.

Rem was even more confused. Flint and steel? "Right here," Rem said, reaching for the pouch at his belt where the stone and the steel rod lived.

Torval tipped the sphere in his hand sideways, to allow that stiff cord protruding from its crown to stand out. "Light it, then. Hurry."

Rem had no idea what Torval was getting at, but he did as commanded. He fished the flint and steel from his belt and began striking them together, producing sparks that never gave Torval the flame he was after.

Rem heard something metallic, far off to his left. It was outside the cart. The Red Raven's cage. Voices followed the ringing and the creaking.

"Hurry," the Red Raven said. "Your hands are shaking."

"Hold your cock," someone else said. "I'll have this popped in a jiff."

"We've got to find Tzimena," the Raven said quietly.

"Forget about her," a third person snapped. This one was female, her voice husky. "Tymon says—"

"Hang Tymon!" the Raven snapped. "I'm not leaving without her!"

Rem looked to Tzimena. She'd heard it, too. The sick look on her face told Rem that she wasn't sure where she'd rather be—sheltering in this cart, or out there on the road, with her secret lover who was about to be freed from his birdcage.

"Hurry!" Torval growled, and Rem realized he'd stopped trying to light the cord. He raked the flint along the steel rod two or three more times before some of the sparks finally did the trick. Suddenly the cord was burning—and the sparkling, sputtering flame moved along the cord's length with startling swiftness.

"Torval," Rem said, staring at the crawling flame. "What is that—"

Torval stood and lobbed the sphere up over the high wall of the cart, off into the woods. The instant the sphere left his hand, he dropped into a crouch again and clapped his hands over his ears.

Rem, Tzimena, and Elvaris all stared.

Torval lifted his hands for just an instant and clapped them back in place again. "Cover your ears! Hurry!" he said.

Rem just managed to do so before a sudden sound like a striking thunderbolt shook the world around him.

CHAPTER EIGHTEEN

Rem felt the cart—the whole forest—shake beneath and around him, some swift, sudden, godlike force that registered as a deep, unsettling vibration in his own chest. A billow of smoke belched up from the forest over the lip of the cart. The air stank of sulfur and char. When he removed his hands from his ears, he could hear the woodland outlaws shouting back and forth to one another: *What was that? Where'd that come from? Crikey, they've got magic!* Behind all their inquiries, there was another sound, close by.

Someone screaming.

Elvaris and Tzimena lowered their own hands from their ears. They stared at Torval as if he'd just awakened a dragon and asked them to pet it.

"What was that?" the Lady Tzimena demanded.

"That, milady," Torval said with an evil grin, "was dwarven mining craft, weaponized."

Rem looked to the open chest, to the five objects remaining, then back to Torval. "Blasting powder?" he asked.

Torval nodded. "The same."

"I thought...I'd heard...I mean, we were taught those were just stories!"

"Well," Torval said, indicating the chest and its deadly contents. "We've got five more stories to tell. Let's not dally, eh?"

Rem nodded, snatched another powder sphere from the

chest, and tossed it to Torval. They repeated the ritual, Rem seeking a spark with his flint and steel, Torval lobbing the blasting sphere after its cord was lit—to the right side of the road this time—the four of them hunkering down and covering their ears just before an earthshaking explosion jostled the cart and filled the world once more with wafting smoke and the stench of sulfur.

"Somebody hit the ox wain!" one of the bandits cried. "Take to the trees if you have to!"

Another: "Up and over, lads! High arcs, just like in practice!"

Rem and Torval were busily trying to light a third blaster when something suddenly thunked down into the bed of the cart not a foot from them. It stood vertical, vibrating a little from the suddenly arrested force of its descent.

An arrow.

Cack.

Elvaris scrambled to grab the riders' shields stowed in the cart. She shoved one toward the Lady Tzimena, tossed another to Rem and Torval, then grabbed a third for herself. She held it over her head as though expecting rain.

"Milady," she said to Tzimena, suggesting the proper positioning for the shield.

Tzimena followed suit, and just in time. Two more arrows thunked down viciously, one landing in Wirren's unfeeling torso, the other just behind Rem and to the right.

Torval snatched up the shield Elvaris had thrown him and tried to position it so that it might cover both him and Rem at once. With his free hand he held the third blasting sphere. Rem's hands busied themselves trying to get a good spark to light the blaster's fuse.

There. A hiss and a hungry flame. Torval lowered the shield just long enough to stand and lob the sphere—forward and to the left this time, farther away than his prior tosses. Just as he fell to his knees and raised the shield again, drawing Rem into an uncomfortably close embrace, a trio of arrows whistled down in rapid succession. One landed an inch from Rem's extended boot; the other two slammed into the upraised shield and held fast. Rem dared an upward glance and saw the leading edge of one arrowhead peeking through the thick wood of the shield's inner curve.

The tossed sphere exploded. Rem, who hadn't had time to cover his ears before the thunderous roar, suddenly heard a terrible ringing. It was like a bell was struck and allowed to ring indefinitely, its knell sounding on and on into eternity, a single, unbroken wall of metallic gonging without interruption. Everything he heard was suddenly distant and muffled, the ringing drowning it all out.

He looked to Elvaris and Tzimena. Each had a shield to herself, which gave them greater protection, but their shields bore several arrows each, while still more stood in haphazard arrangement throughout the cart.

"We can't stay here," Rem shouted at Torval. "If they keep sending these arrows down upon us, one of them will hit its mark sooner or later!"

Elvaris broke in. Rem knew she was shouting, as well, but her voice still sounded deep and far away, as though she spoke from the bottom of a well.

"They'll have snipers in the trees soon!" she said. "If one gets a good angle, they can pick us off!"

Torval yanked his maul near. "Down the hatch, then!" he said, suggesting the ladies' means of ingress to the cart. "You two will have to make a break for the tree line while we cover you!"

Rem stared at Torval, the two of them impossibly close— close enough to kiss—under that upraised shield. The look that passed between them said all that needed to be said: if they left this cart and tried to cover the women while they fled, they'd have very little chance of surviving the encounter.

"There's nothing for it, lad," Torval said quietly. Rem couldn't hear him, precisely, but he knew what the dwarf had said.

"Eyes open, fists clenched, backs to the wall," Rem answered, and offered a mordant smile.

"Let's grab the last of these," Torval said, leaning sideways to try to pluck out the final three blasting spheres.

Something suddenly slammed into the outer wall of the cart. Rem couldn't be sure, because his ears still rang, but he thought it might have been glass, because it made an unmistakable shattering sound upon impact. The shattering was followed by a foul smell—sulfur again, and the unmistakable acridness of burning wood. Rem turned and saw flames visible just over the right-hand wall of the cart.

"Sundry hells," Torval growled. "They've got firebombs of their own..."

As Rem stared at the cart wall, saw the flames leaping over its far side and black smoke starting to swirl away into the woodland sky, his eye caught swift movement. It was an object of some sort—small, oblong—arcing from out of the trees. It looked as if its path would take it right into the cart bed.

He yanked Torval aside, suddenly unconcerned about trying to stay under the protection of the shield. The two of them sprawled toward Tzimena and Elvaris, putting a few more feet between themselves and the space they'd just occupied. As they hit the haphazardly piled supplies scattered around the women, the falling object hit the cart bed. It shattered upon impact.

Flames spread everywhere.

Some of the street urchins in Yenara called them dragon

gobs—bottles or jars of lamp oil or some other incendiary stuffed with a rag or scrap of cloth soaked in the same substance and set on fire.

And now the front end of the cart bed—including poor dead Wirren and the chest of blasting spheres—was in flames.

The blasting spheres!

Rem realized what was about to happen just as Torval yanked him backward, roaring as he went.

"Out the back!" the dwarf commanded, and threw the considerable weight of his compact body against the trifold gates at the rear of the cart. One strike was all it took. The gates flew wide and Torval toppled out onto the road. Rem shoved the women out ahead of him, and the three of them hit the ground running, making straight for an old, half-rotten log near the side of the road. They caught air and dove behind the log just as the blasting spheres succumbed to the flames.

The cart exploded, a roaring wall of thunder, smoke, and blunt concussive force. Rem felt himself hit the ground...was vaguely aware that the ladies had landed in a tangle within arm's reach...dared a glance up and saw the air roiling with poisonous black clouds, swirling embers, and flaming debris. The knelling bell in his ears had changed tone, but not fierceness.

They'll be coming, Rem told himself, trying to will his body to respond to his commands to move, to rise, to arm himself.

Any minute...coming...from the trees...from the road...

Torval? Where's Torval?

He forced himself up onto his knees, half tumbled against the enormous roots of a nearby cedar, blinked, and tried to orient himself. His head was swimming. His ears were useless. The whole world stank of fire and brimstone.

He kept his back to the tree and looked to Elvaris and Tzimena. Tzimena was bent over her bodyguard, studying a horribly bloody wound in the swordswoman's leg. A giant splinter of wood, as big as three fingers side by side, protruded from her thigh, crimson rivers spilling out around the site. As Tzimena struggled to tear cloth from her dress and stanch the bleeding, Elvaris kept trying to push her mistress off and get herself upright.

Rem pushed hard, feet on the ground, back against the tree. Clumsily he managed to get himself standing and drew his sword. He was searching the swirling smoke that swaddled them on all sides, wary of any attackers, when a pair of them simply materialized out of the haze.

They were right behind Tzimena, on the other side of the log the three of them had used for hasty cover. One was a man, nondescript in every way except for his woodsman's greens and the bow drawn tight in his hands. An arrow point gleamed, trained right at Rem, shaking a little as the man struggled to hold the draw. Beside him was the Red Raven. He had a sword in his hand, but it was at rest, hanging in a loose grip at his side.

"Tzimena," the Raven said. Rem could not hear him, of course, but he could read her name on the outlaw's lips easily enough.

Tzimena offered some terse response, barely sparing a glance over her shoulder. She was more concerned with tending to Elvaris's wounded leg. When she did not immediately leave Elvaris's side and answer the Raven's call, the outlaw stepped forward, grabbed her arm, and yanked her to her feet.

Rem lunged, ready to put his sword to use.

The archer at the Raven's side stepped forward, making the lethal closeness of his arrow, the lethal ease of his shot, all too apparent to Rem.

Rem froze. He slowly lowered his sword, but did not drop it.

In answer to his grip, Tzimena jerked away from the Raven

and took a step back. The Raven's face betrayed an instant's frustration and fury. He lunged, holding her arm more tightly this time, and yanked her to him so forcefully that Rem thought her arm might pop from its socket. Tzimena's soot-covered face was streaked with tears, and she beat at the Raven and wriggled in his grasp, eager to be back at Elvaris's side. The Raven seemed to struggle now to control himself. He let her beat at him, but he held her firmly and made no attempt to block her haphazard blows. He seemed to be trying to honestly calm her, to get her to understand that hysteria would not serve her in the present moment.

Elvaris suddenly lurched upright. She swayed for a moment, then drew her sword and leveled it. "Let her go," she commanded. Rem could see beads of sweat on her dirt-streaked face, the way she breathed in ragged gulps. The pain of that leg wound had to be fantastic, and yet there she stood, trying to still do her duty.

"Toffey," the Raven said.

The bowman swung his drawn arrow from Rem to Elvaris. He couldn't hold that draw much longer. Rem could clearly see the strain in his shoulders.

Tzimena suddenly stopped her struggling. "No!" she cried.

"You'll come with me?" the Raven asked.

Tzimena was staring at Elvaris, giving a silent command with her eyes. She nodded. "I will."

Elvaris took a single step. "Milady!"

The Raven drew Tzimena close, an almost loving gesture. Tzimena threw up her hands. "Stand down," she said to her bodyguard. Then she looked to Rem. "Both of you. He won't hurt you if I just go."

Elvaris shook her head. "My job is to keep you alive, milady—"

"This is what keeps me alive," Tzimena said. "And the two of you. For now."

"Sir?" the archer said. "What about this one?" He swung his arrow back and forth between Rem and Elvaris, not sure which was the more important target now. Rem could see the strain sending tremors through his whole body.

The Raven looked to Rem, then to Elvaris. His expression was quizzical—an unspoken challenge. *Well? Will you or won't you?*

Rem threw down his sword. Elvaris did the same.

The Raven smiled. "Smart," he said. "All that remains is to stay here after we've gone. See to that one"—he indicated Elvaris—"she doesn't deserve to die on this road. Not today."

"If you hurt her," Rem said, staring right at him.

"She'll be safer with me than anywhere in this world," the Raven said, smiling with honest satisfaction. "On that, you have my word. Lower your arrow, Toffey."

The archer, Toffey, let out a long, relieved sigh as he simultaneously lowered the bow and slowly released his draw. He turned to the Raven and was about to speak when something long and sharp suddenly bit right into his skull and sent him tumbling sideward. It was an arrow, and it had killed him before he'd even known it was coming.

The Raven yanked Tzimena into his arms and pulled her out into the road, back toward where his half-ruined cage stood on its little two-wheeled cart amid the ruins of the larger ox wain. Rem swung his gaze about, trying to find the sniper who'd put that arrow in Toffey's skull.

She stood about ten yards away, on the verge of the road, nearer the fallen redwood that blocked their retreat. It was Galen, face a mask of icy, lethal determination. The scout held a compact, elegantly curved compound bow, and she already had another arrow nocked and drawn.

"Let the lady go!" she shouted. Rem had no doubt that if she loosed that arrow it would hit its mark.

The Raven stood, arms locked around Tzimena, using her as a shield. Tzimena looked as though she had given up her struggle to be free of him, perhaps waiting for a better opportunity to present itself.

Rem looked back and forth between the two, wondering what would happen. It was only as he swung his gaze toward Galen that he saw another form bleeding out of the smoke swirling behind her.

"Galen, behind you!" Rem cried.

Galen spun, turning fully around in the span of a single breath. Her would-be assailant—another of the Raven's outlaws—charged out of the smoke as she whirled, and took an arrow in his throat. As he fell, choking on his own blood, Galen snatched another arrow from her quiver and spun back to face the Raven again.

But the Raven was on the move. He was yanking Tzimena along, one arm held in an iron grip, across the road and into the dense green foliage on the far side.

Rem snatched up his sword and took off running.

"I'm going to regret this," he said to himself, then plunged into the brush after them.

Twilight fell hard upon them, the sun lost behind the encroaching mountains and many ranks of enormous trees, shadows deepening moment by moment, the forest choked with lingering clouds of smoke from the spent blasting spheres and the Devils' firebombs.

Emerging from the brush on the verge of the road, Rem saw the Raven just ahead, Tzimena in tow, speeding through the ferns and the undergrowth, wending around the enormous trees, due west, toward the river. Even as Rem gave chase, he began to realize that the woods around him were full of activity. He heard the ring of swords and shouted orders, saw the Raven's outlaws retreating on paths of their own off to his left and right. Clearly some of the others in Rem's party—the lord marshal, Wallenbrand, perhaps Tuvera and Redriga—had made it off the road and taken the fight to the outlaws. The outlaws, now seeing their master freed, fell back rapidly, two by two. Half the travelers were dead, and the outlaws had what they wanted; there was no point in fighting any longer.

Rem didn't like all the chaos. His goal was singular: he wanted to wrest Tzimena from the clutches of the Red Raven. He didn't care if the Raven escaped; he didn't care if he had to kill the man or any of his servants in order to succeed; he only knew that, with so many dead and so much blood shed, the only thing that could possibly assuage the sense of failure that threatened to overwhelm him was making sure that the Raven didn't get away with the Lady Tzimena. It was that simple. If they couldn't deliver the Raven himself safely to the Duke of Erald, the least he could do was save the duke's bride-to-be.

Torval, he suddenly thought. *Gods and ministers of grace, what happened to him? He opened the rear gates of the cart and was the first out, but I was so eager to get Elvaris and Tzimena to cover that I lost track of him! What if he's lying back on that road, right now, bleeding, dying, torn to pieces by the explosion?*

Then there's no hope for him, a calm inward voice replied. *The girl is your mission now. Get her away from that smirking bastard from the cage, and you'll have done something worthwhile today. Mourn Torval when you know that he's gone, not before.*

His foot caught a root and Rem nearly went sprawling. Miraculously, he managed to right himself and begin his pursuit again. Somewhere close, off to his right, he caught sight of fleet figures moving through the brush, shouting short, sharp reports and commands back and forth between them. He dared a look and saw that it was two of the Raven's men—the Devils of the Weald—dressed in the same woodland greens and hoods as the two men slain on the road by Galen. Off in the distance, a hundred yards away or more, Rem could just make out other figures moving through the greenery, on the same westward path, stretched out in a broad, spacious line. Clearly the outlaws had a plan and they were now following it, affecting a swift and orderly retreat that would've made a veteran mercenary captain proud.

The river. There must be some way the lot of them planned to cross the river. If they could make it across swiftly and destroy their own means of passage so no one following could use it, that would give them every advantage. There'd be no hope of staying close on their trails or tracking them back to their hidden lair after that.

But I'm not trying to track them all back to anywhere, Rem reminded himself. *My only task is to get Tzimena out of that bastard's bloodied hands. That's all. Nothing more.*

Up ahead the roar of the river increased as Rem drew near. Briefly he lost sight of the Raven and Tzimena on their headlong plunge through the brush, but suddenly, there were two moving bodies cutting north to run parallel to the river instead of heading directly for it. Maybe there was a deer path that they followed? Some deadfall they had to move around? From Rem's vantage behind them, his world an unbroken screen of knotty tree bark, fern fronds, and tree boughs, the finer details of the forest and the terrain were lost. Worse, the light around him was fading fast.

Rem suddenly saw a bare track of earth bending away from the trodden path that he ran upon. It headed right toward the path that the Raven and Tzimena were on, dead-ending on a little rise above and ahead of them.

He made his decision instantly and followed the track. This was his chance. If he could get ahead of them and cut them off—

He made the rise, leapt over a fallen log, hit the ground on the far side, and spun, righting himself. He was in their path now, sword at the ready.

The Raven skidded to a stop. Tzimena kept running, trying to use momentum to yank herself out of his grip and hurry to Rem, but her kidnapper's hold was ironclad. She screamed as her arm was yanked back toward him and her feet slid out from under her. Tzimena hit the forest floor with a cry and cursed. The Raven, his own sword leveled in his left hand and ready for a duel, reached out with his free right hand and dragged Tzimena back toward him by her dress.

Rem waited, trying to size the man up. If he was, in fact, Korin Lyr of Erald, then he would've had good sword training all through his youth and young manhood. If he'd managed to make a living in these woods as an outlaw, that would've provided him even more valuable experience. He was also left-handed, presenting a number of challenges for Rem. No matter what, the contest ahead would be a deadly one, and Rem couldn't afford to lose.

You're also exposed, he reminded himself. *Any one of his Devils could sneak up on you from behind here. They're just a little ways off in the woods, at your back. If one of them sees you here, standing toe to toe with their master . . .*

"Let me pass," the Raven said.

"Let her go," Rem countered.

The Raven yanked Tzimena closer. "She's safer with me than she'll ever be with you."

"Don't do this, Rem," Tzimena said, her face truly pained.

"Are you telling me you want to go with him?" Rem asked.

"I'm telling you I don't want anyone else to die to keep me away from him," she said. "Isn't that enough?"

The Raven shot a glance at her then: shock, hurt. It was as if that was the first time he truly knew—truly *believed*—that Tzimena didn't want to run away with him into the woods to be an outlaw's wife.

"You can't mean that," the Raven began. "I told you—"

She turned on him, defiant and angry. "Aye, Korin, you *told* me—but you never *asked* me."

Rem took a single step to close the distance between them. The Raven's momentary distraction was blown away when he saw Rem's advance. He yanked Tzimena close, into his arms, and held her tightly while still extending his sword in his left hand. She was his shield now. Rem couldn't strike or attack in any way without endangering her.

The Raven's eyes flicked sideward—noting something, focusing on something just over Rem's right shoulder. Rem knew exactly what that meant, even before he heard the low, slight scuff of a boot on the loamy earth.

He spun just in time to parry a dagger thrust from the man who'd been sneaking up behind him. While the would-be knife man cursed and moved to make another strike, Rem brought the pommel of his sword around in a flat, backhand arc that connected hard with the villain's jaw and sent him plummeting to the ground, dazed and bleeding from the mouth.

But he wasn't alone. There were three Devils on hand now, all approaching from what had been Rem's rear just moments ago. Two were men—one with a sword, another with a hand ax—while the third was female—young, ruddy faced, bearing in her hands a longbow with an arrow already nocked but not yet drawn.

Cack, Rem thought. *Not much I can do against these three.*

He heard the rattle of fern fronds and spun again. The Raven wasn't standing alone, either. Two more outlaws had joined him, also armed, also closing on Rem and ready for a fight.

The Raven and five accomplices in all.

Rem was surrounded.

He had only one means of escape: the river. No one blocked his path toward it, and it was only about twenty yards from where he stood. That girl with the bow might be able to hit a moving target, but there was no way he could stand against all these armed assailants and come out on top. He was good, but he wasn't *that* good.

"Drop your sword," the Raven said.

Rem did as commanded.

The Raven smiled—a rather sad smile, Rem thought—then gave a little nod.

Rem knew what that meant and dove just as he heard the twang of the loosed bowstring. He hit the ground, saw the arrow zip lightning-quick through the empty air he'd just occupied, then scurried up onto his feet again and took off sprinting.

"Run!" Tzimena screamed.

"Take him!" the Raven ordered.

Rem faintly heard a bow creak and the string twang again. He half expected to feel the bite of an arrow an instant later, but instead the missile plunged finger deep in the trunk of a cedar that he went speeding past.

The river, make the river, get to the river.

He heard boots pounding the forest floor, the rattle of disturbed underbrush, cries of exhortation and hatred.

"Get him!"

"He's going in!"

"Shoot him, Derva! Now!"

Rem leapt from a little bluff on the riverbank right into the roiling current. The water was cold—colder than he'd anticipated. That bone-numbing cold stole his breath as wet, frigid darkness engulfed him. Rem kicked for the surface in answer, desperate for air, for some sense of control.

He broke the surface and drank in a lungful. Blinking water from his eyes, trying to tread water even as the current swept him along, Rem looked back at the place he'd just abandoned. He saw the Raven's outlaws standing on the shore, receding, staring, cursing, farther and farther away by the second.

The current had him now. It was fast. He slammed into a rock, rolled around it, and was dragged underwater on its far side.

Well, he thought, *if Torval's dead, I'm about to join him . . .*

CHAPTER NINETEEN

Upon leaping out of the ox wain, Torval had scurried under the only cover available: the little two-wheeled cart that supported the Red Raven's cage. For an instant the world was all fire and roar, ringing ears and blunt concussive force. The cage cart bucked and skidded backward in the mud a bit, but Torval was still sheltered beneath it. He might have blacked out—he couldn't be sure—but soon enough, the world around him came into focus again, and the dwarf realized that he was not, in fact, dead and blasted to a million pieces. Only then did he finally stir.

He was shocked to find that the cage cart hadn't just skidded through the mud in answer to the explosion, but collapsed. Its entire ruined bulk lay atop him, and it took a great deal of effort to force himself upright and shrug all the wreckage off himself. When Torval finally managed to do so, he saw a ruined landscape in front of him that looked like the aftermath of a major military action. Every tree limb that had hung too close to the explosion was now splintered or in flames. A dead man lay just a few feet away—an arrow protruding from his skull—while another lay farther on, heaped right in the road beside the fallen tree that now barricaded the road. Smoke and the smell of charred wood clung to everything. The world was hazy and stinking and indistinct. Torval breathed the vile air and thanked a whole panoply of gods he didn't believe in that he was still alive to smell it.

Movement to his left. Torval turned and peered through the smoke. It was one of the Lady Tzimena's guards—Galen, was it?—helping Elvaris to her feet. Elvaris was wounded—he could tell by her uneasy gait—but Torval couldn't tell precisely what had happened to her. The dwarf turned in a full circle to survey the scene.

All that remained of the oxcart were two broken wheels and a lot of charred wreckage. Farther ahead, the ox lay dead in the mud, though it looked as if the animal had succumbed to several of the Devils' arrows long before the wain exploded. Beyond the dead ox still hitched in traces without a cart, Torval saw more prone figures through the swirling smoke: dead horses, dead bandits, dead allies. Only a few live bodies moved among the ruin.

One of them, Torval suddenly realized, was the lord marshal. For the first time, the proud soldier had allowed his shoulders to slump, his weariness and despair to register through his normally strong frame. He was picking out their own dead from among the slain on the road, dragging them away from any beast or bandit who lay too close, gathering them at the verge of the road. Beyond him, Torval thought he saw more moving forms—one sitting, wounded, another tending the wounded person—but the air was too hazy to make out just who it was.

"Torval!" Elvaris called. She sounded very surprised to see him.

Torval turned toward the swordswoman. Blinked. Raised a hand.

"Here," he said weakly, and stumbled away from the cart wreckage to meet her.

Elvaris sat on a fallen, hollowed-out log, one leg stretched out straight along its surface. Galen, the scout from the Lady Tzimena's company, was examining her companion's wound. As Torval tottered closer, he could just make out its particulars: a big, jagged piece of wooden shrapnel lodged in Elvaris's left thigh, blood already coagulating around it. If she hoped to save her leg, that huge splinter needed to come out, but removing it would most likely provoke a new round of bleeding that could kill her.

"That's bad," Torval said, gesturing at the wound. "Needs cauterizing."

"I agree," Galen said calmly. "Care to build me a fire and heat me up a blade?"

Torval nodded. As he turned to shuffle away, Elvaris spoke.

"I thought we'd lost you for sure," she said. "After the explosion—"

"The cage cart," he said with a weak gesture. "I was underneath. I guess it saved me."

"What was that?" Galen asked. "I've seen incendiaries before—lamp oil in jars, like the stuff the Devils employed, or that pitch-based stuff the Magrabaris use in naval warfare—but never anything so . . . so . . ."

"Volatile?" Torval asked.

Galen nodded. Then added a word of her own. "Destructive."

"That's the art of my folk. It has all sorts of names, but the simplest is blasting powder. The recipe is a secret among our alchemists, and it's only gained renown among your kind in the last hundred years or so, and slowly at that. The *welk* aren't eager to let that fiery spirit out of its soul jar."

"So how did those bombs arrive in the bed of the wagon?" Elvaris asked.

"I put them there," someone said.

They all turned to find the lord marshal standing nearby, eyeing them with that familiar, dismissive gaze of his, like a schoolmaster studying a bunch of unruly children.

"Well, thank you, then," Torval said. "We only got to use three of them, but those blasting spheres saved our lives—"

"They were not for you," the lord marshal said, "and they were worth more than all three of you put together. Do you have any idea, you petulant stump, what those bombs cost me? How difficult it was to get any dwarf in that damned city of yours to even speak to me about them, let alone sell them to me? And now they're all gone—expended. And for what?"

Torval felt anger rising in him. "Well, they kept the four of us alive—me and Rem and Elvaris and the Lady Tzimena. My sincere apologies if our survival wasn't your highest priority."

"The Lady Tzimena," the lord marshal said, then made a point of looking around him before throwing up his hands. "Where is she now?"

"The Raven made off with her," Elvaris said. "Rem gave chase."

Torval whipped around toward the wounded woman. "Rem followed them?"

Elvaris nodded and indicated a stand of trees on the far side of the road. "Right through there."

Torval turned and stared into the empty, silent, darkening woods. "Sundry hells," he muttered. The lord marshal spoke then, as did Elvaris and Galen, in answer, but Torval was no longer listening. He was poking through the ruins of the half-blasted cage cart to find his maul, which he was sure still lay somewhere on the muddy ground where he'd been sprawled. When he picked its glint out in the failing light, he snatched it up and took off at a run into the woods.

"Torval, no!" Elvaris shouted. "Don't go out there alone!"

"I won't be alone once I find him!" Torval shouted over his shoulder and carried on into the brush.

He half expected to meet some of those infamous Devils of the Weald in his headlong plunge through the woods, but none materialized. Every now and again, Torval would see evidence of them: blood on leaves, footprints in the loam, broken branches or torn fern fronds, in one case a number of arrows, stuck upright into the earth for easy picking. But warm bodies were in short supply. Any outlaws formerly in the area either were dead or had fled.

Torval called out for Rem as he went—a foolish move, perhaps, if there were still brigands about, but he was little worried by that. That idiotic boy had gone off in pursuit of the Red Raven and his pretty prize, thinking, no doubt, that he could take the man in a one-on-one duel and fight off any of his accomplices who decided to come to his aid. Rem might bristle every time Torval or someone else called him Bonny Prince, but his instincts to protect pretty women from ill use were finely honed and nigh indomitable. He was cautious in a great many things, but if Rem believed there was a damsel in distress, he would rush in like a spring colt, eager to prove just how brave and gallant and dangerous he could be.

Torval had tried to break him of it, knowing it was an instinct that might get the boy killed, but clearly he had failed. Utterly.

And now here he was, in a darkening wood trying to find some evidence of the lad. Where in the sundry hells could he have gotten off to?

Torval's night vision would serve him well, even in the dark, but seeing wasn't his primary concern. He was focused on what might happen to Rem even if he'd escaped death at the hands of the Raven and his companions. What would he do? Where would he end up? Torval supposed a young man of noble birth probably knew how to take care of himself in the woods, but these woods weren't like any others. Rem himself had tried to make that clear. They were vast, dangerous, and teeming with all sorts of unpredictable wildlife, from the hungry bears that innkeeper had spoken of to prowling, screaming hillcats to the outlaws and brigands that haunted the road.

What was that? Something glinting, lying right in the middle of a half-trodden path through the undergrowth, just off to Torval's right. Torval all but sprinted to the spot of trampled grass and earth. When he saw what lay there, something in the center of him seemed to drop, like a floor with the struts yanked out from under it.

It was Rem's sword—the one Torval himself had gotten him when he'd first joined the wardwatch. It was just lying there on the loam, discarded and ignored.

He wouldn't part with that, Torval thought, staring at the abandoned blade, *not by choice. If it's lying here, it's because he had to throw it down.*

But Rem wasn't lying there with it... That was something, wasn't it?

So what had happened? Had he been taken prisoner? Or had they just gotten the drop on him and forced him to throw down his blade before he'd made another run for safety?

Torval searched about him for some sign. He could see just fine, even in the failing light, but he knew nothing of woodcraft. Certainly he could recognize the most obvious and clumsy signs of passage—broken twigs and deep, clear footprints and the like—but he was no tracker, no scout. What could he glean from the world around him now?

The woods were brightening. Suddenly, when there had only been deepening gloom before, Torval realized that he had started to sprout a shadow. Someone was approaching with a light source; he turned to greet them.

It was Galen, the Lady Tzimena's scout, and old Wallenbrand, the lord marshal's lieutenant. Each of them carried a torch, their bright, flickering orange light making the shadows of the forest deeper, spewing the smell of burning pitch.

"Did you find him?" the old man asked. He sounded genuinely concerned.

Torval shook his head. "Here's his sword," he said, snatching up the blade, "but he's nowhere in sight. I don't know where he could be, what he might have—"

"Here!" Galen said, hurrying forward and lowering her torch toward the ground where Rem's sword had been lying. She knelt and reached out, indicating a very shallow, barely visible depression in the forest floor. "That's a footprint," she said, showing Torval. "Looks like a long stride—running. Heading straight that way."

She pointed, then rose and led the way through the bracken and brush, following the line of Rem's headlong rush.

Torval heard the sound and realized what they were moving toward: the river. Rem had been running, straight as an arrow, toward the Kaarten River. Soon he, Galen, and Wallenbrand had reached the spot where the bank suddenly dropped bluff-like toward the river below. It wasn't a long fall—no more than the height of a grown man—but it was certainly abrupt.

Galen knelt on the bank and studied Rem's tracks. "They stop here," she said. "And there's no distress at the edge. He didn't fall or slip—he took a running jump."

Torval stared down into the roiling waters. The river was wide here, but also rocky and uneven. It dipped and curled and bent, the waters tumbling and foaming on a gentle decline off toward the west, back the way they'd been traveling for the last few days. If Rem had leapt into the river and let the current carry him, he might have ended up all the way back at the ford they'd crossed that morning—or even farther!

"I've got to go after him," Torval said, and marched away from the river's edge.

"Torval, no," Wallenbrand said, stalking after him. "I know he's your mate, but we can't go traipsing off into the woods tonight. We have wounded to tend, and we've got to keep watch if we're going to survive 'til morning."

"That sounds like your problem, not mine," Torval said, not breaking stride as he barreled through the brush on a straight path back toward the road. "Our prisoner is gone, as is your duke's precious bride. You lot can see to the two of them—I'm going after my friend."

"He's right, Torval," Galen said. "I know what you're feeling—how frightened for him you must be—but if you go after him now, in the night, there's no telling what could befall you."

Torval had barely spoken to the woman during their travels, but he'd seen Rem talking with her more than once. The Bonny Prince had respected her, so Torval supposed he could just adopt the same position by default. But right now, he didn't want to hear any more attempts to dissuade him. He needed to *move*, to *seek*, to *do* something. He couldn't simply sit, wait, think…

"I can't just abandon him," Torval said, rounding on the female scout. She and Wallenbrand both halted. "He's alone out there, probably lost. He doesn't have my night vision and he doesn't have his sword. How's he supposed to protect himself?"

"He's no fool," Wallenbrand said. "He knows his way around horses, and he's been a good member of this expedition. If he dragged himself out of that river, then he's probably smart enough to stay put. He'll try to build a fire, keep a sharp stick at hand, and wait for us to come looking for him."

"And what if he *didn't* drag himself out of the river?" Torval snapped. "What if he's hung up on a fallen log somewhere, dead and cold? Do you think he'll wait 'til morning to be found then? Or will some hungry beast come along and cart him away? Or worse, what if he's still alive and he made it out of the water, but he's wounded? Hurt? Helpless?"

"Torval," Galen said, "right now, we're all hurt and helpless. Don't make it worse. Come back to camp and help us through the night. Come morning, I'll go with you myself. We'll find him, come hell or high water."

Torval stared at the woman, then at Wallenbrand. He took a number of deep, ragged breaths before he finally relented.

"Fine," he muttered. "First light."

"Impossible," the lord marshal said, once they were back on the road. "I forbid it."

"You what?" Torval asked, incredulous.

The lord marshal was singlehandedly preparing a hasty camp just off the forest road, only a short distance from the ruins of the wagon and the lined-up corpses of their companions. Currently he was seeing to the small fire now crackling in a hasty pit, doing his best to keep it stoked and fed with what little flammable wood they'd managed to scrounge.

"I said there will be no search party for your companion, master dwarf. Not tonight, and not come first light. Our first priority is recovering the Raven and the Lady Tzimena. Your foolish friend is on his own."

"All due respect, Lord Marshal," Elvaris broke in. She was sitting nearby on one of the dead horses. "We don't work for you."

"Ask your captain, then," the lord marshal said. He looked to Captain Tuvera. She was busy trying to clean and stitch up that seeping wound in Elvaris's thigh.

Tuvera didn't even raise her eyes from her work. "Our job here is to protect the Lady Tzimena. That's why her mother pays us. That's the whole reason we came along. If she's missing, she's the one we need to find."

"May I remind you," Galen said calmly, "that our charge ran away from us? She could've fought. She could've kicked, screamed, clawed, punched—done anything necessary to keep that bastard from running off with her. But she didn't."

"It wasn't that simple, Galen," Elvaris broke in. "One of the Raven's archers had Rem and me dead in his sights. Tzimena left with him to spare the two of us."

"How convenient," the hard-faced scout snapped. "Last time I checked, it wasn't the lady's job to keep any of *us* safe."

"Aye, that," Torval broke in. "Rem heard her talking with the Raven last night. Said she knew something was bound to happen. She just took his word for it that no one would be hurt."

Tuvera raised her eyes, staring. Clearly she could not believe what Torval had just reported.

"Did she now?" the lord marshal asked.

"Did I stutter?" Torval asked in return.

"Did you hear her yourself?" Tuvera asked.

Torval shook his head. "No. That's just what Rem told me. I trusted his report."

"And still, you kept this from us?" the lord marshal asked, squaring his shoulders and planting his palms on his knees. "My son lies dead, master dwarf. If you two knew about this attack—"

"Spare me your sanctimony," Torval spat back, in no mood to have such a conversation with a man like him. "We were the odd men out in this company—how did we know who to trust? Certainly not you, you gods-damned strutting peacock. You haven't wanted us here from the start."

"Because you were a burden!" the lord marshal shouted. "You coin-grubbing sons of whores! Unable to take the word of a man of honor—"

"Man of honor?" Torval answered. "If you're so gods-damned honorable, why don't you tell Captain Tuvera and her soldiers who the Red Raven really is?"

The lord marshal's eyes went wide. "What did you say?"

Torval knew it was a rather daring gambit—perhaps even a foolish one—but there was no point being delicate any longer. All cards needed to be slapped onto the table and read, and he would know if Rem's theory about the Raven was correct only if he confronted the lord marshal with it.

And now the man's look of shock and panic told him all that he needed to know.

"What's he talking about?" Tuvera asked.

"Aye, what's he talking about?" Croften added. An arrow still protruded from his shoulder, awaiting ministrations.

"I won't be interrogated," the lord marshal said. "Especially not by a worm-ridden, grub-eating, shrunken little mercenary who extorts whores and thieves for a living."

"Then you'll be interrogated by me," Tuvera said, rising to her feet and facing off with the lord marshal now. "I am captain of a royal honor guard and your peer in this affair. Tell me now, Lord Marshal, what is this dwarf intimating?"

"Nothing," the lord marshal said, determined to stonewall them. Torval saw that he was trying to control his expression and body language now—removing the stricken look from his face, bending forward, letting his balled fists loosen and release. He actually thought he could convince them that his silent panic had been nothing at all.

"Rem heard the Lady Tzimena call the Red Raven by the

name Korin. Tell me, Lord Marshal, have you ever known a man named Korin? Or worked for one?"

Tuvera's blue eyes were large and wondering. Clearly she was starting to understand. "Korin...as in Korin Lyr? Your duke's murdered brother?"

"Not murdered at all, apparently," Torval said, still challenging the lord marshal with a white-hot glare to argue. "Korin Lyr *is* the Red Raven!"

The lord marshal pointed at Torval. "You would believe this foolish dwarf? This illiterate, inbred pickmonkey who makes his living cracking heads and jostling coin from hardworking people?"

"I would indeed," Wallenbrand said bitterly. "That explains a great deal, I think."

"That's who we were hired to help him catch?" Croften asked, face a mask of shock and confusion. "A runaway duke?"

"Hired?" Torval broke in. "I thought you were Eraldic house guards?"

"Provisionally," Wallenbrand said. "We only met the good lord marshal two weeks ago, in Yenara, when he hired us to help him trap and transport a notorious outlaw. Croften, Wirren, and I? We're not house guards—we're mercenaries."

Torval couldn't believe his ears. Hadn't Rem suggested this very thing? Hadn't he noted that all the lord marshal's men seemed to be using private tack and harness on their horses—the sort one owned, not the sort one acquired with a hired nag? Torval hadn't been sure what to make of it, but now it made sense.

These men weren't the survivors of an ambush. They'd been hired by the lord marshal in Yenara. And they were waiting for the Red Raven to show himself. Which meant—

"You didn't lose any of your men, did you?" Torval spat at

the lord marshal. "You didn't chase the Red Raven to Yenara, you were *waiting* for him!"

The lord marshal leapt to his feet. His voice was a roar in the night-silent forest. "I lost men!" he shouted. "They were waylaid here, in this forest, on this very road, carrying missives regarding our rendezvous with the Lady Tzimena!"

"But you weren't among them!" Torval pressed. "You were so eager to capture your prize, you sent your own soldiers into harm's way!"

"Used them as bait," Wallenbrand said. "To draw him out." The old mercenary sighed and shook his head. "It would seem, Torval, that none of us had the whole story."

The lord marshal looked to Captain Tuvera now. Though his aspect remained severe—belligerent—his voice carried a note of desperation. "Captain," he said, "these men are hired hands, and this dwarf is a hanger-on. I swear to you, my only concerns in this are the Lady Tzimena's safety and the Red Raven's final date with justice."

"I don't know a gods-damned thing about your hired hands or this dwarf," Tuvera said bitterly. "But your face is telling me all I need to know about their words and how true they are."

"You lying snake," Elvaris spat. "You knew this whole time! Your own men and our noble lady—just bait to catch your errant prince?"

Galen was shaking her head, trying to keep up with the revelations as they tumbled forth. "That makes no sense," she said. "He's your master—the rightful heir to the throne."

"An inheritance he would rather steal than claim," the lord marshal said bitterly. "A throne he abdicated in favor of this—this banditry! He is a traitor to the Duchy of Erald and a villain of the highest order, and if it is with my last breath, I will see him punished."

A long silence fell among them, each of the party trying to make sense out of what they were hearing, how their predicament had gained an entirely new cast in light of hitherto unknown facts. Torval, for his part, turned what little he knew—what little the lord marshal had said—over in his mind.

"You say he abdicated," Torval finally said. "But you also brand him a traitor. Which is it? It can't be both."

"I owe you nothing," the lord marshal said bitterly. "Least of all an explanation."

"If not him, then the rest of us," Captain Tuvera countered. "If you want any more aid from us, Lord Marshal, you'll tell us everything—truthfully. Otherwise we leave you here beside this road to rot and find your own way out of this forest."

"You would abandon your charge?" the lord marshal asked.

"Not her," Elvaris said. "Just you."

"That goes for us, as well," Wallenbrand said. "We were contracted to deliver the lady and the Raven, period. Not to go hunting through these woods in search of either. Start talking, Lord Marshal, or Croften and I will consider our contract null and void."

Torval wished he had something to threaten the lord marshal with, other than simple bodily harm. But, of course, he and Rem were the ones getting the short end of this stick. They'd come along to earn a reward. Knowing what he knew now, Torval wondered if that gold would have ever been paid...or if the Duke of Erald, eager to see his outlaw brother hauled in and executed to keep all his secrets safe, might have simply arranged for the two of them to disappear.

In some strange way, Torval thought, *this disaster might have saved us. If we'd simply carried on and delivered the Raven to the duke...*

"I was his teacher," the lord marshal said finally. "His teacher, his sworn protector...his friend." His voice was quiet now, gentle, even. The voice of a tired man unloading a heavy burden. As he spoke, he stared into the fire before them. "Since I was only a boy, I've served the House of Lyr, worn the livery of the duke. I was page to Korin's grandfather, then squire and first sword in his father's own ducal guard. I remember when Korin Lyr was first drawn from his mother's womb— may Aemon protect her. For the greater part of my life, my strength, my purpose, all were bent to the protection and nurturing of the House of Lyr. Korin, his brother—the both of them—were like my own sons. In some ways more so, because my boy was never as gifted or as promising as either of them."

Torval suddenly thought of Rem, and his claims about his own father's hard heart and unwavering demands. No wonder his young partner had disliked the lord marshal so intensely upon first meeting him.

"But something in my instruction failed to take hold. Korin Lyr, for all his bravado and skill and apparent charm, was no man of quality. He preferred whores and mummers to the ladies of the court his father tried to pair him with. Sought revels and leisure when he should have been at his father's elbow, attending to matters of state. And for all those years, Verin jostled to make a place for himself. He worked harder, sacrificed more of his time and effort, nigh killed himself in a vain attempt to win his father's favor over Korin's own firstborn primacy. But the elder Lyr would not be moved. Korin was firstborn, and so he would inherit, despite all of his failures, his clear lack of dedication. Verin was told, time and again, that his lot was to serve, to protect, to support, but never to rule."

Torval studied the lord marshal carefully. The man's eyes were downcast, aimed squarely into the crackling flames before him. His voice carried hints of bitterness and regret, anger and frustration, but his self-control remained. Not a single tear glinted in his eyes. His lip never quivered or bent into anything so vulgar as a frown.

"Those of us in the small council hoped a change might come upon the boy once his father passed, but that was not to be. He ascended to the throne, took the crown, and began his rule, but he was the same beast. Missing roundtables, ducking embassies and treaty negotiations to hunt in the woods or go whoring in the city streets. He bedded almost a dozen young women of quality—perfect matches for marriage—assuring each of his good intentions and pledging love and devotion… but he never married a one. We lost vital trade alliances, were threatened with all-out war, saw the honor of the House of Lyr impugned—all because one spoiled boy could not grow up and accept his duty."

"So you tried to murder him," Torval said. "To put his brother on the throne."

The lord marshal raised his eyes. "We did not try," he said. "We succeeded. Or so we thought.

"It was agreed among a small number of us that Verin should rule, that Korin should be removed. We paid two of his more annoyed and embittered companions to accompany him on a long hunt in these woods, to make sure that Korin Lyr did not return. That he met with some fell hazard that would strike no one as strange or extraordinary. What we did not count on were the Devils of the Weald. They, apparently, found the three of them in the midst of conflict."

"How do you know all this?" Captain Tuvera asked.

"One of the two assassins survived the encounter. Barely. When we found him, half in the grave and left to die on the forest road, he gave us the story. He and his partner had made their move on the young duke, but failed to deliver killing blows. They'd given chase, but in the midst of that chase, the

Devils of the Weald found them. They slew his companion, filled him with arrows, and took the young duke prisoner. The Devils demanded a ransom. We offered them twice as much if they'd simply kill the young duke and rid us of him. Curiously, they never responded to our offer."

"How long before you knew they'd let him live?" Wallenbrand asked.

"A year, perhaps. The young duke—the new duke—had insisted on making his own hunt in the Ethkeraldi. Our party was ambushed by the Devils, and in the midst of the melee, I saw him. The boy I'd raised and protected and taught, firing arrows at his own royal house like a common brigand, smiling when I called his name and challenged him. I knew what a terrible mistake we'd made then. The old saying goes, *If you strike a king, you must kill a king, lest his fury be roused*. We tried to usurp a throne from a foolish, self-indulgent boy, but all we did was chase him into the wilds and make him a monster."

"But you couldn't leave him there, could you?" Torval asked. "He was a liability now. Living, breathing proof that the Duke of Erald was a pretender and the small council were a bunch of usurping schemers. That's why you want him so badly now. Why you've spent all these lives in an effort to run him to ground."

The lord marshal speared Torval with a cold glare. "It is no longer simply self-interest, master dwarf. Now, more than ever, it's a matter of honor. With every breath, that boy dishonors his house, his throne, his country. He dishonors my faith in him, all the sacrifices I—and others—made to make *something* of him. On top of it all, he's now taken my son from me—my *only* son!"

"You put your son in harm's way," Wallenbrand broke in. "No one else. Blame yourself for that."

"*He* is to blame!" the lord marshal roared. "And he *will* pay!

On my boy's blood and the graves of forty generations of the House of Lyr, that monster of a man will pay!"

"A monster you made," Captain Tuvera said.

"That may be so," the lord marshal said. "But I can unmake him. I *will* unmake him. And the lot of you, by Aemon, will help me!"

"How do you reckon that?" Torval asked. Was the man mad?

"Because all of you still want something. You, women, want to recover your good lady. You, sellswords and dwarf, want your gold. And I want the Raven. Help me get what I want, and I promise every one of you, you'll get what you desire and more."

Torval said nothing, simmering over the insult implicit in the lord marshal's pronouncement. Gold? Bah! He was far from gold-hungry now. All he wanted—all that would satisfy him—was the recovery of his friend and a safe, speedy journey homeward.

That, and perhaps—just perhaps—the lord marshal's head on a pike.

Chapter Twenty

After Rem's plunge into the waters of the Kaarten, Tzimena was hustled down to the river's edge, where a rope had already been tied across the stream's span, anchored high on a tree nearby and descending gently toward another tree on the river's far bank. Korin crossed with her, the two of them settled into hemp loops, then set loose to slide from one side of the river to the other. More of her onetime lover's accomplices waited on the far side to catch them and make sure they didn't collide with the tree the fly line was anchored to.

Once they were safely across, the rest of those on the river's opposite side joined them. Tzimena saw two more crossing lines farther upriver, widely spaced, and noted that, in all three cases, when it was time for a last person to cross, the line anchoring the rope on the eastern side of the river was undone, the person bringing up the rear was tied to it, then they leapt into the river and were hauled across by their mates. Someone might follow, but they wouldn't be using the Devils' crossing technique. Once everyone was over the river, their widely spaced company set off through the darkening woods at a rapid march, eager to put distance between themselves and their pursuers before night fell.

Tzimena did her best to take account of those whose company she was now trapped in, but it was difficult, seeing as the bulk of the group was scattered far and wide around her in the forest, and the last light of day was fast being sapped from the purpling wood around them. From what she could glean, the band was made up of men and women, most wearing old, ragged forest greens or rough-spuns mimicking the colors of the sylvan landscape around them. She saw women with scars and missing teeth; handsome men with oiled hair and good swords; filthy-faced children and hoary-bearded old men. A motley band, all in all, mismatched in every way except for their skill at hit-and-run warfare. On that count they were unbeatable.

I should've fought harder, she thought. *Refused to follow. Just dropped myself, right there on the forest floor. Made him drag me. Tried to hit him harder, tried to scar him, to hurt him. What have I done, letting myself be taken by these rogues and outlaws? Is he even the man I used to know—*

She suddenly tripped on a gnarled root. Before she sprawled forward and met the ground, facedown, Korin had her, catching her midfall. He held her in his arms—gently, with concern—and stared into her eyes.

"Easy now," he said softly. "The darker it gets, the more the roots will try to trip you. Step lightly."

"Step lively," a tall woman up ahead said over her shoulder. "We need to move faster, not more carefully." She was Korin's height or taller, her mouse-brown hair cut short and swept away from her face. She was the tallest, most powerfully built woman Tzimena had ever seen—and the core of Tzimena's entire house guard was made up of strong, capable women. But the women in her mother's employ tended to be wolves or panthers or even hunting hounds, whereas this one was a full-on mother bear or lioness. Even her bow—a full-length, professional archer's longbow—was larger and more formidable than those wielded by most of the men around her.

"Just keep marching, Tymon," Korin said. "We'll get where we're going soon enough."

The woman, Tymon, though several paces ahead, snorted audibly. There was something between her and Korin, Tzimena could tell: a mutual respect, but also a sense of betrayal or disappointment...as if Korin had done something to offend her, but she had yet to make the nature of the offense known. Tzimena didn't relish hearing about it. Infighting would do little to procure her safety while she tried to figure out how to get away from her onetime betrothed and his merry band of thieves and killers.

"There'll be food when we make it back," Korin said quietly beside her. "Wine and beer, too. We've got barrels and barrels in reserve. We found caves in the woods—a veritable labyrinth, with multiple entrances and exits. It's amazing—wait until you see it!" He sounded like a child reporting the sumptuousness of his home to a newly arrived traveler.

"Food sounds good," Tzimena said with honest relief. "I'm starving."

"Prisoners eat at our discretion," Tymon said over her shoulder.

"She's not a prisoner," Korin snapped back.

Tymon threw a long, wondering glance back over her shoulder without breaking stride. "Isn't she?"

Korin didn't respond. Tzimena didn't like the sound of that.

They walked for hours, until well after the sun had gone down. When the wood was finally too dark to see in, small torches were lit along the advancing line and the group carried on, those still marching in darkness following the lights borne by those leading the way. Everywhere around them the forest came to life: small claws scrabbling on the loam, small bodies rattling the underbrush in their furtive passage, the churring of nightjars, and the wondering hoots of owls. At intervals she heard hillcats screaming in the distance, the sound chilling her blood with how distressed—how human—it sounded. Once or twice, Tzimena thought she heard the sounds of something larger—a deep rumbling, as though in a watching predator's gullet. But each time one of those sounds reached her ears and made her stop in her tracks to examine the impenetrable darkness surrounding her, Korin would gently take her arm and urge her along.

"What's out there?" Tzimena finally asked him.

"Just about everything," Korin said calmly. "Eyes forward. Keep moving. Among us you're safe."

She seriously doubted that, but she did as she was told.

Finally, after an apparent eternity, the land started to slope gently upward. They trudged with the incline, their scattered party gradually coalescing into something like a snaking, single-file line, until eventually, after pressing through a close copse of trees that barely allowed passage for one or two at a time, they broke into a clearing on a sort of promontory, tucked between the rocky outcroppings of a gently rising hillside. Tzimena saw guards posted upon the high rocks ahead and supposed they were guarding the entrances to those caves Korin had spoken of. In the gloom she could pick out at least two small cave mouths, with dim firelight burning deep within them. Below the sharp ledges and sculpted stone of the hillside lay a small encampment made up of lean-tos and stone-circled cookfires, as well as a few random tables standing right out in the open for the preparation of victuals. Moving amid this ad hoc outdoor kitchen, more people awaited them. Tzimena estimated the attack group from the forest consisted of about fifteen outlaws in total; another dozen—men and women, children and elderly—waited here in the lee of the hillside.

"There he is!" an old man wheezed out of the company,

and came tottering forth, one arm outstretched, toward Korin. His left hand was tied up against his body, visible, but clearly withered and useless. "There's our prodigal master, come home again!"

The old man laughed as he threw his good arm around Korin. Korin hugged him warmly, a bright smile on his face. There were torches and lamps spaced around the little amphitheater between the outcroppings, providing much more light than there had been in the woods. After a long embrace, Korin withdrew. The old man turned his protuberant, bulgy-eyed gaze on Tzimena.

"And is this her?" he asked from behind his untrimmed whiskers. "Is this the bride?"

Tzimena shot a glare at Korin. *Bride?*

"This is Tzimena," Korin said, his gaze begging her for both silence and patience. "Tzimena Baya, Holgur Deadhand, one of my most trusted companions."

"I thought we were all your trusted companions," the woman, Tymon, said from one of the tables where food was being prepared. She was greeting a woman engaged in vegetable chopping. They shared quiet words and quick, furtive kisses.

A boy milling among the newly arrived group was looking around, reading all the faces, clearly searching for someone he wasn't finding.

"Where's Mott?" he asked. He couldn't have been more than twelve.

"We lost him, boy," a big bruiser with a war hammer said. The man offered a fell glance to Korin and continued. "We lost many. Too many."

"Do we have a count?" Korin asked, undeterred by the hammer swinger's silent insinuation.

A middle-aged bowman with a shaved head and gold rings in both ears responded. "Mott, Taron, Beidel, Crumbley, and Jinx, by my count."

"Laric and Adolyn, as well," someone else added.

"That's seven," Tymon said, now approaching Korin, her longbow finally laid aside. "Seven of our best, for you"—she looked to Tzimena—"and for that."

That. Tzimena didn't care for the insinuation. It wasn't pride that made those words hurt, it was practical concern; clearly this Tymon was someone of power and influence in the group...and she regarded Tzimena as little more than a piece of property.

And not very valuable at that.

"This was my wish, and you realized it," Korin said. "You have my gratitude, Tymon. Eternally. Now, if you'll give us a moment..."

"A moment?" the woman asked, incredulous, then stepped closer. She spoke to Korin quietly, through clenched teeth. "There are people mourning here, Lyr. Every one of those we lost had a father or a mother or a lover or a sibling or a child here—every one. You'd turn your back on their suffering now so you can entertain your whore?"

"I'm no one's whore," Tzimena said, the words tumbling out before she could catch them. A fury was rising in her, despite the fact that she knew it would not improve her position. "May I remind you, I was dragged here. I didn't come of my own free will."

Korin looked wounded by those words.

Tymon just sneered. "Didn't fight very hard, did you?"

Tzimena felt something inside her contract and bristle, but she knew better than to raise further objections. She was nothing here—no one. A bargaining chip. If she was going to find her way out of this, she had to blend into the background and make these outlaws drop their collective guard...

"Watch your mouth," Korin hissed back at Tymon. "Tzimena is my guest here, which makes her welcome and safe. If that's a problem for you, we can take it up together later. For now we need some solitude—just a little. I need to make sure her head's in the right place."

"Fine, then," Tymon said. "Later. But know, sir, this isn't over. We've suffered losses by hewing obediently to your commands. Sooner or later you'll need to justify yourself and answer for them."

"Later, then," Korin said. Once more he had Tzimena by the arm. "Come on," he said to her quietly, "follow me."

Tzimena let herself be led away. They moved through the crowd around the cookfires, crossed the little clearing, then climbed over a number of rocks shouldering their way out of the hillside until they finally reached a little stone table under an outcropping that lay farther up the slope from the camp. It was like being on a balcony of sorts, and it gave Tzimena a wonderful view of the world she was now engulfed by. What she saw was the camp itself—the outdoor mess area hugging the rocky slopes, sentries and evening strollers moving about on the rocks and ledges above. Now that she was closer, and at a higher vantage point, she could see the cave entrances more clearly, as well as the lights burning within them. A small, shallow stream— spring fed, no doubt—spilled out of a fissure in the rocks, flowed down the rocky hillside, and burbled its winding way through the camp below before heading off into the distant woods. Beyond the caves and the hillside and the camp, however, the rest of the forest below and around them was black as a pot of ink, with no light or sign of civilization anywhere. The stars above were bright and cold in an almost-cloudless sky, a lonely crescent moon frosting the endless miles of breeze-stirred tree-tops and black mountains that bounded the valley in pale silver.

Korin bid Tzimena sit on a boulder. He took the one beside her. It was hard, but not a bad perch. For a time they sat in silence, staring at the activity throughout the camp, listening to the distant wash of sounds drifting up from the forest that surrounded them, studying the stars in their endless millions as they crawled across the firmament above them.

"What now?" Tzimena asked.

"That's up to you," Korin said amiably, as though they were a pair of lovers on holiday.

Tzimena tried to study Korin's face, but there was very little she could discern in the dark. The dim light afforded by the torches and lamps of the camp just picked his silhouette out of the darkness and made him solid. It did little to truly illuminate his features.

"I'm your prisoner," Tzimena said slowly. "I fail to see how I have any choice in what comes next."

"You're not my prisoner," Korin said, "you're my guest."

"Then I can leave anytime?" Tzimena asked.

Korin paused before answering. "Not right away. Better to wait."

"Then I *am* your prisoner."

"Would you prefer to be *his*? Verin's? You know well that a prisoner is what he would've made of you."

Tzimena sighed. "I thought I explained myself—"

"You tried," Korin said. "We had very little time before the lord marshal arrived and I had to flee."

Tzimena shook her head. "What were you thinking? Coming all the way to the city? You had to know you'd be caught, one way or another."

"I honestly didn't," Korin said, chuckling a little.

"And your men? The four who accompanied you? What happened to them?"

He shrugged. "Not sure. I haven't seen them since we were separated in your quarters."

He fell silent again. Tzimena tried to read that silence, could not, but made her own assumptions, at any rate. Korin's infernal coolness was infuriating.

"So," Tzimena said, "four of your men could be rotting in a dungeon or shipped off to a mine right now, and you don't give a damn? Seven of your companions—your friends—died on the road today trying to free you and kidnap me . . . and you don't give a damn?"

"That's ridiculous," Korin snorted. "Of course I give a damn. Those were my people. But once I learned of your betrothal—"

"Once you learned of my betrothal, you couldn't countenance letting your brother have something you wanted . . . even though you left everything else that was yours behind?"

He turned to face her now. She saw the tiny glint of his eyes in the darkness. "That's not fair."

"Oh, I think it is," Tzimena said. "What else could drive the mighty, cunning Red Raven to such foolhardy lengths but unrequited love and undying sibling rivalry?"

"I didn't come to humiliate him," he said, a little too earnestly, "I came because I loved you."

"Once, perhaps," Tzimena said. "But honestly, Korin, what am I to you now? It's been ten years since we last saw one another. Eight since our last correspondence. Or had you lost count? Do you really think I can live here? Thrive here? I can ride and fence and loose an arrow as well as anyone in my country, but I'm a creature of the court. That is where I belong. I can't stay here. Not for any length of time."

"That's not what you said in Yenara." His voice was dark, full of betrayal.

"I said I missed you. I mourned you. And, finding you again, I wished we'd had more time. But this...bringing me here. It won't work, Korin. This place will kill me. And if this place doesn't, your people will."

"That's preposterous," he said. "They are my people. What I want, they want—"

"Is that so?" Tzimena asked. "You are so, so dear to them? Tell me, then—how did you come to be their leader? What makes you so special that you could adopt the mantle of an outlaw who's been terrorizing these woods since we were both children, and get that outlaw's compatriots to follow you?"

Korin's silence was instructive. Tzimena swore she could hear him smiling, but that was her imagination, of course. Nonetheless, if there had been a candle nearby to allow her to see that there was, indeed, a self-satisfied smirk on his face, it wouldn't have surprised her. Korin had always been sweet and dashing and brave and bold and earnest—but he was also entirely too much in love with the stories he told himself. Even the ones that weren't true.

"I'd wanted to hunt in these woods for years, but our father wouldn't allow it. Said it was far too dangerous, what with all the bandits about. But, of course, when he died and the throne fell to me, there was no one to tell me no any longer. So after the dust settled and the duchy was done with its mourning, I finally decided I'd do what I'd always dreamed of doing, and put together a little hunting expedition for myself. Just me, my squire and page, and a pair of trusted companions with their own assistants. I left Erald in Verin's care and told them all I'd be back in a week or two.

"Unfortunately, Verin had paid my companions to assure my death in the woods. Broke my heart, really; they were the two best friends I had, like brothers since we were children."

"But easily bought, apparently," Tzimena said.

"Apparently," Korin agreed, nodding. He drew a deep breath. "They were chasing me, promising to make it quick if I'd just stop running, when the Red Raven and his Devils of the Weald found us. They killed my would-be assassins, then tied me up and dragged me away.

"They knew I was valuable, so they held me for weeks. Finally, word arrived one day that they'd received a message from Verin himself, delivered by a trusted adviser. The new Duke of Erald said that he was assured that his brother had died in the woods, on a hunting expedition, and that anyone the Devils presented as said brother was clearly just an impostor. He advised them to do away with me posthaste, and gave them twice the ransom they'd asked for my return. I must say, I was fairly impressed that he could deny my existence and pay handsomely for my execution with such ease."

Tzimena sighed. "Gods, Korin...Twice the price of your ransom, to kill you instead of returning you alive?"

Korin nodded again. "My dear brother. Honestly, he proved more cunning than I ever would have given him credit for. I knew he was always eager to please Father, but I never imagined him capable of wielding the power he so coveted."

"So what happened?"

Korin shifted on his boulder, turning to face her now. He sat forward, leaning, elbows on his knees, head below hers. "The Devils decided to kill me in ritual combat. They put a wooden stave in my hand, tied my ankle to a stake in the ground, and sent some of their best to do away with me for sport. I killed three and had the fourth on his back before the Red Raven himself—my predecessor—called an end to it. Dumb luck, really. I had nothing to lose, so I fought better than I ever had in my life."

Tzimena reached out then. Her situation was precarious and untenable, true, but there was still a great deal of the old love in her. And now, hearing his tale, beginning to understand what Korin had gone through to survive betrayal and abandonment, only to return to her now as the Lord of the Woodland, an outlaw of great renown...It struck her as most astounding. Almost romantic.

Almost.

But even if she could not entirely countenance his choices, she still pitied him. That was what led her to take his face in her hands and raise it so that she could look into the dark hollows where she knew his eyes to be, even though she could not see them in the deep gloom they occupied.

"Your brother betrayed you," she said. "Twice. There is no forgiveness for that."

Korin shrugged. "Perhaps not. In any case, the Raven gave me a choice: join his company and earn my keep, or die quick—a warrior's death, with honor. I chose to stay and earn my way. In truth, though the going was rough and the Devils never showed me any pity or understanding, I was happy during those months. I was earning my own way in the world, proving my worth. It was a good feeling."

"Did you have a plan?" she asked. "The desire to escape? To return home?"

"Of course I did," he said. "I made plans all the while—for months—trying to decide what I needed to go back to Erald. Money. Weapons. A plan to retake the throne and reveal myself. But one day, I rose and realized something: I simply wasn't that man anymore. If I returned, I'd just be another nobleman's son, wearing ermine and pronouncing edicts, getting soft and fat. But here—in the wild—I was someone. I'd earned the love and respect of my captors. I'd learned to finally love and respect myself. I was capable. I was deadly. I was a man. If I returned, I could only be less..."

Tzimena nodded, understanding. Presented in that fashion, she supposed it made sense. She supposed every child of noble birth wrestled with that doubt, that vague feeling that all the deference and opportunity they were afforded was a sham...an accident of birth...and longed to prove their mettle somehow, by some means concrete and unassailable.

"They adopted you, then," she said. "How did you finally come to lead them? Don't tell me the Raven took a shine to you and named you his heir when he sought to retire?"

"Oh no," Korin said, and she could hear the smile in his voice once again. "Surely not. He was a bastard, the Raven was. Bright and brave and brilliant, but a thorough, unmitigated bastard. My trials and my rise to prominence coincided—by sheer good fortune—with the slow dissolution of his own faculties. Maybe it was hard living—because life out here, make no mistake, is hard. Maybe it was the drink, for he certainly swilled enough. Everyone saw it, though. He started missing shots. Making mistakes during raids and ambushes. Dropping things. Failing to note details that nearly undid us.

"So I challenged him."

"Challenged him?" Tzimena asked.

"Aye, challenged him," Korin said. "To a duel, for the leadership of the Devils of the Weald. He fought hard...but I won. But even after he was stripped and left for the wolves, I knew there was value in the name. Just because the man who'd been the Red Raven died didn't mean the legendary, immortal Red Raven had to. And so I simply became him. And if I do say so myself, I think I've quite elevated the mantle. Some of the best songs now sung about the Raven in the taverns of the west are of *my* exploits since taking over, his own largely embellished or forgotten."

Tzimena was shaking her head in answer to the whole of his fantastic tale, not just its culmination.

"And yet," she said, "you've still chosen to stay here? All this time? To so harry your brother's caravans and military parades that he put a price on your head? And how did he even manage that, seeing as you were once the Duke of Erald?"

Korin shrugged. "I suppose it's not so hard," he said. "How many people ever see a duke, after all? Or a king or queen? And even if they have, isn't it usually from a great distance? No, all Verin had to do was replace most of the soldiers who knew me once he claimed the throne. After that it was easy."

"But you could have come forward," Tzimena said. "Made your own claim! Demanded justice! Shown the whole world that Verin stole what was rightfully yours, and tried to kill you in the process!"

"To what end?" Korin asked, and she heard the ardor in his voice. "I'm free here, Tzimena! I rule by the consent of these people! They chose me, and I keep them happy. We are all cast-offs here... unforgiven convicts, unrepentant sinners, people of no means or renown. Out in the world, we are all targets, or criminals. In here everything is ours, provided we can take it."

"Like you took me?" Tzimena asked.

"I haven't taken you," Korin said, and there was real frustration in his voice. "If anything, I rescued you! Did you really want to marry my brother? Was that your idea? Or his? Or, let me guess, your mother's?"

Tzimena lowered her eyes—a foolish gesture, she knew, since it was probably too dark for him to even see her face.

"Mother," she said quietly. "She vaguely recalled that we once met—many years ago—but she had no idea we'd become so attached to one another. Even across the years. I suppose I managed to keep that secret too well from her. When your brother made his offer to her, she actually explained to me who he was, and where Erald lay on the map...as if I didn't already know."

"To be fair," Korin said, "we were never in Erald together."

"We were barely anywhere together," Tzimena added. "At any rate, I had no good reason to turn down your brother's offer—not in Mother's eyes, anyway. Besides, the one time I met him, he reminded me of you."

Korin shook his head. "Words to pierce me like a dagger..." He sounded as though he were trying to laugh, but she sensed real sadness in his voice, as well.

"Korin," Tzimena said, "when I heard you'd died, I mourned. I mourned for months, silently, alone, because I could tell no one of the secret I'd been carrying. My mother, my companions... They saw the grief in me, but they couldn't reason out the cause. And I wouldn't tell them."

Even now, she felt childish saying it aloud. She had been seventeen when they first met, he nineteen, sent to the university in Toriel by his father. Face-to-face in a students' grogshop on the seedier side of town, they'd been instantly struck by the thunderbolt of some potent and pagan love goddess. While he studied, they carried on their clandestine affair, knowing that, as they were both of noble birth, but separated by a great distance, they could not simply choose one another. He'd been her first love—physically and emotionally—and he'd always sworn that she was his, though Tzimena had her doubts. And yet, during those years, he had seemed earnest. Unwavering. His letters were full of passion and poetry, and their times together nothing short of magical, now all tinged in her memory with the twin crowns of dashed hopes and sweet nostalgia. But then his father had learned of their association and forbidden his son from pursuing it further. He'd withdrawn Korin from the university and had him dragged home. After that Korin continued to write, and they managed once—just once—to meet in the free city of Orbhen for a last week of intimacy and adoration. Korin had left that encounter promising to make it all work; he would convince his father to allow their marriage, or he would simply await the old man's death. They need only be patient, and not give up on one another or their dream of being together.

Then the years flew by. The old duke died and Korin took the throne. The last letter he sent urged her to wait for him, just a little longer. Once he was crowned and settled on the throne, he could finally make their dreams into reality.

And then she'd received word. It was offered as gossip at a holiday feast, visiting dignitaries clicking their tongues and shuddering over the fate of that poor, misguided Lyr boy who'd insisted on hunting in the Ethkeraldi. Tzimena remembered well how she'd felt when she heard them speaking; how she'd assured herself they had the name wrong, or the duchy, and looked into it herself, only to learn that it was all true.

Korin was dead. Gone forever. Never to return. His last promise would remain forever unfulfilled. The strength of her grief was beyond even her own understanding. It had dulled and been packed away in the center of her for years now, but still, if she reexamined it, its potency left her more than a little puzzled and ashamed.

She'd met a young man, had a fling with him, and hoped to marry him. Those hopes were denied. Perhaps they were misplaced to begin with.

And yet something had kept that fire burning in both of them. Something pure and childish and hopeful…and probably lost. They knew there was little chance of their marrying, seeing as their separate homelands were so far apart and their political requirements rarely in accord. Hadn't Tzimena considered it the cruelest of ironies when her mother had first broached the subject of romantic interest from Verin Lyr, the Duke of Erald? *Impossible*, she'd thought. *Erald has never been interested in Toriel, nor Toriel in Erald. Why now? Is this just one more of fate's cruel jokes? First keep me from marrying the man I always loved? Then steal him from me by slaying him in the wilderness? And finally, when he is gone, send his brother a-courting, offering me the alliance I'd always hoped for at last, but with the wrong man?*

She felt Korin's hand on hers. It was rough and warm. It reminded her of everything foolish and youthful and green that she'd always loved in him…

And it mocked the bitter reality of her present predicament.

"If you really want to go, you can," Korin said quietly. "I won't keep you against your will. But what would you be going back to, Tzimena? Marriage to my brother? Or, if you wriggle out of that, betrothal to some new dimwit lord a year or two down the road?"

"You're right," Tzimena said slowly. "Life in the wild, coupled with a murderous bandit who smells like a hog wallow—that's a much better proposition."

She heard him draw breath, as though he was about to respond…but no words came.

She stared down from their perch toward the fire-encircled camp. Something was going on down there. The number of Devils gathered round the primary cookfire seemed to have increased—perhaps they'd slipped out of some unseen cave mouth in the hillside. Wherever they'd come from, there were dozens of them now, holding some sort of palaver. Tzimena could hear nothing clearly, nor even see the proceedings in great detail, but she knew the look of a conclave when she saw one.

Probably deciding whether to ransom me or just feed me to a hillcat, Tzimena thought grimly.

"All right, then," Korin said at last, and stood. "How about this: Make no decision tonight. You're tired. You're also probably a little disoriented and scared. Surrounded by strangers, out in the middle of nowhere, completely unsure of my intentions—"

"Don't flatter yourself," Tzimena said. "I know your intentions. I just question your true motives."

"My motives?" Korin said. "Tzimena, I love you."

Tzimena rose. He offered his hand, but she didn't take it.

"You love a girl who grew out of herself, became someone else," she said, "just as I love a boy who died in these woods years ago."

"That's not true," Korin said, and he meant it. "All I've ever wanted was you. I'd given up on it ever happening, but when I stole those dispatches from the lord marshal and saw the wedding plans…"

"What?" Tzimena pressed. "What, precisely, did that knowledge stir in you? Envy? Jealousy? Wrath? What better way to get back at your hated brother than to intercept and steal his bride-to-be?"

"It was a sign," Korin said, voice catching in his throat. "A sign I've been waiting for. Praying for."

Gods help him, the poor fool actually meant it. Tzimena could at least admit to herself that her own attraction to Korin—still present and powerful, even after years apart—was capricious and illusory; not the love of a real person, in all his complex glory, but attachment to an idea, a dream. Korin, apparently, could not do the same.

She had so many things she wanted to say to him—so much truth that he needed to hear. And yet she was suddenly very tired. Exhausted, in fact. And famished.

"I'm hungry," Tzimena said. "Can I eat something, please? Then sleep?"

"Of course," Korin said. "Let's go."

"Just give me tonight," Tzimena said as they started to pick their way down the hillside. "Let me rest and get my wits about me."

"Take all the time you need," Korin said, and he meant that, too. Unfortunately, Tzimena knew that, even if he was willing to give her all the time she needed, neither of them was likely to have it.

Sooner or later, someone would come for her. Either her own loyal guards would track her down, or the lord marshal would refuse to leave the wood without retrieving her, or Verin would return, with his own ducal guard and an army of mercenaries, and tear the forest apart in search of her. If she could work out her own means of escape before that happened, so much the better.

They descended from their promontory down into the little amphitheater created by the out-thrust rocks of the hillside. All of Korin's people were still gathered there around the main cookfire. Tzimena heard the ghosts of words and argument, questions, considerations, but she could make sense of none of it. A gentle breeze raked the slopes above and below them, and the trees whispered somnolently under the stars.

When she and Korin crossed from the outer dark into the light at the periphery of the camp, the crowd around the fire fell silent. It was sudden, immediate. Their leader and his prize were back in mixed company.

Gods, what now? Tzimena wondered.

"Where's supper?" Korin asked as he led the way toward the cookfire. "You're all here, but I don't see the victuals."

"We held a parley in your absence, sir," said that bald bowman with the matching gold earrings. "It ruined all our appetites."

The tall woman, Tymon, glared at the man when he spoke, as though his words—cryptic and uninformative as they were—were out of turn and unwarranted.

"Parley?" Korin asked. He and Tzimena had arrived at the edge of the cookfire now, right in the thick of the gathered group. Tzimena realized, suddenly, that those at the edge had moved aside to allow them through, then drifted in behind them.

Blocking their withdrawal.

The big man with the war hammer spat into the fire. He had a look on his face like he'd just eaten something bitter. "Options had to be discussed, outcomes weighed."

Korin smiled, though Tzimena could clearly see it was a wary gesture. "Options and outcomes? Sounds like cumbersome business. Honestly, can't we just tap a keg and eat? I can smell the porridge—"

"Fine," Tymon said, as though she'd reached the end of her patience. "If none of you curs will speak, I will!" She looked at Korin across the fire. "We talked of removing you."

"Removing me?" Korin asked. "From what?"

"From your position," the bald bowman said. "Your Ravenhood, I guess you'd say."

"That's ridiculous," Korin said, forcing a laugh that sounded all too vulnerable—all too frightened—to Tzimena's ears. "I am the Red Raven, Scourge of the Ethkeraldi, and you—you motley bastards—you're my Devils of the Weald!"

That old man with the withered hand, Holgur, shook his head. His expression was hard but sad. "No, lad—you're no more the Red Raven than the man you slew to earn the mantle. He could be replaced. So can you."

"And I say you should be," Tymon said with finality.

A chorus of shouted *I say, too*s broke out among those gathered. The consensus was hardly unanimous, but there were enough voices to suggest a majority.

Tzimena felt cool sweat beading on her brow, even though the night wind was cold and getting colder.

"I don't understand," Korin said. "I leave here your leader and come back to a coup?"

"Exactly," Tymon said. "You left us. *Abandoned* us. And for what? For her! You traipsed off to a foreign city, taking valuable men with you—men who have yet to return! And what happened? You were caged. On your way to be hung. And how many died to get you out of that cage? To deliver this highborn whore in her pretty dress to our camp?"

Korin lunged. If he could've passed through the cookfire unharmed, Tzimena believed he would have. "Don't call her a whore!" he hissed. "Insult me all you want, but she's my guest!"

"Wrong," Tymon said, and strode forward, rounding the big cookfire toward where Korin stood and speaking as she came. "She is a prisoner. A valuable one. We'll see her confined and guarded until someone pays her ransom... or refuses to."

Tzimena suddenly felt strong arms grasping her. They had her arms, her shoulders. She didn't even bother fighting, but they crowded around her as if it were her clear intent.

"Let go of her!" Korin shouted. A crowd was forming around him, as well.

"She's a prisoner—and so are you!" Tymon shouted. "Korin Lyr, I charge you with dereliction of your duties, reckless endangerment, and culpability in the deaths of eleven of our brothers and sisters! Tonight you'll be bound and confined.

"Tomorrow, you'll stand trial."

CHAPTER TWENTY-ONE

Rem woke in an instant. No dreary, vague awareness of wakefulness returning; no slow climb back to consciousness; a sudden, jarring, startling instant yanked him up out of a peaceful, exhausted sleep, and made him realize how cold, hungry, and stiff he was.

He lay on a bit of open ground, nestled among banks of ferns and sorrel, a towering redwood at his back. The ashy remnants of a small fire lay before him, cold and dead. It was early morning—still gray, shrouded in mist, no solid sunlight yet peeking over the hilltops or spearing down through the forest canopy. He had pains in his back, his shoulders, his knees. His mouth was horribly dry, and his belly growled resentfully at its emptiness.

Rem rubbed his hands over his face and through his matted hair. His body was trembling and cold, thanks to the death of his fire while he slept. He'd try to relight it again shortly. For the time being, he just wanted to sit upright and let his brain awaken. Maybe once his mind was clearer, he could face the day ahead of him with a little more enthusiasm.

The Kaarten had swept him far downriver. He was fairly certain he'd managed to finally snag the bank and climb out before reaching the river ford crossed by his company the morning before, but that still meant he'd gone a long way. The ford had been somewhere between five and six miles behind them at the time of the ambush. Even if he'd extricated himself from the Kaarten before reaching it, that still put—in the worst possible case—five miles between him and his surviving companions. That was a long way to go without food, water, weapons, or a mount.

Well, he wasn't entirely bereft. He'd leapt into the river with several necessary implements on his belt: flint and steel to light a fire and a single sharp knife. The former two had come in handy the evening before, after he'd pulled himself out of the rushing waters, trudged into the woods in search of some shelter, and finally built himself a little fire as night surrounded and imprisoned him. He'd sat there, in the dark, before the modest flames, naked and shivering while he all but willed his clothes to dry. He at least knew that trying to pass the night in wet clothes in a forest prone to cold nights was foolhardy. He'd been willing to suffer through a naked chill in the short term for the promise of sleeping, clothed, afterward. Luckily, that one thing had gone according to plan. In a few hours, his clothes dried, he slipped back into them, and he curled up at the foot of that redwood to sleep. In his present predicament, there was really nothing more to do.

That was enough. The early-morning cold dug deep into him, down to his bones. He reached into his belt pouch, produced the little round flint and small rod of steel he used for fire making, and went to work. In a few minutes he had the last bits of firewood burning in the hasty pit he'd dug. Knowing he needed more fuel, he left the little fire to go in search of some dead limbs or sticks. It took him a long time—too long—just to find a small amount. This forest, with its damp air and rich soil and enormous trees, offered very little in the way of good kindling. Everything was alive here—green and growing and vibrant and hearty.

And hungry. Just as hungry as he was, no doubt.

He tossed a few more sticks onto the fire and tried to come up with a plan. He had water—there was the river for that—so he need not fear dying of thirst. But he needed food of some sort, and that would be far more challenging. With all the ferns about, he could probably cut some fiddleheads and subsist on those—his father's chief huntsman's lessons about that hadn't left him. He just had to be careful. Too many could make him ill, and he couldn't afford any illness presently. So, at best, fiddleheads were a stopgap—not a real source of nutrition. He still needed more.

He knew there were all sorts of berries and nuts available, as well, to those who knew how to find them, but his memory regarding which were safe and which were poisonous or inedible were less clear. He could positively identify and eat hurtleberries, if he found any, but that was all. Likewise for mushrooms; he vaguely recalled that there were several varieties he could eat, and several more that could liquefy his insides or kill him with paralysis...but he couldn't hope to remember which was which.

That left the forest wildlife: birds, rodents, fish. If he had a few more tools—some twine for snares, the time to weave bark baskets or cages—he could, perhaps, manage to catch something. But he had neither the time nor the resources to do so. He needed something to eat, right now, just to get him started. He intended to start trekking back toward his companions, following the line of the river, but he didn't want to do that empty-bellied and half-crazed.

A spear, he thought. *Make yourself a spear, pick a spot by the riverbank or in the woods, try to spear a fish or a rabbit. But do it quickly, and don't waste too much time in the effort. Every second you sit here, trying to feed yourself, your party is likely to get farther away from you.*

So he found himself a long, straight limb of ash, stripped its leaves and branches, then used his knife to sharpen one end to a deadly point. Satisfied, he marched himself toward the river, telling himself that certainly, with a little luck, he could spear a fish.

As it happened, he could not. The damnable creatures were quite swift in their own element. Though he thought himself nearly successful on several occasions, his thrusts always missed. After a while he'd made such a nuisance of himself that the fish stopped swimming through the shallows where he stood altogether, and he knew it was time to move on. He'd try to find a small stream or pond—the sort favored by animals coming to drink. Perhaps, if he was patient, some unlucky beast would present itself to him.

Of course he found nothing. No tributaries, no ponds, no thirsty animals. Realizing that his plan was folly, Rem decided that all that was left to him was a slow, steady advance northward, back to where he'd left his companions. He considered trekking eastward, to the road, but decided that keeping the river close was more important. He walked for some time, the river always in sight on his left, the road lost in the deep, dark woodlands stretching to infinity on his right.

By the time sunlight began to cut down through the thick forest canopy, marking the beginning of a new, proper day, Rem's hunger had moved him to go in search of sustenance once more. He trudged into the forest and managed to root out a few fiddlehead fronds, as well as a single hurtleberry bush with a handful of sour, unripe berries on its branches. He cut five fiddleheads in all, but only ate two, saving the others for later. They were tough and bitter and very hard to chew, but after he'd managed to pulp them up with his teeth and swallow them, they settled his hunger a little. He hoped the berries would dispel the bitterness of the young ferns, but they were so sour he actually wished he'd just stopped with the fiddleheads. Still, they put some kind of fuel in his belly, and would keep the worst pangs at bay for a little while. Rem supposed that was the best he could hope for. Off he went, back toward the place he'd first leapt into the river.

That was a fool's move, he thought as he marched along. *You could think of nothing else, so you jumped into the gods-damned river.*

He'd been surrounded, outnumbered, and unlikely to survive a direct encounter. He couldn't run back for the road—there were too many of the Raven's Devils blocking his path in that direction—but there was a great, wide gap in their tightening circle that allowed for a straight path to the river. What else could he have done? It was either stand there and possibly end up dead or captured, or run for it and take his chances with the roiling Kaarten.

He'd taken his chances.

He wondered only now what had happened to the others. Had they even made it through the night? If the Devils of the Weald had left even a small contingent behind and attacked once more in the dead of night, while all his traveling mates were bone-tired and still licking their wounds, the outlaws would have had a good chance of victory. He actually created that scenario as he walked, imagining the slow tightening of the cordon of forest outlaws around the sleeping camp; the silent murder of whoever had been tapped for guard duty while the others slept; the panic as those remaining woke and saw their friends already slain in their sleep.

And he imagined Torval—assuming the dwarf had even survived the explosion of the ox wain. The Devils might outnumber him, and might even have approached him while he snored the night away, but if the dwarf woke with any strength in him at all, he'd die hard. No doubt, even if the Devils killed all those remaining, Torval would've been the last to go, only succumbing after wounds sufficient to slay a bull were hacked into him, taking a number of his would-be assailants with him.

Rem shuddered. No. He couldn't imagine it. It was too terrible. They were fine, he told himself. The Devils had probably retreated to their lair—somewhere across the river, he guessed, to put at least one natural barrier between themselves and the outside world—and the survivors back at camp would have passed the night mourning their dead, treating their wounds, and sleeping fitfully, fearful of what might come for them in the dark.

And what of Tzimena? Rem had charged off, half-cocked and eager to wrest her from the Red Raven's clutches, but he'd failed miserably, hadn't he? What had her night been like? Despite hearing her speak with the Raven in loving tones, he'd seen her face when Korin Lyr had taken hold of her and tried to drag her away. She might still feel love for him, depending on the nature of the past and the relationship they shared, but in that instant she hadn't wanted to go anywhere with him. The horror of watching her friends and bodyguards injured or slain in the Devils' ambush had poisoned any affection she might still harbor for the man.

But where was she now? Tied up in a cage of her own? Perhaps treated with deferential kindness and superficial grace, knowing all the while that she was nothing but a prisoner, and escape all but hopeless?

Aemon wept...They'd all made a huge mess of this little road trip, hadn't they? Everyone with their own agendas, their own desires, their own unspoken plans and expectations...all of them blasted, frustrated, and scattered after a single violent encounter with a force they had all but expected to meet.

That's the price of disunity, Rem thought. *A catastrophic unreadiness. Helplessness in the face of one's enemies, because there is no plan—there is no priority. Everyone's out for themselves . . . and everyone pays the price for that selfishness.*

It was a hard lesson, but Rem thought he'd finally learned it. Whatever happened from here on, he'd do his damnedest to make sure it involved everyone. Without some sort of unity, some plan for cooperation, they'd all die out here.

There was rustling in the brush nearby. Rem turned toward the sound, curious, and froze when he had the swishing bush in his sights. Once again there was a minute shudder—a trembling of leaves, a small, small scraping sound as tiny paws moved over loose leaves. Something was in there. Something alive.

Rem gripped his spear and felt himself lowering his whole body into a defensive crouch. If he was lucky—very lucky—some inoffensive little forest rodent would come waddling out of the bracken and move just close enough for him to spear it.

If he was not lucky—and, truth be told, his luck hadn't been terribly well starred since he began this whole expedition—the thing in the bush would be a famished hillcat, a young wolf on the prowl, or a bumbling bear cub whose proximity to an armed human would likely draw the ire of its murderous mother.

Be calm, Rem thought. *Be patient. Breathe. Pretend you're Torval, who wouldn't shrink or run even if the thing in the bushes were a grave wight loosed from the sundry hells.*

He watched. He waited. Once more the brush shuddered. Finally the overlapping fern fronds and weeds at the fore of the little copse broke, and out hopped a mad-eyed brown hare. It took two short hops, then stopped in the middle of the clearing that it and Rem shared.

Rem stared. It was an ugly thing, pop-eyed and rangy,

its limbs long and thin, indicating that it was underfed. So it offered no great storehouse of meat...

But that made little difference. Rem's mouth was already watering. If he could just get the thing skewered on his spear, he was reasonably sure he could skin it and dress it. In an hour he could be sitting by a fresh fire, eating roasted hare, satisfied that he was still a competent woodsman.

He slowly altered his grip on the spear, moving his whole body with ponderous, deliberate slowness to put the point of the hastily made implement forward, toward the curious hare.

The animal didn't move. It snuffled the ground a little, rooted about in the littered loam surrounding it. Nibbled on a patch of sprouting weeds, then withdrew.

Rem drew a deep breath. Blew it out.

And struck.

His speed startled even him. Perhaps it was hunger, or desperation, or who knew what, but the carved point of his long stick shot down with murderous accuracy and thrust right through the exposed flank of the hare. His own movement was so quick, and the hare's flesh so yielding, that Rem had to look down after striking, just to make sure he'd been successful.

There lay the hare, eyes wide in disbelief, twitching its last on the end of his stick. There was something about its movements—so weak, so small—that gave Rem pause.

Hold on, he thought. *That was too easy. What hare doesn't hie at the first movement, the first indicator of trouble?*

Something moved in the leaf-littered loam then—something small and twisted. It was a piece of thin thread. Staring now, still holding the spear in both hands while its point stuck in the earth beneath the bleeding hare, Rem could see that the thread was looped several times around the hare's rear left paw, and snaked off through the bushes the animal had emerged from.

A snare? he thought.

A moment later, when a noose fell over his head and closed savagely around his windpipe, Rem realized the thread on the hare's foot was no snare at all.

It was a leash, however small and primitive.

The hare was bait.

Rem was the catch.

CHAPTER TWENTY-TWO

"Rem!" Torval shouted for the forty-seventh time.

He wasn't sure how far he'd come. He'd set out just before dawn, quietly, so as not to rouse anyone in camp. Galen had been posted as sentry, but she'd just taken up a post north of camp, allowing Torval to slip off in the opposite direction. Part of him hated to abandon them—he wanted to see the girl, Tzimena, recovered, and he'd come to admire and respect every member of her personal guard—but despite those misgivings, Torval had only one burning desire at the moment: he had to find Rem, and once he found Rem, the two of them would head for home. Hang the reward. Hang the lord marshal. Hang the safety of strangers. His partner was lost. Torval would find him.

So he'd been trudging along in the predawn darkness, using the road as his guide but intermittently venturing into the woods for signs of his comrade, for at least two hours now. What sort of distance was that? A mile? Two? If he'd been traveling steadily, in a straight line, he could better gauge, but his frequent off-road tramping and close search of the ground for indicators of Rem's passage frustrated his efforts at truly measuring his progress.

So far he'd found nothing. Heard nothing. Seen nothing.

If the boy was dead—drowned in the river somewhere or already half-digested by a bear—Torval would never forgive himself. He'd made Indilen a promise, hadn't he? The boy was *his* to guard, *his* to protect. They were partners, and he'd failed his partner.

"Rem!"

Forty-eight.

Darkness was yielding to gray, a thin veil of mist snaking between the looming trees and the shaggy fern copses. Torval could clearly hear the river far off to his right, but couldn't say how far away it was. The judgment of distance was not his strong suit, after all. For one thing, he'd been raised on dwarven measures; for another, he'd spent so long among humans that their own measures had tried to replace their dwarven equivalents in his mind; but for a third thing, he'd spent the better part of his adult life living in cities, wandering bounded streets. He thought in terms of blocks and wards, alleys and boulevards, not miles or leagues or furlongs or whatever silly spans one might apply out in this great, wide expanse of overgrown nothingness.

Well, at least he wasn't lost. There was always the road and the river. As long as he had those two things, within sight or hearing, he could always find his way back to camp. Or out of the woods, if it came to that.

But I'm not leaving these woods, he thought decisively. *Not without Rem. If all I can recover is a scrap of his shirt or a boot with a chewed-off foot in it, I'm not leaving here 'til I know that he cannot come with me.*

Something chuffed far off to his left. Torval turned toward the sound, every small hair on his muscular arms standing straight, sweat beading on his bald brow despite the chill in the early-morning air. The chuffing was followed by a long, low bellow and a heavy, ponderous sound, like the dragging of great feet.

Gods, what was that?

Torval stood still, listening—though he had no idea what he was listening for. The bestial groans and dragging subsided into the pale wash of background noise in the woods: the chitter of waking birds, the distant sloshing of the Kaarten, the rustle of trees in a delicate breeze.

There, behind him. Another sound. Footsteps! Heavy boots moving slowly, warily across the soft, damp earth of the forest floor.

Torval found a nearby cedar and backed himself into it. The tree was so tall that glancing up toward its high branches and unseen crown gave him vertigo. Was there a single tower in Yenara that high? In any city in the world? He imagined that if one could climb to the top of the damned thing, one could probably see all the way back to Yenara and the coast.

He was certain that someone—or something—was following him. Tracking him. He waited, trying to still his breathing enough that it would not affect his hearing. Briefly he closed his eyes and listened.

Boots, still moving slowly, cautiously. He heard the scrape of the toe against rustling weeds as they were lifted; heard the crunch of dead pine needles and rain-softened twigs as the heel fell.

Creak. Clink. Armor! Leather, tightly banded, along with some metallic component—maybe scales, maybe chain mail.

Bird wings, rustling eagerly as the creature fled its shrub perch and took flight. Someone's passage had disturbed the bird in its ground-level home...

Torval opened his eyes. He tightened his grip on his maul, then let his left hand fall to one of the daggers at his belt. Slowly, eager not to let even the smallest sound give him away, he jostled the dagger to loosen the grip of its scabbard, then drew it forth.

Blade in one hand, bludgeon in the other. He was ready.

If they have bows, he thought, *I'll be no match for them. I might take one . . . two if I'm lucky . . . but it would only take one good shot to put me down.*

I could negotiate . . .

No.

I could try to be sneaky, to just watch . . .

No.

There's only a fight, then. Steel to steel. Flesh to flesh. Their blood or mine, no mercy.

Yes.

He drew three deep breaths and exhaled them with equal patience, then leapt from behind the great cedar, brandishing maul and dagger as he did.

A bow swung up, arrow already nocked. It creaked a little as the archer drew the bowstring taut for a shot.

"Wait!" cried Wallenbrand.

Galen did not loose. She held the drawn arrow in place, its point trained right on Torval's broad trunk.

Torval stared. Wallenbrand, Galen, and Tuvera. They were all armed—Wallenbrand and Tuvera with their swords in hand, Galen with her compound bow drawn and ready to skewer him. They stood in a broad skirmish line, each ten paces from the next. Clearly they'd been advancing through the woods toward the tree behind which Torval hid.

Torval lowered his weapons. "Sundry hells!" he shouted. "I could've killed you!"

"Unlikely," Galen said with a crooked smile as she lowered the bow and reversed her draw.

"What are you doing all the way out here?" Tuvera demanded. "Alone, no less?"

"Searching for my partner," Torval said, as if it were the most obvious thing in the world.

"It isn't safe, master dwarf," Wallenbrand said, looking strangely as Torval imagined he himself looked when trying to speak sense to one of his children.

"And why should you care?" Torval asked, perhaps unfairly. "We are not your people. We are not your problem. You've got your own recoveries to make, your own wounded to tend to. I won't interfere with your business in these woods, so don't interfere with mine."

"You think we don't want to find him?" Tuvera asked.

"Why would you?" Torval countered. "What are we to you?"

"Look," Wallenbrand said, his voice craggy but eminently reasonable, "I won't lie and say the lord marshal would want any of us out here searching for your friend. He wouldn't. He'll give us all a dressing-down when we get back. But, Torval, honestly... we would've helped if you'd given us the option."

"Maybe it's the lord marshal who kept me from asking," Torval said. "Or you, Captain Tuvera. You and the lord marshal are leaders, and you have to watch out for your people. You've lost too many already. You shouldn't lose any more... not even to help me find Rem. He's my responsibility—a burden I'm happy to bear. Just stay out of my way."

"Give us an hour more," Tuvera said. "Let us help you for just that long, Torval. We'll spread out, march south, and see what we find. If we find nothing by that time, we agree to head back to camp. How does that sound?"

"I won't refuse your aid," Torval said, "but I'm not going back without him."

Tuvera looked to Galen, then Wallenbrand. Clearly they'd all discussed this possibility before they ever left camp. Torval could see it on their faces—the disappointment of an inconvenient but inevitable truth. He wasn't sorry. Let them stamp their feet and argue all they liked, he had but one job now: find Rem and take him home. Nothing else mattered, so far as he was concerned.

"Fine," Tuvera finally said. "We'll keep at it for an hour. At that time, we head back. If you refuse, we can't force you. Fair?"

Torval nodded. "Fair," he said. "Now come on. We're wasting time with all this yammering." He led the way without looking back to see if they followed.

Torval suspected he should be checking the river, but there was a part of him that refused to make that his first order of business. He'd search first out here, in the woods, for any sign that Rem had made it out of the Kaarten alive. Perhaps when he returned to camp he'd follow the river and look for the boy's waterlogged corpse, only after he'd exhausted his woodland options. But some small part of him honestly believed that, so long as he only searched for places where a living, breathing Rem could be, a living, breathing Rem was the only thing he was likely to find.

The sun was up and their hour of cooperative search almost spent when a sudden low whistle off to Torval's left drew his attention. Torval turned and saw Galen, who'd sounded that whistle, standing twenty or thirty yards off, frozen with her bow half-raised, eyes staring intently into a broad line of laurel and lilacs crammed among a thicket of alder and cottonwood up ahead. Tuvera, farther off to Galen's left, was staring at her companion, awaiting information. Torval supposed Wallenbrand, off on his right, was doing the same.

But for the time being, Torval would not move. He stared carefully at the woman scout, the way her dark eyes narrowed and scanned that thick screen of brush ahead, as if trying to pick something out of it.

Torval raised his shoulders a little in a puzzled shrug. *Do you see something?*

Galen caught Torval's movements in her peripheral vision, turned to spear him with her now-intent gaze, then swung her eyes back toward the line of brush again. This time she raised her bow, drew back the already-nocked arrow, and took aim.

Wood snapped, somewhere far off to Torval's right. His head whipped around toward the sound, but he could not see anything that might have made it. Wallenbrand, who had spaced himself about the same distance off from Torval that Galen had, was looking in the same direction. Clearly he'd heard it, too. The sound had been sharp, sudden—a twig broken by a falling foot, followed by no movement whatsoever.

Torval tightened his grip on his maul and his dagger. He decided to take charge of the situation if no one else would. Slowly he picked a path forward, placing his big feet as carefully as he could, looking for a good spot to make a stand on. After stepping over several low tussocks of weeds and through the swaying fronds of some close-packed ferns, he came to a bald spot on the forest floor, just big enough for him to occupy comfortably. It would give him a good range of movement, if he had to fight. He kept his eyes fixed on the screen of brush ahead, the one that he knew Galen had her bow aimed at. Could Torval see something back there? Behind fern fronds and waxy green leaves and the net of swaying branches? The flicker of small, dark eyes? The flat, leathery wrinkles of skin?

"Show yourself!" Torval finally shouted, his voice booming through the forest like the explosion of one of those blasting spheres the day before. "You're surrounded, so you might as well come out right now!"

The brush rustled a little. Someone or something *was* in there.

"Come on out," Torval commanded, "and maybe we can talk! The longer you hide, though, the less friendly we'll deem you to be!"

The brush rustled again. Finally Torval saw something big moving behind the screen, something hitherto crouched at last revealing its considerable height and bulk as it stood straight, the tops of the shrubs around it barely reaching its waist.

It was nine feet tall, maybe ten, and as wide at its enormous shoulders as Wallenbrand was tall. Torval recognized the thick, wrinkled hide, the mottled, dark-gray skin turning lighter on the creature's blunt face and exposed torso—as well as the broad, vaguely hunched shoulders and the small, round head thrust forward on a thick, bullish neck.

A mountain troll, very far from its home. And judging by the fact that it wore bracers of wound leather and fur around its enormous forearms and a cured leather loincloth around its middle, Torval guessed that it wasn't just some wild wanderer. The only trolls that wore clothing—even the smallest scrap— were domesticated.

Torval's nostrils then caught a swirl of familiar scents on the cool breeze: sweat, animal musk, dung, and the tang of some- thing vaguely astringent. That was a scent Torval recognized all too readily.

He felt his heart start to beat in double time…then triple. It was a wholly unconscious reaction, one his body repeated every time it was in the presence of his old enemies…the slay- ers of his family…the scourge of all human- and dwarfkind.

The troll wasn't alone. There were orcs about.

Torval wasn't sure what to do. He wanted to charge, to lay

into the thing with blade and bludgeon, to hurt it and bruise it and tear it down...

But if it wasn't alone?

If it was part of a group?

He threw a look back at Galen and Tuvera. She was shaking a little—Torval could see it in her shoulders and in the hovering point of the arrow. It wasn't fear, though; the stony look on Galen's face told him that. No, it was simple strain: the scout had held that draw for too long. She'd have to loose it soon, or else—

Torval caught movement. He turned back toward the troll just in time to see the hulking brute raise its enormous, apelike arms above its head.

"*Hrzhat*," the troll said through its fierce underbite.

Hold, it had said in a common orcish dialect.

Too late. Torval heard the subtle twang of Galen's bowstring and suddenly an arrow appeared, buried to half its length in the troll's right pectoral, just above its nipple. The troll gave a groan, followed by another pair of words.

"*Djaba!*" it roared. "*Bowhra!*"

Torval heard the twang of another bowstring, sensed something suddenly splitting the air just before his nose, and heard a small *thunk* as something buried itself in the earth off to his left. He turned and saw an arrow fletched with crow feathers buried in the loam at an oblique angle. It must have passed just in front of his face, fired from somewhere off to his right and above.

He turned, followed the imagined trajectory, and found another body moving on the lowest branch of an enormous ash, a little ahead and to the right of Wallenbrand. This was neither a troll nor an orc, but something small, thinner of bone, knobbier of joint. Its evil, grinning face was garishly elongated and sported a large, protruding, bat-like ear on either side.

A goblin—yet another rare sight in this part of the world. The little imp was already reaching for another crow-feathered arrow from its quiver as Torval stared at it, perched there on the tree limb.

"Galen!" Torval shouted, and beat a hasty retreat toward the cover of a redwood some distance behind him. "Archer! In the trees!"

From the corner of his eye, still moving, Torval saw Galen nock and draw another arrow, take three steps forward, and swing herself round until she had a perfect bead on the goblin sniper in the trees. She loosed her arrow. Torval heard it strike something, but didn't bother looking until he'd made it behind the redwood and knew he wouldn't be skewered in the next instant.

He peered back. Galen's arrow had struck the tree trunk, missing the goblin by about three feet. The needle-toothed little archer was already moving out along the tree limb. He loosed an arrow as he went.

Torval turned to make sure Galen wasn't hit. He was relieved when he saw she'd already retreated for cover, as well, leaping behind a fallen pine and yanking another arrow from her quiver. Tuvera crouched behind the same pine, scanning the woods around them, looking for signs of more enemies.

The sound of pounding bootheels and the rattle of armor reached Torval's ears just before Wallenbrand called out.

"All sides! Orcs!"

Torval searched the forest. Wallenbrand was right. They seemed to be everywhere. A young, muscular orc bull had appeared from behind the same ash where the goblin archer sat and now charged Wallenbrand, a small shield strapped on one arm, a nasty-looking war hammer in his other hand. A tall, trim orc with patchy, discolored skin—large, pale blotches spaced haphazardly over the visible portions of its elegantly muscled body—closed from far behind Wallenbrand and Torval, bearing in one hand a long spear tipped with a blade almost as long as a sword. Still farther behind, following the same track Torval and company had advanced from, a stocky, pot-bellied specimen loped steadily, lifting a big battle-ax above its head as it came. On the opposite flank, beyond where Tuvera and Galen sheltered behind their fallen pine, yet another orc advanced: a female, the sides of her head shorn close while the rest of her thick, black hair cascaded from the crown of her head. The charging bitch wielded a long, forward-swept saber, poised and ready to sweep down with lethal force.

Four orcs, a goblin archer, and a troll hiding in the bushes. What in the sundry hells had they stumbled into?

All at once, the world was a storm of ringing steel and hoarse war cries. Torval had just enough time to see Tuvera engage the orc female while Galen simultaneously nocked an arrow and fired at the fat one approaching from the rear. He then spun back toward Wallenbrand.

The young buck was closing. Wallenbrand stood ready, sword held two-handed, gaze sweeping back and forth between the young hammer swinger and the slowly approaching spear-man. The buck was closer, moving faster, so Wallenbrand turned to meet him just in time, parrying three hard blows from the hammer.

Torval saw the spearman spring forward, his slow advance becoming a hard charge in a single breath. That big spear-tip cut through the air ahead of its master, plunging right toward Wallenbrand's exposed back.

Torval's feet moved before his conscious mind even realized the old man needed help. Unbidden, his maul swept down in a savage two-handed arc and he drove the seeking spear point into the earth at Wallenbrand's feet, just inches from where the old mercenary now shuffled in his duel with the young orc.

Wallenbrand landed a hard blow to the young buck's shield and sent it reeling. Without hesitation he spun toward the spearman—still stunned from Torval's intervention—and immediately went on the offensive. Wallenbrand was clearly no master swordsman, but he was fast and strong, and his blows drove the orc spearman back. But the orc, to Torval's amazement, proved to be an artist with his weapon. With practiced assurance and moves that could only be described as graceful, the spearman parried every blow Wallenbrand landed, long spear shaft and fearsome blade dipping, whistling, sweeping, and clashing.

Torval would have intervened again, but he saw the young buck, now recovered, charging for another attack. He rushed to meet it and laid into its shield before the youngster could even poise its hammer for another attack.

Torval was ready to bring his maul around, seeking a small span of exposed rib cage on the young orc's right side, when a great shadow fell over him. The young orc's gaze rose, taking in something tall behind Torval. The buck retreated a single step.

Torval spun, knowing well what he'd find: that troll, towering over him, ready to crush him with a single, furious blow.

The troll roared, raised one huge, wide foot, and brought it crashing down. Torval barely sidestepped it.

Another roar. A fist rose and fell. Torval threw himself to his left and once more narrowly escaped the crushing blow.

Snarling, the troll drew its fist back—low this time, as though to uppercut an opponent in a boxing match. The fist barreled forward. Torval dove, its outbound arc just missing him as he hit the forest floor. As his body rolled, Torval saw the troll's swinging fist collide hard with the young buck, who'd been sneaking in from behind to try to put Torval down while the brute kept him busy. The young orc flew a good ten feet before landing with a crash in a groaning heap.

The troll made a strange sound—a gasp—and clapped its big hands over its gaping mouth. Torval saw his chance to escape. He scampered forward, right between the big beast's squat, bowed legs, and scurried away on the far side, eager to put as much distance as possible between himself and the troll.

Torval drank in air. He was panting, a sharp stitch already digging into his side.

But there was no time, not even for a pause. Just a few feet away, the short, fat orc with the battle-ax was almost upon Galen—and the scout was out of arrows. The young woman had unsheathed her sword, but the blade was narrow and elegant. It wouldn't hold up to the heavy blade on that orc's ax.

Torval shot forward and threw himself onto the short, fat orc. For an instant their bodies entangled, the stink of the beast filling Torval's nostrils and making him gag audibly. The gambit worked, though: Torval had built up enough momentum to send the stocky bastard reeling sideward. Down the orc went, its ax clattering from its thick, knotty fingers. Torval landed atop the huffer. Before his adversary could regain his senses, Torval rose up above the orc, straddling it, and raised his maul for a merciless strike.

That's when something strong seized him. Torval felt crushing force around his torso, and his feet left the ground, the whole world falling away. For a moment the woodland loam filled his vision—there the downed orc; nearby Galen and Tuvera—then he was turned, and his vista changed. Now there were only sun-kissed treetops, a broad dome of bright blue sky, and the broad, flat face of the troll. The creature had snatched

Torval up in one hand, like an oversize doll, but as it drew him close to its face, its other hand fell upon him, and now Torval was locked in its viselike grip. It would be nothing—a minor expenditure of force—for the hulking brute to simply press its big hands together and crush Torval like an unwanted pest.

But the troll didn't do that. Instead it held him high, staring right into his face, its own green, wide-set eyes studying Torval intently. Its mouth was curled into a frowning snarl, but its eyes bespoke something else...something less impulsive. Was that curiosity?

Torval truly didn't care. Staring into the beast's face, he opened his mouth and sounded a defiant dwarven battle cry. He followed that barbaric yawp with a hard strike from his maul, right between the troll's eyes.

The troll shrank from the blow. Its brow furrowed. The maul strike hadn't damaged the creature, but it had clearly hurt it.

The troll roared.

Just as Torval prepared himself to strike once more—even if the beast crushed him in the next instant—another sound reached his ears. It wasn't the troll's roar, but something clearer...more acute.

Orders.

"Swu tushtathro!"

The troll swallowed its roar.

Every orc in the clearing froze.

Torval, still held in the troll's grip, craned his neck about, looking for who had shouted those orders.

There, standing at the tree line just over Torval's left shoulder, a broad-shouldered orc male, surveying the battleground with bright, blazing eyes and a toothy scowl. Its head was bald save for a topknot woven into three thick braids that swung easily behind it, and it wore a well-wrought suit of armor plates over banded leather and chain mail. Its left hand and forearm were covered by a bit of orcish smithery that Torval had seen only once or twice before: a hybrid between a gauntlet and a buckler, favored by some orcish warriors because it allowed one to deflect heavy weapons without the cumbersome weight of a full-size shield. In its right hand it held a curved broadsword, fearsome in its weight and inelegance.

This had to be the leader.

"*Mu obuwathro*," the chieftain barked.

Torval knew those words. *We go.*

Then, after another sneering appraisal of the enemies before them, the chieftain spoke again: "*Nadju nuzhwathwar.*"

That was a phrase unfamiliar to Torval...but he didn't like the sound of it.

The orc chieftain's orders were obeyed at once. The orcs in the clearing all withdrew in haste, never taking their eyes off their enemies or turning their backs to them, but clearly raising their weapons and holding them aloft—the very opposite of a threat—as they retreated.

The troll's eyes swung from its master to Torval. Its look of fury had evaporated. It now looked like a child being called home, wishing it could still play, if only a little while longer. With a low, throaty groan, the troll dropped Torval, turned, and lumbered away through the trees. Torval hit the ground hard. By the time he'd managed to get himself upright again, the orcs, the troll, even the goblin sniper were all gone.

Tuvera, Galen, and Wallenbrand slowly gathered around him, scanning the tree line and the now-empty forest around them, all wearing similar looks of shock and confusion.

"What happened?" Tuvera asked, her whispered words betraying her disbelief.

"They had us," Wallenbrand said. "Had us dead to rights."

"Aye, that," Galen said. "One minute, we were surrounded. The next, they all stopped. The chief gave his orders and off they went."

We go. Torval blinked, staring again at the empty forest now surrounding them. No. That couldn't be. Orcs didn't engage and then leave off like that. It was unheard of!

"That can't be," Torval said, almost to himself.

"Torval," Galen said, "you took a hard knock. Are you squared?"

"I'm fine," Torval snapped impatiently. "Just…addled."

"I think," Wallenbrand said, "our time's been spent. We should head back."

"No," Torval said, but he wasn't even sure he meant it. His head was still swimming. He was still staring into the brush and woodland around them, all but willing the orcs to return. "Rem's still out there."

"And so are those orcs," Tuvera said softly. "This time, they decided we weren't worth the effort. We might not be that lucky if we meet them again."

Torval watched. Waited. The woods were silent but for the song of birds and the soft stirring of breezes in the pine boughs.

"Lucky," he said. "Sure."

Something was amiss here, bent and twisted and out of joint. Torval wished he could make sense of it, but still, his thumped head made clear thought all but impossible.

I want my friend, he thought miserably as he searched the high grass and weeds for his fallen maul. He found it readily. *I need my friend*.

That thought haunted him—hounded him—all the way back to camp.

CHAPTER TWENTY-THREE

They came for the two of them around midday, when the sun was highest. The group that collected them for the trial was almost identical to the one that had escorted them to the make-shift jail the night before, led by a towering, broad-shouldered bruiser named Orhund. Accompanying him was the bald fellow with the matching gold earrings—Dedrik Firebow—and a pair of jostling, uncivilized-looking brothers who (Korin had informed her) were twins, though not identical—Zayber and Lyme.

Tzimena noted that Korin—who'd exhausted every mode of conversation and bargaining with his jailers the night before—now looked too wounded to even bother treating with them. He offered no quips, no jests, no remembrances of shared good times or stolen rewards now, opting instead for sullen silence as they opened his cage, urged him out, then tied his hands with a series of complex knots ending in a cord that looped around his throat. When Korin was secure, they opened Tzimena's cage and helped her out. They didn't bother tying her up. The fact that there were no bonds indicated they probably didn't see Tzimena as a flight risk—too posh, too weak, or too clumsy to run away from them—and this vaguely insulted her.

From the cave they were led down the hillside to the open ravine where the primary camp stood. The cookfires were low and smoldering under the afternoon sun.

It looked as though the entire encampment had been gathered: men and women, children and the elderly, a company of about forty in all, if Tzimena's estimations were correct. Sitting at one end of the group, on an old chair—a lovely, well-carved antique that looked rather out of place here, in the middle of the woods—was the woman Tymon. An empty chair sat on either side of her. The hard, sour look on her face made it clear that she had no relish for the business that was about to be attended to.

Tzimena and Korin were ushered into the midst of the gathering. Another chair—this one far more simple and rustic than that which Tymon sat on—was produced for Tzimena, and she was made to sit. Korin stood, Zayber and Lyme on either side of him. Orhund and Dedrik wended separate paths through the crowd to the empty chairs flanking Tymon and took seats of their own. Finally the old man with the withered hand slung against his chest—Holgur—turned and surveyed everyone present.

"We now bring one of our own to trial to face charges of reckless endangerment, unbridled lust, and the unintentional but negligent deaths of his fellows. He who stands accused is Korin Lyr, called the Red Raven, and he is our leader."

A murmur ran through the crowd, a punctuation of some sort to Holgur's opening statement and invocation.

"Received," they all said in unison.

Formal call and response; clearly this was not the first time one of their own had been put on trial.

"Our brother shall now be tried and judged by his peers. If he is found guilty of his crimes, he faces one of the three allowed punishments: permanent marking, exile, or death."

"Received," they all said again.

Permanent marking, exile, or death. Tzimena idly wondered which of those she might prefer if this were her trial and not his.

She studied Korin: shoulders slumped, eyes downcast, mouth turned down in a sullen frown. All the bravado he'd displayed last night, when they were led to their prison, seemed to have left him...

"Don't be a fool, Orhund," Korin had said as they were marched up the rocky slope toward the Devils' caves. "You've prospered under me, don't try to deny it!"

"Won't," Orhund said.

"Tymon's just having a bit of a piss," Korin offered, as if the two men were sharing a private joke. "Let's let her calm down, then you can suggest she come to her senses and set me free."

"Nope," Orhund said.

Korin tried very hard with that one, to no avail.

Desperate for some reprieve, he next turned to Zayber and Lyme for comfort.

"Come now, boys," Korin said. "Haven't we had good times? Wasn't I like a father to you? Brought you through your youth to strong manhood?"

"Like a father," Zayber said.

"But not a father," Lyme finished.

"Still and all," Zayber added, "we're most appreciative. Don't think us ingrates."

"Right, exactly," Lyme said hastily. "This has nothing to do with gratitude or good times shared, Raven, sir—it's just a shifting of priorities."

"Shifting priorities?" Korin had asked incredulously.

"Aye, that," Lyme continued. "In your absence, there was a great deal of conversating—"

"—And debating," Zayber said.

"Debating, conversating, and argumentation, that is," Lyme finished. "To wit, at issue: your leadership, and the relative value of your decision-making skills, especially insofar as your relations with the city of Erald and its administration goes."

"And women," Zayber said. "Don't forget the women."

"There are those, as well," Lyme said agreeably.

"The women?" Korin asked. Tzimena heard the combination of panic and feigned innocence in his voice. She wasn't fooled.

"Shut up, the both of you," Orhund grumbled.

They were inside the cave, having moved through its low-ceilinged entryway into the main cavern beyond. Light came from torches, lamps, and candles placed all about the great, open space, and there were a dozen or so people moving about, seeing to one task or another, or simply lounging on boulders to chat. A large body of water dominated the far side of the cavern, rippling lightly in the dim, diffuse light. They remained close to the right-hand wall of the chamber, however, angling toward a set of natural stone stairs up ahead that rose into a low, dark side passage.

"Dedrik, please," Korin had said then. "Can you please, please talk sense to this lot? To Tymon?"

Leading the way, Dedrik mounted the stone stairs and had to duck a little to keep from knocking his forehead on the low ceiling of the black passage beyond. The torch he carried illuminated what lay within: a long, rambling throat of stone with sturdy makeshift cages set into the stone itself on either side. When Dedrik reached a point just beyond the first two facing cages, he turned and stood, watching as the prisoners were ushered forward. He had sad, introspective eyes, the eyes of a very old man, though by his appearance, Tzimena placed him at just past forty. He might have been older, but if so, he was well-preserved. But those eyes—they were positively weary.

"What the lads are trying to say, Korin," Dedrik said as

Orhund undid the locking mechanisms on the first cage, "is that you've got a cunny problem."

"Oi," Zayber said, shaking Tzimena in his grip. The brothers were on either side of her. "Lady present!"

"Apologies, miss," Lyme whispered to her. "No offense."

"None taken," Tzimena muttered.

Orhund shoved Korin into his cage then, closed it, and locked it. He shuffled past Tzimena and began the process of opening her cell.

"What are you talking about?" Korin asked from behind his hand-hewn bars. "You've heard me talk about Tzimena a hundred times, Dedrik!"

"More like a thousand," Dedrik said passively.

"She's the only one I've ever wanted," Korin said pleadingly, and Tzimena almost believed him. Almost. "The only one I've ever loved!"

Dedrik shook his head, his largely implacable face still imparting a deep, earnest sadness. "That may be," Dedrik said, "but I think the other men are tired of the way you make use of their women to assuage your broken heart."

Korin's mouth worked, as if seeking a response. "Make use...," he said weakly.

"But that's the least of our concerns," Dedrik carried on. "Presently—and most pointedly—the issue before us is the wisdom of your continued leadership. Ever since waylaying that caravan and finding that dispatch about the royal wedding, you've been unreliable and distracted. And running off to Yenara—"

"For love," Korin said.

Dedrik shrugged a little. "*We're* your family, lad. Where's your love for us? Going after this young lady"—he indicated Tzimena, now locked in her cage—"put us all in danger."

Orhund looked over his handiwork, studying the prisoners in their separate cages, then rubbed his hands together as if wiping off something foul. "Enough. Let's go. Zayber, Lyme—you're on first watch. Go out to the passage entrance so you won't be tempted to chatter with these two."

"First watch?" Zayber brayed.

"And who's to relieve us?" Lyme asked.

"And when?" Zayber added.

Orhund turned and glared at them both. His bushy eyebrows turned down. "I don't know who and I don't know when. Get your arses out there and keep your eyes and ears open. I find either of you sleeping, I'll snap you over my knees."

The two young men nodded and scurried back to the passage entrance. Orhund left without looking at Korin or Tzimena. Dedrik backed toward the entrance, still bearing the torch, but didn't say anything for a long time.

"Dedrik, please," Korin said. "I know I've made mistakes... but this?"

Dedrik cocked his head a little, like a parent scolding a child. "Let it play out," he said quietly. Before leaving, he turned to Tzimena. "There are a couple blankets in there, milady. I gave you his."

With that, the one called Firebow was gone, and Tzimena and Korin had been left alone in that nearly pitch-black tributary passage in their separate cages, the only illumination being the faint, secondhand glow of candle- and torchlight from the main cavern beyond the mouth of their own. Tzimena heard the sigh and moan of winds snaking through the caves, allowed ingress by small, naturally occurring vents and chimneys in the hillside. She also heard the placid burble of the spring water that filled the cistern in the main chamber. Closer, more immediate, were the sounds of Zayber and Lyme's hissed chatter, an argument about something she couldn't discern. Where they sat in the passage was very nearly black as a moonless night. She could only make out the faintest suggestion of Korin's cage bars opposite her own, and see Korin's movements, but no details of his form.

"I'm sorry," Korin had said. His voice sounded tired and very far away, even though the two of them could probably touch if they stretched their arms toward one another through the bars.

"As am I," Tzimena said glumly.

Still foolish, she'd thought at some point before sleep took her. *Here we are, trapped and facing an unknown fate, and I'm still more worried for Korin than I am for myself. The worst betrayals are from friends, after all, or loved ones. If these people were truly his family for the last five years . . .*

She knew no more until golden torchlight crept into the cave and woke her. The night had passed. It was early morning and the two of them were being fed—water and some sort of acorn paste that Korin assured Tzimena was nutritious, if not precisely tasty. After breaking their fast, they'd been left alone again for hours. Though the passage was still dark, secondhand daylight from the world outside the caves filtered in sufficiently to provide a slight extra measure of illumination. Their passage was no longer nearly black as pitch, but more of a slate gray, with forms and movement more readily visible. Through those hours, Tzimena and Korin talked from time to time, but their conversations were separated by long gulfs of awkward silence. The subjects ranged far and wide.

"Is it true?" Tzimena asked at one point. "The women?"

"Don't sound so sanctimonious," Korin had said.

"I'm just asking a question," Tzimena countered.

He took a long time to answer. "I didn't force anyone," he said, as if that explained everything and made it better.

"And a few men, no doubt," Tzimena said sardonically. Korin didn't bother to argue with that last comment. She didn't really give a damn if he liked to lie with boys as well as girls—it was the greed of it that upset her. The sense of entitlement in him that told him it was all right to use those who looked up to and respected him, to betray those who trusted and supported and protected him. Clearly his hunger knew no bounds.

"Will they kill us?" she asked.

"They might," Korin said, not looking at her. He was playing with some stray gravel between his folded legs. "Though you're probably valuable, so I'd guess they'll try to ransom you."

There hadn't been much to say in response to that.

After another interminable silence, so long that Tzimena had started to daydream, it was Korin who restarted the conversation.

"I meant it, you know," he said sheepishly. "I love you. I've always loved you."

Tzimena raised her eyes. He was looking at her now through the bars of his cage. She could be wrong, but she thought the sad look in his eyes and the set of his mouth suggested earnest intent—a true statement, with no adornment.

"You could've come for me at any time," Tzimena said. "Handed the mantle of the Red Raven to someone else, then struck out on the road south until you'd made it to Toriel. If you'd come to me sooner and told me your tale and shown me—*shown me* with your journey—that you truly loved me, I would've run away with you. I don't give a damn about inheriting my mother's lands and titles, Korin—at least I wouldn't if I thought I had an honest chance to seize true love.

"But you didn't do that, did you?" she continued. "You waited five gods-damned years, until you found out I was betrothed to your brother—"

"I couldn't let you marry him!" Korin hissed.

"You mean you couldn't stand to let him have me!" Tzimena answered. "Only then—seeing your brother once more get the best of you in something—did you tear yourself away from your little woodland kingdom and come to find me."

Korin had lowered his eyes then. Shrugged. "It must be nice, being so sure in all things."

"I'm not sure of anything," Tzimena said. "But I do know that if you really want something, you go after it—whether someone else is threatening to take it away or not."

He had nothing to say to that.

"I defer to our judges," old Holgur concluded. "Tymon called Longstride, Dedrik called Firebow, and Orhund, called the Lesser." With that Holgur withdrew, found a bit of empty ground, and sat himself upon it, legs crossed beneath him.

Korin let his blue eyes sweep over all assembled. "Ingrates," he said quietly. "After all I've done for you—"

A series of murmurs ran through the crowd. Tzimena heard none of their whispered words, but the looks on some faces told her all she needed to know: many of these people, despite being wronged, were yet uneasy about punishing their leader.

"You'll have your opportunity to speak," Tymon said loudly, clearly intending her voice to move not only Korin to silence, but everyone else, as well. "First we offer the charges. You, Korin Lyr, called the Red Raven, and hitherto our leader and first bow, are accused of endangering the lives of your companions and peers for the sake of your own pleasure and satisfaction; of abandonment of your post and duties upon the occasion of your journey to the city of Yenara in order to treat with the Lady Tzimena of Toriel, who is present; and of responsibility for the deaths of eleven of your companions in the prosecution of your intentions.

Those who went to Yenara with you have not returned, and more lives were spent when you were freed from captivity yesterday on the Ethkeraldi Forest Road."

"I didn't ask you to rescue me," Korin said.

"But you expected it," Dedrik offered. "Did you not?"

Korin said nothing.

"Likewise," Tymon continued, "you are charged with the misuse of your power and privilege as first bow in your wanton seduction of no less than five women and two men in this company, who are, themselves, pledged openly to men or women who serve you. Let it be noted that there is not a single claim suggesting that our leader forced himself upon these lovers of his—yet the fact remains that he is our leader, and that few would—until recently—have refused him anything he asked of them."

"Is that what we stand for now?" Korin asked. "Outdated marriage laws and notions of propriety? A free person as a piece of property?"

"You know well that no such laws exist among us," Orhund interjected. "But we do have rules regarding the misuse of the trust of companions. That's why we still hold to the ritual of pledging when people so decide—so that no one pledged may be arbitrarily seduced or taken advantage of by another."

"Then why are the men and women who indulged me not up here on trial, as well?" Korin asked.

"Because they are not in the position of power that you have been," Dedrik said quietly. "Their transgressions are personal—against the partners they were pledged to. Your transgression is public, for it affects everyone in this company."

"A leader who will take from his or her companions is a tyrant," Tymon said. "The Devils of the Weald do not countenance tyrants."

"Fine," Korin said. "Get on with it."

Tymon studied him. For the first time, Tzimena saw something in her eyes that betrayed real feeling—a deep well of competing, roiling emotions that her anger and resentment had masked until now. Slowly the tall woman sat forward in her chair, planting her hands upon her knees.

"Do you not understand, Korin? Are all these charges falling on deaf ears?"

"You speak of betrayal," Korin said quietly. "I am the one betrayed. I left here secure in the knowledge that all of you, my people, would be safe and protected by my chosen lieutenants—namely you, Longstride—in my absence. I return now to charges of dereliction of my duties. Who's been whispering in all your grubby little ears, eh? Was it Tymon? Has she been angling to take my place all along? Or maybe Dedrik? He's the subtle one, after all...the smart one. Certainly not Orhund—he wouldn't have the stomach or the brains for this."

Tzimena watched as Korin ranted. The three judges winced perceptibly as their names were invoked. Their faces betrayed mixtures of anger and loss and pain—as if they were watching someone they'd once loved dearly make a fool of himself. When Korin pronounced Orhund both cowardly and stupid, the big man looked like he might bound out of his chair and tear his onetime captain limb from limb.

But nothing happened. Korin brayed. They listened. The people exchanged fell glances and whispers.

"Clearly," Tymon said at last, her voice quiet and measured, "you have not entirely forgotten what it meant to be highborn, for only someone highborn could so easily mock his comrades when faced with honest grievances. Tell me, Korin—were we always so base in your eyes? So contemptible and worthy of disrespect? If so, why did you work so hard to prove yourself among us? To become a good leader for us?"

"Because I could," Korin said bitterly. "Clearly, if any of you could have challenged and ejected my predecessor before my coming, you would have."

"So you are a man of many talents," Dedrik said. "A man of great capability and means. Does that entitle you to berate us? To sleep with our wives or husbands? To run off without a by-your-leave to snatch some prize of your own"—he indicated Tzimena—"no matter what your absence—or your possible capture—might mean for your people?"

"I am the Red Raven, Scourge of the Ethkeraldi," Korin said slowly. "I go where I will. I do as I like."

"You are only the Red Raven because we *allowed* you to be," Tymon answered coldly. "And that which we have given you can be taken away. In an instant."

"I'm your leader!" Korin shouted.

"You are first among equals," Orhund said. "You said so in your oath when you took the mantle, did you not?"

Korin gave no reply.

Orhund stood and roared like a bear. "Did you not?"

Korin actually shuddered where he stood when the big man's voice boomed through the ravine. He stood in awe, in shock, at how Orhund's towering frame shook with rage, not a stone's throw from him. Finally Korin managed to square his shoulders, raise his eyes, and look at his onetime friend directly.

"That was my pledge," he said. "First among equals. First to give, last to take."

"Tell us, then," Tymon said, now standing herself and moving closer, "how your actions reflect that position. Should a first among equals betray the trust of their companions?"

Korin shook his head. "No."

"Should a first among equals abandon their office for the sake of fetching a trophy wife? Especially when doing so endangers everyone associated with them?"

Korin lowered his eyes. He could no longer tolerate Tymon's level, accusing gaze. "No," he said quietly.

"And when lives are spent rescuing that person—that reckless, selfish, self-indulgent person—from his captors, should that person yet be allowed to lead? To exercise the power they so clearly do not respect or wield responsibly?"

Tzimena admired this woman, this Tymon Longstride. Though she might yet prove Tzimena's undoing, her sense of honor and her ability to articulate the problems at hand were rare faculties even at court, let alone in the woodland hideout of a band of outlaws. What had brought her here, to banditry and a life on the margins? she wondered. What might she have been if the world hadn't chased her to its frayed and ragged edges?

Korin, meanwhile, said nothing, did nothing. He waited, hands tied, eyes down.

Tymon stood before him now. She glared, daring him to raise his eyes and meet her gaze.

"We loved you," she said quietly. "All of us. That's what makes this betrayal—this failure—all the more hurtful."

Korin raised his eyes to her. Though Tzimena's view was poor, she could still see the glint of tears in Korin's eyes. When he spoke, his voice was rough and strangled.

"Give me another chance," he said. "I swear to you, Tymon—to all of you—I swear I shall make you proud again!"

"Too late for that," Orhund said from his seat.

"No!" Korin begged. "No, come now—it's never too late."

Tymon nodded. Tzimena could see the sadness apparent on her face now. "It is, Korin."

"One last time, before we deliberate," Dedrik chimed in. He stood and addressed Korin directly. "How do you answer the charges, brother?"

Korin looked as if he was trying to find the right words, some means of rescuing his dignity, his authority—even just his life. Watching his mouth move while no words presented themselves made Tzimena terribly sad. She had always believed—even after she thought him dead—that Korin Lyr was one of the smartest, cleverest, bravest young men she'd ever known, with a quip to answer every insult, an insult to answer every challenge, a challenge to answer every slight or sign of disrespect. And there he stood, accused of crimes by the people who'd been his family for the last five years...speechless.

"He has no answer," Tymon said dismissively.

"Guilty," Korin said.

Tymon, who'd been on the way back to her chair, stopped midstride. Everyone watching the proceedings drew breath or gasped. Orhund settled back into his seat, as if happy to finally be done with an unpleasant task. Dedrik leaned forward and stared off into space, indicating to Tzimena that, as far as he was concerned, he wasn't done with anything. In fact, he looked like a man whose unpleasant tasks were only beginning.

"Say it again," Tymon commanded, rounding on Korin and returning to him. "Reckless endangerment?"

"Guilty," Korin said flatly.

"Exploitation of your power? Betrayal of your vows?"

"Guilty."

"The wrongful deaths of our comrades?"

"Guilty," Korin said with finality. "Happy now?"

Tymon almost answered, then stopped herself. Once again, Tzimena could see emotion on the woman's face. There was a trembling—ever so slight, barely perceptible—in her lower lip, and her eyes had grown dewy. This task, no matter how aggressively she attacked it, clearly gave her no pleasure.

"You all heard?" Tymon asked the crowd.

Murmurs of assent all around. A few of the watchers started to shout proposed punishments, or even to cast boos and hisses at their onetime leader. Orhund shot to his feet and glared at the troublemakers, instantly silencing them.

"Very well, then," Tymon said. "Korin Lyr, known among us as the Red Raven, I hereby strip you of your rank as first bow, the mantle of Red Raven, and the authority previously granted you to lead this company."

"What's my sentence, then?" Korin asked.

Tymon said nothing.

Orhund said nothing.

Dedrik said nothing.

The world was still and silent as everyone waited for an answer to Korin's question, and no one rushed to offer it. Tzimena waited, as well. She assumed it would be nothing good—nothing merciful. She only hoped she might escape the same fate.

"That shall have to wait," Tymon said, then looked to Zayber, Lyme, and another pair of outlaws lingering nearby. "Take them back to their cages."

Tzimena felt Zayber's and Lyme's hands on her arms, pulling her back to her feet again. The other two men flanked Korin and moved to usher him away. Korin looked as though he'd just seen something terrible—something beautiful, irretrievably broken. His eyes were downcast, and he remained silent.

"How long shall we wait?" Tzimena cried, finally finding her own voice. "You've adjudged him guilty—now he's got to sit and stew while you lot come up with the worst punishment imaginable?"

Tymon moved quickly, crossing the space between herself and Tzimena in three long strides. Before she'd even arrived in the space before Tzimena, one long arm had snapped out, and one strong hand raked hard across Tzimena's cheek. The sound of the slap in the quiet forest was loud and flat and ugly.

"Keep your mouth shut or I'll gag you," Tymon said through gritted teeth. "This is your fault as much as his."

Tzimena was truly dumbstruck. *Her* fault...?

"Get them out of here," Tymon commanded, and their guards obeyed this time. Tzimena wondered, all the way back to the cages in the cave, just what Tymon Longstride had meant by that remark.

This is your fault as much as his.

Impossible, she thought. *How? What did I do? What am I guilty of?*

No answers were forthcoming. She wasn't even sure she wanted them.

CHAPTER TWENTY-FOUR

"Wakey wakey," a croaky voice said, accompanied by a waft of
fetid air that Rem assumed was the speaker's rancid breath.

He didn't really want to open his eyes. His head felt too
large for his shoulders and ponderously heavy, like an over-
filled wineskin. He managed, however, and was most puzzled
by what he saw.

Everything was upside down.

No, that couldn't be right.

He was upside down. He could feel it now—his tied feet far
above him, his arms hanging below, his body and head swaying gently on the end of his tether like the clapper in an iron
bell. His mouth was dry enough to sand lumber with, and his
throat felt as if someone had tried to hang him and mucked up
the job. He tried to draw a deep breath, gagged, and launched
into a terrible coughing fit. The spasms that racked him as he
coughed made him swing in a slightly wider arc. Trying to
stop the coughing and catch his breath while hanging head
downward like this was nigh impossible.

But he supposed, at present, that was the least of his worries.

What truly concerned him was not how terrible he felt,
nor how helpless he was, hanging by his bound feet about an
arm's length above a wood plank floor. No, what unnerved
him—what terrified him, really—was the rustic ugliness of his

surroundings and the hideous, troglodytic visages of the three figures who stood before him.

One wore a mask—a human face, Rem realized with dread and astonishment. Or rather pieces of human faces, sewn together into an unholy patchwork.

It wasn't orcs after all, Rem thought. *This is where that poor fellow's face got off to . . .*

Behind the flesh-masked man was another, tall and muscular, but twisted, as well, like a gnarled oak, shoulders uneven, a hump on one shoulder blade, head bent at a strange, sideward angle, one arm ending in a stunted, two-fingered hand held against his big chest, the other arm dangling at his side, impossibly long.

The third figure was an old woman. Her face looked as though it had been carved from a sun-seasoned piece of old tree bark, lined and weathered and bleached and creased, framed by thin wisps of white, tangled hair. She only had one eye—where another had been was nothing but an empty black well—but that single orb threatened to pop right out of her head, bulging against the failing restraints of her eyelids.

She was the closest. The one who'd blown her rank breath into Rem's face as she'd urged him back to wakefulness.

Merciful Aemon, gods of the Panoply and saints of grace and fortune, don't let me die here, Rem thought suddenly. *Anywhere else—in the woods, in the river, tossed from a cliff, mauled by a bear . . .*

But not here.

Not among these things . . . these half people, errant from a nightmare of big witches and child-snatching ogres.

"There he is," the old crone croaked. She was bent double, her head craned almost upside down to match the position of Rem's. She stood uncomfortably close to him, and he could smell her even when she wasn't speaking. She had a reek like rotting flesh and sickness.

The big one with the twisted body clapped its mismatched, misshapen hands. "*Gar gar gar,*" it babbled in a low, throaty voice. "*Gar norf ner wender kop.*"

Rem thought it might be speaking the common tongue— there was something familiar in those words. But the thing's horrid mouth, tongue, and palate—pure wreckage, all, like the gaping entrance to a collapsed mine shaft—kept it from forming its words correctly.

"Siebel says he wants the leg, great-mother," the one with the quilt-like human face mask said. "I'll settle for the soft bits. His bobs and his black-nappy and the red-ropes."

"Wallow your hogs, Swifty," great-mother said impatiently, her face still an inch from Rem's. "There's questions need answerin'."

"*Kefrums?*" the big one, Siebel, said.

"You heard me!" great-mother snapped, now standing to her full height—which was only a little taller than Torval. The old crone was so withered by time, so bent by the blows of fate and circumstance—and, Rem guessed, inbreeding—that she looked almost like a butcher's hook on legs. She turned, addressing someone unseen.

"Brown Bon! Fopsy! Stoke that fire! We need the cauldron boiling!"

"Stoked," someone said. It sounded like a woman, but Rem couldn't be sure.

"Sundry hells it is!" great-mother crowed, then stalked toward whomever she was addressing, giving Rem a casual shove as she did so. Suddenly Rem found himself spinning on his tether, the whole topsy-turvy world around him whirling in lazy circles, with no means of stopping in sight.

He caught scattered impressions of the place they were in. It was a cottage of some sort, roomy inside, with a high ceiling and a great deal of space between the visible walls. It was sloppily made, wide gaps between most of the clapboards that made up the outer walls allowing pale sunlight in from the outside. Every inch of the place was littered or decorated with the cast-offs of these terrible, bloody-minded wood folk: small fragments of bone, crumbs, old dried leaves, and desiccated clumps of moss littering the floor; ragged furs and half-cured pelts and great swaths of flayed and half-tanned skin nailed to the walls or hanging from curing hooks; iron tools from an age already ancient when Hobb's Folly had been full of life and hope; strange bottles and jars filled with all sorts of horrifying, quasi-identifiable flora, fauna, or body parts; and ill-made, tilting furniture that would have been comical if it hadn't been found in such a hideous, hellish place. All around him was the smell of death and decay—the coppery tang of blood, the astringent stink of piss and the low, mulchy odor of excrement, as well as a horrid, rotting scent that reminded Rem of both worm-ridden fruit and fish left to ferment under a hot sun.

The others, Brown Bon and Fopsy, stood behind Rem, shuffling around a great, stone-ringed firepit—built inside this firetrap of a house, brilliant—attending to a giant iron cauldron hanging above crackling flames. Fopsy was, indeed, a woman—thick through the middle, barefoot, thin, stringy hair having mostly fallen out in clumps, wearing an old, ragged dress that had clearly been taken from a rich owner five or ten years ago. Brown Bon had his back to Rem, so he could see little of the man, no matter how many times he passed through Rem's spinning vision. From the back he wasn't so fearsome— just a man, thin, bony, a little hunched—but Rem guessed he'd be just as vile once he got around to revealing himself.

Gods, what had he gotten himself into?

The one-eyed old woman—great-mother—turned back

toward Rem from the cooking cauldron. She shuffled nearer and lowered her terrible, time-furrowed visage close to Rem's. Before speaking she reached out a single bony hand and arrested Rem's spin, as well.

"Now then," she said, once more blowing that rancid breath into Rem's face. "Let's us have a palaver, eh? How would supper like that?" He was entirely too close. He could not only see that she had no teeth, but could make a close examination of the yawning, black wells in her gums where teeth used to be, every time she spoke.

And did she just call him *supper*?

"Palaver," he managed, "absolutely. As you wish, madam. Ask me your questions and I'll answer honestly, you have my word."

She hit him headwise. "Shush, now, supper. You talks too much."

"Forgive me," Rem said, trying to maintain some modicum of restraint. "How came I to be here, may I ask?"

She hit him again, harder this time. "Quiet, says I! That's talking, ain't it?"

The one with the human face mask—Swifty—slid into Rem's field of vision now. His body was rocked by strange spasms. When an odd sound emanated from the strange goblin of a man seconds later, Rem realized he was laughing, snickers that rocked his whole body as if he was in on some hilarious joke that Rem himself had missed entirely.

"You stalked the coney," he said, fingers fluttering like an excited child's, even as his height and deep voice told Rem that he was probably at least thirty or forty years old. "That was mine! My trick! My trap! Swifty caught you, didn't he? Caught you good!"

He launched into another laughing fit. Watching that patchwork mask of noses, eyeholes, mouths, and ears stretch and contort as he brayed beneath it was going to give Rem nightmares for the rest of his life, if he did get out of this mess alive. He wondered if the effect might be less loathsome—less disturbing—if this Swifty just wore a single face at a time, instead of this hideous, slapped-together monstrosity.

Great-mother drove one fist into Swifty's gut and he spat out a breath, wheezing. He bent double and moaned as the old witch turned back to Rem.

"Clap that hog trough," she muttered. "Idle, prattling, foolish boy."

"That hurt, great-ma," Swifty said.

"And good thing it did!" she hissed. "Elsewise you might not get the message carried, eh?"

"Look," Rem said, voice calm, eminently reasonable. "I was separated from my friends. They'll be looking for me. If they find me in this state"—he indicated his topsy-turvy position—"they're liable to be quite cross with you. What say you cut me down and see me on my way?"

Great-mother smiled a little, then made an offer of her own. "What say we cut your throat like a pig, dress you like a deer, then stew you like a stringy old horse?"

Rem weighed those words. She was utterly serious. Even pleased by the prospect. "Not my first choice," he said.

"Let me do it, great-ma!" Swifty begged, having found his breath and his voice again. "Let me bleed him!"

Siebel shuffled into view now, the big, twisted oaf with the misshapen limbs and bent neck. "*Ma tu, ma tu!*" he chuffed. "*Nyet ma dommer um. Bas? Baaaas?*"

Rem could see his face more clearly this time, and he shuddered at the sight. The creature was, he thought, human—or some small part so—but a primitive existence and spoiled lineage hadn't been kind to him. His head was a misshapen oblong covered in seeping boils and lumpy tumors that threatened to split the skin, his eyes small and dark and deeply recessed under a sloping brow, his nose a mashed, broken appendage all but spread across his face like a piece of soft, rotten fruit. His mouth was the worst, though—soft palate cleft, lips strangely puckered and leathery, hanging loose as though they'd been glued on by their horrid architect at the last moment, teeth a tangle of yellow and black discoloration against livid red gums.

"Where's the little 'uns?" great-mother asked.

Swifty shrugged. "Chuck hunting. Birding. Egg picking. How should I know?"

Rem fought the urge to cry out. Little ones? Here? Among these?

You've got to stall them, Rem thought. *As long as possible, any way possible. Maybe if you stall them long enough, you'll think of something . . . formulate a plan . . . see a way out of this . . .*

But he imagined there was no way out of this. He'd already reached his hands up quickly and subtly to his belt and found his dagger gone. The one in his boot might still be there—it was hard for him to tell, at present—but summoning the strength and speed to reach up and grab it before his captors could hurt or kill him? That was a long shot. Great-mother and Swifty each had a collection of knives, shoved naked into the hemp ropes they both used to bind their tunics round their thin waists. Maybe if one of them got close enough, he could grab a blade and . . .

No. That was foolish. He was hanging upside down. Even if he could snatch a knife and stab whoever stood right in front of him, whatever wound he gave them, even if fatal, would take forever to kill them. They'd have plenty of time to cast him into the dark ahead of them. Or any of the others might intervene.

Stall anyway, he thought. *You've got nothing to lose. Every breath earned is hope. Try to remember that . . .*

"I'm sorry," Rem said. "I've totally forgotten my manners. Might we introduce ourselves?"

Great-mother, Swifty, and Siebel—all gathered in a tight cluster beside the cauldron and the cookfire—turned to stare at Rem as though he'd just uttered words in Old Horunic. Fopsy and Brown Bon gave him odd looks, as well, pausing briefly in their ministrations to the fire and the contents of that big iron pot.

"My name's Rem," Rem said, placing his hands on his chest to suggest himself. "I've come from Yenara, on my way to Erald. Who am I speaking with?"

Great-mother surprised him then by taking two long, swift strides across the littered floor and grabbing his balls with one of her clawlike old hands. The crone squeezed hard, and Rem screamed to wake the dead. Gods, but that hurt. It hurt bad. Worse than anything he'd ever experienced.

"You've got a name, and it's supper, supper!" great-mother snarled around her pitted gums. "As for who's come claiming you, ain't you knowin' nothing about the Big Wood? Ain't you heard who's the first, last, and best crow feeders hereabouts? I's the great-mother—oldest and wisest—of the Bosker clan, and these here striplings are my bloody brood. Welcome, keener, to the family citadel!"

She gave his scrotum one last, hard squeeze, then released it. Rem felt on the verge of vomiting, the pain of her assault and his long period inverted both threatening at once to overwhelm him. He coughed, sputtered, drew breath like a man who'd been drowning. He realized that his eyes were wet with tears, and he might have uttered a sob or two as she'd squeezed.

"Pleased to meet you," he croaked.

"We's the jeepiest, hereabouts—the shiniest, the broviest, the bloggiest! Why, people sing songs of we, the Bloody Boskers, far and wide! If you come mopsing through this wood unknowing, you's a fool indeed."

"Fool indeed," Rem parroted, the agony between his legs now subsiding to a dull, throbbing ache.

"Squidge him again, great-ma!" Swifty urged. "I like it when he blargs like that!"

"Please don't," Rem begged.

"Fine, then! On to business!" the old woman said, cackling as she did. Clearly she was pleased with herself for causing Rem so much pain. Now she shuffled nearer again. "How many?" she asked.

"How many what?" Rem asked in return.

Great-mother hit him across the face. The touch of her rank skin, however brief, was enough to make him gag. "How many come you? You's not alone, not in these woods! We seen your snaky train!"

"If you saw," Rem said, "then you know how many."

"Can't count," Swifty said apologetically. "Not well."

"Shut your gullet!" great-mother snapped, then returned her attentions to Rem. "Tell us, now: How many? Give us the trues and we'll do you quick, supper. No pain. Just *whoosh*— fast and neat. Out like a candle."

"There were forty of us," Rem lied. "And we're expecting a hundred more. The duke was to meet us, with a full-company honor guard, somewhere west of the river ford."

"Forty and a hundred!" Swifty gasped. "That's more than twenty! Maybe even more than thirty!"

"*Bot hanken warty*," Siebel snuffled.

Great-mother wasn't convinced. Rem could see it in the way her single eye narrowed suspiciously, probing into him like the point of a sharp bodkin. "Lies, I says. Wasn't more than a score, most like. Maybe less."

"Fine," Rem said, thinking of another approach. "You've found us out. We're outlaws, here to trade with the Devils of the Weald."

To Rem's surprise, great-mother suddenly stood upright—at least as close as she could come to it—and screamed in horror. It was a sound of shock and disgust and distress; a woman finding a rat in her larder, calling for someone to come kill it.

"Devils, bloody Devils!" great-mother shouted. "Curse them, crush them, mush them, tush them! Peel all their skins and crack their bones and let their eyes pop, jellified, on the fires and feed the ants and snails! He names the Devils!"

Swifty scurried forward and bent to speak to Rem. "She hates them Devils," Swifty said, as though in confidence. "Best not mention them again."

"Devils, proud! Devils, pretty! Devils, pure! Devils, true! Bah! I shit on the Devils! I blast all the stinking, unholy smoke in my bum toward their groves and caves and I piss venom on their cookfires!"

Swifty threw Rem another reproving glance—*Please, sir, don't mention them again*—then withdrew. The fact that Rem had just shared an intimate moment with a man wearing a mask made of human faces, that he'd seen that man's eyes deep within the mask's torn eyeholes, and that those eyes, though veined and rheumy, were anything but mad or inhuman, made Rem vaguely ill.

But that was neither here nor there. Clearly great-mother hated the Red Raven and the Devils of the Weald. Saw them as proud, upstart competitors, no doubt. He could most definitely use that to his advantage ...

"And just what was it?" the great-mother demanded, moving

nearer now. "What was it you blighters brought to trade with those poxy louts?"

Rem tried to think of something that might interest them. Would they be pleased to hear that it was the Red Raven himself they'd been transporting? Would they be tempted if he mentioned weapons? Would they respond to need if he suggested they'd been trading provisions? What on earth could these backward, twisted people possibly want that would, for a moment, anyway, keep them from killing him?

He opted for weapons. "You heard the booms, yes?"

Siebel and Swifty both nodded emphatically.

"Oh yes," Swifty said. "Heard that. Loud, they was! Like ground thunder! Smelled the smoke when the wind changed, too! Was that some wonder-worker? Some magic man calling the thunder out of the sky and the fire out of the earth?"

Rem shook his head. "It was a weapon. Dwarven blasting powder. They use it underground, for making tunnels and caverns of their own."

"Fool talk," great-mother spat. "Ain't no low folk here-bouts."

"No, indeed," Rem said, wishing his own familiar dwarf would come barreling through the door of this mean little den about now. "But the men in the armor—the strong men, the shiny men—they bought this blasting powder to use as a weapon! Against the Red Raven and the Devils of the Weald!"

"Against?" great-mother asked thoughtfully. "I thought you said trade?"

"It was a trap, in truth," Rem said, knowing there was at least some veracity in that statement. "We came saying we'd trade with the Raven and his Devils, but we sought to eradicate them."

Swifty tried on that word. "Eradi..."

"Stamp 'em, break 'em, burn them to ash!" great-mother

shouted at him. "That's what *eradicate* means! Now pinch your top-cunt or I'll pinch it for you!"

Swifty closed his mouth. Despite his fearsome mask and his strong frame, he looked like a scolded little boy.

Great-mother was, indeed, intrigued now. "So you says these blasties were meant to fire the Raven and the Devils, and Swifty here says he hears 'em. Ain't none left?"

"Indeed," Rem lied. "Many. You've only to waylay my companions and steal them for yourself. I'd say neither the Raven nor his Devils nor any other pretenders in these woods would cross you after that! You'd have something none of them would have!"

"That sounds lovely, great-ma!" Swifty said. "Let's do it! Siebel and I can go!"

"*Ta woom*," Siebel said, clapping his misshapen hands. "*Boddy boddy baes?*"

In the distance Rem heard a hoarse barking that launched into a fierce, whining howl. He wondered what kind of beast could make such a noise—too wild to be a dog, too high pitched to be a wolf. Then he remembered: they were in coyote country.

The sound froze everyone present. Great-mother raised her head and listened. Swifty and Siebel bent close to each other. Even Fopsy and Brown Bon, by the cookpot, paused in their labors of chopping edible roots and tossing sprigs of wild herbs into the roiling water to raise their heads and listen.

The sound came again, barks becoming bays. Rem couldn't judge precisely how far away the animal might be, but he guessed within a quarter mile.

"That's Cobby, south side," Swifty said.

"What do you know?" great-mother hissed. "All those beasties sound the same."

"Not true, great-ma," Swifty countered. "I can tell! Each one's got his own bark, his own larf, his own howl."

"We should cook 'em," Brown Bon muttered.

"We can't and you won't!" Swifty shouted, looking suddenly agitated by Brown Bon's suggestion.

"He's just baiting you, Swifty," Fopsy said. She returned to chopping whatever twisted root she'd been peeling, tossing chunks into the stew cauldron.

Once more the coyote barked, but its call was altered this time. Barks devolved to a howl...but the howl was suddenly cut off. In its wake silence reigned.

"Oh no," Swifty said, rheumy eyes widening within the darkened holes of his human skin mask. "You hears that?"

"Those flea-bitten beasts are your problem," great-mother grumbled. "I's with Brown Bon. Shoulda cooked 'em long time ago! Thieving things!"

"They's the guards!" Swifty said, and moved toward the far side of the room now, out of Rem's field of vision. What was he doing? "I's gotta go. Siebel, you come, too."

Siebel shuffled to follow.

"Siebel, stay!" great-mother snarled. "Swifty, too!"

Swifty appeared to Rem again. He was carrying a big, unwieldy weapon now—a hammer of some sort, the handle long and thick, the head small but clearly heavy, probably pure iron. It looked like a comically enlarged version of the maul Torval was so fond of carrying.

"They bark because someone comes," Swifty said desperately. "I's goin' to sight it."

"They barks 'cause they's dog-rodents, that's why!" great-mother said. "Now put that hammer down! We's ain't done with supper yet!"

"Supper can wait," Swifty said, sounding for all his height and bulk like a whining child eager to go out and drop his fishing pole in the stream one more time before dark.

Great-mother opened her mouth to respond, but the words were swallowed by the sudden thunder of the door to the vile little cabin being torn off its rusted hinges. Hanging there, helpless and topsy-turvy, Rem wondered just what could do that—what could tear a door right off its hinges and cast it aside. He thought he saw a big shadow outside—something broad and hulking—but the setting sun poured in from beyond, igniting the cloud of stirred-up dust that accompanied the ruin of the door and making it opaque.

The big shadow responsible for the door's removal stepped aside then, and new forms rushed through the door, one after another. The first was small and low, walking in a strange, side-sliding, crab-like manner.

Rem had never seen a living goblin before, only drawings and mummers' masks made to resemble them. This had to be one, though: the long, pointy chin, the sharp cheekbones, the flashing, recessed little eyes, and the broad, toothy grin. It looked no taller than Torval—four feet at the most—but of much more slender cast.

The fleet little creature had a small compound bow in its knotty hands. As he scurried into the cabin, he nocked an arrow and drew, aiming the point toward the largest target, which was Siebel. He did not, however, loose.

Following in the goblin's wake: orcs. They hurried through the torn-away door, one after another, filling the large single room of the shabby little cabin, fanning out and brandishing their cruel weapons with relish.

Swifty shouted something—Rem could make no sense of it—and shook his big hammer in threat.

Great-mother shouted, as well, yammering at Swifty and Siebel and the two hunched over the stew pot.

One of the orcs started barking orders in its own tongue.

Everything was noise and shuffling feet and rattling weaponry. Threats, orders, confusion.

Another rattling: some other door on hinges. It was coming from just behind Rem. He tried to crane his neck round to see what was happening. He heard before he managed a clear view; whatever strong, large creature had yanked the front door off its hinges now did the same with its counterpart at the rear. Rem heard heavy boot-falls rushing forward. He was at a terrible angle to see clearly, but what he did catch from the corner of his eye gave him no comfort.

More orcs. The one in the lead had an enormous, curved saber...and breasts.

A female?

Indeed, a female. And she was charging right at him.

Cack, Rem thought.

CHAPTER TWENTY-FIVE

Torval winced as Galen drew the catgut taut, closing the gash on his right bicep. With practiced efficiency the scout knotted the stitch—bringing another wince from Torval—and bit off the excess thread. Torval studied the dressed wound and offered a cursory nod.

"Good work," he said, then rose from where he sat, took up his maul, and made for the road. They were camping west of it; he had a long walk ahead if he was going to resume his search for Rem.

"Where do you think you're going?" the lord marshal demanded. "I should think one bloody encounter with an orcish war band enough for one day. Don't you?"

Aye, one encounter was enough. But it had struck Torval as strange that the orcs had retreated so quickly after the fight was joined. Steel had rung, blows had been traded, wounds had been gouged, and blood had flowed, but in the midst of the melee, when things were just getting savage, the orcish chief had called off his warriors, and they'd retreated into the woods.

Why would they do that? That wasn't normal orc behavior, by any stretch. War bands fought to the death when they engaged...unless they had specific orders to do otherwise, a larger goal that a small conflict could interfere with.

So what was that larger goal? What was so important that it kept those orcs from fighting to the death?

"I asked you a question," the lord marshal pressed. "Have you been struck dumb suddenly, master dwarf?"

Torval turned slowly and stared at the lord marshal. He'd grown to hate the man in an astonishingly short time. He didn't discount strength, or honor, or the necessity of command, but there was something in this Harcta Kroenen that set his teeth on edge—a hard-nosed, overbearing pride that threatened to crush the man and all around him. There was, likewise, the issue of his presumption. For the better part of a week, during the first half of their journey, the man had made it clear how much he did not want Rem and Torval along, how little he respected them, what a drain on resources they were. And now that half the company was dead and Rem was missing? Suddenly the lord marshal claimed command over everyone—including Torval—and the right to decide who was worth searching for and who wasn't.

If he persisted, he would have to be taught a lesson. Torval would be happy to teach him.

"There's still light," Torval said. "I plan to return to where we were attacked and resume my search. If night falls, I'll just camp where I find myself and keep searching in the morning."

"I've given you no leave to do so," the lord marshal said.

"I've asked none," Torval answered through clenched teeth.

Captain Tuvera stepped in. "Lord Marshal, the dwarf is concerned for his mate. Let him search."

"Aye, let me search," Torval said bitterly. "I ask for no companions, no assistance. I just want to be left alone. Carry on to Erald for all I care."

"There is still the matter of the Raven," the lord marshal said. "Have you forgotten?"

Torval couldn't help himself. He stalked up to the lord marshal and snarled up into his smug, frowning face. "Keep. Your. Fucking. Gold."

"I'm not talking about gold, master dwarf," the lord marshal countered. "I'm talking about duty. You and your foolish young companion had one task to complete on this journey: to keep the Red Raven locked in his cage. Now that he's loose, you would simply abandon us? Abandon your duty?"

"My duty," Torval countered, "is to my friend and my watch. I owe you *nothing*, Lord Marshal Kroenen, nor anyone else here."

"Perhaps you were working with him, then," the lord marshal said, a sneer forming at the corner of his lips. "Perhaps, as I'd suspected all along, that outlaw managed to bribe you and your companion into helping him escape. I was not present, after all, when he was freed from his cage. You claim it was one of his own, but it would have been easy enough for you to set him free—"

"The Lady Tzimena knows the truth," Elvaris broke in. She had just finished re-dressing her wounded leg and now stood on it, clearly in pain. "I do, as well. If you accuse Torval of lying, you're accusing me, also."

"And who are you?" the lord marshal asked, swinging his gaze toward her. "One more sword-strumpet in your lady's company? You rode at the rear, as well. Could you, also, not have been bought?"

"That's enough," Tuvera said coldly. "You won't accuse my soldiers of treason, Lord Marshal. So much as suggest it again, and we'll settle it right here, steel to steel."

The lord marshal's hand fell to his sheathed sword. His smirk became a cold smile. "Try me, you braying cunt."

Tuvera's sword was free of its scabbard in a breath. Elvaris drew her own, though doing so forced her to shift her weight onto her good leg and risk being thrown over by a light shove. Galen was up, arms out in placation, trying to calm everyone. The wounded Croften and Wallenbrand had their weapons out now, as well. Everyone was shouting, hurling challenges, warnings, insults.

"Stop it! The lot of you!"

Torval's voice split the commotion like one of those blasting sphere explosions. As they all suddenly fell silent, turning their wondering gazes upon the dwarf, Torval felt his own face twisting into a contortion of disgust, his own fell gaze sweeping over them all, tired of their bickering.

"You lot can kill each other when I'm gone," Torval said. "I don't give a grizzly fart for all your quarrels. And you, Lord Marshal—any other man who'd impugned my honor in the way you have would, were I in my own city, already be dead on the ground, his skull split by this maul in my hand. Since we are in a rare predicament here, however, I'll honor my partner's memory by forgoing the righteous killing I'd like to visit upon you now. Even if Rem's dead, at least he'll be proud of me for exercising a little restraint."

"Threaten me again, dwarf," the lord marshal said.

"Shut up," Torval answered. "Now, I'm going to find my partner, dead or alive, and when he's found, we're going home. We'll walk all the way—keep your gods-damned horses. If I need to, I'll carry the boy on my back. But as I live and breathe, you shall not stop me."

"Let me convince you otherwise," Captain Tuvera said, still holding her sword toward the lord marshal.

"There's no convincing," Torval said, shaking his head. "I wish you well, Captain. You're brave and true, and your swordmaids should be honored to serve under you."

"We need you, Torval," Tuvera said then. She let that sink in as she slowly withdrew from her guarded stance and resheathed her sword. She faced Torval now, and he saw the look of need on her face.

"We only had one task on this journey, as well. That was to protect the Lady Tzimena, to see her delivered safely to her new husband and her new home. As of now, we've failed in that mission. But I think we can still find her."

"I think so, too," Torval said. "So you should go after her."

"But we need every hand," Tuvera said earnestly. "You know the Red Raven will have a great many outlaws in his camp. And finding that camp will be hard enough, though not impossible, seeing as we've got two first-rate trackers with us." She indicated Galen and Croften. "If we're to stir up that nest of snakes, we need more hands to cut them down."

Torval could sense her need, feel it, even. Under other circumstances he would have aided them happily. The Lady Tzimena was, after all, a victim in this. Wasn't that Torval's job? To protect innocents from the predations of evil?

But Rem was out there somewhere, lost and alone.

"My partner needs me," Torval said quietly. "Were it not so I'd stand by you."

"Consider," Wallenbrand broke in. "You almost reached the ford in your search, and with our aid. We found no sign of him—not even a corpse. All we did find was that orcish war band, and they very nearly tore us to bits."

"That's why it must be me alone," Torval said. "I won't have anyone else hurt or suffering for my partner and me."

"That's not my point," Wallenbrand said, moving forward.

"Leave him, Wallenbrand," the lord marshal said. "He's nothing to us."

"Pardon me, sir," Wallenbrand said, "he may be nothing to you, but he drove aside an orcish spear aimed at my beating heart. From where I stand, this dwarf is a boon companion. So, with all due respect, shut your mouth and let me finish."

The lord marshal was stunned into silence.

Wallenbrand continued. "We looked for him and didn't find him, Torval. Rem could be anywhere. But the Lady Tzimena—we *know* where she probably is. We can track her and recover her. Help us do that. Let's all get that one thing right, and then maybe everything else—Rem, the Red Raven, your reward—will fall into place."

It was a sensible argument, Torval knew, but he was still loath to agree to it. As Wallenbrand said, Rem could be anywhere. He might have survived and pulled himself out of the river on the north bank. He might simply be sleeping under a fern somewhere and he hadn't heard them searching for him, calling for him. He could also, just as easily, be alive and wounded. A bone broken. An ankle twisted. Even a nonfatal injury could become fatal if left to fester too long in these accursed woods, or simply because it would keep Rem from finding his way back to them and getting the food and water he needed to survive.

And yet... Wallenbrand was right. Rem could be *anywhere*. Finding him in these woods—even if he was alive and mobile—could take a very long time. Shouldn't saving an innocent girl, now held prisoner by robbers and thieves, matter more? Wasn't that what Rem and Torval did, every single day, on the streets of Yenara?

The dwarf hung his head. Sighed. He wanted Osma's good counsel. He wanted his children's hugs and kisses. He wanted his partner here, to talk sense to him. To convince him.

But Rem was gone, and Torval would have to convince himself.

"Forgive me," he muttered under his breath.

"What's that?" Tuvera asked.

"Fine. You have me," Torval said with a sigh. "What's the plan?"

CHAPTER TWENTY-SIX

"So," Tzimena asked, tired of the silence between them for the past few hours, "what was your plan, precisely?"

It was well after dark now, the passage they occupied once more swathed in darkness. The silhouettes of two guards haunted the open mouth of the passage, sharp against the dim, flickering light of torches and candles emanating from the larger cavern chamber beyond. That distant, secondhand light from outside allowed Tzimena to just make out the narrow vertical stripes of Korin's cage bars. She imagined Korin's view of her cage was no better.

"What does it matter now?" Korin asked. His voice was hoarse, soft. The voice of despair. The voice of defeat.

"It matters because, if one or both of us are to die, I'd like to share something true with you. Just once. Just so we both know exactly what we believed might happen."

Perhaps it's a foolish hope, she thought. *But it feels appropriate somehow, like the last gold we can mine from the tapped vein of our love for one another. It was a childish love, of course, a love built on dreams and infatuation, not reality, but maybe, just maybe, truth could now redeem it, could make the memory of it not so bitter.*

Korin sighed. "I honestly don't know," he said. "I swear, my intentions were honorable."

"I doubt that," Tzimena said quietly.

"Earnest, then," Korin said. "When we ambushed the honor

guard from Erald and I found that dispatch indicating that you and Verin were to be married, it stirred something in me. I know you don't believe me, Tzimena—and I suppose I don't blame you for doubting—but I really did think of you every day while I was making a life out here. They were idle thoughts, true—where is she now, what's she doing now, who's she loving now—but my memory of you, and my desire for you, never left me."

Damn him, he sounded as if he meant it. There was a weariness in his voice, a sense of capitulation, that suggested he was too tired to lie, too beaten. Then again, she'd begun to suspect that Korin, for all his passion and single-mindedness, was also quite adept at fooling himself. If there had ever been a man who could have talked himself into believing he carried a torch for someone through the years, when in fact they'd never been more than a tiny adjunct to his everyday idylls, it was Korin Lyr. The man loved a good story, the more doomed and romantic the better.

"All right, then," she said. "I never left your thoughts. Something stirred in you when you found out I was betrothed to your brother. Then what? It would've taken you a week or more to get to Yenara once you set out. What on earth did you think would happen once you got there, if you were able to fool my keepers and get close to me?"

Korin was silent for a time. She imagined him shrugging in the dark, but of course she could see nothing. He was only a voice buried deep in a well of shadow.

"I really don't know. I think, in my mind, I told myself that you would never want to marry Verin—not unless your mother forced you into it. Maybe, I thought, once you knew that I was alive, you'd decide you wanted to be a part of the life I built here, if only to escape the one waiting for you."

"The Red Raven and his errant bride," Tzimena said, half to him and half to herself. "Would I get a colorful nickname, too?"

"The Ladyhawk," Korin said. She heard a smile in his voice. "Or maybe the Bloody Robin?"

"Clearly you hadn't thought it through," Tzimena said. She, too, was smiling now. She rather fancied the Raven Queen.

"Was I wrong? Was that wholly impossible?"

Tzimena paused. Searched herself, desperate to give him an honest answer. "I don't know," she finally said. "There's a part of me that might have wanted that...might have liked that. In truth, when you came into my chambers and I saw you, I was too shocked to think of anything. You were speaking, Captain Tuvera was speaking, all sorts of words swirled around me, but I couldn't focus. All I could do was try to reason out why the captain of the honor guard sent to fetch me looked so much like you."

"Then you sent Tuvera away," Korin said. "Had you realized what was happening by that time?"

"I think so," she said. "But we didn't have long, did we?"

"No," Korin said, regret putting a sharp edge on his voice. "No, we didn't."

"I don't know what I might have done, had you managed to paint a better picture of what might be for me," Tzimena said. "But once you fled, once I had time to think and reflect, I knew which way I was leaning. And my answer would have been no."

Korin said nothing. She could actually hear him breathing in the dark. Aemon, was that answer so unexpected for him? So shocking?

"Why?" Korin finally managed. "How? How could you just...stay?"

"Because it's my life, Korin," she said. "I was raised to rule. I was raised to lead. I was raised to *give* something to the world. I have my days when I hate that responsibility and wish I could flee from it, but it will not leave me be. And so I think I would have said no."

"But the words we shared on the road. Stolen, in the darkness—"

"I was still wrestling with myself," Tzimena said. "I knew I wanted to see you freed and away…but I was never entirely certain I would go with you."

Again silence. He was fuming, she could tell. She could almost imagine his face, frowning in the dark, his eyes downcast, his brow knit angrily.

"Why did you come with me when I fled, then?" he asked.

"I didn't," Tzimena countered, feeling anger rising in her now. Was he really this blind? This foolish? "You threatened our companions and forced me to go with you."

Korin said, "I just assumed—"

"Well, you assumed wrongly," Tzimena countered. "I did everything I could short of grabbing a weapon and wounding you, Korin, but you used me as a human shield and dragged me off anyway. Besides, when I saw you'd cut down anyone who followed, and that that boy, Rem, wouldn't leave off, I was forced to decide: Would I let him die saving me, or would I relent and maybe save him? I chose the latter."

"Who is he to you?" Korin said.

"He was innocent," Tzimena said. "Caught in the middle of all this. Unlike you, Korin Lyr, I won't have innocent people suffering on my behalf, or dying for my lost causes."

Perhaps that was a low blow, but she didn't care anymore. She was determined now to make him see. If some terrible fate awaited him, she wanted him to die with clarity, with the truth lodged at the center of his heart and mind like arrow points that were impossible to extract.

His love for her did not justify hazard to innocent lives.

His love for her did not obligate her to abjure her responsibilities simply to feed his desires, his ego.

And her love for him, no matter how pure once upon a time, could not save him from the reckoning that his actions demanded. He had to be punished for his wrongs. Perhaps she would have to be, as well.

Maybe that was the difference between them. She was ready to suffer for her sins. He'd spent five years in the wilderness running from his own.

"So," Korin finally said, "our love *is* a lost cause? Is that what you're saying?"

"I suppose so," Tzimena answered. "Or rather...I do love you, Korin. When I realized that it was you in that Eraldic livery—that you were alive, that you hadn't died under a brigand's knife in these woods—it lifted a weight from me. It gave me hope for all sorts of things. Maybe not our love—because that was something from the past, something young and hopeful, no longer even real—but if you could be alive, so miraculously, then, maybe, all sorts of miracles were possible. Maybe marrying your brother wouldn't make me miserable. Maybe ruling by his side in Erald wouldn't be the end of something but a beginning. Maybe the road ahead was actually just as bright—just as full of possibility—as I thought all the untraveled roads behind me were."

"And what of me?" Korin asked, and she could hear the anguish and bitterness in his voice—the self-centered sort borne only in the hearts of religious zealots and love-struck young men, a bitterness fueled by a monstrous sense of entitlement, suddenly denied all that it had claimed as its own by right. "What of the love I felt? The hopes I held, that were thrown down and trampled?"

Tzimena weighed her response carefully. She wasn't trying to hurt him now, but to help him. To awaken him. To make him see something, clearly, for the first time in his moonstruck, daydreamy life.

"I never wanted to hurt you, Korin," she said. "But I couldn't lie to you, either. If you would not hear my words and know that I spoke truly, I'd have to break away from you and let you figure it out in time...apart from me."

He fell silent again. Outside, far away, an owl screeched.

"You're cruel," he said with a sigh.

She wanted to respond that she was not—that it was only his frustrated need, the denial of his satisfaction, that made it seem so. But what was the point?

Perhaps some people couldn't be helped.

Perhaps some people would never listen, no matter how clearly and directly you spoke to them.

Tzimena decided to change the subject. "What do you think will happen now? Honestly. No lies, no bravado."

Korin didn't answer for a long, long time. "They'll kill me and sell you," he said finally.

Tzimena felt the sting of tears. She wished she could see him. Look into his eyes, so that he knew that cruel was the last thing she wanted to be right now.

"I wish it could be otherwise," she finally said, having nothing else to offer.

"Why should you?" Korin asked, and she heard that bitterness again. "Clearly you don't care what happens to me...or who you're sold to, for that matter."

It was her first instinct to respond with rancor. To hurl a few insults of her own at him and put him in his place. How dare he judge her! How dare he accuse her of being so coldhearted? So mercenary?

But could she really have expected anything else? Had he given her any cause to hope for more?

The man who Korin Lyr might have been died in these woods, she thought sadly. *The thing left in his place is the boy, frozen forever despite age and experience, a young soul expecting all the world to bend to his will, to feed his desires, to spare his feelings and the stirrings of his heart.*

I'd like to hate him . . . but I only pity him.

"I'm sorry you think so," were the only words she could find. He offered no response to them.

After a while the darkness and silence proved too delicious to resist. Tzimena Baya let sleep take her, and she didn't open her eyes again until morning.

CHAPTER TWENTY-SEVEN

It was strange, Rem thought, how far the passage of a single day could take one from one's imagined place or destination in the world to a wholly different one. How quickly comfort could turn to desperation, how suddenly failure could be spun around and transmogrify into victory.

This morning, he'd awakened on the ground, in the woods, lost and alone, separated from his companions.

By midday he'd been hanging upside down in the cabin of a clan of wilderness cannibals, praying to find some way out of his predicament, hoping against hope that, at the very least, he would not breathe his last breath in that fetid cabin and end up in someone's stew pot, to be consumed and shat out at a later date.

Now here it was, well after dark, and he was no longer alone, and no longer being threatened with murder and consumption.

He was, however, taking his evening meal with an orcish war band, wholly unsure if he was their guest or their prisoner. He wondered if Torval could ever believe such a thing possible, let alone forgive him for such a lapse in etiquette.

Inbred and backward those Bloody Boskers might have been, but from the instant the orcs tore into the cabin and charged, Rem's captors had fought like rabid wolves to protect their home ground. Old great-mother herself—so bent and frail, a victim of hard living, too many years, and poisoned, consanguineous lineage—had snatched up a meat cleaver from a nearby butcher's block and gone to work, charging the big troll that had torn the cabin's front door off its hinges before removing a broad portion of the cabin's rear wall. Great-mother hacked at the big beast with abandon. Watching her bloody attack on a much larger opponent, Rem was reminded of Torval's brave fight with an angry albino orc almost a year earlier.

Siebel and Swifty, meanwhile, had done their level best to hold off the orc band that charged through the cabin's front door. The little goblin archer in the company had studded the pair with a bevy of arrows, but that hadn't stopped them. Like the dumb beasts they were, lumbering, twisted Siebel and flesh-dressed Swifty had been cut and bloodied and pierced but had fought on. Siebel had been neutralized only when one of the orcs—a fierce-looking, mottle-skinned buck wielding a rather nasty-looking long-bladed spear—had run him through and pinned him to the cabin's wall. Only then could another of the orcs—a fearsome female wielding a deadly, curved saber that looked to be of eastern make—move in for the kill and finish the monstrous thing. Swifty, meanwhile, had gotten close enough to the goblin archer to snatch his bow from his hand and try to throttle him. He'd only gone down when a stocky, potbellied orc with a battle-ax chopped one leg out from under him. It had been the spear wielder who then stepped in, drew a strange knife with a forward-curving blade, and hacked off Swifty's head to still his murderous, grasping hands.

In the midst of the chaos and carnage, Rem's pendulous, upside-down position was suddenly compromised. As great-mother fought the big troll, the hulk had stumbled into the center of the cabin, its long arms flailing all about to both defend it and seek a weapon to use against the bloody-minded matriarch. Unintentionally, the troll's big, waving arms had struck the overhead beam that Rem was tied to, cracking the lumber in an instant. When the beam dipped and shattered, the ropes holding Rem to it slid from it and down he went, his head smacking hard on the plank floor of the cabin before the rest of him followed in a bound-up heap.

Rem refused to lose the moment, however. Even as his head ached and his vision swam, he started wriggling and grasping, trying to pull the ropes loose and free himself. His vision had only begun to clear by the time his legs were free. Rem searched around him for some sign of imminent danger, and saw it already looming.

Brown Bon, the stooped male who'd been helping young Fopsy by the cookpot, was roaring down upon him, a big, rusted old knife in his hands, stinking, near-toothless mouth open and shouting incoherently as he charged. Rem, desperate and enraged, scrambled to his feet and charged right at the ugly bastard, just managing to stop his falling knife hand before driving Brown Bon backward. Up close, he could smell the terrible stench of the man's breath and sweat, the unwashed, oily hair, the vague undertone of shit and filthy skin. Just being this close to the vile bugger made Rem want to flee and retch, but Brown Bon wasn't giving an inch. He'd gone blood-wild and kept trying, with all the considerable strength in him, to plunge that dull, rusty knife he held into Rem's face or chest.

They hit the cook pot. The huge cauldron jostled under their weight and sloshed scalding stew onto Rem's right arm. It hurt like the sundry hells, but Rem refused to give in to the pain. He was in a fight for his life now, and there was no time for niceties or licking wounds. A moment later, their feet scrambled together on the floor and Rem suddenly felt something burning creeping up his leg. He dared a glance and saw that, having ventured too close to the cookfire, his right leg was aflame.

That slew Rem's desire to keep grappling with Bon. He

threw all his weight against his opponent, pressing Brown Bon hard against the stew pot and launching himself backward. Rem lost his balance instantly and hit the floor, but he was astonished when he blinked and raised his eyes and saw that Brown Bon himself was now on fire. Not just his trouser leg or boots, either; he'd been shoved so far into the fire beneath the cauldron that the flames had licked up his legs and torso instantly. The cannibal screamed and wheeled round, trying to douse the flames as they began their hungry gnawing at him. As the fire engulfed his head and shoulders, his hair smoking, the whiskers on his face in flames, his screams screwed higher and higher, toward an almost birdlike pitch.

Fopsy, who'd been lurking at the periphery of their duel, screamed, the sight of her onetime cooking companion going up in flames clearly a painful one.

Brown Bon lurched forward, his eyes glaring out of his blackening face and fixed on Rem, eager for one last deadly blow. He took one step, another, raised the knife.

Then the troll intervened. The big, galumphing brute picked up the still-attacking great-mother by her bent legs and swung her sideward like a club. Great-mother slammed hard into the now-blazing Brown Bon, and the two fell silent in the same instant. Their broken bodies were cast aside. The troll gave an audible sigh of relief.

Fopsy was still screaming, arms flailing, mad with fright and grief and who knew what other primitive emotions. Something in Rem suggested—even through his desperation—that he should try to comfort the girl, to silence her. But that was not to be. Just as Rem moved to approach her, the orc female swept in from the side and cut down the screaming woman with her saber. Fopsy gave a last rasp, a rattle, and died.

Suddenly the cabin was quiet. The only sounds were the

twitter of birds in the twilit woods outside and the crackle of popping fat as Brown Bon burned.

Rem had looked around him, realizing that he was now all alone, surrounded and hopelessly outnumbered by an armed orcish war band with its collective blood up.

He hadn't been sure what to do in that instant. For a long time he'd sat there on the floor, staring, trying to get some sense of what might happen next. Little by little, the orcs, the goblin, and the big troll had all closed in around him. That troll looked particularly out of place in the shabby hovel, its big head and shoulders hunched low to keep from thumping against the uneven rafters above.

Rem counted six: there was a big, broad-shouldered, well-armored male sporting three long braids trailing from his crown—the leader of the group, if Rem was not mistaken; the spear wielder; the female; the goblin archer; the fat, stocky orc with the battle-ax (who struck Rem as what Torval might look like if transformed into an orc); and finally the troll.

Rem was just about to offer a greeting, the silence between them persistent and pregnant, when the troll suddenly reached out, seized Rem's shoulders, and yanked him to his feet. He also spun Rem around so that he could look right into the troll's big, broad face. In that instant Rem thought he might finally throw up, as he'd feared doing for the past hour—though whether from fear or simply from dizziness, he could not say.

For a long time, Rem and the troll simply stared at one another. The thing studied him closely, considering him, as though he were the most puzzling of artifacts or buried treasures. Just as Rem was starting to fear that the big oaf might tire of him and crush him where he stood, ending him at last in one swift stroke, the troll spoke.

"*Naca hwar izhgrafa roshe*," it said. Its voice was low, the rumble of a war drum, but something in its tone suggested concern... sympathy, even.

"*Yashno dze djawdwornoc*," the spearman added, stepping into view at the troll's elbow.

The female appeared on the troll's opposite side. "*Bulan*," she said. "*Daco dahna. Omi ba djacla dakwu dzwar?*"

"*Ryudzha*," one of the others said, the word spat as though it was a curse. Rem could not clearly see who spoke, or where they stood. "*Brdjawa ropowi. Wadyo zha raca kordja dze noshura?*" The speaker was somewhere behind him.

"*Tcha djame unta sha, tu'um?*" another said. It sounded like a question.

"*Ba, swa dja wardzana . . .*," another added, the statement an intimation of an unspoken possibility. The voice was high and nasal. Rem assumed it was that of the goblin archer.

"*Na*," one of them countered. "*Frozhatu on.*"

To Rem's great surprise, there had been no questions. Not then, at any rate. Oh, he'd had plenty of his own, but after he'd sputtered all sorts of things at the outset—*Who are you? Where are you from? Thank you, so much, for saving me. What happens now?*—the female finally stepped forward and laid her hand flat across Rem's mouth. Her flesh was dry and rough and smelled of animal musk and sweat.

"Shush," she said around her big, protruding bottom teeth.

The leader had stepped in then—the big one with the trio of braids.

"Fought well, you," he said, and indicated Brown Bon, body still burning on the floor and spewing sickening smoke.

Rem shrugged. "Thank you?"

The orc chieftain bent his head sideward, studied Rem

again, then spoke. "Are safe, you. Come you will, with us. Talk not now. Later."

His syntax was unorthodox—not so unusual, for orcish syntax was notoriously strange to humans—but Rem was surprised by how clearly the orc spoke a human tongue.

Rem nodded that he understood, and the female removed her hand. After that he'd been led outside under the watchful eyes of the female and the troll, while the others tossed the cabin for any useful forage. When they finally emerged, flames were visible inside, and smoke began to pour from between the wood slats and the skin-shaded windows. Clearly they meant to leave nothing behind.

Rem considered the young ones mentioned. What would they think when they returned to find this? In a way he was glad they hadn't. He hoped to never see—to never know— what kind of young ones those monsters could have brooded.

Rem marched along with them, off into the darkening woods, having no idea where he was in relation to his companions or their camp or even the river or the ford. For the first time, he felt truly lost, deep in the wild, so far from the river that he could neither see it nor hear it. The direction of the declining sun suggested that west was off to his left.

He almost opened his mouth to ask questions once or twice, but thought better of it. They'd marched for a long time, until well after the sun went down and twilight gave way to night. Without even the last, purpling light of the sun, Rem could barely see, but the female had laid her hand on his shoulder and begun to guide him, holding him back to grunt one order or another when they came to a slope up or down, a big root that had to be stepped over, or the like. She clearly had good night vision and proved a handy guide. After a rather long march over treacherous ground, Rem noted a faint light off in the woods far ahead of them. It turned out to be the orcs' camp, a small fire still burning, a bent and crusty old orc sitting beside that fire, turning a great haunch of meat spitted on huge sticks above the flame. Another orc—a young male—sat nearby, scouring chain mail with sand and coagulated animal fat. The haunch over the fire looked and smelled like wild boar, but Rem wouldn't swear to it.

The old orc looked up and squinted to study them as they filed into the little clearing. When he saw Rem, his beady, deep-set eyes grew wide.

"*Djha da hrovo?*" he gasped.

"Prisoner," the leader said.

Rem thought it telling that the leader had used that word—a word Rem would understand—instead of a word in their own orcish tongue.

The old orc studied Rem as Rem was guided into the little circle of stones and logs that surrounded the firepit. He got a look on his face as if he smelled something foul.

"Bah," he finally said, dismissing Rem with a wave and bending back to his cook's duties.

The female thrust Rem down onto a log. She sat on his right. The short, fat one sat to her right. The spearman took a seat opposite to Rem's right, while the top-knotted leader sat to Rem's left. The goblin and troll settled in beside one another to the chieftain's left. For a long time, they all sat in silence, staring at one another. Occasionally one orc or another would grunt and mutter in their own tongue, but the leader's eyes never left Rem. Rem did his best not to stare back—he would hate to provoke the creature, after all. It seemed, however, that no matter how long he kept his eyes averted, no matter how infrequently he tried to steal a glance, the leader kept on staring.

"May we speak now?" Rem asked sheepishly, the silence grating on him.

"Spoken have you," the leader said. "Begin."

Rem stared at him, puzzled. "Let what begin?"

"Speaking," the leader said.

Rem looked at all of them around the fire. "Do you all speak a human tongue?"

"Not they," the leader said. "I."

"I me," the troll said suddenly, then held up two fingers, closely spaced. "Small little."

"Corrected am I," the leader said. "Speaks a little, Hrozhna."

Rem looked across the fire at the troll. What was that curious expression it wore? He couldn't quite tell if it was a friendly smile or a hungry snarl.

"Hrozhna," Rem said, addressing the troll. "Is that your name?"

The troll nodded. Now, the smile was clear. "Name me," he said, looking to the others, as though no one had ever spoken his name before.

Rem turned to the leader. "And you? If I may—"

"Gnusha," the orcish commander said. He sat straight backed on his log, big hands on his knees, shoulders squared. "These"—he indicated the whole of the band around the fire—"are blades, of mine. *Ushrakha ub Gnusha.* Gnusha's Blades."

Rem let his eyes move over each in turn. They all stared at him, studying him, scowling as if suspicious or just disgusted. Or maybe that was just their natural expression?

"I'm Rem," he said, placing his hand on his chest. "I come from Yenara. You know Yenara?"

"Know Yenara I," Gnusha said. "Know the free cities all. Know the duchies and north Marches all. Range far and wide, we. Trade steel for coin, blood for treasure, we."

Steel for coin? Blacksmiths? No. *Steel for coin, blood for treasure.* "You're mercenaries," he said.

Gnusha nodded. "That word. Yes."

Rem considered carefully just what he should ask them—if anything. Would he offend them if he asked the wrong question?

"So," he said slowly, "you are in these woods to earn coin?"

Gnusha nodded. "Yes."

"Hunting something?" Rem asked.

"Hunting men," Gnusha said.

Rem did his best to remain calm. "Oh. All right..."

Gnusha suddenly shook his head and waved his hand. "No. Not all men. Stealers. Bleeders. Takers."

"Thieves?" Rem asked.

Gnusha pointed, indicating that was it. "Thieves," he said. "Yes."

Rem stared, amazed. "You were hired to hunt bandits?"

Gnusha stood and stepped nearer. He drew something from a pouch at his belt. "To hunt men, hired by men," he said, and produced a rolled scroll that he placed in Rem's hands.

Rem studied the scroll, then studied Gnusha, then glanced at the female orc beside him. She stared back, looking about as impatient and annoyed as possible. Rem looked away from her and unrolled the scroll.

The wording was fairly typical of a bounty agreement and warrant to enforce a lord's will. What surprised Rem even more was the ducal seal at the bottom of the warrant. Had he not already seen it, only days before, he might not have immediately recognized it.

"Let it be known," it said, "that the orcish war band presenting this to any human authority who challenges it operates with my express authority and permission, and has been retained for

the purpose of enforcing law and order in the Ethkeraldi Wood
and its environs. Vouchsafe and extend to it every courtesy.

"Attested and avowed, by my decree, Verin Lyr, Duke of
Erald."

Rem blinked.

What in the sundry hells had he stumbled into?

They'd eaten after that, the old orc tearing portions from the
roasting boar above the fire and handing them off to the various
members of the company. Gnusha was served first, followed
by the troll, Hrozhna. After that the portioning out proceeded
according to size. Rem was offered a portion second to last, just
before the little goblin archer.

The needle-toothed, bat-faced archer scowled at him
through the fire. He was small and wiry, but Rem hoped he
never had to tangle with him. He looked the sort who might
casually bite an ear or a finger off during a scrap.

Rem did his best to suppress just how thankful he was for
the meat. He said thank you, of course, but what he didn't
want them to know was that he was starving. He hadn't eaten
anything since those bitter and unsatisfying fiddleheads and
a handful of sour hurtleberries that morning. The boar was
unseasoned, but rich and delicious nonetheless. His body felt
better the moment he began to digest it.

As they ate, Gnusha introduced his company. The big troll,
as Rem already knew, was Hrozhna. The imposing spearman
who'd skewered Siebel was Otha, the female warrior Tludjaba,
the fat ax wielder Budash, the little goblin archer Wudji, the old
cook Tadj, and the young buck scouring chain mail when they'd
arrived Thuwat. The soldiers continued to chat among themselves in their own heavy, sibilant tongue as Rem and the chieftain ate in silence, only occasionally speaking with one another.

As the first portions were eaten, the old orcish cook, Tadj, withdrew from the fire and went rooting around in a giant sack sitting nearby. After drawing out several unwanted finds—a frying pan, some smaller sacks whose contents remained a mystery, some dried meat wrapped in cheesecloth—he finally laid hands on something big and squidgy waiting at the bottom of the sack. This he drew out and held high for all to see. It was a sealed goatskin that clearly contained something liquid, for it sloshed and jostled as it was displayed. The cook offered it to the chieftain first. Gnusha politely refused and indicated Rem.

"*Brwo gu,*" Gnusha said quietly.

Tadj turned and offered the sack to Rem. Rem stared, wondering just what sort of vile orcish brew might be sloshing about in there. What did they drink, for that matter? In Yenara they always seemed to be beer-and-ale sorts, but out here in the wild, was that what they were like to carry with them? Or was it something else? Maybe they had a taste for wine? Or mead?

Apparently he'd hesitated too long.

"Take," the old cook grunted.

Rem must have made a face that betrayed his trepidation, for Gnusha spoke an instant later.

"Mare's milk," the orcish chieftain said. "Good. Fills belly. Kills hunger."

Mare's milk. Really? Out here? In a wineskin? Wouldn't it spoil and sour? If he drank the stuff, it was like to make him vomit.

"Drink," Gnusha said, more insistently. "Offer first to you. Refuse is insult."

Rem nodded and snatched the big, heavy skin from the cook and uncorked it. That settled it. Vomit or no, he didn't care to offend these excellent orcs, who thus far had been disinclined to slay him, cook him, and eat him for supper. As he drew the skin to his mouth, he smelled the brew within: yeasty, pungent, a smell somewhere between an overripe apple and a cold-cured sausage.

That combination of smells gave him no pleasure, but what could he do?

He drew a deep breath, laid the cork-hole of the skin to his mouth, and drank a long, deep draught of what lay within.

It was surprisingly light for something made from milk, but on his palate the stuff was just as bizarre as his momentary whiff of it had suggested. There was sourness, acidity, more of that strange taste of a browned apple coupled with something meaty and funky, halfway between the cured sausage he'd smelled and an aging cheese. It was frothy, too, full of bubbles.

And there was alcohol in there, clearly. It wasn't just milk; it was a fermented brew.

He finished his deep swig and drew the skin away, hoping that he wouldn't immediately throw it all up. The bubbly mixture burned a path down his throat and thumped unceremoniously into his gut, where it gurgled and roiled and burned.

"Good," he said, positive that his face betrayed that he lied. "Very good. Yes. Thank you." He coughed and gagged a little.

The cook handed the skin back to the chieftain, Gnusha. Gnusha took the skin, gulped down several mouthfuls of the stuff, then handed it back to the cook. The cook started around the fire, offering the skin to each warrior in turn, starting with Hrozhna the troll.

Rem hastily chewed the rest of his roasted boar, hoping that maybe the taste of the pork would banish the strange stain of the fermented mare's milk on his tongue and throat. After a few minutes, when all his boar was gone and the milk-skin had made a round through all gathered, Rem knew the mare's milk wasn't likely to come burbling back up through his esophagus. Feeling this, he relaxed.

Even stranger, when Tadj took the milk-skin from Wudji the goblin and offered it once more to Rem, Rem decided he wanted more.

Why? he wondered as he accepted the skin and put the cork-hole now wet with orcish saliva to his own mouth and squeezed out another mouthful of the vile stuff within. *Why should I want more? Didn't it almost make me sick before? Wasn't I sure it would all come back up?*

Truth be told, he didn't really care why. He only knew that the stuff in that sack, odd as it was, was also eminently satisfying, settling his hunger more thoroughly than a whole joint of that roasted boar could.

And the way it affected his thought processes didn't hurt, either. For the first time in the last day and a half, Rem actually felt at ease. Comfortable. Unworried.

He looked to Gnusha after the orcish chieftain had enjoyed his own swig again. The chieftain smiled, his fangs and tusks flashing savagely. Rem smiled back and nodded in salute.

"My thanks, Gnusha," Rem said. "Sharing your food, your drink...You are a most generous host."

"Not generous," Gnusha said, shaking his head. "Fair. Give to you do we. Give to us do you."

"Give to you?" Rem asked, suddenly worried. "What could I possibly give to you?"

"Seek in these woods," Gnusha said, eyeing Rem carefully to seek out any prevarication or attempt at trickery. "Called Devils, they are. Slay them we would. All."

Rem stared, not sure what he had to offer.

"Tell us all will you," Gnusha said gravely, his tone making it clear there was no room for negotiation. "Help us find."

CHAPTER TWENTY-EIGHT

Torval had, more than once in his life, considered becoming a mercenary. The life would have suited him, he thought, had he not had children he loved who needed his attention. If it were just him, alone, he could happily live on the march, drifting from place to place with his unit, collecting pay purses that he never got around to spending, most of his money going to improve his weapons, his armor, to pay for new tattoos or the occasional coupling with a camp follower, just to break up the monotony. He suspected, when wistful (which was a rare state for him), that such a life might have agreed with him, right down to his bones. No fixed home, following orders, slaying enemies, then carrying on to the next job. There was simplicity in it. Honor. Elegance.

So he'd thought, before they'd spent the better part of a day, a night, and a morning trying to locate some sign, some trail, that could take them to the hidden redoubt where the Devils of the Weald made their beds. Before they'd seen the camp, folded into a deep recess in the hills, with rocky outcroppings and stone bluffs hemming it in on three sides like a fortress. Before they'd waited and waited for hours for a report from Galen and Croften regarding possible approaches. Before they'd arrived at their deadly plan and closed their cordon on their unsuspecting prey. Before they'd used fire and smoke to sow discord and killed, injured, or captured a few dozen in the subsequent chaos.

In short, before Torval had realized just what a monster he now found himself working for, and just what lengths that monster would go to in pursuit of his quarry.

They'd used the waning light of the day before to get themselves on the west side of the river. Once that was accomplished, they made another camp—small, hasty, easily abandoned if the need arose—and sent Galen and Croften in search of signs of the passage of the Red Raven's outlaws, anything that might indicate what direction they'd marched in or where their hideout might be located. Croften, fighting a mild fever and the persistent pain of the arrow wound in his shoulder, had managed to find a few shallow footprints and broken twigs, indicating that someone had moved through a given area, but it was Galen who ultimately picked out the trail and followed it. While the rest of them waited by the riverbank, the night gathering around them, no fires lit because they did not care to be seen, Galen and Croften picked their way through the darkening wood, over fallen trees and sometimes round in circles on half-eroded deer paths, until they'd managed to tease out a definite direction of travel. Having located a trail, they returned to camp. Everyone passed the night in the same near darkness, watching as a sliver of moon drifted slowly over them, wheeling from east to west.

Torval had expected they might ask him for his help following the track after the sun left the sky. He was a dwarf, after all, and his night vision was far more reliable than any of his human companions' tracking skills. But they had not asked for his aid—not then, anyway. Instead they decided they would set out before dawn with Torval in the lead and follow the Devils' track back to their camp. As soon as morning came, they'd trek out to the spot where Galen and Croften had abandoned their search and carry on from there. The next day would probably bring a great deal of danger. The closer they got to the Devils' camp, the greater the likelihood of armed sentries and bloody fighting.

Unfortunately, by well after sunrise the next morning, Torval almost wished they *had* encountered a sentry, or some straightforward fighting. Galen and Croften used small, makeshift torches to light their path through the woods to the place where they'd abandoned the trail the night before. Upon reaching that spot, Galen had shown Torval just what to look for— not only obvious signs like footprints, but also the more subtle sorts—trampled leaves, broken or bent boughs, narrow pathways suggested by the gaps between certain shrubs and trees. And then they'd doused the torches and let Torval use his night vision to lead the way. Whenever he reached a point where he could see no sign, he'd call Galen or Croften up to examine that spot more closely, and they would determine which way to continue.

They lost hours that way, essentially roaming in circles and into numerous dead ends where the tracks they thought they'd discovered ultimately ran out at the base of a big cedar or in the burbling beds of rocky brooks and tumbling streams. By the time they realized just how lost they were, light had already crept into the world, the forest around them gray and mist-shrouded, more visible by the moment, yet still hiding its most cherished secrets in the many shadows that the still-coming sunrise had yet to banish.

It was just as the sun peeked over the hills to the south and shot its first broken rays through the high forest canopy— almost four hours after they'd first risen and set out—that Galen, scouring the brush desperately for some new indication of the right path, returned and said she thought she'd found something. Since the sun was up now and Torval was no longer needed, she and Croften followed the lead. A short while later, they returned to report that at last they'd located a path worth following. The weary company set out.

They came upon their first sentry an hour later, Galen suddenly holding up her fist to silently order a hold to their march, then waving to indicate that everyone should hunker down and take cover. Torval sheltered behind a big pine and searched the broad face of the woodland before them, a riot of tree boughs and green leaves and needles and shadowy recesses. When Torval heard something crunch—teeth, biting into an apple—he managed to finally pick out their quarry, about fifty yards on.

The man perched high in a forest oak, humming placidly to himself and breaking his fast on that small, crunchy apple. At this distance, and with a screen of branches between him and the target, Torval could not tell if the man was actually proving an effective sentry and watching the forest, or if his humming and loud snacking were signs of foolhardy dereliction. A moment later, though, it hadn't mattered.

Galen killed the man with a single arrow. He gasped a little—shocked at the steel point that had just burrowed a hole through him—then fell from his perch before his surprise could be given voice. Torval wagered he was dead before he hit the ground twenty feet beneath him.

They dragged the man's lifeless body under a copse of ferns, then took cover again and waited. Without any idea how many Devils there might be in total, it was difficult to gauge just how closely their sentries might be spaced. That long, quiet pause in the wake of the guard's murder allowed them to see if his fall had immediately been noted, or if their way was clear.

No one cried out. No one came. They carried on, slow and steady. Beyond the sentry post, they found clearer tracks through the underbrush, persistent footprints along the path indicating that it was well trodden and probably a primary route into the camp.

The sun was well up and the morning mists burned away by the time they found the camp itself. It lay just beyond a little ridgeline, nestled into a sort of ravine in the hillside, jagged, rocky shoulders protecting its north and south sides, the hillside rising at its back, to the west. From their vantage point, secreted in the tree line down the slope, Torval and the others could clearly make out the dark depressions in the hill's face denoting caves where the Devils made their proper homes while the walled clearing served as a makeshift kitchen and open-air great hall. There were guards on the hillside, perched on rocks and among the crags, staring outward, the morning sun probably blinding them a bit, since it shone right in their faces.

They conferred in hasty whispers.

"They're well entrenched," the lord marshal noted.

"I wouldn't try to take that camp," Wallenbrand said with a scowl. "Not unless there were three times as many of us."

"Head-on's no good," Tuvera offered. "Too much open ground between the tree line and the bluffs. They'll see us coming and pick us off. And some of us can't cross that ground at speed."

She suggested Elvaris. The swordmaiden sat with her back to an ash a stone's throw away, looking drawn and weary, hastily changing the dressing on her bloody leg wound.

"There might be a way," Galen broke in. "We could use the trees for cover and go farther up the hillside, try to hook around from behind."

"What good would that do?" Torval asked. "They're still burrowed into those caves."

"Look up the slope," Galen said. "See that thin column of smoke? And that other, over there?"

"Chimneys," Croften said quietly.

"Precisely," Galen agreed. "We could plug up the chimneys. Maybe even drop something burning down into them, smoke them out—"

"We'll see to it," the lord marshal suddenly broke in. Clearly something about that plan appealed to him. "Wallenbrand, Croften, and I. The rest of you, stay hidden here until we drive them out."

"Wait a minute," Torval grumbled, "is that it? That's your plan? The three of you try to creep up and plug those chimneys while we wait for a signal?"

The lord marshal's face was still, implacable. "Your time will come, master dwarf. Just do as I say."

Off they went, the lord marshal, Croften, and Wallenbrand, disappearing into the woods south of their position, leaving Torval alone with Tuvera, Elvaris, and Galen. The four of them settled in for a long wait.

"They know what they're doing, I'll give them that," Tuvera said at one point.

Torval, who'd been wondering idly if he'd ever see Rem, or his home, again, raised his eyes. "What's that?"

Tuvera suggested the Devils' camp. "Safe. Secure. Hard to find. How many hours did we waste trying to track them down?"

Galen nodded admiringly. "Those Haita hill brigands we rousted out back in Estavar? They couldn't have done better. No wonder these Devils have made such a name for themselves."

Torval took a moment to look out upon the camp then, to

really study what he could see from their hiding place beyond the tree line. "There are women and children up there," he said, almost to himself.

"Whole families, probably," Elvaris said. "Families by blood or families made by the exigencies of hard living. Not so unusual, really."

Torval thought of the many times he'd arrested pickpocket children who'd ultimately proven to be the brood of grown thieves he'd arrested previously. Yes indeed. Not unusual at all.

He settled in after that. Little by little, the interminable waiting ate at him like swarming ants. His whole body was tense and weary all at once, eager for action and wholly unsuited to it. What he desperately wanted was to go find a quiet copse of woodland shrubs and curl up for a long nap. If only—

A loud clap of thunder shook the hillside and sent birds fleeing in terror from their canopy roosts. As Torval and the swordmaidens all turned and stared, they saw the Devils visible in the little camp screaming, waving their arms, running to and fro. A thick pillar of smoke belched from one of the cave mouths above them.

Without warning there came a second explosion. Yet another cave mouth vomited a cloud of white smoke. Screams sounded out of the hillside into the hitherto-still air of the forest.

Torval felt a fury rise in him. Instantly he recalled that locked chest full of dwarven blasting spheres: nine compartments containing six spheres, with three compartments yawning emptily.

Clearly the lord marshal had kept a few on his person for just such an emergency.

Torval had no idea what kind of chaos was now being wrought, but he could hear the screams, the shouted names, the calls for a bucket brigade, even at this distance.

"I'd say that's our signal," Tuvera said.

Torval only grunted. The four of them broke cover and charged up the hillside.

They met little resistance. A few of the Devils—men and women alike—saw the strangers rushing into their midst and took up arms to repel them, but the chaos was too great. Galen laid two men out with well-placed arrows and wounded three more, forcing them to yield. Torval felt vaguely sick as they rushed in, slowly realizing that the people they now attacked had been cleaning up after their breakfast, or preparing a midday meal, just moments before. One woman charged him, sounding a full-throated battle cry as she did, brandishing a woodsman's ax. Torval sprinted into the arc of her ax-swing, threw his arms around her waist, lifted her and tossed her aside. He had no intention of using maul or blade on a woman if he could help it. When the explosions sounded, many of the women in the clearing below the caves had gathered the children in a recess cut into the rocks, allowing no easy entry save through a pair of camp wives now standing sentry, one wielding a sword, another a battle-ax. Up on the promontories beneath the cave mouths, people stumbled and rushed about, survivors reeling out of the haze with bloodied, soot-covered faces, hacking and doubled over from the thick, sulfurous smoke, while able bodies plunged into the roiling clouds in search of injured survivors. The lord marshal, Croften, and Wallenbrand were sweeping along the broad ledge, herding the excited survivors back toward the path that led down to the ravine and the clearing. One man tried to attack them. Big Croften picked the fellow up and tossed him off the ledge without hesitation. After that there weren't many eager to fight their attackers.

★   ★   ★

Now, here they stood. A haze of yellow smoke from the blasting spheres still hung on the promontories while new smoke—thick and black—poured from the cave mouths and curled into the blue morning sky. Something in the caves had been set alight by the explosions, and it burned now, unhindered, unopposed. The survivors of the sneak attack had all been gathered in the rock-walled clearing beside the now-dead cookfires, about thirty of them. As Torval had feared, there were women and children among them—a good many, too. He supposed some were blood relations, while others were part of ad hoc families formed when parents died, or when children taken in road raids were added to the Devils' numbers to someday join the ranks. There were a number of old men, as well—those bent by time or cut down by bad luck and circumstance, who could no longer function as competent warriors and rangers. These, Torval guessed, probably took on the roles of elder statesmen and artisans, kept the central clan unit attended to while the Red Raven and his bandits went out on long patrols in search of booty.

At least half of those now gathered bore injuries of some sort: burns, lacerations from flying shrapnel, lungs full of smoke that set them hacking up blood at intervals, or wounds earned in brief conflict with Torval's band of ambushers. Those untouched busily tended their injured comrades, or kept the few children of the camp safe and settled. Torval had no idea how many of the Devils had died in the caves or fled into the woods, but those remaining had clearly had all the fight knocked out of them.

Croften had taken a spear-thrust to his lower right side, but the wound looked as though it might not prove fatal. Clearly the big scout simply presented too tempting a target. He sat aside with a scowl on his face as Wallenbrand hastily sewed him up.

The lord marshal studied the cowed and injured outlaws now gathered before him. He was uneasy, pacing like a caged panther. They'd executed a sneak attack on the most notorious outlaw band in the woods, beaten it, even, and now controlled its secret hideaway... but of the young lady they sought, or the Red Raven himself, there was no sign.

It made Torval angry. These Devils had sins to pay for, no doubt, but they'd just been attacked with explosives, in the very place where they took safe refuge, without any warning or opportunity to parley. Part of Torval understood the bloody logic of the lord marshal's stratagem—even admired the ruthlessness of it—but there was another part of him, the part that tried to hew to honor and some sort of code of conduct, that could not countenance what they'd just done. Even in the name of recovering Tzimena... or Rem.

Captain Tuvera marched up to the pacing lord marshal and spoke. She made no effort to whisper or keep her words from their prisoners' hearing.

"Something's not right here," Tuvera insisted. "No sign of the Raven? No sign of the Lady Tzimena?"

"Spirited away, no doubt," the lord marshal said.

"Or burning in those caves," the captain spat back. "Casualties of your bloody bomb attacks! Why didn't you tell us what you had planned?"

"Because he knew you'd object, that's why," Wallenbrand said angrily, pausing in his ministrations over Croften's spear wound. "He certainly knew I'd object. He didn't bother to warn us, either. Here I thought we'd find those chimneys and smoke them out, slowly. Next thing I know, this yellow-plated bastard is lighting the fuses on those dwarf blasters and tossing them into the caves!"

"It worked, did it not?" the lord marshal asked.

Torval saw Tuvera's eyes suddenly widen in disbelief. "You're still trying to kill him! You didn't care if he and Tzimena were in the caves, or if those blasts took her out! As long as the Raven was dead, you'd consider anyone else wounded or killed an acceptable loss!"

Torval felt his stomach tighten. Yes, that was it, wasn't it? He waited for the lord marshal to argue, to offer another explanation. He did not. Instead the man simply turned back to the prisoners and nodded toward them.

"I am inclined to see an interrogation or two as our only options," the stiff-backed son of a whore said, as though Captain Tuvera had not just accused him of trying to murder her charge. The lord marshal then turned to Torval. "What say you, dwarf? You interrogate prisoners regularly, do you not? Have you any skills to offer in this situation?"

"We could ask them," Torval suggested.

"Ask?" the lord marshal repeated.

Torval nodded. "Before we jump to the formal interrogations. Look at them, Lord Marshal. Most of them are women and children. The strong among them are still young—pups, for the most part—and the old ones are all scarred or damaged somehow. These aren't the cream of the Devils' crop."

"Begging the question of where the cream hied off to," Tuvera said nervously.

Torval guessed this group was perfectly capable of charging their captors and overpowering them...but something kept them from doing so. The lord marshal's blasting spheres had proven just how relentless—how merciless—their captor could be. Knowing that he would stop at nothing to get his way, they also knew bravery would profit them little.

The lord marshal offered a nod and a dismissive wave.

"You have a little time, then," the lord marshal said. "Draw some out and question them."

"Very well," Tuvera said, and began marching toward the prisoners.

Torval shot out ahead of her. "Forgive me, Captain, but let me handle this. This is what I do, after all."

He didn't wait to hear an affirmative from her. As quickly as he could, he presented himself to all gathered there.

"Listen up!" Torval shouted, his voice echoing between the rock walls of the ravine around them. "My name is Torval, and I'm here to ask some questions! Answer me plain and true, there'll be no trouble. Lie to me or trouble me, you'll be sorry. Does anyone disbelieve me?"

They all stared back, looking neither worried nor convinced. Most of them wore hard faces and frowns, clearly irritated by having been caught off guard but not terribly troubled about it. Those were the faces, Torval knew, of people who were used to losing more often than they won, people who treated losses—however bitter—as little more than temporary setbacks or dues to be paid.

Hard folk. Survivors.

He wasn't entirely sure he could break them or convince them.

"We're only after two people," Torval said. "If you can point us toward them, we'll leave you be."

He imagined he heard a gasp from the lord marshal, far behind him, but he didn't bother turning around to see if that was true. That blue-clad bastard might have his own ideas, but Torval meant to keep his word, even if he had to use force of arms to do so. They'd left far too many dead already. If they couldn't extract what they needed without undue coercion, they had no business seeking it.

"First and foremost, we want the Lady Tzimena Baya, alive and well. Barring her whereabouts, we ask for the Red Raven. We know he's your leader, but his surrender could buy freedom for the lot of you."

A tall, handsome woman surrounded by children snorted and made a dismissive face at the word *leader*. Torval stepped nearer, spearing her with his gaze.

"Care to disagree?" he asked.

The woman stared right back. "He's not our leader. Not any longer."

A number of the women present hissed and bade the speaker shut her mouth.

"Bite me," she said in answer. "I'm telling them nothing that they might not learn soon enough."

"Not your leader?" Torval asked, stepping closer. He heard footsteps behind him and glanced over his shoulder to see who was approaching. It was Tuvera and the lord marshal. They had looks of incredulity and astonishment on their faces.

"He was tried and convicted and stripped of his powers," the woman said. She drew a squirmy baby closer to her breast and yanked a wandering toddler at her feet closer. "That's our way. When we lose confidence in a leader, they're removed."

Torval threw a glare at the lord marshal. "A sound plan."

"Where is he, then?" the lord marshal demanded, striding forward. "Tell us, now, and there will be no need for further violence."

Captain Tuvera didn't even try to hide her displeasure. "Lord Marshal, if I may remind you, the Lady Tzimena is who we're after—"

"Who *you're* after," the older man snapped. "I have scores of my own to settle." He turned back to the speaker from the crowd. "Tell me, woman, or so help me I'll snatch that babe at your breast and—"

Torval stepped into the lord marshal's field of vision. "And what?" he asked.

"Stand aside," the lord marshal growled.

"Make me," Torval countered. "I promised these people safety in return for their cooperation—"

"A vow you had no business making," the lord marshal said. "You have no power here, master dwarf."

Torval took a step closer. "Last time I checked," he said slowly, "I was still armed, and so are you. If you want to presume to give me orders again, you'd better draw steel—"

Tuvera stepped between them, clearly eager to break up their standoff, but equally keen to reach the woman in the crowd and speak directly to her. "Tell me," she said, with real need in her voice, "where is the Lady Tzimena?"

Torval turned as the woman responded to Tuvera's petition.

"They were both locked in the cave, up there," the woman said, nodding toward one of the rocky outcroppings protruding from the hillside, still bleeding smoke. "But they were taken out early this morning, a couple hours before you lot came upon us."

"Shut your mouth," an old man said, rather forcefully, Torval thought. The threat in his voice was implicit.

"Shut your own," the woman said. "I might die for my children or any one of you, but I won't die for that philandering brigand and his royal whore!"

Torval saw Tuvera tense beside him, responding unbidden to her ward's being branded a whore.

"Where?" the captain pressed again.

The woman stood and pointed eastward. "That way," she said. "Through the birch wood. It was most of the leadership that took them—Tymon Longstride, Orhund the Bear, Dedrik Firebow, and a half dozen others. I don't know where they were headed, exactly, but I heard them talking before they fetched the Raven and the girl to set out. They had an appointment to keep."

"An appointment?" Torval asked.

The woman nodded. "A buyer," she said. "Someone eager to trade for both the Raven and the girl."

"No," the lord marshal said quietly.

"I'll swear on the heads of my four children, every word is true," the woman said. "There are others here who know just as well as I do. Ask them! One or two of them are bound to back me up—"

"We need to go," the lord marshal said.

Torval and Tuvera stared at him. "Go where?" Torval asked slowly. "Do what?"

"He's still out there," the lord marshal said, then addressed the group. "Take what you can carry and go, all of you. If you linger or challenge us, you'll be cut down. Find other holes to crawl into—this camp is yours no more!"

Wallenbrand approached his commander. "Now, see here," the old man said, "Croften's hurt, and we barely know where we're going."

"You still have a contract to fulfill," the lord marshal said. "Refuse to follow me now, you can march back to Yenara without so much as a copper in your pocket. I didn't ask you—any of you—whether you agreed. Our quarry is waiting east of here, and we're wasting time."

The lord marshal set out down the slope, eastward.

Someone limped up beside Torval. It was Elvaris, still favoring her wounded leg. "I hate that man," she said quietly.

Torval could only nod. Aye, that. He hated him, as well.

He only longed for the right pretense—the right conflict—to make splitting that bastard's hard skull an unavoidable action.

CHAPTER TWENTY-NINE

Tzimena had no idea how Korin's people could see anything for that first hour, the world was so muddy and dark. They set out just before dawn, when the first gray light of the sun was a thin band rising over the hills to the east, and descended into the woods, following a winding, narrow path. Their company carried only two lights, tiny tin lamps borne by the outlaws at the head and tail of the column. Beyond the modest glow of those small, half-hooded lamps, however, everything was blackness and cold. And yet, somehow, they managed to find the necessary track and carry on, with few interruptions or respites, through a dark and silent world of towering, ancient trees, gradually stirring birds, and curious beasts.

At last light seeped into the world, and the wild landscape around them faded into view, a washed-out slate gray at first, then bruised purple, then watery blue. The gathering twilight of morning gave to everything an ancient and pensive quality that Tzimena found alternately beautiful and frightening. One didn't really know what the word *wilderness* truly meant until one was lost in the middle of the Ethkeraldi. There was, literally, no civilization here, no mark of human passage, no indication that human thoughts or desires could do any more than notch a tree or leave a footprint that would soon be erased by a fall of leaves or the seep of groundwater. Tzimena briefly considered trying to break from the group and flee, to run south, toward the river, and throw herself in as that boy Rem had, and thus take her chances with the current. But in the end she knew she was not so daring. She could endure just about anything, including whatever vile captivity she was about to be traded into. Wait and see, that was her strategy. She could always flee later, fight later, kill herself later. But she could not do any of those things, could not take any wild chances, without first seeing what her alternatives were.

The sun was well up by the time they saw a figure in a hunter's cloak emerge from a stand of trees some distance ahead of them. Tzimena heard words exchanged by Dedrik Firebow—who led their way through the wood—and the stranger on the far side of the clearing they traversed. She was, however, too far away to hear just what those traded words were. After a brief exchange, Dedrik stepped from the line and called back down its length.

"He wants to see the prisoners," he said, voice echoing blasphemously in the early-morning stillness of the ageless forest.

Tymon, who'd trudged along behind Tzimena all the way to their destination, took Tzimena roughly by her arm and dragged her sideward, out of the line, where she could easily be seen by the stranger. Up ahead, towering Orhund yanked Korin out of the line in the same manner. For a long time, the two of them stood like that, held by their handlers, on display, until at last the stranger in the hunting cloak raised his hand in agreement, then started waving the party on.

Tzimena was shoved back into line, and the whole group carried on.

They crossed that little clearing, were swallowed by another tree line, and wound along another barely perceptible path before coming, at last, to another clearing, much larger than the first. Well shaded by a perimeter of tall spruce, redwood, and ash, the great glade's edges were demarcated by spidery ferns interspersed with beds of mounding sedge, cream-colored yarrow, and manzanitas squatting in the shadow of the trees. A little brook wound through the center of the clearing, filling a small pond rippling in the sunlight on the glade's western edge. Men in hunter green and sturdy cloaks milled about, drinking hot brews warmed over a small fire crackling near the pond. A number of horses were gathered round the pond, dipping their heads to drink or cropping at the moist grasses at its edge. They were good animals—sturdy, well cared for, adorned with first-rate tack and harness.

Tzimena counted the men, then counted the horses. There were ten mounts, but only seven men.

There are more in reserve somewhere, she thought. *Probably surrounding us.*

She also thought it strange that the men visible were dressed like common woodsmen or hunters, while their mounts—as well as their tack and saddles—were clearly expensive. Those weren't the stolen mounts of forest brigands at all.

The cloaked herald who'd met them at the edge of the clearing, who had led them into the grove where his superiors waited, now turned and faced the outlaws. He drew back his cowl, revealing a thoroughly ordinary face with a neatly trimmed beard and hair recently shorn and oiled.

That's no outlaw, Tzimena thought. *That's a courtier.*

"We welcome you," the man said expansively. "I trust this place was not hard to find?"

"We know these woods better than you ever will, sir," Tymon said from her place in line behind Tzimena. "What say we dispense with pleasantries and get down to business? Where is your buyer?"

One of the men at the fire lifted his head as though hearing his name. He set down the steaming mug in his hands, rose from his seat on a flattened old tree stump, and approached the party. As he did so, the rest of the men around the fire fanned out in a broad line behind him. No one moved quickly or deliberately; their movements were measured and patient, calculated to look as unthreatening as possible.

But they were preparing for something, weren't they? At least the possibility of something.

The cloaked man from the fire approached the group. "May I see the prisoners?" he asked, his face still shadowed by the cowl of his cloak.

Orhund shoved Korin out of the line again and presented him. Tymon did the same with Tzimena.

"Bring them forward," the man said, halting.

Tymon and Orhund directed Tzimena and Korin to the front of the line to meet their buyer. Tzimena began to have a suspicion about who was under that cowl, and it gave her no pleasure.

It can't be, she thought. *He wouldn't dare. To be so brazen, so bold...*

The man drew back his cowl and revealed himself: young-ish, early thirties, with a blandly handsome face, a perfectly groomed mustache, and hair the color of honey. He smiled as though greeting old friends in the most unexpected of places.

Tzimena heard Korin snarl a single name. "Verin."

"Good morning, Brother," said Verin Lyr, the Duke of Erald, as he stepped forward and put his arms around Korin, the man he'd stolen a duchy from. "You look as though you've had a hard time of it."

Verin embraced his brother and hugged him tightly, clapping his back with manly emphasis, then drew away again. Korin, of course, had made no effort to return the gesture. He stood, hands tied before him, staring with narrowed eyes and knit brows at the man whose treachery had routed his life into its present dead end.

Verin Lyr turned to Tzimena and smiled. "And this," he said, "must be my blushing bride." He approached her, studying her as he did, clearly enamored by what he saw. "The portraits were lovely, my dear, but in person—even in such dire straits—you are more stunning than I ever could have imagined. It's a pleasure to finally meet you."

Tzimena stared back, doing her best to offer neither venom nor bravado. Neither would serve her in the present instant. "The Duke of Erald, I presume?" she asked.

He bowed magnanimously. "At your service, milady. And most charmed—"

He reached out to take her tied hands and kiss them. Tzimena jerked them away and took a reflexive step backward. Tymon caught her and shoved her forward again.

"Fair enough," Verin Lyr said with a sigh. "I do understand, this is not the optimum circumstance under which the two of us should meet. What can one do, though? These are strange times."

"To business," Tymon said shortly. "State your offer again, so that all can hear it."

Verin nodded, turned to his herald, and gave a little nod. The man who'd met them hurried back across the clearing to the camp and set about extracting some large leather sacks from the saddlebags on one of the horses.

"Our agreement," Verin said, "was for the delivery of these two individuals in return for four hundred pieces of gold and a privateer's contract between myself and your organization."

Tzimena felt her mouth fall open. She hated the man for shocking her so, but that agreement was, indeed, a most brazen and unbelievable gambit.

"Three years?" Tymon asked. She was clearly the leader of the Devils now that Korin was out of the picture.

Verin Lyr nodded. His herald had returned now, bearing with him two large, heavy sacks adorned with actual locking mechanisms, as well as a leather dispatch case. He set down the heavy burden of the bags of gold and handed the case to his master. Verin extracted a rolled scroll from the dispatch case, gave it a quick review, then offered it to whoever would take it. Dedrik stepped forward to do so.

"Three years to make of the wood what you will, free of my interference or the attentions of my soldiers, so long as I receive one-fifth of your take, four times a year. It's all there. You can read, can't you?"

Dedrik—who had already been studying the scroll—threw a hateful glare at the duke, then offered the scroll to Tymon.

"Of course I read," she said bitterly.

The duke shrugged. "My apologies. I try to make no assumptions."

"So that's what this has all been leading to?" Tzimena asked incredulously. "A crowned duke receiving tribute from outlaws and brigands in exchange for free rein?"

Verin Lyr held out his hands. "Politics, milady. Why eradicate one's enemies when one can simply buy them? Better to let a single outlaw band hold the wood and maintain some semblance of order—while paying me tribute—than to leave it the chaotic mess that it is presently. Besides, when someone has something you want..."

She didn't care for the way he stared at her and let that statement trail off into the empty air. Not at all.

"If you think I'll marry you now," she said, shaking her head.

"Oh no," he said. "I'm sure you won't. No, milady, I've

bought you to make sure you're disposed of in a manner befitting your station—and wholly exonerating myself. All of this—this devil's bargain, the whole mess—is for him." He pointed to Korin. "He's the one I've been after all along. You were just a convenient political device. And bait."

Korin suddenly turned, his pained eyes seeking those of his onetime companions. He looked to Orhund, to Tymon, to Dedrik. "Please," he said. "Don't let him do this. I'll go with him—won't even put up a fight—but don't give him Tzimena. She's innocent in this."

"I would argue otherwise," Tymon said. "For her sake, you endangered us all."

"And I'll pay for that," Korin said. "But she shouldn't."

Dedrik suddenly moved closer to Tymon and whispered something. Tzimena could not hear just what was said, but Tymon instantly shook her head and spoke her response at full volume. "No," she said loudly. "I won't consider it."

"Are we still negotiating?" the Duke of Erald asked, endlessly amused. "I thought we'd settled all this. Here's your gold, there are my prisoners, let's exchange and be on our separate ways."

"Hold it," Dedrik said, stepping away from Tymon to place himself just beside Tzimena, halfway between his chieftain and the duke as they stood staring at one another. "Let's offer a counterproposal."

"Dedrik, get back in line," Tymon said, "or I'll sell your hide, as well."

Dedrik looked to Orhund. "This isn't what we do. You both know it."

Orhund threw a pitying glance at Korin, then shrugged. "The Red Raven is dead, old friend. It's a new world, with new rules."

Dedrik looked back to Tymon. "The girl, Tymon. It's not fair—"

"Little is fair," Tymon snapped in answer, "without blood or gold making it so."

"I like that," Verin Lyr said. "I'm stealing that."

"Tzimena, run," Korin hissed. "Now."

"No," she said, still staring at the duke.

Verin Lyr saw the determination in her eyes and nodded approvingly. "Clever girl."

"Tzimena," Korin said, begging now, "you need to—"

"I won't," she said flatly. "I'm through running. Being a prize. Or a pawn. Let this bastard do with me what he will. I won't even give him the satisfaction of a scream."

The Duke of Erald smiled broadly at that. "Oh, milady... challenge accepted. Besides, I think you know running would be pointless. My bowmen are well placed, after all."

He gave a single gesture, waving one hand lightly and pointing toward one of the Devils near the front of the line. From somewhere in the distance Tzimena heard a faint twang, and suddenly an arrow buried half its length in the man's chest. The life went out of him instantly, heart pierced, and he crumpled to the forest floor.

Tymon grabbed Tzimena and yanked her close, holding her before her like a shield. Orhund had done the same with Korin. Dedrik was on his knees, having already drawn an arrow from his quiver and nocked it, eyes scanning the trees for the hidden archer.

"There are several of them," Verin Lyr said. "Well hidden. Do not try to cross me, or you'll see just how deadly their aim can be."

Tymon responded, and though she was behind Tzimena and

remained unseen, Tzimena heard something peculiar in the brigand chieftain's voice.

"Cagey, sire. Very cagey."

From the corner of her eye, Tzimena saw Tymon give a gesture of her own, indicating the herald who had met them at the tree line and who had now delivered the gold. An instant later another arrow flew from the trees behind them and found a home in the man's left eye. Down he went.

Verin Lyr stared at his dead companion, then raised his eyes to Tymon. He looked mildly annoyed, not angry or aggrieved or even fearful. "Fair enough," he said. "We've both got bowmen hidden in the trees. With a few more gestures, we could each shower this glade with enough steel points and goose feathers to slaughter the lot of us. But what good would that do?"

"I agree," Tymon said. Tzimena could hear the nerves in her voice—the tight control exercised over her natural inclination to fight or flee, her fear tempered by rage and defiance and a desire to just be away from here with the reward that lay just a few feet away on the ground. "We've both shown what we're capable of," Tymon continued. "What say we forego mutual destruction and just transact some business?"

Verin Lyr nodded, then indicated the bags of gold lying on the ground nearby. "There's your bounty," he said. "Give me my prizes and you can be on your way."

Tzimena was about to make a counteroffer of her own when Tymon shoved her roughly forward. Tzimena went plunging toward the Duke of Erald and landed in a heap at his feet. She raised her eyes and glared at him.

If he touches me, she thought, *I'll bite his fingers off. Let him kill me if he likes . . . I won't be bought and sold like a broodmare.*

"Get up, darling," Verin Lyr said from above her, bending down and offering his hand. "This has already taken long enough..."

Tzimena was just about to pull herself up from the ground so that Duke Verin would not lay hands on her. That was when she heard the voice from the tree line. It was a female voice, strong, clear, and familiar.

"Touch her and you'll never know what hit you," Captain Tuvera said.

CHAPTER THIRTY

Torval would have preferred that they make themselves known in a less threatening fashion. Clearly there was already a tense standoff underway here—prisoners being traded for gold, two men lying dead with arrows in them, probably hidden archers in the trees surrounding the clearing. Sundry hells, if those same hidden archers hadn't been so bloody intent on what was happening in the clearing instead of around it, they might have actually heard the approach of Torval and company as they picked their way through the brush—their stealthiness notwithstanding.

The lord marshal and Wallenbrand had circled around to the right—on the eastern side of the clearing—while Croften and Elvaris had gone left, to the west. On the south side of the clearing, directly behind the party from the Red Raven's camp, Torval had joined Captain Tuvera and Galen. The group had agreed to remain quiet and hidden until either help was needed or the lord marshal led an attack. That much they had all concurred upon and deemed "the plan."

Unfortunately, when that big woman from the Devils shoved Tzimena to the ground and the man in the cloak who appeared to be buying her made a move to help her to her feet, Captain Tuvera and Galen had thrown the plan out the window. Torval didn't know precisely what was going through their heads, but he guessed it had to do with their sworn duty to protect the young woman at all costs. One moment they'd all been hunkering down behind a hump of mounded sedge; in the next instant, Tuvera had given Galen an order.

"Draw," the captain said quietly. Galen obeyed without question, smoothly couching an arrow on her bow, nocking it and drawing it as the captain stood and strode from her hiding place.

"Touch her and you'll never know what hit you," she said loudly, forcefully.

Everyone in the clearing turned toward the sound of her voice. Sheathed weapons were drawn. Weapons at rest were lifted and brandished. Torval made a hasty count: six Devils, the buyer who stood above Tzimena, four guards close to him, three more lingering at the pond with their horses. Two of the men in the Raven's company readied their bows, arrows nocked and drawn. The four cloaked swordsmen behind the buyer spread out in a broad line behind their master. All readied themselves, their stances telling Torval that they were professionals, probably full-time soldiers, not just some other brigand band trying to trade valuable booty with the Devils of the Weald.

Something was wrong here.

Captain Tuvera stood alone—armed, yes, armored, certainly, but all alone—with only a single archer hidden in the brush at her back to cover her. Torval turned and searched the treetops nearby, trying to see if he could pick out a hidden archer or two. He thought he saw another secreted guard about twenty yards westward—off to his left—but the greenery was too thick and he couldn't be sure. He desperately wanted to bolt from cover to stand at Tuvera's side, but something in him kept him rooted to the spot, a strange sense that this was not his fight unless dire need dictated otherwise, a sense that this was something the captain and her scout would have to play out together, alone.

For the moment.

The man in the cloak who'd been moving to help Tzimena to her feet studied Captain Tuvera, threw an irritated glance at Tzimena—still on the ground—then planted his hands on his hips.

"Who are you, then?" he asked.

"Captain Tuvera, house guard to the Countess of Toriel, and that young woman's protector. Step away from her, now, or you'll be the next corpse on the ground."

The man smiled, showing a mix of admiration and irritation. Torval didn't like that look at all. Who was this man? He didn't look rough, like the Raven or his own men. Moreover, his exasperated confidence indicated an ingrained sense of superiority that made Torval uneasy.

"Well, Captain Tuvera, house guard to the Countess of Toriel, and this young woman's protector, I suggest you drop your sword and tell your archer not to loose that arrow, because you're speaking to Verin Lyr, Duke of Erald and this young woman's rightfully betrothed husband."

"Cack," Torval said under his breath.

Galen lowered her bow and looked to Torval. She looked just as puzzled, just as worried, as he was.

"I don't care who you are," Tuvera continued. To her credit, there was no trepidation in her voice—no indication that she was scared. "That girl is my responsibility until she's safely ensconced in her new home. Since we're still in the wild, I'd say I'm still on duty."

Torval saw that something was happening. The parties in the clearing were moving. It was a subtle drift, but it was noticeable nonetheless. The swordsmen behind the duke were closing on their master, but fanning out farther around him, putting more space between them to allow for greater range of movement when the fight began. The Raven's Devils, meanwhile, were also slowly dispersing, aware that there were new parties on the scene, and that the chance of a confrontation was rising with each passing second. They were scattering themselves— however slowly—so that they wouldn't present such knotted targets. At least one of them—a bald man with earrings shining in each ear—scanned the tree line calmly, searching for all possible avenues of egress.

They're no fools, Torval thought. *They know what's coming.*

"Milord!" someone called from far off to the right.

Torval and Galen looked. The lord marshal had appeared. He marched out of the tree line, sword sheathed, arms raised in deference. Clearly he didn't want to be mistaken for an attacker and shot.

"Good help, at last!" the duke said with a laugh. "Lord Marshal Kroenen, good to see you, sir!"

Wallenbrand had emerged from hiding, as well. He trailed some distance behind his commander, looking far more suspicious about what was underway and how it might turn out. The lord marshal, for his part, kept his eyes on his master and addressed only him.

"The people in the brush are mine," he said. "Two over there"—he pointed to where Torval and Galen were still concealed—"and two more on the far side of the clearing. Let them show themselves. Tell your archers not to fire, if you please."

The duke raised his hands and made two tight fists. That done, the lord marshal addressed everyone waiting for his promised signal.

"Show yourselves!" he called. "The time for games is over! This all ends, here and now!"

A big, broad man in the Raven's group drew the bound Red Raven closer to him, a convenient human shield. "What is all this?" he growled.

That tall, muscular woman who'd thrown the Lady Tzimena at the duke's feet now reached for her and yanked her back into her arms. She drew Tzimena close, a knife to her throat, and began a slow turn, scanning the whole of the clearing and the tree line surrounding it.

Torval looked to Galen. "It's time," he said.

Galen nodded and stepped out of the brush. Torval followed from the opposite side of the tree that had been sheltering them. Over on the far side of the clearing, Croften and Elvaris had appeared, moving forward slowly, cautiously. Two of the three guards on horse duty left their charges and approached the swordmaid and the mercenary, probably to dissuade any hasty action. Torval hated the thickness of the air—the sense of menace and hazard—now laying heavily upon the glade. This was when things went awry, when there were too many beating hearts and bared blades in one place at one time.

The duke finally lowered his balled fists and surveyed the scene, betraying no trepidation, only endless amusement.

"A dwarf?" the duke said upon seeing Torval. "Where'd you acquire a dwarf, old friend?"

"One of the city guards from Yenara," the lord marshal explained. "He and his partner—lost to us—were the ones who caught your brother."

"Watchwarden!" Torval barked. "Not city guard!"

"You couldn't shake him?" the duke asked, eyeing Torval as if he were a stray cat that kept begging for milk.

The lord marshal shrugged. "He and his companion were coming to claim the reward, sire. The gold pieces promised on the Wanted circulars."

The duke nodded, then indicated the bags of gold lying before the Devils. "Bad news, my little friend. I'm cash-poor at present... unless you can solve that problem for me."

Torval stared back at the grinning fool. "And how do you propose I do that?" he asked. He hated the man instantly—the smug, entitled, little whelp.

"Well, it's very simple," the duke said, raising his voice so that all in the clearing could hear. "I am the Duke of Erald. I am fabulously wealthy. And if I'm not mistaken, these poor, shabby Devils of the Weald are now far outnumbered. So if the lot of you who came here with the lord marshal could just assist my men in mopping them up—"

Torval heard a gasp. It was Tzimena. The tall woman who held her at knifepoint had suddenly tightened her hold, forcing that surprised breath out of her prisoner.

"Try it and she dies," the woman said, pressing the blade of her dagger against Tzimena's dark, olive-skinned throat.

The big man holding the Raven was playing the same game, his big war club having been thrown down in favor of a jagged knife of his own, its point pressed into the Raven's ribs.

"Is this how you'd betray those who would treat with you fairly, good duke?" the big man asked.

The archers in the Devils' midst had their bows half drawn now, circling, searching for potential threats and targets.

Torval could feel the situation spiraling out of control. He tightened his grip on his maul. It would happen soon now. Any moment...

In answer to the big man's challenge, the duke nodded. "It

is. I was perfectly happy to pay you and get my prizes in return, but now the situation has changed, and I'd like my gold back."

"There will be no prizes," the woman who held Tzimena said. "Threaten us again and your bride-to-be dies."

"Did you not hear my intention to kill her myself?" the duke asked.

Torval heard Captain Tuvera draw a breath. No, she hadn't heard that.

"So go on," the duke continued. "Kill them if you like. Then my soldiers will kill you, and I can go back to my city knowing that my gold will remain in my coffers and these two unfortunate walking, talking complications will be beyond my concern."

Where would it come from? Torval wondered. Who would start it? And when it did come, whose side would he be on? Whose side would anyone be on? If Tzimena died, would her bodyguards make for the duke, to kill him in answer? If Torval fought alongside Tuvera and Galen and Elvaris in Tzimena's name, would he be fighting Wallenbrand? Croften? The lord marshal? And there was still the matter of how many men the duke actually boasted. Seven visible in the glade, but there had to be more in the trees…

Too many variables. Too many complications. Too many threats to be rightly assessed and prioritized.

Someone screamed—pure shock and surprise. That scream mingled with a sound like something enormous being broken, the bones of a giant snapped by a bad fall, the creaking of old wood and the rustling of leaves.

Movement drew all their eyes to the southeastern edge of the clearing. A big cedar on a knoll just beyond the tree line was swaying back and forth, bending forward toward them. Up in it, an archer was clinging to a thick limb for dear life, legs already loose, dangling, kicking empty air.

Something gigantic and angry was twisting the tree, pressing on it, applying pressure until—

Its roots tore loose and the whole tree teetered. The sound was slow, gradual, but the effect came suddenly. One moment the tree shook and bent precariously, the next it was falling. The archer on the high limb lost his grip and plunged along with the toppling tree. The huge trunk, almost a hundred feet high, swept right down into the clearing like the hand of an angry god falling out of the sky to swat an unrepentant sinner. All those in the middle of the clearing scattered like ants, and the cedar came crashing down. Its impact sent up a great cloud of dust, dirt, and fallen leaves, obscuring the world around them and shaking the ground.

Torval retreated instinctively. As he coughed dust from his lungs and blinked stinging earth from his eyes, he tried desperately to scan the clearing again and figure out what was happening, what had brought that tree down into their midst like that.

And then, he saw it, standing tall and proud and ugly where the base of the cedar now stood, its torn-up roots stretching every which way in an arboreal corona.

It was the troll. That gods-damned, bone-snapping, flesh-eating troll from the day before! The beast stood there, blinking dumbly, as though it was just as amazed at its feat as any witness might have been. Then it looked to the clearing, saw the staring eyes and pale faces of everyone who'd just scrambled to avoid being crushed, and roared. The roar was long and loud, one of challenge and defiance.

Its companions showed themselves: the female, the young buck with the war hammer, the ax swinger, the spearman, that blasted goblin with its deadly bow—and finally their chief: the big orc with the triple braids trailing from its otherwise-shorn skull. Arrayed for battle, the orcs roared and raised their weapons high before bounding down the knoll-side, charging toward the humans scattered about the clearing on either side of the great fallen tree.

Finally Torval had a target, knew whom to fight—whom to kill.

He raised a hoarse, hearty battle cry of his own and rushed to meet them.

CHAPTER THIRTY-ONE

Rem watched from hiding—helpless, hopeless—as Gnusha's Blades charged down the gentle slope toward the clearing and the groups of armed fighters waiting there. It wasn't his plan to stay here indefinitely, but he'd wanted to get some sense of what was unfolding, who the combatants were, and just what was at stake before he ran—unarmed—into the midst of all that insanity and tried to find his own useful place in it.

As they'd watched the proceedings, hadn't he urged Gnusha to do the same, if unsuccessfully?

Just minutes ago, they'd been quietly hidden up here, wholly unknown to those in the clearing below.

"They're making a trade," Rem had quietly explained to his captors. They were too far away to hear any of the words spoken if they were not shouted, but Rem recognized Tzimena and the Red Raven well enough, even at a distance. "That man in the cloak is buying those two prisoners."

"Buying, he," Gnusha rumbled thoughtfully. He looked to Rem. "Being brigand, must be. Buying, selling people, do only brigands."

Rem nodded. Anytime Rem was tempted to dismiss Gnusha's thought processes as slow or backward simply due to his halting speech, he needed only look into the orc's pale-green eyes to remember how wrong he was. This war band leader, however fearsome and brutish he might appear, was an individual of uncommon charisma and a warrior of unparalleled valor. Speaking another tongue was never easy, after all. How much harder would it be if your mouth and jaws weren't even shaped for it?

Rem was about to suggest a plan of attack—which he knew Gnusha would immediately dismiss—when he heard voices raised and heated words exchanged. When he looked, he saw Captain Tuvera on the south side of the clearing, her sword drawn. She was leveling some threat at the man making the buy. Clearly she had hidden backup, probably Galen, ready with her bow in the underbrush.

That complicated things. Before, there had only been Tzimena and the Red Raven to worry about extracting in one piece. Now, if Tuvera and Galen were present, that could mean...

"Oh gods," Rem whispered.

"Gods, what?" Gnusha asked.

Rem pointed to Tuvera. "She's an ally. That means there may be more allies nearby. If there's a fight, you mustn't hurt them—though they may try to hurt you."

Gnusha stared back, as if awaiting explanation.

"Well," Rem said, mightily embarrassed to have to say it plainly, "you're orcs. They'll see you rushing in and just assume you want to do them harm."

Gnusha stared at Rem, then looked to his companions, letting his grim glare meet all their expectant gazes. Finally he shook his head.

"*Washab*," he muttered. The orcish word for *human*, spoken in a manner clearly indicating exasperation.

More raised voices. Rem turned his eyes back to the clearing. He saw a familiar figure striding out from the tree line a few hundred yards off to their right, his hands held high, his blue surcoat unmistakable despite the grime and soot now covering it.

"That's the lord marshal," Rem said, pointing him out to Gnusha. "He was the leader of our expedition."

"Spare him too we?" Gnusha asked impatiently.

Rem was about to answer in the affirmative when the exchange between the lord marshal and the man making the deal to buy Tzimena and the Raven suddenly reached his ears, spoken as it was over a great distance, in raised voices. He couldn't make out everything they said, but—

"Milord," the lord marshal had said.

"Good help, at last!" the mysterious buyer answered with a hearty, delighted laugh. "Lord Marshal Kroenen, good to see you, sir!"

Then realization dawned. Though he was at least a hundred yards from the man, Rem could yet recognize the features of his face, especially when he smiled.

He and his brother had almost identical smiles.

"That's the Duke of Erald," Rem said. He turned to Gnusha, knowing that his shock was apparent on his face. "That's your employer, Gnusha!"

Gnusha stared down into the clearing, squinting. "Met never a duke. Blooded warrant by herald."

Rem didn't have to wonder much what Gnusha meant. He had interacted with orcs in Yenara just enough to know that, when they were trying to speak in human tongues, the terms *bonded* and *contracted* and *agreed to* were often translated as *blooded*. For orcs considered all agreements bound by blood, even if no such ceremonies were observed.

And there he was, down in that clearing, trying to buy his brother Korin and Tzimena from the Devils of the Weald.

Rem supposed the duke could be attempting to ransom

them both away from their captors...but somehow he thought that the duke's ultimate intentions might not be wholly benign. After all, if he wanted his brother executed, and he realized Tzimena knew who he really was...

"Listen to me," Rem said to Gnusha, "I think there's something wrong unfolding here. Something sinister."

"Attack now we?" Gnusha asked.

"Just listen," Rem begged, wondering how long he could hold them off. "The duke is trying to buy that man and that woman to murder them. The man is his brother! The duke stole his throne and already tried to kill him once. The woman is the duke's betrothed, but she knows that the duke's brother—supposed dead by the rest of the world—isn't."

Gnusha stared, face twisted in perplexity.

Rem tried to decide just what Gnusha and his Blades needed to know—what might sway them to target only the right people in that clearing, and not go in hacking and slashing indiscriminately.

"We have to save her!" Rem said, pointing to Tzimena, who—he now saw with dread—had been snatched into the arms of one of the Raven's people. She was being held at knifepoint. The situation down there looked tense. Dire.

"Save her," Gnusha said. "Kill the rest, we?"

"Not the women in the red tabards," Rem said hastily. And then he saw another familiar face down among those in the clearing—a face he'd almost hoped not to see, considering he was crouched at the edge of the scene with a band of orcs spoiling for a fight.

"And that dwarf," Rem said, pointing. "He's my partner. My friend." He searched his storehouse of a dozen or so orcish words and phrases, picked up in his year on the watch. "*Hrughar*. Friend. *My* friend. I beg you—"

Gnusha was already on his feet and giving orders. He looked to the troll.

"Hrozhna," he barked, then indicated a nearby cedar. *"Uscatlu frawu'du."*

The troll nodded and went to work. They'd silently slain one of the duke's guards hidden in the tree line where they'd crept forward, but apparently they'd missed another secret soldier: an archer, mounted high in the tree that Hrozhna now bent to toppling. The moment Hrozhna threw his weight against the tree and the whole trunk swayed, the archer in the boughs above suddenly screamed, terrified to realize that his perch was now under attack. He'd either completely failed to notice the party of orcs beneath him, or he'd stayed silent in fear of discovery. Either way, he'd given himself away now. Hrozhna threw his huge, thick body against the cedar, again and again, slowly but surely snapping the trunk and edging it toward collapse. Above, amid swaying branches, Rem saw the hidden archer trying to cling first to the big trunk, then to the thick branch he'd been mounted on. It did him no good. When the tree finally fell, the archer tumbled from his perch headlong with a cry and was buried when the tree thundered to rest in the clearing.

That was when Gnusha and the others showed themselves, standing tall and proud along the ridgeline of the knoll, raising their weapons and sounding hoarse battle cries to the open blue sky. The orc war cry sent the horses by the little pond scattering in all directions. The Raven, held prisoner by one of his own men, turned on the big fellow and started grappling with him. Galen spun and fired an arrow into the tree line at her back, probably aiming to take out a hidden archer she'd marked when the troubles began. The orcs charged down the slope. A number of the soldiers in the clearing charged to meet the orcs. Rem watched, helpless, as his captors bounded down the shallow slope toward their enemies, weapons and voices raised, dead set on chaos.

And that's when he heard another battle cry coming up from below. There was a great deal of confusion and shouting, of course—the duke's soldiers running to meet the incoming orcs, the Devils not in possession of Tzimena or Korin Lyr taking up position to do the same, arrows loosed, swords drawn—but there was only one voice down there raised in a full-throated battle cry that portended the rending of flesh and the spilling of blood wholesale.

It was Torval.

The instant he'd seen the orcs, his blood had boiled and he'd sounded his beastly intent to meet them, head-on, and trade deadly blow for deadly blow.

Already he was sprinting toward the slope to meet Gnusha's Blades.

Rem took off running.

"Torval, no!" he shouted, waving his arms like a lunatic as he rushed down the slope of the knoll. "Torval, stop! Don't engage them! Torval!"

Torval had almost reached the nearest orc to him—Thuwat, the young champion, with his fierce war hammer and heavily scarred shield, eager for the glory that killing a fierce dwarf in combat would earn him. Torval barreled on with all the fury and might his compact, muscular body could summon, wholly unafraid of the bigger adversary with the heavier weapon and a means of protection ready at hand.

No matter how loudly Rem shouted, his partner could not hear him—would not, more precisely. All he could hear right now was his own battle cry and the thump of his pulse in his reddened ears.

Rem would have to take him down.

He ran faster.

Steel rang through the clearing, the battle joined. From the corner of his eye, Rem saw that little Wudji, the goblin, had mounted the fallen cedar and was scampering along the trunk, darting among the upturned braches and boughs, stopping at intervals to take rapid shots at any adversaries with bows, knowing that eliminating them was a good first step toward victory. The Devils so armed returned fire, everyone's desperation meaning they missed nearly every shot they took. On the north side of the tree, Wallenbrand was engaged in a fight for his life with one of the duke's soldiers, that match of mercenary versus house guard telling Rem that the duke and the lord marshal had decided, in light of all the adversaries present, to slice right through their remaining liabilities. If they were openly trying to kill Wallenbrand, then Croften and Captain Tuvera's troops would soon follow. Off on Rem's right, hulking Hrozhna advanced before his comrades like a one-troll cavalry, wading right into the heaviest fighting and using his big, apelike arms to sweep adversaries aside like mowed weeds.

Aemon, this was going to get out of control fast. Rem couldn't even see Tzimena or the Raven any longer. The knot of bodies near where they were being held were all jostling and moving, surrounded by a cloud of swirling, boot-stirred dust.

And here came Torval, closer and closer as Rem poured on speed. The collision, he knew, would hurt like the sundry hells.

Torval saw him closing only at the very last second. Rem saw the dwarf's furious face suddenly elongate into a mask of wonder and amazement, his eyes wide as saucers; then Rem launched through the air and slammed hard into his partner, enfolding him in his arms and letting his momentum knock the oncoming dwarf to the leaf-strewn forest floor. They hit the ground hard and rolled a little, and Rem struggled to raise his eyes and see what Thuwat had made of the situation.

The young orc stood with his war hammer high and his shield wide, frozen in midstrike, staring.

Rem waved him off. "*Hrugahr,*" he said, again and again. "*Hrugahr modja.*" *Friend. My friend.*

Thuwat made a sour face—robbed of a victory, robbed of glory—then shook his head in frustration and rushed off into the midst of the unfolding battle.

Torval punched Rem in the gut—or maybe he was just shoving? Rem wasn't sure. He only knew that something heavy hit him in the middle and his breath was stolen and he fell right onto his back. Torval coughed and lay on his back beside him, but made no move to rise.

"Are you out of your fucking mind?" Torval snarled. "I had him, gods damn you!"

"They're friends, Torval," Rem wheezed. "I've been with them most of yesterday and through the night."

The dwarf sat up. "Impossible!" he spat.

"I knew you wouldn't believe me and I knew you wouldn't hear me screaming at you as I came bounding down that hill because you were too intent on killing them, but I swear it! They're a mercenary company, hired by the duke to scour the forest and clear it of brigands!"

Torval stared. His mouth was bloody. Rem tasted copper and realized his probably was, too.

The two partners turned and surveyed the scene. It was pure chaos. Orc fought Devil; Devil fought Eraldic soldier; Eraldic soldier fought Eraldic soldier, for that matter—for now it was clear that the duke's men had been ordered to take down Wallenbrand and Croften and the women in Tzimena's retinue. Everything was twanging bows and flying arrows and ringing steel and cries and curses and dust whirling in the slanting sunlight amid moving bodies.

Where was Tzimena? Rem could no longer see her. Was she wounded? Slain? Stolen away by the Devils?

"Well, what now?" Torval asked. "This isn't our fight, lad." Rem heard a note of sadness in his voice, as if Torval wanted to enter the fray but couldn't justify the decision.

Rem saw a flash of shining black hair and a snatch of red fabric. There! On the far side of the insanity, making a break for one of the last trio of horses on the far side of the clearing that hadn't bolted!

There was Tzimena. The Red Raven appeared to be with her, shoving her along, watching her back. Her hands were unbound now, but his were still tied.

And who was that, wending through the chaos toward them? A cloaked figure, indiscriminately hacking a path through the bloodshed toward his two most wanted prizes.

Verin Lyr, the Duke of Erald.

"Wrong," Rem said. "It's still our fight. You help Tzimena's guard. Keep the orcs off them. Fight side by side with those orcs if you have to—just don't let those brave women die in the midst of all this! They need allies, and you and I and those orcs are all they've got!"

Torval looked as if he was about to object to being told to fight alongside an orcish war band. Rem didn't let him.

"I'm going after Tzimena and the duke."

"Tzimena and the duke?" Torval parroted.

Rem was already up and running. His plan was to skirt the melee and stop the duke from pursuing Tzimena. Barring that, he'd steal a horse of his own and go after them.

"She doesn't deserve to die here, Torval!" Rem shouted

back over his shoulder...and then his partner was far behind him, and the world was fury and bloodshed all around.

On the far side of the clearing, Tzimena had just swung up into the saddle of one of the horses belonging to the duke and his men. She turned and said something to Korin, and then, before she'd even finished, the Red Raven shoved her animal's face, to wheel it around in the opposite direction, and slapped its rump hard. The horse bolted, straight for the woods on the north side of the clearing. Tzimena bent into the headlong rush like a champion rider.

Rem was closer now, but not close enough. In the midst of the chaos, he saw Elvaris engaged with an Eraldic guardsman, her Taverando flashing divinely in the choked sunlight of the glade. Some distance from her, nearer in Rem's vision, Captain Tuvera was being driven back by another of the duke's men—only to be rescued a moment away from a killing blow by Gnusha himself. The orcish war chief grabbed her attacker by the trailing hem of his forester's cloak, yanked him backward, and nearly cut the man in half with his huge, curved scimitar. Even as he ran, trying to concentrate on his ultimate goal, Rem clearly saw the fear and wonder on Tuvera's face as she stared at the orc who'd just saved her.

And what good could Rem do? At the moment he wasn't armed. What in the sundry hells did he plan to accomplish with his bare hands? Where could he find a sword or a weapon? He scanned the world to his right, where the fight was underway. A few bodies lay in the dirt, one moving, three others still. Rem noted that one of the dead men, skewered through an eye by an arrow, had a sword still sheathed at his belt.

Rem dove for it. In seconds he had the weapon in hand and had launched back toward his destination.

Across the clearing the duke was almost upon the Red Raven, his sword drawn and bloodied from his passage through the chaos, making straight for his brother. The Red Raven had his back to the duke, watching Tzimena's escape, more intent on her flight than on his surroundings, the hazard bearing down on him, second by second.

"Korin!" Rem shouted, hoping his voice carried over the ringing steel and curses and cries.

The Raven heard. He turned just in time to see his brother closing in, raising his sword and drawing back for a savage overhand thrust. With a practiced nimbleness Rem could have mustered only in a dream, the Red Raven threw himself backward, hit the ground flat, then tucked in his legs and rolled aside. The duke's thrust hit empty air and sent him stumbling forward— momentum carrying him toward a target that wasn't there— as the Red Raven disappeared beneath one of the tied horses and sprang back to his feet on the animal's far side. The duke regained his footing and moved to round the tied horse. Korin turned to the next horse in line. Something sharp and shiny protruded from one saddlebag, hard for Rem to see at his distance, but clearly metal. A woodsman's hatchet or some similar implement. The Raven rubbed his bonds against the glinting blade and quickly cut through them.

The duke, though, had slapped the aft end of the horse blocking his advance and now drew back for another fierce strike, this one a sideward chop instead of a thrust.

The Raven charged his brother before the strike could come full round toward him, landing inside the arc of the swing and throwing the duke back in a fierce tackle. The two brothers stumbled backward, the duke struggling mightily to keep himself from falling under his brother's hand-to-hand attack. He failed. Both men went down, duke on bottom, outlaw on top, the sword in the duke's wildly waving right hand.

Rem had a plan now. If he could just get there while Korin had his brother pinned, he could strike the sword from the duke's hand—or plunge a well-aimed thrust right into his rib cage, ending him with a single blow.

Are you ready for that? he thought absently. *A poor, simple watchman slaying a duke? Especially when said duke is fighting for his life against a notorious outlaw? Don't fool yourself that there won't be consequences for that action.*

Fine, then. He'd try to disarm him without killing him. Give Korin an advantage without saving him entirely. But first he had to get there.

The brothers were wrestling savagely. The sword had fallen from the duke's grip and they were rolling about on the loam like a couple of drunken Kostermen brawling outside a tavern. Rem knew the look of such a fight—brutish and ugly, two men unwilling to back down, each ready to do the other in with his bare hands.

Korin landed a good, solid punch to the duke's face. The duke landed a pair of his own to Korin's ribs. Korin pulled the duke's hair, bringing a scream from his noble brother's throat. The duke reached for his belt, drawing something.

"No!" Rem screamed, in spite of himself.

The knife bit deep into Korin's left side. The Red Raven threw back his head, teeth gnashing, and bellowed in pain. Verin, satisfied, shoved his brother off and tossed him aside. Korin caught himself in a half crouch and knelt there in the dirt, the hilt of the little dagger protruding from his belly. The duke, meanwhile, rolled sideward, scrambled across the dusty ground, and snatched up his sword again.

Rem was there to meet him. As the sweaty, flush-faced duke rose shakily to his feet, sword in hand, he caught sight of Rem, skittering to a halt just a few feet from him and leveling his own blade.

The duke blinked, wholly confused. "Are you one of his, then?" he asked between gulps of air.

"'Fraid not," Rem said.

The duke didn't have anything more to offer. He lunged, offering a withering onslaught of varied attacks that Rem fought desperately to parry and redirect. Upthrust, slash, downward thrust, backward slash, slash, overhand chop—again and again, faster than almost any opponent Rem had ever faced, clearly making the most of his nobleman's martial education.

Maybe I won't have to worry about killing him after all, Rem thought absently as he struggled to stay alive. *I'll be lucky to walk away from this.*

"Brother!"

The duke spun, mercifully sparing Rem a killing blow, just in time to see Korin Lyr, the Red Raven, his own brother, charging for his own attack. Rem advanced from behind, intent on shoving the duke forward, to throw off his balance and give Korin some advantage—

—but the duke heard Rem's heavy-footed advance and countered it with a swift, high backward strike. The duke's elbow and Rem's face collided and Rem saw darkness strewn with whirling stars and felt himself moving backward and downward. Then his back was on the ground and he was blinking furiously, trying to regain his vision and his sense.

He heard steel on steel, the grunting of men in a duel to the death. As his vision returned, Rem raised his head to see that Korin had purloined a sword from one of the tied-up horses and now met his brother with a furious series of his own attacks. Unlike a proper gentleman trained in dueling by other proper gentlemen, he didn't just rely on his sword's point or his sword's edge, either. He regularly interspersed backhand strikes with his sword's blunt pommel and hilt strikes toward his brother's face in an effort to break his brother's defenses and counter his more classical blade work.

Rem propped himself up on his elbows, desperate to catch his breath, waiting for his vision to clear entirely, wondering just what he should do. He really couldn't kill the duke unless the man was threatening someone innocent—that, at least, would provide a cover story if anyone tried to bring charges against Rem. But duke and outlaw, dueling on equal terms in a forest clearing? Rem didn't care to be the one to strike the killing blow on the outlaw's side in that contest.

Then the duke made Rem's choice for him. He countered a series of attacks from Korin with practiced assurance, and managed to slip one savage thrust through Korin's defenses. From where he lay, still half-dazed and struggling for breath, Rem saw the Duke of Erald run the Red Raven through like a speared boar.

Korin Lyr, to his credit, snarled and spat blood in his brother's face. As Rem watched, the onetime duke turned outlaw struggled along the length of the blade, reaching out for his murderer, desperate to lay hands on him, to choke him, to gouge out his eyes—to do anything that could end the match in his favor, despite his own imminent death. It was too late. That wound was fatal, probably ripping right through the outlaw's liver. Rem knew he'd be growing weaker with each desperate breath, the life and strength gushing out of him.

Rem scrambled to his feet, desperate to join the fight, to stop the injustice unfolding before him…but as he stood upright, his vision swam again and he pitched forward. He was down on his knees in an instant, the whole world whirling around him. He raised his head and managed to catch sight of Korin Lyr hitting the ground in a heap as his brother, Verin Lyr, the Duke of Erald, strode past him, heading for one of the tethered horses.

Rem crawled across the loam toward the Red Raven. By the time he reached him, his head was still throbbing, but he thought he might be able to stand without falling again. A quick glance told him the duke was mounted, whipping his horse with its reins, already bolting off into the woods.

Along the same track as Tzimena.

Rem had to go. Immediately.

He looked into Korin Lyr's watery eyes. Blood kept gurgling from his open, working mouth as he tried to form words.

"Tzi—Tzi—Tzi," he hissed.

Rem nodded. "She's safe. I swear it."

The Red Raven stopped trying to speak, relaxed. Rem felt he should stay with the man, not abandon him to bleed his life out upon wild ground in the middle of a forest, all alone . . . but he had something far more important to do. Feeling the sting of tears in his eyes and a murderous rage in his heart, Rem shot to his feet, pounded across the ground to the nearest horse, untethered the animal, and swung into the saddle.

Save her, he thought. *That's all that matters now.*

Kill him if you have to.

Hang for it if you have to.

Don't let him take her, too.

CHAPTER THIRTY-TWO

Torval had counted seven soldiers in the clearing before everyone began to emerge from hiding. Four of them stood in a broad semicircle around their master, while the other three hung back, near the big pond on the west side of the clearing where their horses drank. That count proved to be misleading, however, when the fight was joined. Suddenly there were more men in the clearing who, though wearing no livery, were clearly intent on wiping out the Lady Tzimena's bodyguards and the outlaws who'd come to trade her. Intermittently arrows flitted down in shallow arcs from the tree line on all sides, indicating that at least two—perhaps as many as three—archers remained in hiding.

And here stood Torval, caught among the lot of them and a stone's throw from an orcish war band already on the rampage among his enemies.

Fight side by side with those orcs if you have to, Rem had said.

Don't let those brave women die, he'd said. *They need allies, and you and I and those orcs are all they've got.*

Torval's confusion and frustration made his whole body shake. How he longed for a good, straight brawl in a Yenaran tavern, where his own job was stopping the fight and dragging a few belligerents into the watchkeep when it was all over and done with. Pure. Simple. Uncomplicated.

The world around him was a storm of complications. Chaos

everywhere. Ringing steel. Spat curses. Hasty orders. A few quiet pleas for mercy. Fists on flesh and blunt instruments cracking bone. The lord marshal had joined the fight alongside the duke's house guard, rallying a tight knot of troops to defend themselves from the oncoming orcs while ordering small contingents of two or three against the rest of their enemies—newly declared, still haunting the clearing.

"There! Stop them! Bottle their escape!" he cried, indicating the remainder of the Lady Tzimena's swordmaidens.

"Traitors!" he shouted, clearly indicating Wallenbrand and Croften, the last two mercenaries remaining who had been—until just moments ago—his loyal companions and in his employ. "No mercy!"

"The outlaws!" he called to the men on the farthest side of the clearing. "Leave none of them alive! Not a one!"

Strangely, the orcs seemed the least of the lord marshal's worries. But even as he struggled to keep the men of the duke's house working in concert and aware of the consequences of failing to prevent the escape of their declared enemies, the orcs lumbered among them, seeking contest and demanding bloody attention whether the lord marshal had formally declared them enemies or not.

There, that big, sleek, spear-wielding orc, moving slowly and steadily among the fighters, parrying blows and plunging in his blade with an elegance and deliberateness Torval had never seen among the hack-and-slash orcish raiders from the mountains, or even in the streets of Yenara.

Or that female, sword flashing swift and true as she waded in among her human adversaries, her muscular curves sliding and tautening beneath her gray-green skin as she lunged, whirled, parried, and slashed, a fencer of unparalleled ferocity and savage grace.

The troll, by contrast, had no technique at all: he just stomped about, snatching up anyone who seemed to be threatening one of his mates, disarming when possible, tossing sloppily when disarming proved too difficult. As Torval watched, the big, hulking brute took a pair of arrows from adjacent firing positions, roared in defiance, then snatched up one of the duke's house guards and threw the man overhand as though he were flinging a stone. The guardsman arced through the air and collided with an archer hidden in a tree some distance away, and both men fell end over end through the branches to the ground, landing together in a bloody, broken heap.

And what was this? Here came an orc! Short, fat, stocky, a huge battle-ax lifted over his bald head, barreling forward on thick, squat legs, right at Torval. Was he mad? Hadn't Rem said the orcs knew Torval was an ally? That they wouldn't attack? Torval tightened his grip on his maul. This was how far you could trust orcs! Once their blood was up, they'd kill anyone—any*thing*—that got in the path of their onslaught. And here came this green bastard, howling for blood, ready to cleave Torval's skull in two!

Torval raised his maul and charged, closing the space between him and the orc in three long strides. He drew back for a hard strike, planning to come in under the orc's lifted ax blade and double him over with a solid blow to the ribs. Then, to his great astonishment, the fat orc skittered to a halt, seemed to hesitate, and nodded frantically, his ax still hovering in the air above him.

"*Nazhud washa!*" he shouted.

Torval knew more than a few words and phrases in the foul orcish tongue, and this was among them.

Behind you.

He spun and struck, just in time for his already-drawn-back

maul to describe a wide, flat arc and slam hard into the leather-armored gut of one of the lord marshal's loyal comrades. The soldier, who'd been ready to bring his own sword down in a killing blow on Torval's shoulders, bent double at the impact of the maul and almost yanked Torval to the ground with him as he fell hard and hit the forest floor. The man groaned as Torval yanked his maul free. Just as Torval stumbled backward to try to regain himself, the man moved sloppily. He seemed to be trying to rise, sword still in hand.

The ax-wielding orc brought his blade down, adjusting his swing from high to low, like a mower wielding a scythe. The blade bit deep into the fallen man's middle and his groan became a startled yelp. He was dead an instant later as the orc yanked his blade free.

Torval stared, blinking. That man...he'd been coming up from behind, ready to end Torval with a single unseen blow. And that charging orc...

The huffer shook now, delighted that he'd made his first kill of the day. He pumped his ax into the air, exultant. "*Bohrutu mu! Bohrutu mu!*"

We fight! We fight!

Torval could only nod.

"Yes," he heard himself say, "we fight."

Yes. They fought. Side by side. Allied.

Gods, what a strange day this had turned out to be.

Then, before he could even wrap his head around what was happening, the ax wielder sounded another curt battle cry and hurried off, intent on a new adversary awaiting his hungry blade.

Torval watched him go, wondered what had just happened, what might happen next, how he'd ever gotten himself into such a mess. He was wondering about that—pondering that in stunned silence—when another human soldier suddenly charged him, this one with a sword in one hand and a small, light shield in the other, ready for a more equal contest.

Torval rushed him. Time to fight. Time to kill.

His opponent was on the ground, skull bashed in by his maul, in moments. Torval's fevered brain, finally starting to orient itself and formulate a plan, reeled off fragmentary standing orders in an effort to get his pumping blood and pounding heart set to a task.

Bolster the orcs.

Stand with the women.

Bolster the orcs. Stand with the women.

There, not twenty yards away. Tuvera, Elvaris, and Galen, back to back to back, the two swordswomen taking on all comers while the bow-wielding scout laid down steady, well-placed cover fire against any distant enemies who might join the shrinking cordon around them. They were holding their own, but they were clearly outnumbered. Galen's quiver—visible to Torval—had only three arrows left.

Torval searched the melee, trying to find someone to back him up. There was Croften, the big scout from the lord marshal's company, currently fighting off two members of the duke's household, covered in blood and mud and roaring like an angry dragon as he hacked and slashed and struggled to defend himself. His blows were wide and wild, yesterday's arrow wound and the fresh injury from that morning both torn open and bleeding again. He wouldn't last long if he didn't get relief.

And he'd be a fine companion if he could be saved.

Torval charged one of Croften's attackers from his undefended flank, collapsed the man's right knee joint with a well-placed strike of his maul, then planted the spike of the maul in the man's skull when he fell prone. Torval was ready to attack the second man, now closing on Croften's right, but that man's momentary shock and concern for his fellow proved his undoing. As he turned and shouted the name of the soldier Torval had just slain, Croften took the opening and slashed sideward. His bloodied sword planted itself in the man's neck and threw his now-limp body to the ground. The falling corpse took Croften's sword with it. The scout didn't have the strength to hold on to it. He waited until the body came to rest before stepping forward to try to fetch his weapon.

"My thanks, half-pint," Croften said between ragged breaths.

"Save it," Torval said. "I need your sword. Tuvera and the others—"

Croften yanked his blade free from the dead man's half-cleaved neck. He looked pale, ragged. How much blood had he lost from those open wounds?

"Let's go," he answered, summoning a grim smile. He marched, tottering visibly, toward Tuvera and the rest. Torval followed. He yanked a few arrows from downed adversaries along the way.

They were just in time. Galen had fired her last arrow and resorted to her own hitherto-sheathed sword. She, Elvaris, and Captain Tuvera were struggling mightily to defend their shrinking perimeter, but someone had set a great many of the duke's men upon them. The three women were surrounded by half a dozen soldiers.

Torval and Croften arrived just as Tuvera parried a probing thrust from one soldier only to feel the bite of another's sword. Elvaris fought savagely on her side of the shrinking circle, her work with that fancy blade that Rem so admired a wonder to behold—but her wounded leg put her at a distinct disadvantage. More than once during their short, desperate approach, Torval saw her lunge and threaten to topple, the leg making it impossible for her to keep her balance as she might in an unwounded state.

Torval indicated the right side of the contingent. "You take those," he barked at Croften. "The rest are mine."

Croften nodded gravely and waded in. "Understood, master dwarf."

The first man was cut down before he even realized Croften was closing. The second and third, however, adjusted and attacked quickly.

Torval had no time to watch. He'd joined the fight on his own terms by then, downing one man with a hard blow from behind to his unprotected crown, then diving forward to throw all his weight into another man's gut and send him sprawling. He caved in that one's face with his maul before the third, just a few steps away and currently engaged with Elvaris, saw what was happening and tried to make allowances.

His moment's distraction was enough. Elvaris ran him through. Down he went.

For a moment Torval and Elvaris stood, satisfied, gulping breath. Then, suddenly, the swordswoman's eyes grew wide.

"Torval!" she shouted, and lunged forward. Torval was about to spin on his heels, sure that she saw something or someone charging from behind, but he had no time; the Estavari swordswoman shot right past him and all but knocked him aside with all the weight of her body as she went. As Torval stumbled and turned and tried to keep himself from falling, he heard the ring of steel and saw what he'd been saved from.

It was the lord marshal himself. He'd crept up on Torval, almost unnoticed in the fray, then charged at the last instant for a killing blow. Now, as Torval watched, Elvaris met the lord marshal, blade to blade, parrying every strike he made and daring more than a few of her own. The two adversaries were well matched, the lord marshal's forceful, direct style frustrated at every hack and slash by Elvaris's smooth, confident blade work. It occurred to Torval that she was as good as Rem—probably better, if she was still so deadly while wounded. The grunts and curses that escaped both as they dueled made it clear no love was lost between them, either. Clearly this was a contest to the death, fueled by rage and hate.

But already Torval could see that Elvaris was flagging. It was that wound in her left thigh. No amount of stitching, cauterizing, or bandaging could have kept it closed once the battle was joined. Blood stained the swordswoman's torn leather trousers, the pool getting wetter and tackier by the instant, and Torval could see in Elvaris's increasingly unsteady movements, the way she favored that bad leg and kept stumbling about, that she couldn't stay upright much longer. He had to get her out of there, and fast.

But how? More than once he'd thrown himself at Rem and knocked him out of a fight—literally—in order to take his place and finish things, but doing so now struck the dwarf as rather foolhardy. Putting himself into the middle of that contest might just get Torval wounded, or Elvaris killed. And no matter how Torval circled and tried to approach from the rear, to creep up on the lord marshal and get the better of him while his back was turned, the moment could not be found. Every time he was ready, the two combatants reeled or whirled, and their blades would dance into the dwarf's line of sight, keen and deadly, ready to bite if he got too close.

The lord marshal laid into her with a series of fierce, terrible overhand blows. Elvaris met each one, but the speed and weight of the onslaught was too much, too fast. She retreated

under the blows step-by-step...and finally her bad leg gave
out. Torval saw the knee bend, saw Elvaris lose her balance and
go reeling backward, arms wheeling. The lord marshal saw his
chance: in an instant she would be on the ground, on her back,
and he could finally end her. He raised his sword and took the
three strides forward necessary to put him above her.

Torval lowered his head, ready to charge now that there was
an opening—but it proved unnecessary. In the next instant, a
scream sounded—rising on the air as though barreling closer
second by second—and something big and heavy slammed
into the lord marshal. He and the thing that hit him—a flying
guardsman, now unconscious from the impact—turned end
over end and sprawled a stone's throw away.

Torval turned. Across the clearing he saw the troll, standing
tall with four or five arrows protruding from it, front and back,
yet seemingly unperturbed. The troll was looking right at Torval. It raised its hand and waved. Torval even imagined the
beast smiled, like a child proud of a lucky bowling pitch across
a village green.

Torval could only raise a hand in answer: *Thank you.* He was
sure his face registered only shock and confusion.

Now, back to the struggle at hand. Torval saw that the lord
marshal, though clearly stunned by the impact of that flying
guardsman, was already moving, trying to regain his sense and
get back to his feet. It wouldn't happen. Not if Torval could
help it.

The dwarf sprinted from where he stood and all but threw
himself on the prone lord marshal. He laid his weight on his
fallen adversary and straddled him.

Where was his sword? There! In his hands, rising, rising—

Torval brought his maul down hard. He thought he had
the spike turned down and hoped to spear the nobleman's

arm to the forest floor, but somehow his weapon had been turned around in the struggle. It was the blunt side—the hammerhead—that came crunching down upon the lord marshal's wrist. Torval heard bones break, heard the lord marshal cry out, and the sword fell from his fist. Having disarmed his foe, Torval turned the maul sideward and laid its breadth across the lord marshal's throat. He held it at either end and laid all his weight on it. The lord marshal struggled to keep the maul's handle from crushing his windpipe, but with one ruined, broken wrist and the weapon already so close, he had little leverage. His face bloomed red, eyes bulging, the breath from his half-crushed throat ragged and thin.

Don't let him live, Torval thought.

Take every last breath, Torval thought.

Add this notch to your maul handle, Torval thought.

But that was mercy, wasn't it? Escape. If he killed the lord marshal now, the man would never face trial, never be publicly shamed and made to pay for all the trouble he'd caused, all the lives he'd ended and ruined and endangered.

"Torval."

It was Elvaris. He heard her, but of course he could not see her, because she was somewhere behind him, and all that Torval could see right now was the lord marshal's blood-engorged, straining face, his bulging eyes and open mouth and lolling tongue.

"Torval," she said again, and he felt her hand on his shoulder. "Let him up now. We can't just kill him—we have to make sure he pays for this. For all of it..."

Torval knew the sense of that, could feel the rightness of it in his gut. But there was equal rightness in the way his steel maul handle kept lowering against the big, proud man's windpipe... the way he was gasping for a last breath... the way his eyes bulged and fluttered and rolled in his beet-red face.

Elvaris limped into view. She was no longer behind him now. Instead she moved toward the lord marshal's fallen sword. When she reached it, she kicked it aside, far beyond the prone man's grasp, even with his good hand. Then she fell to her knees. She was right in Torval's line of sight now, leaning on her own beautiful blade.

"Stop it, Torval," she said. Not a plea...an order.

Torval did as she commanded. He wasn't sure why...only that something in him told him this way would be better. More *right*. More *just*.

The lord marshal coughed and sputtered, gasping for breath and drawing it in in desperate, ragged gulps. His broken wrist was swollen and discolored under his bracers and chain mail now.

Torval struggled to his feet. For a time he stood over the lord marshal, enjoying the sight of the desperate man's struggles to regain himself after being so horribly beaten. When it looked as though that recovery was progressing—as though the lord marshal might regain both the ability to breathe and the ability to speak imminently—Torval made another decision. He planted one thick foot beside the lord marshal's calf, to brace the man's leg, then gave the lord marshal's foot a hard swipe with his maul. Again bone broke. The foot dislocated from the ankle joint and bent at a horrid angle.

Torval nodded, satisfied. "That's so you don't slip away, you bastard."

CHAPTER THIRTY-THREE

Even at a breakneck gallop, Tzimena's horse picked out a path more effectively than she could have. It was a deer track of some sort, narrow and, in some places, precariously over-grown, littered with old, broken limbs and stray stones deposited by old mudslides. The path was likewise overhung with all sorts of healthy trees, their limbs threatening, time and again, to knock Tzimena from the saddle or catch on her billowing dress and yank her from her seat. She had no idea where she was going, what direction they were heading in, where any meaningful landmarks like the river or the mountains might be. Her entire world was speed and the thunder of hooves and the threat of being struck by looming foliage or thrown from a tripped horse.

And yet she would not slow.

Round a bend to the right, back again to the left, down a small dip, through a gully, up a short slope, past huge cedars and towering redwoods and rustling pines.

Were those hooves, pounding closer, behind her? Was someone trailing her? Tzimena dared a glance back, keeping her head low, beneath the rippling screen of her mount's mane. She saw nothing.

Perhaps it was an illusion—the echoes of her own horse's hooves through the woodland around her? Surely, if someone was going to follow, they'd be far behind, wouldn't they?

She turned her eyes forward again. There was an enormous fallen ash ahead, its old, dead trunk overgrown with moss and lichen, blocking the narrow little deer path like a brick wall.

She whipped her horse, lowering herself to hug its withers.

"Jump it," she said. "You can do it, darling, I know it. Don't let it stop you, just—"

The horse screamed, tossed its head back, and dug in its hooves. It would not jump, and it would hear no more nonsense from her about it. For a moment Tzimena was certain she could hold on, avoid being thrown—she'd lowered herself, after all, there was no way the horse could—

But it did. It dipped its head low and dug its forehooves in deep, and in the next instant Tzimena was tumbling forward, right out of the saddle, sliding over its withers and head. Something slammed hard into her tumbling body, and she realized it was the fallen ash. Breath left her. Sense left her. Everything was darkness and shock and pain—bone-deep pain. She was sure that every bone in her body must have shattered. But her fall wasn't done just yet. She'd hit the log, but there was still the matter of the earth itself, and gravity. Down she went, landing in a heap, in agony, her brain scrambled, her only thoughts the desire for a deep breath and the vague question of whether she'd ever draw one again.

Her head swam. Her chest hurt when she tried to inhale. She wondered if a rib or two were broken.

Get up, she thought. *Move.*

What was that? Hooves approaching? Someone following?

Get. Up. Move.

Tzimena raised her head. Blinked. Her vision cleared, little by little. Her horse had moved to the verge of the little path, staring off into the green underbrush, its big, brown eyes blinking innocently, as if it hadn't just tried to kill her.

She got her arms underneath her and tried to push herself up. That would be enough if she could accomplish it: up on all fours, not sprawled flat on the ground, that was it. If she could attain just that much...

She did. She tried breathing again and felt that pain in her lower ribs again, like a thorn-studded belt, constricting her. She also noticed something red dripping lazily onto the damp earth beneath her. Tzimena raised a hand to her face and realized her nose and mouth were both bleeding.

A little blood. No worries. You survive a hemorrhage worse than that each month. Move, damn you! Someone's coming.

She sat upright, legs folded beneath her, like a penitent kneeling before a holy shrine. For a long time she only breathed, working hard to regain her strength, her control, to make sure that if she dared to stand, she wouldn't lose consciousness and collapse again. Every part of her ached, but no part of her refused to move. Aside from those possibly cracked ribs, nothing seemed broken.

The hooves were getting closer.

Tzimena braced herself against the fallen ash and stood. Immediately her head swam and she fell back against the dead tree, vision full of dancing motes. Her horse's ears had pricked up now, and the animal had turned its head toward the sound of an approaching four-legged companion.

Her vision was clearing, but not fast enough. Tzimena searched the area around her for a hiding place. She saw ferns and bracken and thick shrubs and tall trees, but nowhere sufficient to secret herself. Nor, she thought, did she have the strength to just start running. Soon, perhaps, but right now? Impossible.

The hoofbeats were almost upon her.

Tzimena reeled toward the verge of the deer track, determined to just go stumbling into the brush and hide behind a tree if she had to.

But it was too late. At the far end of the deer path, from the direction she'd come, a huge black destrier appeared, bearing upon it a familiar rider: the Duke of Erald. He looked red-faced, sweaty, and winded, but he reined in his mount when he saw her and studied their surroundings as if half expecting a trap of some sort.

Tzimena felt all the fight go out of her. Oh, she'd claw his eyes out if he got close enough—he could count on that—but there was no point running any longer and making a fool of herself. She'd just have to stand here and either kill him herself, or force him to kill her. Either way, she'd fight until she had no breath left in her.

"Really," the duke said, spurring his horse into an easy canter to advance, "what was the point of all this?"

"To get away from you," Tzimena said. She spat out blood and saliva. "Simple enough."

The duke approached. When he was just about three yards from her, he reined his horse in. "Curious," he said. "You agreed to marry me readily enough."

"Don't flatter yourself," Tzimena said. "My mother agreed that I should marry you. I was less eager, but I had no better offers. Besides, I didn't know you at all—for good or ill—let alone what a snake you were."

The duke shrugged, a most nonchalant gesture for a man who looked as if he'd just fought to save his own life and was now moments away from taking hers. He spoke as he dismounted.

"Well, if it's any solace," he said, "my intentions were true. Mostly, anyway. Partially, I suppose. If you had made it to Erald, safe and sound, and met me and married me and come to love me,

I would have been happy. Your beauty, after all, was not exaggerated. But, alternately, if you drew out my brother and made it possible for me to finally do away with him...that would've been fine, as well. Even if I had to lose you in the process."

Tzimena blew out a breath. "You bastard."

Verin Lyr threw out his hands, a gesture of apology. "Strategic principles, that's all. If you can undertake an action that could result in several possible outcomes, and more than half of those possible outcomes are in your favor, take the action. Simple enough. Now..."

He drew his sword. There was still blood on it. Tzimena wondered whose blood it was.

Were those hooves she heard approaching?

Wishful thinking, she thought. *There he stands, armed and ready to do me in. Here I stand, broken and without protection. How far will my fists or my nails or my teeth get me against that bloodied blade of his?*

"...I have no wish to make this painful for you," Verin said, moving closer slowly, cautiously, the sword at his side. "If you'll get on your knees and turn around, I can make it quick."

Tzimena spat blood at his feet. She wasn't imagining it. There *was* a horse approaching!

He heard it, too. Likewise, he saw that she heard the hooves.

And that made him strike.

He moved quickly, sweeping up his sword and bringing it down in a vicious overhand arc that fell right toward her. Tzimena had received a great deal of martial training in her youth—all Estavari women did, noble or not—but her years of drilling were far behind her, and she was out of practice. Still, she knew that if someone was coming at you with a sword, and you had nothing, the best thing you could do was get close to them, inside their swinging or thrusting range.

And that's what she did. She barreled forward as the blow fell, throwing all her weight against Verin Lyr's torso, wrapping her arms around him and doing her best to drive him backward and throw him off balance. The impact brought a deep, stinging pain from the ribs she imagined cracked, but she bent into the tackle nonetheless. Her life depended on it.

He was too practiced, though. The duke managed to get a foot behind him, to save his thrown balance, then gripped her by her dress and twisted sideward. Using his body for leverage, he threw her round him and she hit the ground hard, now lying on the deer path between him and his unmounted horse. The horse, for its part, was startled and cantered backward, nearly clearing the path.

The approaching hooves were loud now, very close.

Hurry up, she thought. *Whoever you are, hurry!*

She raised her head and looked to the duke. He was charging toward her, sword raised again.

Tzimena rolled backward, desperate to get away from the sword falling toward her. She managed to avoid the first blow but kept rolling as the duke straightened and prepared for another. As he drew back, this time for a sideward thrust, Tzimena scrambled to her feet and retreated up the path, away from the barrier of the fallen ash. Just as she made her feet, the approaching horse and rider rounded the bend, pounding toward them.

She had only an instant to see the rider's face, but there was no mistaking the red hair and freckles, even under two days' worth of dirt and grime.

It was Rem. He had a sword in hand, and he charged right toward the duke, clearly prepared to counter him.

Of course, Tzimena stood between them.

She threw herself aside as Rem galloped through the space she'd lately occupied, heading straight for the duke.

The abandoned horses on the sides of the road fled into the brush, affrighted.

Rem brought his sword down in a savage arc, but the duke was ready for him. Their swords met in the air and rang loudly in the forest. Just as Tzimena thought Rem would drive his stolen horse right into the fallen ash, he yanked the beast's reins and it reared and wheeled. Again Tzimena was terrified—the horse was overbalanced! It would fall, surely, pinning Rem beneath it!

But clearly the young man knew how to ride. The horse's upright, wheeling bulk stayed vertical and its wheeling hooves struck out at the duke. Verin stumbled backward, eager to avoid the metal shoes that nearly crushed his skull. As the horse finally placed all four hooves on the ground again, Rem swung out of the saddle on its far side—to make sure he got good footing before the duke could charge—then slapped the animal's rump and sent it off into the woods.

The duke and the red-haired city watchman charged at one another and launched into a fierce duel, far more terrifying and impressive than any Tzimena had ever seen in a tournament or melee, because the stakes here were the highest: life and death.

She'd had a feeling about Rem all along—a sense that he wasn't just the humble watchwarden that he claimed to be—and his sword work proved her right. He met every blow the duke offered with practiced assurance, took every opening offered with deadly intent. The duke, for his part, was a frighteningly skilled opponent—fast, confident, ferocious yet always controlled—but Rem, whoever he was, held his own beautifully.

And yet...as the match wore on, Tzimena started to get a sinking feeling. How long could Rem last against the duke? A single minute? Two or three?

And would she just stand here, letting this brave boy risk his life just to save hers?

Steel notched steel. The men grunted, barked, sliced the air, and managed, at intervals, to land minor hits against each other. The duke left a nasty cut on Rem's left arm. Rem managed to get his point in, just the slightest bit, at the duke's right shoulder. Round and round they went, each knowing the other wouldn't yield until he was put down for good.

Tzimena searched around where she stood. Something. Anything. There had to be—

There, beneath the shading fronds of a fern, half-buried in the dirt between the spreading roots of the tree at her back! Tzimena fell to her knees and dug in with her hands, desperate to loose the treasure waiting there.

"I don't know who you are," the duke grunted between strikes, "but you're quite good. If I weren't about to kill you, I'd offer you a job."

"I already have a job," Rem said, still attacking, "and I'm doing it."

Tzimena almost had it—a large stone, the size of a small melon. She scratched and clawed at the earth around it, trying to pry it loose, but the earth held it. Already ants and other small insects were streaming out from beneath it. An earthworm breached the loam and her clawing fingers tore right through it as she kept digging.

Grunts. Steel ringing. Someone cried out, taking a hit— Rem, she thought, but she couldn't be sure.

"Just know how pointless this all was," the duke said, sounding smug even as he snarled. "You died to defend a woman whose death will follow hard on yours, to avenge a man you never knew—never could have known."

Korin? Did that mean...?

Tzimena screamed, pure fury, desperation, need. She tore into the earth so hard her nails tore and her fingers began to bleed. As she yanked, again and again, the stone started to move.

"Gah! Gah! Gah!" someone shouted, each bark punctuated by the ring of blade on blade—a bevy of strikes, seeking to end the match with overwhelming force.

The stone tore loose. Tzimena had it in hand. She yanked it up—it was far heavier than she'd imagined—took to her feet, and dashed across the path toward the two combatants.

The duke was driving Rem back toward the fallen ash, blow after blow in merciless succession, Rem helpless to do much more than hold his sword high and horizontal in the hope of parrying the onslaught.

Tzimena nearly rammed right into the duke, but managed to skid to a halt just short of him. Careful to avoid his blade as he brought it back for each overhand strike, she raised the big, heavy stone in her hand and brought it crashing down on Verin Lyr's unprotected skull.

The stone was unwieldy. It hit hard before glancing off. The duke's attack on Rem paused, sword in midstrike, and the duke spun on her, shocked and amazed. For an instant Tzimena thought she might have missed, or failed to hit him hard enough. Then she saw that his openmouthed face was suddenly stained by a sheet of blood from his rent scalp. As the blood poured down from his head, Rem struck from behind. His sword point burst out of the duke's gut, just below his rib cage. The bleeding duke lowered his eyes to see what had suddenly bitten through him.

Tzimena brought the stone down again on his lowered head. She took him high, on the back of the skull, and Verin Lyr hit the forest floor limply, like an overstuffed sack of turnips. She took a step back, horrified at what she'd done, at all the blood welling up from his cracked skull, at the finality and the ugliness of it.

Then she saw his right hand twitch.

Tzimena brought the stone down one more time. She felt his skull split this time, the hard shell and the soft, gray innards all yielding to the elemental weight of the stone she held. Something warm and wet hit her face.

To her own astonishment, she didn't stop. She hated him. Cursed him. Hoped to hurt him—to torture him—to unman him.

She lost track of how many times she brought that stone down, but it was Rem who finally put his arms around her and drew her off. He whispered to her, his voice soft and easy and understanding.

"He's gone," he said. "Drop it, Tzimena. It's over. It's all over."

She was crying, her vision blurred by tears and blood, the taste of copper and bile in her mouth, a terrible, empty hole in the center of her. She did as Rem bade and dropped the stone. For an instant, just an instant, she studied her grim work: the shattered skull, the mottled bits of flesh and hair, the brains and blood, dashed out upon the ground and slopped about like the produce of a slaughter yard.

And then she realized she never, ever wanted to see such a thing again, let alone be responsible for it.

Tzimena threw herself into Rem's arms, sobbing. He held her, his embrace strong, speaking quietly to soothe and comfort her.

CHAPTER THIRTY-FOUR

Six weeks following the bloody battle in the forest—six weeks to the day—Rem and Torval were back in Yenara, enjoying an evening like any other in the King's Ass. Indilen was at Rem's side, the smell of her and the warmth of her a welcome balm after what felt like years on the road. Torval's family was present, as well, along with Aarna. Though technically on duty, the taverner still spent a great deal of time at their corner table, assuring herself that her two most annoying patrons were well cared for. Questions were fired like arrows from Galen's bow, and anecdotes of their journey reeled off with such frequency, and such a complete disinterest in order and chronology, that Rem lost track of almost every episode they tried to narrate. It was a fine summer night, all the windows and doors thrown open to let in the cool bay breezes that cut razor sharp through the otherwise balmy air. Though the taproom rumbled with laughter and conversations, it was not so crowded as to make their welcome-home feast unpleasant, nor so raucous as to seem an ill-chosen venue for a family supper. Flush with their promised reward, Torval and Rem each bought rounds for the place and filled a minstrel's cup with coin, to keep him and his lovely singing partner performing all through the night.

It was perfect, the exact sort of homecoming Rem had dreamed of for all their time away...and yet something still ate at him. It was an itch at the back of his brain, an insistent, dirgelike chord of sullen doom sung by an unseen chorus of alien voices within him. For the first part of the night, he'd done his best to wrestle it down, deep into the shadowy corners of his psyche, far away from his joy at having returned to his love and his adopted city safe and sound after such a perilous journey.

But the shadow would not be banished. It lurked at the periphery of his awareness, squatted in the low, dark corners at the edge of his conscious thoughts, brooded, silent and sullen, even as Torval regaled his children with a much embellished—and much sanitized—version of their harrowing adventures through the Ethkeraldi.

"There I was," the dwarf deadpanned, face grim, voice a hoarse whisper, "surrounded by three armed killers in ducal livery and another pair of those outlaws called the Devils of the Weald. They had me—dead to rights!—though I was armed and willing to drag each and every one of the bastards down to the Eternal Forge with me if they dared charge—"

"And where was Uncle Rem?" Lokki asked.

"Uncle Rem had a mission of his own," Torval said, "saving that poor pursued maiden of Estavar from her horrid suitor!"

Indilen, head on Rem's shoulder, one arm wrapped around Rem's own, gave him a teasing squeeze and glanced up at him. "Always running after damsels in distress," she said with a smirk.

"Old habits die hard," he said, forcing a smile and kissing her softly. Then, he leaned nearer. "Besides, at the end of the day, *she* saved *my* skin—not the other way around."

Her eyes narrowed. The smirk became a sly smile. "I'm sure you were oh so grateful."

Rem didn't answer, but offered a smirk of his own. He turned back to Torval, who suddenly leapt up from his chair and beamed the empty pewter mug in his hands at the trio of wooden cups arrayed on the table before him. As the mug slammed hard into the cups and scattered them with a rattling crash, Torval shouted—

"Crash! There they went! All my enemies bowled aside at a single blow by an unlucky horse pitched straight as a skipping stone! And who do you think saved me in my hour of need? What avenging angel swooped down from the high heavens at that very moment—when I was cornered and ready to die in a storm of blood and dashed bone under all those enemy blades?"

The children all stared, wide-eyed, waiting for the answer. Ammi threw a worried look at her aunt Osma. Osma rolled her eyes, knowing all too well what a tale spinner her brother could be.

"Standing across the clearing," Torval continued, staring into the middle distance as though he could conjure up the image before him, "head and shoulders above everyone else in the melee, stood a bloody, knotty-skinned mountain troll— twelve feet high if he was an inch! I know not why it took pity on me in that moment, but it was that very beast that pitched the horse and saved the day for me. I raised my maul in salute, to pay homage to the big brute. It raised a single fist in answer."

Rem leaned toward Indilen. "That's not precisely how I remember it," he whispered.

He did not hear her reply, though. The moment he spoke, his mind yanked him back, unbidden, to the moment that he and Tzimena returned to the clearing and took in the aftermath of the battle just finishing there.

Rem remembered thinking, *No. This isn't right. It can't be. This is the aftermath of a war. We were just passing through the woods, delivering a prisoner . . .*

*   *   *

When Rem and Tzimena returned to the clearing—trailing the two extra horses, one of which carried the duke's dead body draped over it, his cloak and hood concealing his ruined head—the fighting had wound down. Prisoners were gathered in the middle of the clearing—two Devils of the Weald, a young soldier from Duke Verin's private guard, and the lord marshal himself—while the dead had been separated and laid out on their backs, to better identify them. Croften and Tuvera were among those slain. They lay alongside the Red Raven, two unknown Devils of the Weald, and almost a full dozen of the duke's private guard.

Torval, Wallenbrand, Galen, and Elvaris had taken command of the situation. Gnusha and his mercenaries stood aside, seemingly aware that their presence, though tolerated, was hardly welcome. Rem had to admit, he was relieved to see Torval and the orcs moving about the same space, attending to their separate business without even a fell glance or show of weapons. Elvaris sat on a fallen beech, fresh bandages soaking up seeping blood on her thigh, while Galen stitched up a small slash wound on her forehead.

When Wallenbrand saw Rem and Tzimena return, he strode across the clearing to meet them. Tzimena, who'd been riding behind Rem, arms around his waist, face buried in his shoulder, dismounted first and moved to meet the salty old sellsword before Rem could even climb out of the saddle.

"He gave chase," she said flatly, suggesting the dead duke. "He threatened to kill me. Rem fought with him, but in the end I killed him."

Wallenbrand stared. "You, milady?"

"Me," she said. "Rem fought to defend me, but the killing

blows were mine. If there are charges to be brought, punishments to bear, I shall bear them."

Wallenbrand shook his head. "Milady, I'm just a simple soldier—a hired one at that—but if I have any say, there shall be none. Come away, now, you're bleeding."

"It's not my blood," she said, still sounding like someone half-gassed on witchweed. "It's his." Her half-hearted nod suggested the dead duke.

Rem made sure the horses were hobbled, then approached Tzimena. The old soldier smiled a little and nodded.

"Good to see you safe, lad. I know Elvaris and Galen will be grateful for your defense of the lady."

"The lord marshal?" Rem asked, seeing the proud commander sitting awkwardly with the other prisoners.

Wallenbrand nodded. "Turned on us. Stood with the duke's bodyguards and tried to slay Croften and me, along with the Lady Tzimena's soldiers. Left wrist and right ankle are shattered—courtesy of your dwarven partner—but he'll live."

Rem shook his head. "He's your commander, Wallenbrand. How—"

"*Commander,*" Wallenbrand scoffed. "He hired me—hired all of us—to help hunt down and kill a single man. He spent the lives of his own men—men who obeyed him and trusted him—to see a single man punished. My word may not count for much, but I'll tell anyone who asks just what I think he deserves."

Rem nodded, understanding completely. He admired the old man. If they were back in Yenara, he'd make a fine prefect of the watch. Without a word, Rem left Tzimena and Wallenbrand where they stood and trudged on. He wanted to make sure there could be peace between Gnusha's Blades and his combative partner.

"Did you meet them?" Rem asked as he approached Torval. "My saviors?"

Torval threw a dark glance at the milling orcs and snorted. "Saviors," he muttered. "Captors, more like."

Rem stepped closer and spoke quietly. "When they found me," Rem said, "I was hanging upside down, a yet-to-be-slaughtered supper for the Bloody Boskers. But they cut me down and took me among them—even fed me. I wouldn't be here right now if they'd been as wicked as you'd like to think them."

Torval lowered his eyes and shrugged. "Maybe," he said.

"Come meet them," Rem said. "Say thank you."

Torval raised his eyes again, clearly not fond of that idea.

"Then come with *me*," Rem offered. "Let *me* say thank you. You can just stand there and see what orcish honor looks like."

Without waiting for his partner to agree, Rem strode past Torval and approached Gnusha. The orcs all looked dirty, dusty, and bloodied, but little worse for wear. Hrozhna, the troll, sat on the ground, staring at some freshly picked wildflowers in wonder, as though he'd never seen such beautiful things before. Half a dozen arrows were buried in his thick gray hide, but they did not seem to trouble him. Wudji the goblin had one arm in a bloodied sling and sat staring forlornly at his bow, the string now cut or broken. Tludjaba, the female, was having a bloody gash on her arm stitched by Thuwat, the young champion.

Gnusha stood tall as Rem approached. His mighty, forward-swept saber was sheathed at his side, his large hands empty.

"Did you wet your blade, Gnusha?" Rem asked.

Gnusha nodded. "Paid to kill bandits, we. Kill them, we. Earn purse, we did."

Rem glanced sideward and saw Torval lingering at his elbow, shifting uncomfortably from foot to foot, clearly not wanting to engage with the orcs directly or even look at them. Rem decided his presence was enough and resisted the urge to try to make him say anything.

"I have bad news, Gnusha," Rem said, and indicated the corpse flung over the horse he'd led back to the clearing, far across the field. "The duke is dead. I caught him trying to murder that girl. He had to be put down."

Gnusha stared at the body across the clearing, then looked to Rem again, then back to the body. Finally he shrugged. "Paid in advance, did he. Lose nothing do Gnusha and his Blades."

"Well, that's a relief," Rem had said, smiling and honestly meaning it. "What happens now?"

Gnusha studied the killing ground: the dead, the prisoners, his comrades. He weighed Rem's question heavily.

"Killed bandits. End to oath maker, end to oath. Go, we."

"Go where?" Rem asked.

Gnusha shrugged again. "Go, we, where there is good money for good fight. Have good fight, we."

"Have good fight, you do," Rem said. "I must thank you, Gnusha. My woman, back home, she thanks you, too. You saved my life, and you treated me with honor. If there is ever a favor I can do you, a favor it's in my power to do, I swear, it shall be done."

He offered his hand. A furtive glance sideward told him that Torval's eyes were as wide and white as two of his pickled eggs. No doubt he wanted to reach out and slap Rem's hand away.

Make a pact with an orc? he might shout. *Be in the debt of an orc? Are you out of your mind, boy?*

Rem wondered. He might be. But fair was fair. When someone did you a good turn, you repaid it.

Gnusha, to Rem's great surprise, reached out and took his hand—or, more accurately, his wrist. The orc's big hand wrapped around Rem's wrist and Rem did his best to grasp

Gnusha's own—though it was far too thick for his fingers to stretch very far. They locked gazes for a moment, eye to eye.

"Are brave, you, *Hramba*," Gnusha said, trying his best to render Rem's name in his own tongue. "Meet again, we, be it as *hruga*."

Hruga: friends.

"*Ba*," Rem said, using one of the very few orcish words he knew. "*Djac-ba*."

Yes. Great yes.

Hopefully, Gnusha would forgive his scant grasp of the orcish tongue.

Gnusha smiled then. With his fangs and tusks, it was a most fearsome expression...and yet it made Rem feel good. Their handshake broke and Rem stepped away.

That's when Torval spoke.

"*Hraba du, dja*," the dwarf said. Rem knew those words, as well, though he'd heard them seldom enough in Yenara, from orcs or from his own partner's lips.

I thank you, Torval had said.

Gnusha nodded in acknowledgement. "Is good friend, he," the orc answered. "Keep safe, you."

And with that Gnusha turned and moved to join his band. Rem urged Torval to withdraw, and they turned and headed back across the clearing.

"That was big of you," Rem said quietly.

"I suppose," Torval said, "your soft, courtly manners are rubbing off on me."

"Careful now," Rem said with a smile, "you might start reciting poetry next."

"Where are you?" Indilen asked.

Rem blinked. Torval had disappeared, though his children

and Osma were still at the table, munching nut biscuits and quaffing summer cider. Rem looked to Indilen as if for some explanation. Clearly she saw the shock and confusion on his face, because she only shook her head and touched his hand where it lay in his lap.

"He stepped away," she said quietly. "Probably for a piss in the jakes. But where were *you* off to? I saw the way your eyes glazed over."

Rem tried to smile, but he was certain he failed. "Just taken back, that's all. To the woods."

Indilen studied him. Sometimes, when certain people studied him so closely—eyes boring into him, weighing the unseen, incorporeal parts of him that were most personal and private—he felt insulted, violated, even ashamed. But there was something warming in Indilen's appraisals, something that told him he was not being judged but examined, as a mother looked over a child after a hard fall, in search of injuries in need of attention.

"Do you want to tell me?" she asked. She did not elaborate—but then again, she didn't have to. Rem knew exactly what she meant. They hadn't talked much about it since his return, his close calls and trials on the road largely unelaborated upon.

Torval was away. The children and Osma chattered to themselves. Even Aarna was nowhere to be seen, probably back in the kitchens, seeing to the firepits or waiting for a fresh gooseberry pie from the hearth. This might be a good moment, Rem thought, for him and Indilen to talk more directly—good enough to start the tale, anyway, even if he could not finish it.

"It just weighs on me," he said, lowering his eyes. "The meanness. The waste. Just like Geezer and Rikka...but bigger. Uglier."

Indilen placed a single warm hand on his cheek and drew

Rem into her arms. He held her tight. Words fell out of him in a hoarse, rapid-fire whisper, right into her ear.

"Stop," she said gently. "Come away with me."

In the woods they'd talked long and hard about what to do with the prisoners.

Two Devils were among the dead, while one—the tall woman called Tymon Longstride—had escaped during the fight, even managing to take a satchel of gold with her. But two men remained: a bald fellow with gold rings in each ear, known among his folk as Dedrik Firebow, and a great bear of a man called Orhund. Once disarmed in the midst of the fray, they had offered no further resistance.

"What would you have us do with you?" Tzimena asked them.

"To be honest," Dedrik said, "you'd be within your rights to kill us, milady. We threatened you with as much."

"You actually tried to sell her to someone intent on killing her," Elvaris responded coldly, "which is infinitely worse."

Dedrik nodded. Outlaw he might be, but he was clearly a reasonable man.

"What of you?" Tzimena asked the bigger one, Orhund.

"I agree with Dedrik," Orhund said. "We wronged you. You should put us down. We deserve no less."

"Did you hear that, Lord Marshal?" Elvaris called toward where the patrician sat on the ground. "These men—these thieves—have more honor than you ever could."

Tzimena studied the prisoners for a moment before asking her next question. "Tell me true: What became of the soldiers sent into this forest? The ones bearing the missive that sent your master after me?"

"They died to a man," Dedrik said. "Honestly, we wanted

prisoners, for ransom. But they were strong men...brave men. They wouldn't surrender even when we offered quarter. We were forced to kill them because they wouldn't stop fighting."

"How many?" Tzimena asked, gaze cold.

Orhund and Dedrik exchanged a glance. It was Orhund who responded. "Eleven," he said. "I remember well because it seemed an odd number for a cavalry troop."

Tzimena turned and speared the lord marshal with her cold glare again. "Eleven men," she said quietly. "Your own. Men who trusted you. Who fought and died to preserve *your* honor—used like worms baiting a fishhook."

The lord marshal remained silent for a time. Then—

"I would not resist if you saw fit to kill me," he said soberly, sitting awkwardly with his broken arm and broken leg, the latter still unsplinted and horribly swollen. "I have failed my master and his crown and dishonored my office. That makes me unfit to see another sunrise."

Rem noted that the lord marshal made no mention of endangering the rest of them, nor of the many deaths now attributable to his actions.

"Which is why you shall," Tzimena snapped. "We're delivering you alive to your masters in Erald, Lord Marshal. And if there's any justice in this world, they'll give us the satisfaction of seeing you publicly shamed and executed."

The lord marshal said nothing to that. His eyes remained downcast.

Tzimena then turned back to the Devils. "Let these two go," she said. "I think there's been enough killing for one day."

Dedrik and Orhund stared, both gape mouthed and flabbergasted.

"Milady," Dedrik began.

"Go swiftly," she said, "before I change my mind."

★   ★   ★

They'd met an Eraldic cavalry unit in Pyka, a small, fortified settlement on the eastern borders of the Ethkeraldi. That unit escorted them the rest of the way to Erald, where ten days of arch and awkward tribunals and inquiries unfolded before the city's lord mayor, the duke's grand chancellor, and the city's high priest of the Church of Aemon, along with an army of privy council advisers, secretaries, notaries, and solicitors. Rem and Torval were housed in adjoining rooms in one of the meaner wings of the palace—probably chambers reserved for the servants of visiting dignitaries—while Tzimena, her last remaining swordmaidens, and old Wallenbrand were ensconced elsewhere—unknown and apart from the two watchwardens.

They were not misused or abused in any way—far from it, in fact. They were given use of the servants' bathhouse, their beds were comfortable and the bedclothes changed often, and food arrived in their chambers three times a day, regular as the tide. And yet the two of them could not entirely relax in their seemingly benign surroundings. Even after they'd decided they could trust the food and bathe in relative safety, neither of them could shake the fear of being quietly murdered in their sleep, victims of some fiction hatched by the Eraldic court to save the late duke's good reputation. And so, despite the relative comfort of their beds, the regular changes of sheets and blankets, and a steady diet, Rem and Torval had continued to take shifts through each night, one remaining awake while the other slept. By the third night, they'd both admitted they felt silly doing so, that their paranoia was probably excessive and misplaced.

But they hadn't stopped.

Neither one of them slept all the way through the night until the day finally came when all the survivors of the lord marshal's ill-starred train were gathered in the same tribunal chamber and heard the determinations of the Eraldic court.

The public comments offered by the ministers of the tribunal suggested that the late Duke Verin's plundering of the royal coffers to fund orcish mercenaries, privateering contracts, and clandestine ransoms was both illegal and hitherto undiscovered. Apparently there was a great deal of coin missing from the royal treasury. Its vanishing could only have been Verin's doing—though Torval and Rem each suspected that more coin might have vanished in the days since their return...riches that could easily be pocketed, their theft attributed to a dead man.

The lord marshal was found guilty of dereliction of duty, misuse of crown resources, and reckless endangerment. He would hang, and the inherited title of lord marshal, protector of the realm and sword of the duke, long a source of pride in his family, would be stripped from his heirs.

Lady Tzimena Baya, having defended herself from misuse and murder, was guiltless. She—along with her two swordmaidens—would remain in Erald as guests of the court until a large honor guard could arrive from her home country to escort her in safety back to where she'd come from.

The two watchwardens from Yenara, having arrested a wanted fugitive in the line of duty and embarked upon the long, dangerous journey to Erald in good faith, would be rewarded: fifty gold pieces were theirs, along with the court's sincere hope that their homeward journey would be uneventful, and that neither of them would find need to visit Erald again. Ever.

Indilen frowned upon hearing that. "Hardly sporting, making you feel so unwelcome."

Rem shrugged. "It was an ugly business for them, I suppose, and we were just a pair of unfortunate complications. Their cut into the reward rankled us both, but I suppose it was better than disappearing into an Eraldic coal mine or dying in our sleep, eh?"

They were outside now, having taken the lull in the festivities as a signal to seek a little privacy. They settled themselves into the cozy herb-and-vegetable garden Aarna kept, sandwiched between the King's Ass's aft end and the walls of its immediate neighbors on the block. There they sat, upon the wooden frame of a planter sprouting sweet basil, savory rosemary, and spearmint, a cool breeze twisting down into the narrow confines of their curious cloister from the open sky above.

Rem heard something: a slight, low moan, the sort one might offer in pleasure or relief. Indilen stiffened beside him; she'd heard it, too. The two of them peered into the darkened recesses of the narrow alley just beyond the wide-open back gate of the garden, searching for some sign of life.

There. Another low, sensual moan. It was a small sound, audible only when the wind subsided. Indilen finally patted Rem's leg and pointed toward the shadows. About ten yards off, two shadowy forms squirmed in the dark alleyway, pressed against one of the stone gateposts marking the edge of the garden. Those intermittent moans, it seemed, were offered between soft caresses and passionate kisses.

Rem and Indilen shared grins and stifled giggles.

"Should we leave them?" Indilen asked quietly.

"It's a public garden and I'm settled here now," Rem said. "If we keep quiet, they'll never notice us."

Rem put his arm around Indilen then and held her close. He buried his nose in her hair. Inhaled. Savored. Truth be told, he'd like to take her to his own dark corner about now...or back to their rented rooms.

"Were you there," Indilen finally asked, "for the end?"

"Of the lord marshal?" Rem asked.

Indilen nodded.

"We were," Rem said with a sigh. "Partially because the court demanded it—some Eraldic pap about bearing witness to the results of one's sworn testimony. I suppose we also wanted to know he'd gotten what was coming to him. Big turnout—right in the city's main square, beside that waterfall Brekkon had told us about." He shook his head. "As it should be, I suppose...but it gave me no pleasure."

"But they heard you," Indilen said. "They heard you *all*, and your words brought about justice."

"Justice," Rem said, almost wistfully. He knew it was true, of course. Tzimena's sincere gratitude and her last tearful goodbye to him had proven that. It really hadn't hit him until that moment—offering farewells and trying to finally treat her like the noble lady he knew she was—but her words, her tears, and the warmth of her embrace had made the profundity of his actions clear at last.

Please, milady, he'd said as she'd held him tightly, *I was just protecting someone in need. Doing my job.*

You saved my life, she'd answered. *That's no small thing. If I can ever repay you...*

No, he'd said, pulling himself away and trying to smile so that she knew he honestly wanted nothing from her. *No, milady, you owe me nothing. Knowing you're safe is enough.*

Send him one of those fancy blades, Torval had broken in, indicating Elvaris. The swordmaiden stood just a few feet behind her mistress, a striking figure in a new suit of silk and linen, her plate and chain mail being cleaned by the duke's own armorers. Though she was dressed as a civilian, the handsome lady still wore her Taverando at her hip.

Torval, shush, Rem snapped.

Tzimena, to Rem's great relief, hadn't been embarrassed or insulted. She'd only smiled. *The girl you told me of*, she said, *is very lucky to have you, Rem. If only I could find a man of noble birth with half your character . . .*

The sound of kisses from the couple in the alley invaded Rem's thoughts: soft, wet. Another moan. A low, gravelly sigh.

"Do you ever miss it?" Indilen asked, her voice still low so as not to disturb their snogging neighbors.

Rem turned to her. "Miss what?"

"Before," she said. "The court."

Rem thought about his answer before offering it. "Sometimes," he said, "I miss the ease. I miss good food and fine clothes. I miss a castle keep to call my home and a stable full of horses I handpicked. I miss sunny afternoons hawking and presiding over feasts or fetes—when I felt like I was giving something instead of taking it."

He stopped, studied her. Indilen's face was open, understanding. She wasn't asking for a comparison—old life versus new—simply a window into his heart.

"I should think anyone would miss those things," she said.

"But all those things," Rem continued, "as pleasant as they are, came with too high a price."

"Civilization," Indilen said, "at its most decadent and sumptuous."

Rem shook his head. "No, civilization at its most naked—its most base. The everyday people that crowd this city—blacksmiths, greengrocers, brewers, and day laborers, all struggling to get by, creating mechanisms and institutions to make the collective effort less taxing, less terrifying—*that's* civilization. What Korin Lyr couldn't escape and what his brother and the lord marshal followed through on . . . that was savagery.

It might have worn ermine and silks, but it was primitive none-theless: plotting, backstabbing, power wrested and fought over and wrested again. Nature itself isn't half so vile or treacherous."

Indilen nodded, seeming to understand. For a moment she lowered her eyes, gathered a thought, then lifted her gaze again and met Rem's own. "I've thought about him, ever since that day you left. My whole experience of him came solely from the walk between the watchkeep and Roylan's Square, but something about him stuck with me."

Rem stared, not sure where this was going.

"He reminded me of you," Indilen said.

Rem wasn't sure how he felt about that. "Oh?"

"A young man desperate to make his own way, to forge his own path—to be a thing of his own making, secure in himself and beholden to none."

"You gleaned all that?" Rem asked. "Just from a walk and a few glances?"

"Well," Indilen said, "your tales of what came after have filled in a few blank spaces for me. But you shouldn't act so shocked. You saw it, too. That's what's weighing on you now, I think: You're wondering how much the two of you might share. If you, deep down, may be just like him."

Rem was stunned. He wanted to refute her words, her assumptions... but he couldn't. For the life of him, he couldn't.

"But," Indilen hastily added, "there is one great difference between you, so far as I can see. He didn't have your character. You ran off to test yourself—to *find* yourself. That one—I don't think he ever found anything. He was just a scared little boy, hiding in the woods. Playing roles, but never sure who he was when the mask was off."

Rem exhaled the breath he'd been holding. Nodded. That did make sense. In truth, he had thought about Korin Lyr a number of times since they buried him. He, too, felt the kinship between them...and imagined more than a few ways in which, given the right circumstances, Rem could have become him.

"I know the feeling," Rem said, and felt the sting of a tear in his eye. Aemon's bones, not now! This was not the time or the place. But when he carried on speaking, he heard a quaver in his voice—low, but present nonetheless. "In truth, I sometimes wonder who I am, now that I'm no longer the man I was—"

Indilen kissed him. It was quick, soft, but heartfelt and eager, a gesture of comfort and reassurance. "I know who you are, because I see what you do, every day."

Rem held her face in his hands. "I was going to say—when those questions subside, when I know who I am, it's because I have *you* to assure me. Maybe I did run off to hide in the wilderness...but you're the one who found me and saved me from myself. I can never repay you for that."

Indilen smiled and laid her head upon his shoulder. "That sword cuts both ways," she said. "We saved each other."

He held her for a long time, rocking her gently, the sounds of the city swirling around them as the shadowed couple in the alley continued their amorous liaison and an old lover's ballad wafted from the open windows of the King's Ass. Rem had never known such warmth, such contentment, as he did in that moment. He was just about to lift Indilen's face again, to kiss her again, when he heard a great commotion: a table overturned, pewter plates and ale steins clattering across the rush-strewn floor of the tavern, the metallic slither of blades leaving scabbards. A woman screamed. Someone begged: *None of that! None of that!*

Indilen stiffened beside him. She heard it, too.

"No no no no," Rem muttered. He'd so been enjoying the evening...

The couple in the alley heard the commotion, as well. At the first clatter of dishes, their kissing and groping ceased. With the sound of drawn blades, one of them stepped out of the darkness and into the light.

Rem had to stifle a burst of laughter. It was Torval who'd just stepped into the dim secondhand light from a lamp by the back door of the King's Ass. Just behind him, emerging from the shadowy alleyway, was Aarna. Her dark curls were disheveled and the upper laces of her bodice hastily undone.

"Oh my," Rem said.

"About time," Indilen added.

Torval stepped toward the door, eager to break up the erupting fight—but he froze when he realized that Rem and Indilen were there, staring at him. When Aarna saw them, sitting so close and staring with (Rem imagined) bald shock on their faces, she did what came most naturally to her: she burst out laughing, long and loud.

"So much for a secret rendezvous," she said between howls.

Torval did his best to look unperturbed, though Rem did relish the fact that—for the very first time in his memory—Torval actually looked embarrassed, like a child caught in some naughty act. The dwarf powered through it, though, immediately scrunching his face into his customary scowl and jerking his head toward the doorway. Inside, insults were hurled and feet thumped over floorboards as people scurried for safety or a good view of what about to unfold.

"Well?" Torval growled, and marched inside.

Aarna propped herself against the stone gatepost of the garden's outer wall now. She was still laughing.

Rem looked to Indilen. Indilen indicated the door. "They need you, good watchwarden."

"I'd really rather not," Rem said.

"I know," Indilen answered. "But then who would you be?"

He smiled. Clever girl.

With a sigh he rose from the planter and strode toward the door. As he stepped back into the warm, bread- and meat-scented air of the King's Ass, he heard Indilen joining Aarna in raucous laughter behind him.

ACKNOWLEDGMENTS

Here we are, at the end of another adventure, settling back into our daily routines, awaiting the next call—whenever it might come—to leave our cozy nests and venture out into the wide world. I sincerely hope you've enjoyed what I've come to think of as "Rem and Torval's Road Movie" and assure you that, Fates willing, our two miscreants shall return for more buddy love and two-fisted adventure on Yenara's cramped and muddy streets. This outing was brought to you by the amazing team at Orbit, including my hardworking, keen-eyed editor, Bradley Englert, whose notes and insights keep my work both narratively consistent and emotionally honest. Great editors are worth their weight in gold, and Bradley is a great editor.

Special thanks, as well, to my ever-loyal agent, Emily Keyes, for her continued support and hustle. Writers are strange and squirrelly creatures at the best of times, thus to make long-term investments of time, interest, and enthusiasm in such mercurial beings is an act of tremendous faith. I can't say thank you enough for Emily's faith in me.

As usual, I'd be remiss if I did not offer shout-outs to my family—my lovely Liliana; my beautiful son, Gabriel; and my parents, Carol and Jim—whose faith in me never waivers, even when I have none in myself.

And finally, readers, I'd like to thank all of you. At the end of the day, Rem and Torval live, breathe, laugh, love, and fight because of the power of your belief in them. To all of you who've walked Yenara's streets with me, who've reached out to tell me that you love these characters, that you enjoy the time you spend in their world, and that my words made a hard day better, a long night less lonely: sincerely, I cannot thank you enough.

So as the prefect says, keep your eyes open, your fists clenched, and your backs to the wall. The streets are mean, the alleys winding, and the going hard, but with the right partner by your side, you'll make it to the dawn.

Dale Lucas
January 2019

extras

www.orbitbooks.net

about the author

Dale Lucas is a novelist, screenwriter, civil servant, and armchair historian from St. Petersburg, Florida. Once described by a colleague as "a compulsive researcher who writes fiction to store his research in," he's the author of numerous works of fantasy, neo-pulp, and horror. When not writing at home or trapped in a cubicle at his day job, he loves travel, great food, and buying more books than he'll ever be able to read.

Find out more about Dale Lucas and other Orbit authors by registering for the free monthly newsletter at www.orbitbooks.net

if you enjoyed
THE FIFTH WARD: GOOD COMPANY

look out for

THE THOUSAND DEATHS OF ARDOR BENN

by

TYLER WHITESIDES

Ardor Benn is no ordinary thief – a master of wildly complex heists, he styles himself a Ruse Artist Extraordinaire.

When a mysterious priest hires him for the most daring ruse yet, Ardor knows he'll need more than quick wit and sleight of hand. Assembling a dream team of forgers, disguisers, schemers and thieves, he sets out to steal from the most powerful king the realm has ever known.

But it soon becomes clear there's more at stake than fame and glory – Ard and his team might just be the last hope for human civilisation.

CHAPTER

1

Ardor Benn was running late. Or was he? Ard preferred to think that everyone else in the Greater Chain was consistently early—with unreasonable expectations for him to be the same.

Regardless, this time it was all right to keep his appointment waiting. It was a stew tactic. And stew tasted better the longer it cooked.

Ard skipped up the final stairs and onto the third floor. Remaught Azel clearly wasn't the big fish he purported. Rickety wooden tri-story in the slums of Marow? Ard found the whole thing rather distasteful. Especially after Lord Yunis. Now, that was something! Proper stone mansion with a Heat Grit hearth in every room. Servants. Cooks. Light Grit lanterns that ignited with the pull of a chain. Ard half suspected that Lord Yunis wiped his backside with lace.

Different island. Different ruse. Today was about Remaught Azel, no matter how unaccommodating his hideout appeared.

Ard shifted the Grit keg from one arm to the other as he reached the closed door at the end of the hallway. The creaking floorboards would have already notified Remaught that someone was coming. *Interesting*, Ard thought. *Maybe there is something useful about holing up in a joint like this. Floorboard sentries.*

The door swung open, but before Ard could step through, a hairy, blue-skinned arm pressed into his chest, barring entrance.

"Take it easy," Ard said to the Trothian man. This would be

Remaught's bodyguard. His dark, vibrating eyes glared at Ard. Classic. This guy seemed like a tough son of a gun, although he was obviously past due for one of those Agrodite saltwater soaks. The skin on his arm looked like it might start flaking off.

"I'm a legitimate businessman," Ard continued, "here to do... legitimate businessy things."

He glanced past the large bodyguard to the table where Remaught sat, bathed in sunlight from the western window. The mobster wore a maroon velvet vest, a tricornered hat, and a shoulder cape, currently fashionable among the rich folk. Remaught seemed tense, watching his bodyguard detain Ard at the doorway.

"Search him."

"Really?" Ard protested, holding the Grit keg above his head so the bodyguard could pat his sides. "I left my belt and guns at home," he said. "And if I hadn't, I could easily shoot you from where I'm standing, so I find this whole pat down a little unnecessary, and frankly uncomfortable."

The bodyguard paused, one hand on Ard's hip pocket. "What's this?" he asked, his voice marked by a thick Trothian accent.

"Rocks," Ard answered.

"Rocks?" Like the bodyguard had never heard of such things. "Take them out—slow."

Ard reached casually into his pocket and scooped out a handful of small stones that he'd collected on the roadside before entering the building. "I'll need these for the transaction."

In response, the Trothian bodyguard swatted Ard's hand, sending the dusty pebbles scattering across the room.

"Now, that was quite uncalled-for," Ard said to the mobster at the table. "I find your man to be unnecessarily rough."

"Suno?" replied Remaught. "Three cycles ago, he would have fed you those rocks—through your nose. Going soft, I fear. Fatherhood has a tendency to do that."

Ard wondered what kind of father a mobster's bodyguard would be. Some fathers made a living at the market or the factories. This guy made a living by stringing people up by their toes at the whim of his boss.

The Trothian moved down, feeling around Ard's thighs with both hands.

"At the very least, you should consider hiring a good-looking woman for this step," Ard continued. "Wouldn't hurt business, you know."

The bodyguard stepped back and nodded to Remaught, who gestured for Ard to enter the room.

"Were you followed?" Remaught asked.

Ard laughed as he set the Grit keg gently on the table, stirring a bit of dust that danced in the sun rays. "I am never followed." He adjusted the gaudy ring on his index finger and sat down across from the mobster. "Except occasionally by a bevy of beautiful maidens."

Ard smiled, but Remaught Azel did not return the gesture. Instead, the mobster reached out for the Grit keg. Ard was faster, whisking the keg away before Remaught could touch it.

Ard clicked his tongue. "How about we see some payment before I go handing over the Grit in a room where I'm unarmed and outnumbered?"

Remaught pushed backward in his chair, the wooden legs buzzing against the floor. The mobster crossed the room and retrieved a locked safe box from the window seat. It was no longer than his forearm, with convenient metal handles fastened on both sides. The Regulation seal was clearly displayed on the front beside the keyhole.

"That looks mighty official," Ard said as Remaught placed it on the table. "Regulation issue, isn't it?"

"I recently came by the box," replied Remaught, dusting his hands. "I like to keep my transactions secure. There are crooked folk in these parts."

"So I hear," answered Ard. "And how do I know the safe box isn't full of sand?"

"How do I know that Grit keg isn't empty?"

Ard shrugged, a smirk on his face. They had reached the part of the exchange that Ard called the Final Distrust. One last chance to back out. For both of them.

Remaught broke the tension by reaching into his velvet vest and producing a key. He slipped it into the lock, turned it sharply, and lifted the lid.

Ard squinted at the coinlike items. They looked real enough in this lighting. Most were stamped with seven small indentations, identifying them as seven-mark Ashings, the highest denomination of currency.

"May I?" Ard plucked out a coin before Remaught granted permission. Ard lifted the Ashing to his mouth and bit down on the edge of it.

"Taste real enough for you?" Remaught asked. Ard's relaxed nature seemed to be driving the man continuously more tense.

Ard studied the spot where his teeth had pressed against the coin, angling it in the sunlight to check for any kind of indentation. He preferred to gouge suspicious coins with a knifepoint, but, well, Remaught had made it pretty clear that weapons were not allowed at this meeting.

The Ashing seemed genuine. And if Remaught wasn't planning to slight him, there would be 493 more in that safe box.

"You ever been to the Coinery on Talumon?" Ard flicked the coin back into the open box. "I was there a few years back. On legitimate business, of course."

Remaught closed the lid and turned the key.

"Coining," Ard went on. "Sparks, that's an elaborate process. Just the effort it takes to grind those raw scales into perfect circles...And you know they follow up with a series of chemical washes. They say it's for curing and hardening. I hardly think a dragon scale needs hardening…"

Across the table, Remaught was fidgeting. Ard suppressed a grin.

"Is something wrong, Rem? Can I call you Rem?" Ard pressed. "I thought this information would be of particular interest to a man in your line of work."

"Perhaps you can save the details for some other time," Remaught said. "You're not my only appointment today."

Ard leaned back in his chair, pretending that the mobster's words had really put him out.

"I'd prefer if we just get along with the transaction." Remaught gestured to the Grit keg. "What do you have for me there?"

"One full panweight of Void Grit," said Ard. "My source says the batch is top quality. Came from a good-sized block of indigestible granite. Passed through the dragon in less than five days. Properly fired, and processed to the finest of powder." He unlatched the cap on the Grit keg and tilted it toward Remaught. "The amount we agreed upon. And at an unbeatable price. I'm a man of my word."

"It would seem that you are," answered the mobster. "But of course you understand that I'll need a demonstration of the product."

Ard nodded slowly. Not all Grit could be demonstrated, especially indoors. But he had been expecting such a demand for this transaction.

Ard turned to the Trothian bodyguard, who leaned in the doorway like he was holding up the frame. "I'll be needing those rocks now."

Remaught grunted, then snapped at his bodyguard. "Suno! Pick up the blazing stones."

Wordlessly, the man hunted across the floor for the stones he had slapped away. As he searched, Ard quickly picked up the safe box, causing Remaught to jump.

"Relax," Ard said, crossing the room and carefully setting the valuable box on the wooden window seat. "I'll need the table cleared for the demonstration."

A moment later, Suno handed the rocks to Ard and lumbered back to the doorway, folding his dry, cracking arms.

There were nine little rocks, and Ard spread them into a loose ring on the tabletop. He unclasped the Grit keg and was about to reach inside, when Remaught grabbed his arm.

"I pick the Grit," the mobster demanded. "No tricks."

Ard shrugged, offering the container to Remaught. The man slipped his hand inside and withdrew a pinch of grayish powder. Ard pointed to the center of the stone ring and Remaught deposited the Grit in a tiny mound.

"That enough?" Remaught asked, as Ard brushed the pinch of powder into a tidier pile.

"More than enough," Ard said. "You trying to clear the whole room?" He clasped the lid on the Grit keg and set it on the floor behind him. "I assume you have a Slagstone ignitor?"

From his vest, Remaught produced the device Ard had asked for. It was a small steel rod, slightly flattened at one end. Affixed at the center point along the rod was a spring, and attached to the end of the spring was a small piece of Slagstone.

Remaught handed the ignitor to Ard, the tiny fragment of Slagstone wobbling on its spring. "With the amount of Void Grit you've laid down, I'd expect the blast radius to be about two feet." Ard said it as a warning. Remaught caught the hint and took a large step backward.

Ard also positioned himself as far from the table as he could, while still able to reach the tiny pile of gray Grit. He took aim and knocked the flat end of the steel rod against the table. The impact brought the spring down and the small piece of attached Slagstone struck the metal rod.

A respectable spark leapt off the Slagstone. It flashed across the wooden table and vanished instantly, with no effect.

"Ha!" Remaught shouted, as though he'd been waiting to make an accusation. "I should have known no one would sell a panweight of Void Grit at that price."

Ard looked up. "The Grit is legitimate, I assure you. This Slagstone ignitor, on the other hand..." He held up the device, gently shaking the spring as though it were a child's toy. "Honestly, I didn't even know they sold something this cheap. I couldn't ignite a *mountain* of Grit with this thing, let alone convince the spark to fall on that pinhead target. Allow me to throw a few more sparks before you let Suno rip my ears off."

The truth was, the tiny pile of powdered granite hadn't lit for two reasons. First, Remaught's Slagstone ignitor really was terribly inaccurate. And second, the Void Grit was definitely fake.

Ard leaned closer to the table, pretending to give the ignitor a close inspection. With his right hand hovering just above the pile of gray powder, he wriggled his fingers, spinning his heavy ring around so he could slip his thumbnail into a small groove and slide the face of the ring aside.

The gesture was subtle, and Ard was drawing Remaught's attention to the ignitor. He was sure the mobster hadn't noticed the fresh deposit of genuine Void Grit from the ring's secret cavity.

"Let's see if this does the trick." Ard repositioned himself, bringing the ignitor down, Slagstone sparking on impact.

The genuine Void Grit detonated instantly, the powder from Ard's ring creating a blast radius just over a foot. It wasn't at all like a deadly Blast Grit explosion of fire and sparks. This was Specialty Grit, and the particular demonstrated effect was far less dangerous.

A rush of energy emanated from the pinch of Void Grit, like a tremendous wind blasting outward in every direction from the center.

It happened much faster than Ard could withdraw his hand. Caught in the detonation, his arm was shoved backward, the Slagstone ignitor flying from his grasp. The stones on the table flew in every direction, the Grit pushing them to the perimeter of the blast, their momentum sending them bouncing across the floor.

The Void Grit was spent, but hovering around the table where the detonation occurred was a dome of discolored air. It would have been a spherical cloud if it had detonated midair, but the tabletop had been strong enough to contain the underside of the blast.

Remaught stumbled a step closer. "How did you do that?"

Ard wrinkled his forehead. "What do you mean? It's Void Grit. Digested granite. That's what it does." He bent down and retrieved a fallen pebble. "It voids a space within the blast radius. Clears everything out to the perimeter. The effect should last about ten minutes before the blast cloud burns out."

To prove his point, Ard tossed the pebble into the dome of discolored air. The little stone barely touched the perimeter before the effect of the Grit pushed it forcefully away.

Remaught nodded absently, his hand drifting to his vest pocket. For a brief moment, Ard thought the mobster might pull a Singler, but he relaxed when Remaught withdrew the key to the safe box. Remaught stepped forward and set the key on the edge of the table, just outside the hazy Void cloud.

"I'm ready to close the deal," he said, producing a few papers for Ard's inspection. Detonation licenses—or at least forgeries—which would allow him to purchase Grit.

But Ard wasn't interested in the legalities of the transaction. He dismissed the paperwork, picking up the keg of false Void Grit and holding it out to Remaught.

"Of course, I'll need a receipt," said the mobster, tucking his licenses back into his vest.

"A receipt?" That sounded frightfully legitimate to Ardor Benn.

"For my records," said Remaught. In a moment, the man had

produced a small square of paper, and a charcoal scribing stick. "Go ahead and notate the details of the transaction. And sign your name at the bottom."

Ard handed the Grit keg to Remaught and accepted the paper and charcoal. Remaught stepped away, and it took only moments for Ard to write what was needed, autographing the bottom as requested.

"I hope we can do business again in the future," Ard said, looking up from his scrawling. But Remaught Azel didn't seem to share his sentiment.

"I'm afraid that will not be the case." The mobster was standing near the open doorway, his Trothian bodyguard off to one side. Remaught had removed the cap from the Grit keg and was holding the cheap Slagstone ignitor.

"Whoa!" Ard shouted. "What are you—"

Remaught brought the ignitor down. A cluster of sparks danced from the impact, showering onto the gray powder housed in the open keg.

"Did you really think I wouldn't recognize an entire keg of counterfeit Grit?" Remaught asked.

Ard crumpled the receipt and dropped it to the floor, lunging for the key on the edge of the table. He scooped it up, but before Ard could reach the safe box, the Trothian bodyguard was upon him. In the blink of an eye, Ard found himself in a headlock, forced to his knees before a smug Remaught.

"I believe I mentioned that I had another appointment today?" Remaught said. "What I didn't tell you was that the appointment is happening now. With an officer of the Regulation."

A man appeared in the doorway behind Remaught. Not just a man—a veritable mountain. He had dark skin, and his nose was somewhat flat, the side of his face marked with a thin scar. The Regulator ducked his shiny, bald head under the door frame as he entered the room.

He wore the standard long wool coat of the Regulation, a cross-bow slung over one shoulder and a sash of bolts across his broad chest. Beneath the coat, Ard thought he could see the bulge of a holstered gun.

"Delivered as promised," Remaught said, his tension at an all-new high. The Regulator seized Ard's upper arm with an iron grip, prompting Remaught's bodyguard to release the headlock.

"What is this, Remaught?" Ard asked between gasps for air. "You're selling me out? Don't you know who I am?"

"That's just it," said Remaught. "I know exactly who you are. Ardor Benn, ruse artist."

"Extraordinaire," said Ard.

"Excuse me?" Remaught asked.

"Ardor Benn, ruse artist extraordinaire," Ard corrected.

The giant Regulator yanked Ard to his feet. Prying Ard's fingers open, the man easily removed the key to the safe box before slapping a pair of shackles around Ard's wrists.

"Now wait a minute, big fella," Ard stalled. "You can arrest *me*, an amicable ruse artist trying to eke out a humble living. Or you can take in Remaught Azel. Think it through. Remaught Azel. *He's* the mobster."

The bald Regulator didn't even falter. He stepped forward and handed the key to Remaught with a curt nod.

"The Regulator and I have an understanding," answered Remaught. "He came to me three weeks ago. Said there was a ruse artist in town selling counterfeit Grit. Said that if I came across anyone trying to hock large quantities of Specialty Grit, that I should set up a meet and reach out to him."

"Flames, Remaught! You've gone clean?" Ard asked. "A mobster of your standing, working with a Reggie like him? You disgust me."

"Clean? No," Remaught replied. "And neither is my Regulator friend."

Ard craned his neck to shoot an incredulous stare at the Regulator holding him. "Unbelievable! A dirty Reggie and a petty mobster make a deal—and I'm the victim!"

Remaught addressed the big official. "We're good, then?"

The large man nodded. "We're good. I was never here."

The Regulator pushed Ard past Remaught, through the doorway, and into the creaky hallway, pausing to say one last thing to the mobster. "You got him to sign a receipt like I told you?"

Remaught scanned the room and gestured to the crumpled piece of paper on the floor. "You need it for evidence?"

"Nah," said the Regulator. "This lowlife's wanted on every island in the Greater Chain. The receipt was for your own protection. Proves you had every intention of making a legal transaction. Buying Grit isn't a crime, providing you have the proper licensure." He gave Ard a shove in the back, causing him to stumble across the rickety floorboards. "Give me plenty of time to distance myself before you leave this building," the Regulator instructed. "Understood?"

Ard glanced back in time to see Remaught nodding as the door swung shut. Ard and the Regulator descended the stairs in silence, the huge man never removing his iron grip from Ard's shoulder. It wasn't until they stepped outside into the warm afternoon that Ard spoke.

"Lowlife?" he said. "Really, Raek? That seemed a bit much. Like you were enjoying it."

"Don't lecture me on 'a bit much,'" answered the Regulator. "What was that whole 'ruse artist extraordinaire' slag?"

"You know I like that line. I saw an opportunity and I took it," Ard answered.

Raek grunted, tugging at the collar of his uniform. "This coat itches. No wonder we can always outrun the blazing Reggies. They're practically choking themselves on the job."

"You almost look convincing," Ard said. "But where's the Reggie helmet?"

"I couldn't find one that fit," answered Raek. "And besides, I figure I'm tall enough no one can see the top of my head. Maybe I'm wearing a tiny Reggie helmet. No one would know."

"Sound logic," Ard said as they turned the corner to the west side of Remaught's building. "You swapped the key?"

"Child's play," Raek answered. "You leave the note?"

"I even drew a little smiling face after my name."

Raek led them to a sturdy hay wagon hitched to a waiting horse.

"Straw this time?" Ard asked, finding it difficult to climb onto the bench with his hands still shackled.

"Should pad the landing," Raek replied.

"Look at you! Good idea."

"You're not the only person who can have one, you know." Raek pulled himself onto the bench beside Ard and stooped to grab the reins. "You're getting bored, Ard."

"Hmm?" He glanced at his friend.

"This little stunt." Raek gestured up to the third-story window directly above them. "It's showy, even for you."

Ard dismissed the comment. Was there a simpler way to steal the safe box? Probably. But surely there wasn't a more clever way.

Remaught had to be feeling pretty smug. In his mind, the exchange had gone off without a hitch. The mobster had been gifted a Regulation-issue safe box, partnered with a crooked Reggie, and taken some competition off the streets by having the ruse artist arrested.

By now, Remaught was probably reading Ard's note on the receipt—a simple message thanking the mobster for the Ashings and informing him that the Reggie was as fake as the Grit. This would undoubtedly send Remaught scurrying to the safe box to check its valuable contents. All he needed to do was thrust Raek's replacement key into the lock, and... *boom*.

Any moment now.

The idle horse stamped its hooves, awaiting Raek's directions.

"We're sparked if he moves the safe box," Raek muttered after a moment's silence.

"He won't," Ard reassured. "Remaught's lazy."

"He could have the bodyguard do it."

"Suno was going soft," Ard repeated what he'd heard from Remaught. "Something about fatherhood. I'm more worried that the window won't break…"

Three stories above, the glass window shattered. The safe box came hurtling out on a perfect trajectory, landing in the back of the hay-stuffed wagon with a thud.

Remaught Azel was blazing predictable. Classic mobster. Maybe Ard *was* getting bored.

"I'm actually surprised that worked," Ard admitted, as Raek snapped the reins and sent the horse galloping down the street.

"That doesn't give me much confidence. Tampering with the safe box was *your* idea."

"I knew *that* would work," Ard said. They'd tipped the replacement key with a tiny fragment of Slagstone and filled the inside of the lock with Void Grit. The detonation would have cleared everything within the blast radius, undoubtedly throwing Remaught backward. The box of Ashings, still latched shut, was hurtled outward by the force of the Grit, smashing through the glass panes and falling three stories to the hay wagon waiting on the street below.

"I had full trust in the Grit." Ard gestured behind him. "I'm just surprised the box actually landed where it was supposed to!"

"Physics," Raek said. "You trust the Grit, but you don't trust physics?"

"Not if I'm doing the math."

"Oh, come on," said the large man. "Two and a half granules of Void Grit detonated against a safe box weighing twenty-eight pan-weights falling from a third-story window…"

Ard held up his still-shackled hands. "It physically hurts me to hear you talk like that. Actual pain in my actual brain."

Behind them, from the shattered window of Remaught's hideout, three gunshots pealed out, breaking the lazy silence of the afternoon.

"Remaught? He's shooting at us?" Raek asked.

"He can't hope to hit us at this distance," answered Ard. "Even with a Fielder, that shot is hopeless."

Another gunshot resounded, and this time a lead ball struck the side of the wagon with a violent crack. Ard flinched and Raek cursed. The shot had not come from Remaught's distant window. This gunman was closer, but Ard couldn't tell from what direction he was firing.

"Remaught's shots were a signal," Ard assumed. "He must have had his goons in position in case things went wrong with his new Reggie soulmate."

"We're not soulmates," Raek muttered.

A man on horseback emerged from an alleyway behind them, his dark cloak flapping, hood up. The mob goon stretched out one hand and Ard saw the glint of a gun. He barely had time to shout a warning to Raek, both men ducking before the goon fired.

The ball went high. Ard heard it whizzing overhead. It was a Singler. Ard recognized the timbre of the shot. As its name implied, the small gun could shoot only one ball before needing to be reloaded. The six-shot Rollers used by the Regulators were far more deadly. Not to mention ridiculously expensive and illegal for use by the common citizen.

The goon had wasted his single ball, too eager to fire on the escaping ruse artists. He could reload, of course, but the process was nearly impossible on the back of a galloping horse. Instead, the goon holstered his Singler and drew a thin-bladed rapier.

"Give me the key," Ard said as another horseman appeared behind the first.

"What key?" replied Raek. "The one I swapped from Remaught?"

"Not that one." Ard held up his chained wrists and jangled them next to Raek's ear. "The key to the shackles."

"Oh." Raek spit off the side of the wagon. "I don't have it."

"You lost the key?" Ard shouted.

"I didn't lose it," answered Raek. "Never had it. I stole the shackles from a Reggie outpost. I didn't really have time to hunt around for keys."

Ard threw his chained hands in the air. "You locked me up without a way to get me out?"

Raek shrugged. "Figured we'd deal with that problem later."

A cloaked figure on foot suddenly ducked out of a shanty, the butt of a long-barreled Fielder tucked against his shoulder.

Raek transferred the reins to his left hand, reached into his Regulator coat, and drew a Roller. He pointed the gun at the goon with the Fielder, used his thumb to pull back the Slagstone hammer, and pulled the trigger.

The Slagstone snapped down, throwing a spark into the first chamber to ignite a pinch of powdered Blast Grit in a paper cartridge. It detonated with a deafening crack, the metal gun chamber containing the explosion and throwing a lead ball out the barrel.

The ball splintered through the wall of the shanty behind the goon. Before he could take proper aim at the passing wagon, Raek pulled back the Slagstone hammer and fired again.

Another miss, but it was enough to put the goon behind them. Raek handed the smoking Roller to Ard. "Here," the big man said. "I stole this for you."

"Wow." Ard awkwardly accepted the gun with both wrists chained. "It looks just like the one I left holstered in *my* gun belt at the boat."

"Oh, this gun belt?" Raek brushed aside the wool Reggie coat to reveal a second holstered gun. "You shouldn't leave valuable things lying around."

"It was in a locked compartment," Ard said, sighting down his Roller. "I gave you the key."

"That was your mistake."

Behind them, the Fielder goon finally got his shot off. The resounding pop of the big gun was deep and powerful. Straw exploded in the back of the wagon, and one of the side boards snapped clean off as the Fielder ball clawed its way through.

"Why don't you try to make something of that Reggie crossbow?" Ard said. "I'll handle the respectable firearms."

"There's nothing disrespectful about a crossbow," Raek answered. "It's a gentleman's weapon."

Ard glanced over his shoulder to find the swordsman riding dangerously close. He used his thumb to set the Slagstone hammer, the action spinning the chambers and moving a fresh cartridge and ball into position. But with both hands shackled together, he found it incredibly awkward to aim over his shoulder.

"Flames," Ard muttered. He'd have to reposition himself if he had any hope of making a decent shot. Pushing off the footboard, Ard cleared the low backboard and tumbled headfirst into the hay.

"I hope you did that on purpose!" Raek shouted, giving the reins another flick.

Ard rolled onto his knees as the mounted goon brought his sword down in a deadly arc. Ard reacted instinctively, catching the thin blade against the chains of his shackles.

For a brief moment, Ard knelt, keeping the sword above his head. Then he twisted his right hand around, aimed the barrel of his Roller, and pulled the trigger. In a puff of Blast smoke, the lead ball tore through the goon, instantly throwing him from the saddle.

Ard shook his head, pieces of loosely clinging straw falling from his short dark hair. He turned his attention to the street behind, where more than half a dozen of Remaught's men were riding to catch up. The nearest one fired, a Singler whose ball might have taken him if Raek hadn't turned a corner so sharply.

The wagon wheels drifted across the compact dirt, and Ard heard a few of the wooden spokes snapping under the strain. They were almost out of the slums, but still a fair distance from the docks. Raek's stolen hay wagon was not going to see them to their journey's end. Unless the journey ended with a gut full of lead.

Ard gripped the Roller in both hands. Not his preferred way of aiming, but his best alternative since his wrists were hooked together. Squinting one eye, he tried to steady his aim, waiting for the first goon to round the corner.

The rider appeared, hunched low on his horse. Ard fired once. The man dropped from the saddle, but six more appeared right behind him. And Ard's Roller only packed two more shots.

"We need something heavier to stop these goons!" Ard shouted. "You got any Grit bolts on that sash?"

Raek glanced down at the ammunition sash across his chest. "Looks like an assortment. Anything specific you're after?"

"I don't know ... I was hoping for some Visitant Grit," Ard joked as he reached over and pulled the crossbow off Raek's shoulder.

Raek chuckled. "Like you'd be worthy to summon a Paladin Visitant."

"Hey, I can be downright righteous if I need to be," he answered.

Ard didn't favor the crossbow. He preferred the jarring recoil of a Roller, the heat from the flames that licked out the end of the barrel. The lingering smell of smoke.

"Barrier Grit." Raek carefully reached back to hand Ard a bolt from his sash. The projectile was like a stout arrow, black fletchings fixed to the shaft. The Grit bolt had a clay ball serving as an arrowhead, the tip dyed bright blue.

The bolt was an expensive shot, even though Barrier Grit was one of the five common Grit types. Inside the clay arrowhead, a chip of Slagstone was nestled into a measurement of glittering dust: digested shards of metal that had been dragon-fired and processed to powder.

Ard slipped the bolt into the groove on the crossbow, fitting the nock against the string he had already pulled into place—a difficult task with chained wrists. The goons were gaining fast now. Definitely within range.

"What's the blast radius on this bolt?" Ard pulled the crossbow to his shoulder and sighted down the length.

"The bolts were already on the sash when I stole it," answered Raek. "I'm guessing it'll be standard issue. Fifteen feet or so. You'd know these things if you bothered to keep up your Grit licenses."

Ard sighted down the crossbow. "Seriously? We're riding in a stolen wagon, you're impersonating a Reggie, we're hauling five hundred Ashings we just swindled from a mobster…and you're lecturing me about licensure?"

"I'm a fan of the Grit licenses," Raek said. "If anyone could purchase Grit whenever and wherever they wanted, the islands would be a mess of anarchy."

"I'm not just anybody," Ard replied. "I'm Ardor Benn…"

"Yeah, yeah. I got it," Raek cut him off. "Ruse artist extraordinaire. Just shoot the blazing bolt already."

Ard barely had to aim, the goons were riding so close now. He leveled the crossbow and pulled the trigger. The bolt released with a twang, finding its mark at the foot of the leading horse. The clay ball shattered on impact, and the Slagstone chip sparked, igniting the powdered metallic Grit.

The blast was nearly large enough to span the road. The discolored cloud made an instant dome, a hardened shell trapping two of the horsemen inside it. Their momentum carried them forward, striking the inside perimeter of the Barrier cloud.

The two horses went down, throwing their riders and crumpling as though they had galloped directly into a brick wall. A third rider also collided with the outside of the barrier dome, unable to stop his horse in time to avoid the obstacle suddenly blocking the road.

The two men within the Barrier cloud wouldn't be going anywhere until the Grit's effect burned out. They were trapped, as though a giant overturned bowl had suddenly enclosed them. Although the Barrier cloud seemed like it had a tangible shell, it couldn't be moved. And this dirt road was compact, so they wouldn't have a prayer at burrowing under the edge of the dome.

Ard grinned at the successful shot. "Haha! That'll buy us some time to reach the docks. Teach those goons not to mess with Ardor Benn and the Short Fuse."

"Come on, Ard," Raek muttered. "You know how I feel about that name."

"It's a solid name for a criminal Mixer like you." Ard understood why Raek thought it was unfitting. Raekon Dorrel was neither short nor impatient. Several years ago, during a particularly sticky ruse, Ard had referred to his partner as the Short Fuse. It was meant as little more than a joke, but somehow, the Regulation ended up circulating it through the streets until it stuck.

"Still don't think that's a respectable weapon?" Raek changed the subject, pushing the exhausted horse as they moved out of the slums.

"I'll leave the Grit shots to you." Ard handed the crossbow back to the driver. "I'll stick with lead and smoke."

Here, the road opened to a few grassy knolls that led right up to the cliff-like shoreline. The steep path down to the harbor was just ahead, where the *Double Take* was moored and waiting. Ard could see flags waving atop several ship masts, but with the high shoreline, it was impossible to see the harbor clearly.

"Clear ride to the docks today," Raek said. Now that he mentioned it, Ard thought the thoroughfare, usually bustling with pedestrians and the occasional cart or carriage, seemed abnormally still for a summer's afternoon.

"Something doesn't feel right," Ard muttered.

"Now, that's what you get for eating oysters for breakfast."

"I think we should stop," Ard whispered.

"Definitely," Raek replied. "We wouldn't want to outdistance those goons…" Raek was cut off as the wagon wheels hit a shallow trench across the dirt road.

Ard saw the sparks as the wheels struck a buried piece of Slagstone. He didn't even have time to grip the side of the wagon as the mine detonated.

Drift Grit.

A lot of it.

The blast radius must have been at least twenty yards, the center of the detonation occurring directly beneath the wagon. The discolored air hung in a hazy dome as the Grit took effect.

Ard felt his stomach churn as a bizarre weightlessness overtook him. The jolt from hitting the mine sent the wagon floating lazily upward, straw drifting in every direction. The horse's hooves left the road, and the poor animal bucked and whinnied, legs continuing to gallop in the sudden weightless environment.

"What was that?" Raek shouted. He still held the horse's reins, though his body had drifted off the wagon bench, his long wool coattails floating around his huge form.

"We hit a mine!" Ard answered. And the fact that it was Drift Grit didn't give him much hope. Barrier Grit would have been an inescapable trap, but at least they would have been safe inside the detonation. Adrift as they were now, he and Raek would be easy targets to anyone with a firearm. "They were waiting for us."

"Remaught?" Raek asked. "Sparks, we didn't give that guy enough credit!"

They were probably ten feet off the ground, Ard's legs pumping as though trying to swim through the air. He'd forgotten how disorienting and frustrating it was to hang suspended without any hint of gravity.

Now upside down, facing west toward the harbor, Ard saw more than a dozen mounted figures cresting the steep trail and riding out to meet them. He didn't need to see them upright to recognize the wool uniforms and helmets.

"Remaught didn't plant the mine," Ard shouted to Raek. "The Regulators did it. They knew we were coming."

"Flames!" Raek twisted in the air to see the horsemen Ard had just announced.

A gunshot pealed, and Ard saw the ball enter the Drift cloud. The shot went wide, exiting the detonated area just above their heads.

"We're sitting ducks!" Raek called, sun beating down on his bald head, dark skin glistening. "We've got to get our feet back on the ground."

Even if they could, exiting the Drift cloud now would put them face-to-face with an armed Regulation patrol. Perhaps they could flee back into the slums. Nope. From his spot hovering above the road, Ard saw four of Remaught's goons riding toward them.

"I thought you said this ruse was going to be low risk," Raek said, also noticing the two groups closing on their position.

"Did I? You're putting words in my mouth," Ard said. "How long until this detonation burns out?" He knew there was no way to know exactly. A standard Drift Grit blast could last up to ten minutes, depending on the quality of the bones that the dragon had digested. Raek would make a more educated guess than him.

Raek sniffed the discolored air. "There was Prolonging Grit mixed in with that detonation," he said. "We could be adrift for a while."

There was another gunshot, this one passing below their feet. Ard didn't know which side had fired.

"What else have you got on that sash?" Ard asked.

"More Barrier Grit." Raek studied his chest to take stock. "And a couple of bolts of Drift Grit." He chuckled. Probably at the irony of being armed with the very type of detonation they were trying to escape.

More gunshots. One of the lead balls grazed the side of the bucking horse. Blood sprayed from the wound, the red liquid forming into spherical droplets as it drifted away from the panicking animal.

Raek drew a dagger from his belt. Using the reins to draw himself closer, he slashed through the leather straps that yoked the animal to the wagon. Placing one heavy boot against the horse's backside, he kicked. The action sent the horse drifting one direction, and Raek the other. The horse bucked hysterically, hooves contacting the wagon and sending it careening into Raek.

Ard caught Raek's foot as he spiraled past, but it barely slowed the big man, tugging Ard along instead.

Their trajectory was going to put them out of the cloud's perimeter about thirty feet aboveground. They would plummet to the road, a crippling landing even if they didn't manage to get shot.

"Any thoughts on how to get out of here?" Ard shouted.

"I think momentum is going to do that for us in a second or two!"

They were spinning quite rapidly and the view was making Ard sick. Road. Sky. Road. Sky. He looked at Raek's ammunition sash and made an impulsive decision. Reaching out, Ard seized one of the bolts whose clay head bore the blue marking of Barrier Grit. Ripping the bolt free, he gripped the shaft and brought the stout projectile against Raek's chest like a stabbing knife.

The clay arrowhead shattered, Slagstone sparking against Raek's broad torso. The Barrier Grit detonated, throwing a new cloud around them midflight.

The bolt contained far less Grit than the road mine, resulting in a cloud that was only a fraction of the size. Detonated midair, it formed a perfect sphere. It enveloped Ard, Raek, and the wagon, just as all three slammed against the hard Barrier perimeter. The impenetrable wall stopped their momentum, though they still floated weightlessly, pressed against the stationary Barrier.

"You detonated on my chest?" Raek cried.

"I needed a solid surface. You were available."

"What about the wagon? It was available!"

A lead ball pinged against the invisible Barrier. Without the protective Grit cloud, the shot would have taken Ard in the neck. But nothing could pass through the perimeter of a Barrier cloud.

"Would you look at that?" Raek muttered, glancing down.

The Regulators had momentarily turned their attention on Remaught's goons. Apparently, the Reggies had decided that an enemy of their enemy was not their friend.

"We've got about ten minutes before our Barrier cloud closes," Raek said.

Ard pushed off the invisible perimeter and drifted across the protected sphere. Since Prolonging Grit had been mixed into the mine detonation, their smaller Barrier cloud would fail before the Drift cloud.

"How do we survive this?" Raek pressed.

"Maybe the Reggies and goons will shoot each other and we'll have a free walk to the docks."

"We both know that's not happening," Raek said. "So we've got to be prepared to escape once these two clouds burn out on us."

"I plan to deliver you as a sacrifice," Ard announced. "Maybe I'll go clean. Become a Holy Isle."

"Right," Raek scoffed. "But they won't be able to call themselves 'holy' anymore."

"Just so we're clear, this isn't my fault," said Ard. "Nobody could have predicted that Suno would sell out his boss."

"Suno?" Raek asked. "Who the blazes is Suno?"

"Remaught's bodyguard," he answered. "The Trothian in need of a soak."

"How does he figure into this?"

Ard had worked the entire thing out as they drifted aimlessly in the cloud. That was his thing. Raek figured weights, trajectories, detonations. Ard figured people.

"Remaught wouldn't have double-crossed us like this," Ard began. "It would put too many of his goons in danger, sending them head-to-head with an armed Regulation patrol. Our ruse was solid. Remaught thought he got exactly what he wanted out of the transaction—a dirty Reggie in his pocket.

"Suno, on the other hand, wasn't getting what he wanted. The bodyguard recently had a kid. Must have decided to go clean—looking for a way to get off Dronodan and get his new child back to the Trothian islets. So Suno sold out Remaught for safe passage. He must have told the real Reggies that one of their own was meeting with his mob boss. Only, the Regulators checked their staffing, saw that everyone was accounted for, and determined…"

"That I was a fake." Raek finished the sentence.

Ard nodded. "And if you weren't an actual Reggie, then you wouldn't be heading back to the outpost. You'd be headed off the island as quickly as possible. Hence…" Ard motioned toward the patrol of Regulators just outside the Drift cloud.

"Flames, Ard," Raek muttered. "I wanted to wring somebody's neck for this setup. Now you tell me it's a brand-new dad? You know I've got a soft spot for babies. Can't be leaving fatherless children scattered throughout the Greater Chain. Guess I'll have to wring your neck instead."

"You already killed me once, Raek," Ard said. "Look how that turned out." He gestured at himself.

Ard knew Raek didn't really blame him for their current predicament. No more than Ard blamed Raek when one of his detonations misfired.

Every ruse presented a series of variables. It was Ard's job to control as many as possible, but sometimes things fell into the mix that Ard had no way of foreseeing. Ard couldn't have known that Suno would be the bodyguard present at the transaction. And even if he had known, he couldn't have predicted that Suno would turn against his boss.

Maybe it was time to close shop if they survived the day. Maybe seven years of successful rusing was more than he could ask for.

"There's no way we're walking out of this one, Ard," said Raek.

"Oh, come on," Ard answered. "We've been in worse situations before. Remember the Garin ruse, two years back? Nobody thought we could stay underwater that long."

"If I remember correctly, that wasn't really our choice. Someone was *holding* us underwater. Anyway, I said we aren't *walking* out of this one." Raek emphasized the word, gesturing down below. Their Drift cloud was surrounded. Goons on one side, Reggies on the other. But Raek had a conniving look on his face. "Take off your belt."

Ard tilted his head in question. "I don't think that's such a good idea, on account of us being in a Drift cloud and all. Unless your plan is to give the boys below a Moon Passing. You see, this belt happens to be the only thing currently holding up my trousers. Take it off, and my pants might just drift right off my hips. You know I've lost weight over this job, Raek."

"Oh really?" Raek scoffed. "And how much do you think you weigh?"

Ard scratched behind his ear. "Not a panweight over one sixty-five."

"Ha!" Raek replied. "Maybe back on Pekal. When you were with Tanalin."

"Do you have to bring her up right now?" Ard said. "These might be my final moments, Raek."

"Would you rather think about *me* in your final moments?" Raek asked.

"Ah! Homeland, no!" cried Ard. "I'd rather think about cream-filled pastries."

"Like the ones you used to eat whenever we came ashore from Pekal...with Tanalin."

"Raek!"

The big man chuckled. "Well, Ard, you're not usually the type to let go of things." He let out a fake cough, saying Tanalin's name at the same time. "But I have to say, you've really let yourself go. You're a hundred and seventy-eight panweights. Pushing closer to one eighty with every raspberry tart."

Raek had a gift for that. The man could size up a person, or heft an object and tell you exactly how much it weighed. Useful skill for a detonation Mixer.

"Still less than you," Ard muttered.

"Actually, given our current gravity-free surrounding, we both weigh exactly the same—*nothing*."

Ard rolled his eyes. "And you wonder why you don't have any friends."

"Don't mock the science," said Raek. "It's about to save our skins. Now give me your blazing belt!"

Ard had no idea what the man was planning, but nearly two decades of friendship had taught him that this was one of those moments when he should shut up and do whatever Raekon Dorrel said.

In a few moments, Ard's belt was off, a surprisingly awkward task to perform while floating with both hands shackled. A gentle toss sent the belt floating to where Raek caught it. He held the thin strap of leather between his teeth while digging inside his Reggie coat for the gun belt.

"How many balls do you have?" Raek asked.

Ard made a face. "I'd think someone so good at mathematics wouldn't have to ask that question."

Raek sighed heavily, his developing plan obviously stifling his sense of humor. "Lead firing balls. In your Roller."

"Oh, right." Ard checked the chambers. "Coincidentally, I have two."

"Reload." Raek sent four cartridges drifting over to Ard, who caught them one at a time. The cartridges housed a premeasured amount of explosive Blast Grit in a thin papery material. At the top of the cartridge was the lead ball, held to the cylindrical cartridge with an adhesive.

Ard set the first cartridge, ball downward, into an open chamber. Twisting the Roller, he used a hinged ramrod on the underside of the barrel to tamp the ball and cartridge tightly into place.

It took him only a moment to reload, a practiced skill that couldn't even be hindered by his shackles. When he looked up, Raek was floating sideways next to the wagon, holding Ard's other Roller and making use of the belt he'd borrowed.

"What kind of arts and crafts are you up to?" Ard asked, seeing his friend's handiwork.

Raek had taken every spare cartridge from Ard's gun belt, a total of more than sixty rounds, and used the belt to lash them into a tight bundle. The barrel of the Roller was also tied down so the Slagstone hammer would make contact with the bundle of cartridges. The whole thing looked ridiculous. Not to mention incredibly dangerous.

"Our Barrier cloud is going to close any second," Raek said. "I'll get everything in position." He shut his eyes the way he often did when required to do complicated mathematics under stressful circumstances. "You should probably get the safe box."

Ard felt a sudden jolt of panic, remembering the whole purpose of the ruse. Glancing down, he was relieved to see that their stolen prize was still floating within the confines of their Barrier cloud, not adrift and unprotected like the poor horse.

Ard judged the distance, reaching out to feel the Barrier wall; solid and impenetrable. He shoved off, a little harder than intended, his body spinning and coming in at the wrong angle.

Ard's forehead struck the safe box. A painful way to be reunited, but it gave Ard the chance to reach out and grab it. For a moment he expected the box to feel heavy in his arms, but weight didn't exist in a Drift cloud.

Ard was just bracing himself to hit the bottom of the Barrier cloud when it burned out. He passed the spot where the invisible perimeter should have stopped him, momentum carrying him downward through the weightlessness of the lingering Drift cloud.

Ard slammed into the road, a clod of dirt floating up from his impact. A gunshot cracked and a lead ball zipped past. Normally, Ard enjoyed having his feet on solid ground. But with the goons and Reggies standing off on the road, he suddenly found himself directly in the line of fire.

"Ardor!" Raek shouted from above. "Get back up here!"

Lying on his back on the road at the bottom of the Drift cloud, Ard saw Raek and the wagon sinking almost imperceptibly toward him. The full strength of the Drift cloud had expired. Prolonging Grit kept it from collapsing entirely, but the effect of pure weightlessness would continue to diminish until both types of Grit fizzled out.

Gripping the safe box against his chest, Ard kicked off the road and sprang upward, the Drift cloud allowing him to float effortlessly upward.

"Gotcha!" Raek grabbed Ard's sleeve, pulling him against the flat bed of the empty wagon.

Raek carefully reached out, taking hold of a thin string. It looked strange, lying flat in the air like a stiff wire. "What we're about to do is among the more experimental methods of escaping."

"You mean, you don't know if it's going to work?" Ard said.

"I did the math in my head. Twice. It should..." He dwindled off. "I have no idea."

"Do I want to know what's tied to the other end of that string?" Ard asked.

"Remember how I lashed your other Roller onto that bundle of Blast Grit cartridges?"

Ard's eyes went wide. "Flames, Raek! That's going to blow us both to..."

Raek pulled the string. Ard heard the click of the gun's trigger on the other side of the wagon. The Slagstone hammer threw sparks, instantly accompanied by one of the loudest explosions Ard had ever heard.

The two men slammed against the wagon as it grew hot, fire belching around them on all sides. The energy from the explosion hurtled the broken wagon on an upward angle, a trajectory Ard hoped was in line with whatever blazing plan Raek had just committed them to.

They exited the top of the Drift cloud, and Ard felt gravity return around him. It didn't seem to matter much, however, since both men were sailing through the air at breakneck velocity. The burning wagon started to fall away behind them, like a comet soaring over the heads of the Reggies.

Raek reached out, grasping Ard's coat at the neck to keep the two of them from separating in the air. Ard had a lot of questions for his big friend. Namely, *How the blazing sparks are we going to get down?* But Ard couldn't breathe, let alone speak.

They were at the apex of their flight, any moment to begin the death-sentence descent, when Raek reached up with his free hand and ripped something off his ammunition sash. It was a Grit bolt, but the clay arrowhead was a different color from the Barrier bolts Ard had used earlier.

Raek gripped the shaft in one hand. Reaching back, he smashed the clay tip against Ard's left shoulder. The Grit detonated, throwing a fresh Drift cloud around them.

Ard felt the weightlessness return, along with a throb on his shoulder from where Raek had detonated the bolt. Guess he had that coming.

In this smaller, new Drift cloud, high over the road, the two men were no longer falling. They were shooting straight through the air, their velocity and trajectory maintained in the weightless environment.

In a flash, they had passed out the other side of the cloud. But before gravity could begin pulling them down, Raek detonated a second Drift bolt, this time shattering the clay tip on Ard's other shoulder.

They were flying. Sparks! Actually *flying*! High over the heads of their enemies, leaving both Regulators and goons behind. A few lead balls were fired in their direction, but there was little chance of getting hit, moving at the rate they were, spinning dizzying circles through the air.

One after another, Raek detonated the Drift bolts, the discolored clouds slightly overlapping as the two men shot horizontally through the air.

The concept of propelling an object over long distances through a series of detonated Drift clouds was not unheard-of. It was the basis for moving heavy materials used in the construction of tall buildings. But for a person to fly like this, unsheltered, the only calculations done impromptu and under gunfire. This was madness and genius, mixed and detonated on the spot.

The two flying men cleared the cliff shoreline, and Ard saw the harbor and docks just below. They exited the latest Drift cloud, the eighth, as Ard was made painfully aware from the welts on his back, and finally began to descend. Gravity ruled over them once more, and Ard judged that they'd slam down right against the first wooden dock.

"Two more!" Raek shouted. He crushed another Drift bolt on Ard's back, maintaining the angle of their fall and buying them a little more distance. As soon as they exited, Raek detonated the last bolt. They soared downward, past the docks and moored ships. Ard saw the *Double Take* below, docked in the farthest spot, a tactical location to speed their getaway.

They exited the final cloud and Ard watched the rapidly approaching water. He had hoped for a more elegant ending to their haphazard flight. Instead, he'd be hitting the bay at tremendous speeds, shackles locked around both wrists, holding a terribly heavy safe box.

Well, I'm certainly not bored, thought Ardor Benn. He took a deep breath.

~

It begins here. Although, for me, I suppose this is something of an ending.

By Dale Lucas

The Fifth Ward

First Watch
Friendly Fire
Good Company

"It
on
ab
or

ab
Yo

a b

ex
ke

it,

hi

soaking wet. Nabbing you might be the only bright spot in our evening, truth be told."

"Just remember," the man said as he began his walk through the rain back to the watchkeep. "I warned you. You could've saved yourselves."